ALL THE LITTLE SECRETS

S.J. SYLVIS

AUTHOR'S NOTE

All the Little Secrets is a full-length standalone enemies-to-lovers high school romance intended for **MATURE** readers. Please be aware that it contains triggers that some readers may find bothersome.

ALL THE
LITTLE SECRETS

PROLOGUE

OLLIE

SECRETS. They were what drove a wedge in reality. They were the bridge between the past, present, and future. They were everywhere. Everyone had secrets. Some bigger than others, sure, but we all had them.

And she knew my deepest, darkest one.

Piper sat beside me in the back of my brother's Charger as he reluctantly stepped out and climbed up the side of a drab, shithole of a house to get to Hayley's bedroom.

I couldn't even fathom the amount of secrets those two shared. Old best friends turned enemies with enough sexual tension to light this entire fucking town on fire. But Hayley was Christian's little secret, and no one liked to reveal the truth.

Leaning back in the Charger, my lip lifted as I glanced over at Piper. The interior of the car was dark, the window tint blocking the glow of the moon, almost as if it had disappeared altogether. Small specks of illuminating blue light from the dashboard dotted the side of Piper's delicate cheek. Her soft features were drawn tight as she stewed in her hatred for me.

"Stop staring at me," she hissed.

I chuckled, the deep sound reverberating in my throat.

"Are you angry because I'm right or because I'm wrong?"

"I'm angry because you tricked me into thinking my best friend was in the car. You all but kidnapped me from the party!"

A jealous side of me emerged as I thought back to an hour ago when I'd walked into the Wellington Prep party. Piper was too close to one of their own, and it irritated me. Fire fanned over my skin as if she were actually mine. It was the reason I'd revealed my hidden ace in the first place.

I slowly shook my head back and forth in Piper's direction. "That's not why you're angry."

Her eyes flared to mine. I couldn't see their color, but I knew they were a jade green, just like the leaves of the evergreen trees that lined the back of English Prep.

She scoffed. "Then please enlighten me as to why I'm angry."

I answered matter-of-factly, "You're angry because I know it was you that night."

Her face didn't so much as twitch. Her pink lips stayed straight. Her eyelashes didn't flutter closed. Nothing. Not even a tick of her cheek. And that right there, my friends, proved that I was correct in my assumptions. She knew if she reacted, she'd give away her poker face and crumble.

I leaned in a little closer, watching Christian through the Charger's window, following after Hayley as she stormed across the street. I breathed in Piper's soft scent as I dipped my lips down to her ear. "I know your secret, Piper. You aren't *nearly* as innocent as you lead people to believe." She held her breath, not daring to make a move. The heat from her body put the interior of the car at a solid 100 degrees, and it stirred up something unholy inside of me. "But that means you know mine, too."

CHAPTER ONE

PIPER

THE SECRET KEEPER. If I ever had a title at English Prep, other than *Friend of Hayley's*, that would be it. Piper: The Secret Keeper. My gaze lazily moved around the room as I sat perched on top of the kitchen island inside Eric's parents' cabin, mentally counting all the secrets I knew of my fellow classmates.

The group of cheerleaders huddled in the far corner of the living room, all gulping cheap beer from their cups filled to the brim, had secretly sexted the PE teacher last year for an easy A. That was secret number one. I shifted my eyes over to Eric, one of Christian and Ollie's best friends, as my feet kicked back and forth below. Eric, with his sobering dark features and stoic expression, definitely had a plethora of secrets, all of which revolved around Madeline, the ex-queen-bee of English Prep. That was intriguing in itself, considering Madeline was Christian's ex-girlfriend. But that brought me to secret number three: mean, callous, bitchy, spiteful, vindictive Madeline. Madeline wanted *everyone* to believe she had a perfect life, the happiest of families. But she didn't. She was lonely and drowning in self-pity. The many windows in her house rarely had any lights on when I'd drive past, and her father was in and out of her and her mother's life, which of course meant that Madeline had to watch her own mother bring stray men to their house whenever she *did* come home. Madeline was like a Pandora's box. She had many secrets that she held close to her heart.

Much like me.

I was drawn to the hidden depths inside my peers. Gathering illicit information on people was my favorite pastime. I could see right through faces that were masked with fake serene. I observed, watched, and waited. I wasn't sure why I was like that. Maybe it had something to do with the fact that I had my own imperceptible, deep secrets buried down underneath my skin that no one truly knew—not even Hayley, my best friend, who was staring directly at me from across the party as she sat on her boyfriend's lap.

Hayley crinkled her eyes and tilted her head, her dark hair falling past her shoulders. She was silently asking if I was okay.

I gave her a short nod with a tiny, fake smile and averted my eyes around the room once more.

It was funny. A month ago, I was the one all but begging Hayley to go to Eric's cabin for the hyped, you-don't-live-until-you-go-to-the-cabin party, but now it was the opposite. Hayley begged me to hang out with her, Christian, and Ollie almost every day, and that would be fine, except for Ollie.

I hated Ollie. Loathed him. Or...at least that was what I told myself.

He and I shared a past. A past that I pretended didn't exist, and he dangled it in my face every single time we were alone together.

But Ollie had secrets, too.

I always toed the thin line of hate that I drew in between us, acting as if I couldn't stand him. And, in a way, it was truthful. I got edgy when he was around, but it was only because he *knew*.

And I didn't like that.

Of course, he'd only ever once came out and said it in an attempt to get me to fall at his feet, but typically, we both pretended like that night didn't exist. It was a raw, heavy, secret-sharing night underneath covers in a black-as-onyx room that neither one of us wanted to touch.

He knew something about me. And I knew something about him. Every time I locked eyes with his baby blues, it was like we were in an impasse. My stomach clenched; my heart thumped a little faster; my blood rushed. Looking at Ollie gave me a rush, but in the worst way possible.

My eyes skipped past Hayley and Christian, his head nuzzling her neck, as I spotted Ollie. A burning hole tore through my belly as I watched his casually cool facade whoosh a fellow classmate right off her feet. He was wearing a tight, plain t-shirt with his backwards baseball cap on, and my breath caught when his large hand cupped her tiny waist. Amber's fingers gripped his forearm, and I clenched my teeth in an envious rage. That was another reason why I hated him; he brought out the worst side of me. The feisty, hot-headed, red-haired girl reared her ugly head whenever he flaunted his excessive flirting in front of my face. He did it on purpose, and I knew it, because each and every time I'd catch his stare, his devilish smirk would appear, and he'd have a twinkle in his eye. I wanted to smack that stupid, sharp jawline of his so he'd stop tormenting me.

But I wouldn't.

Because that would give away everything I was hiding.

I finally casted my eyes away as my phone vibrated in my hand. My heart paused as I read the incoming text.

Mom: The silent alarm went off. Is that you at home?

Two things bothered me about that text. One, she didn't even have the decency to say "hello," even though we hadn't talked or seen each other in over a month—which, to be honest, was nothing new. And two, it wasn't me that had set the alarm off.

Panic shot down my spine as I hopped down from the counter. As soon as my feet hit the floor, it felt like my stomach did, too.

I had a couple of different options. I *could* tell my mom it wasn't me who tripped the alarm and get on with my night of watching Ollie sweet-talk Amber and simmering in pure loathing. Or, I could dip out of the party and go check for myself, because I was pretty certain I knew why the alarm was tripped.

My heart skipped as I stood in the middle of the cabin's kitchen, clutching my phone in my hand as my peers partied and chugged their keg-filled cups of malty beer. I was frozen. My shoes were planted to the wooden floor, the warm lights above my head shining down on me as if I were in the spotlight.

I slowly pulled my phone up and hovered my fingers over the keyboard. *You already know what you're going to do, Piper.*

Me: Yeah, it's me, sorry. Can you turn it off? I'm about to jump in the shower.

I bit my lip as I waited for my mom to text back. *Please don't question it.* The one benefit to my relationship with my parents was that they trusted me. We didn't talk much. My father always traveled for work, and my mom—who was his assistant—went along with him. They checked my bank account every day, waiting for the red flags that they'd learned to recognize in the past, but other than that, they weren't protective at all. Paranoid? Yes. Protective? Not so much. As long as I kept my ducks in a row, they stayed at a distance, and I liked it that way.

My phone buzzed again as I stared a hole into the side of Ollie's head. His perfectly plump lips traced along Amber's neck, and it made my stomach coil like a bundle of snakes. *Do you remember what those lips felt like?* I scowled at the tiny voice in the back of my head. *Shut up.*

Mom: I disarmed it from my phone. Your father and I are thinking of getting cameras hooked up for extra caution. We don't particularly enjoy panicking.

I wanted to text back and ask what exactly they were panicking about. Were they afraid things would get stolen again? Or were they fearful that I'd be in a house with someone who was unstable at best? *Or* were they afraid their business trip would get cut short, and they'd have to deal with the repercussions of their parenting skills? I'd never know.

I rounded a group of football players who eyed me briefly as I walked over to Hayley and Christian. Hayley's cheeks were painted pink as Christian whispered something in her ear. His hand was clamped down on her inner thigh, and I wanted to puke at how perfect they were. Months ago, they hated each other, and now they were *#goals*. The king of the school and the broken girl had somehow found a way to fall in love, and basically everyone in our class foamed at the mouth when they were near. We all wanted what they had. Even me.

"Hey, I'm gonna head home."

Hayley sat up taller and elbowed Christian when I spoke. "What? You just got here! Here, I'll come hang out with you." She shot Christian a scowl, as if it was his fault for distracting her.

I held my hand up and laughed.

"Hayley, it's fine. I'm just tired. You know I'd be over here hanging with you two if I wanted to be."

I hated lying to her.

Hayley's bottom lip jolted outward as she tucked a piece of dark hair behind her ear. Christian was still frowning at the spot on his stomach that Hayley had elbowed. "Are you sure? Maybe I should just leave with you and have a girls' night."

I quickly shut that idea down. A girls' night with Hayley sounded perfect, except that I wasn't sure what was waiting for me at home. "Let's plan that for next weekend. Stay here. Hang out with Christian."

As soon as the words left my mouth, Christian pulled Hayley further back onto his lap, clasping his hands around her middle. "I agree with Piper. Stay here with me." He bit the side of her ear, and I rolled my eyes playfully.

Hayley was fighting a smile. "Okay, but..." Her eyes scanned the living room until they landed on Ollie.

"No!" I rushed out, stepping in front of her gaze. Christian stopped toying with Hayley's ear as he flicked his eyes up to mine. "I don't need Ollie to follow me home, Hayley."

"*Piper.*"

Christian's eyes bounced back and forth between us.

"I'm fine. The threat is gone. It's been *months* since we were chased off the road. The men were caught. And plus, you're the one they wanted. Not me. I can handle driving twenty minutes to my house."

Hayley's shoulders dropped, and I realized I may have been a little too rude with my response. It was nice that she cared about me. *At least one person did.*

"Listen," I started. "I promise I'll be okay. Stay here with Christian. Have fun. That trig test wore me out today. I'm exhausted, and I'm volunteering tomorrow morning at the soup kitchen. I swear we can have a girls' night next weekend, okay?"

Christian interjected, "And I swear I won't interrupt it."

A light laugh came out of my mouth. "You always say that, and yet, you and your brother somehow always show up."

Christian's lip tilted upward in the form of a smirk as I looked away, searching for Ollie one last time. As soon as I found him, he was staring at me intently with his head tilted to one side. Amber was still beside him with her arm draped around his lower back, but his eyes were on me. He raised an eyebrow, I'm sure silently asking me where I was going, but I hastily turned my attention back to Hayley.

"You have to swear it, Christian!" I heard her say.

Christian smirked again. "Scout's honor. I swear I won't interrupt your girls' night with Piper next weekend."

I laughed when she made him pinky promise her after she blurted, "You are the furthest thing from a boy scout. Use a different saying!"

"Okay, I'll text you tomorrow, Hay. Bye, Christian."

"Later. Be careful. Call us if something seems off."

I nodded and made my way out of the party. The last few months had been scary, at best. Hayley's past was messy, ugly, and twisted with threats, and of course that put all of us in harm's way. Christian, Hayley, Ollie, Eric, and I were the only ones who knew the truth about what had happened in Hayley's life before she started attending English Prep. And even though we didn't all wear matching friendship bracelets, we all watched out for one another. The guys kind of became protective over Hayley and me, hence why they wanted Ollie to follow me home.

But that was the *very* last thing I wanted.

What my friends didn't know was that I had a past of my own. A past that kept trying to become the present, and Ollie was the last person on this planet that I wanted to share it with.

The beating of my heart grew as I crept along my cobble-stone driveway. My fingers tingled with little prickles as I shifted into park and turned my ignition off. *Relax.* I blew out a breath when my hands dropped into my lap, clutching my keys with so much force I'd be surprised if I didn't have small dents on the inside of my palm. I quickly flipped down the visor and glanced at myself in the mirror. Soft, orange light splayed on my cheeks, showcasing my freckles underneath the worn-off makeup from this morning, and I gave myself a stern talk.

"Take a deep breath, Piper."

My puffed cheeks grew smaller as air left my mouth with each deep breath I took. I shook my head angrily as I flipped the visor back up, snapping it into place, and opened my door. I wasn't fooling anyone. Even the little twinkle in my eye was downcast by fear and anxiety.

The cool night air bit at my cheeks as I stepped out of my car and glanced up at my house. Three stories of perfectly laid brick, glossy wood floors, soft, plush carpet, and expensive furniture was what awaited me every single day, but not a single ounce of love or security resided inside. I remembered the day my parents told me we were moving to a different house, in a different town, like it was yesterday. Their faces were bright with excitement and new possibilities. It was like they thought a new house and school could actually erase the past and rearrange the future. I was absolutely baffled at the thought, and to be honest, I still was. *Nothing* could change the past. Not even denial.

My eyes darted to each and every window on the front of my house. *All dark. Not a single light on.* There were no other cars in the driveway, no movement outside at all besides the swaying trees dancing with the sudden gust of wind. Another sigh left my lips. I knew what I was walking into. But just because I'd been here before, in this exact position, didn't mean I was mentally prepared for it. Could I ever be mentally prepared for this? Would I ever be okay with feeling like my heart was lodged in my throat as panic seized my body?

My hair swayed with the breeze as I walked up to my front door. It was hard seeing someone destroy themselves. It was like a broken piece of glass becoming more jagged with each new memory, and that piece of glass felt like it was slicing away at my flesh each and every time I got close.

But nonetheless, I kept coming back. I kept caring. Because that was just who I was.

As soon as I stepped foot inside the foyer, noting the alarm had been disarmed, my heart grew weaker. My pulse was racing, and my hands were shaking even more than before. I reiterated aloud, "*It's fine, Piper.*" Then, as I shut the door behind me, I called out, "Jason?" I knew he was here, and if he heard my voice instead of my parents', he'd come out. So I waited. I flipped the light on as I walked farther into the hallway and instantly paused near the opening of the kitchen.

My eyes widened as I spotted a line of red-dotted toilet paper trailing through the hallway from the washroom. *What the hell?* My heart went into triple speed as my voice grew panicky. "Jason? Where are you? Are you okay?"

I picked up my pace and all but ran up the stairs, skipping over the tiny, random bits of torn toilet paper, all of which had blood on them. They were like little clues to a scavenger hunt. A scavenger hunt that didn't have a gleaming treasure at the end.

As soon as I was in front of Jason's *old* bedroom, I pushed the door open. It was dark in his room, except for a small stream of light pouring from the bathroom. There was a quiet rustling of noise coming from inside, and it should have made me proceed with caution. Or it should have at least prepared me for seeing the shell of a human my older brother had become. But it didn't. Instead, I all but ran and pushed the door open wide, taking in the sight quickly, like downing a shot of potent vodka.

"Jesus Christ, Jason." I quickly stepped in front of him and tilted his head back by the tips of his hair, peering down into his bloodshot eyes. One was so swollen it barely opened, and there was a trickle of dried blood coming from his mouth. His red t-shirt was ripped at the collar, and as I further investigated his body, I noticed small cuts lined his elbow all the way down to his wrist. "What the hell happened?"

"Where are Mom and Dad?" Jason's words were muffled, probably due to the swelling of his busted lip.

"I don't know. China, I think. They don't know you're here, even though you tripped the alarm."

He dropped his head but brought it back up slowly. "Wait...they changed the code?"

Obviously.

"Because of me?"

I didn't answer him because it was redundant. Of course they changed the code because of him. What did he expect after stealing hundreds of dollars' worth of things from them last time he made an appearance? He knew he wasn't allowed here, yet he continued to come back, trying his hardest to get around the fact that my parents had completely given up hope on him.

I turned around and grabbed the white hand towel sitting on the vanity top and ran it under cold water. "What happened?"

My brother shook his head, cringing. He shut his eyes, small crinkles forming on his skin. He took a heavy breath, and I held mine, waiting for his answer.

"I fucked up."

Always the same response.

I began blotting at the flakes of blood on his chin. I felt nauseated, sick to my stomach, and even though I'd been in this spot so many times over the years, the disappointment never got any easier to deal with. Seeing my brother like this was a hard pill to swallow. "Is that why you stole so much shit from Mom and Dad last time you were here?"

He nodded, just barely—like if he didn't admit it, then it wouldn't be true.

"Jason," I exhaled, still blotting at his face. Tears threatened to spill down my cheeks, but I bit my tongue to keep myself together. "They're done with you. You know that, right?"

It was true. My parents were so done with my brother and his never-ending fuck-ups. They set their life-after-Jason plan into motion the second he stole from them. Their hope had vanished into thin air, leaving me the responsibility of being the only one to care.

Jason's eyes flashed open, the green in them so much more potent against the red, bloodshot color that surrounded them. "But you're not. Right, sis?"

I should have said no. I should have told him that he needed to leave. That I, too, was sick of his shit. That I couldn't keep watching him do this. That I resented him for the last few years of my life. That I hated him for what he did to our family. But I didn't.

I swallowed back a lump as I wrung out the white towel in the sink, wetting it once more. "Who do you owe this time?"

"His name is Tank."

My hand paused as I peered down at his tattered jeans and ripped shirt. "I don't think I'm familiar with him," I answered.

My brother winced as he sat up a little taller along the vanity cabinets. "That's a good thing, little sis."

A sigh left my lips as I blotted his face again. "How much do you owe?"

The metallic taste of blood filled my mouth as I bit my cheek, waiting.

He paused and averted his eyes away from me.

"Answer me, Jason."

His chin tipped, and I could see the remorse plain as day. "Twenty thousand."

The cloth from my hand dropped to the floor with a whoosh. My ears felt hot; my chest squeezed a little tighter. "Wh...what?"

His gaze shot right through me. "I owe him twenty fucking thousand, and if I don't get it to him by tomorrow night, he'll kill me, Pipe. He'll fucking kill me."

I caught my pale reflection in the bathroom mirror and muttered, *"Shit,"* under my breath.

CHAPTER TWO

OLLIE

BEING a Powell was both a curse and a blessing. Everyone thought they knew me. They thought they knew exactly who Ollie Powell was. The younger (barely) brother of Christian Powell, the alpha of English Prep. The nicer of the Powell boys, the one who was like a ray of fucking sunlight—much the opposite of Christian, who was like getting a glimpse into the midnight sky. But here was the funny thing... They were all wrong. They were so fucking wrong.

Sure, I had the light features: light hair, glimmering white, pearly smile—*thank you very much, Crest whitening toothpaste*—charismatic as fuck. I mean, a tip of my chin and a wink had girls falling at my feet. The women faculty of English Prep—even Ms. Boyd, the old bat of a secretary—blushed when I shot a dazzling look their way. The only person not affected by my charm or tricked by my amiable personality was Piper, but that was a whole different story.

Regardless, people thought they knew me.

But they didn't.

I had secrets.

One secret turned into another secret, and before I knew it, it was like I was living a double life. The first was filled with long days at English Prep, followed by football practice, with nights at my best friend's cabin, drinking warm beer and tongue-fucking girls. But the second was filled with adrenaline, exhilaration, distraction, and a group of people who knew absolutely nothing about me. Nothing but my first name and the type of car I drove.

And that was exactly how I wanted it.

A distraction was something I needed, something I craved. It set me free, allowing me to relish in my anger and perplexity of the situation I was in. I mean, I had to put all those heavy, suffocating feelings into *something*, something that was away from Christian and my friends.

Which was what led me to this place right here.

An old dirt road out on the outskirts of Pike Valley, surrounded by the smell of pine and gasoline. Pike Valley had four valleys: the two wealthier ones—which was where I lived —and then the two others that were filled with middle-class folk and the poor. I was currently smack-dab in the middle of the valleys, waiting for my turn to get a taste of adrenaline.

"You ready for tonight? I've got money on you, bro."

I tipped my chin up to Brandon, one of the guys who had already raced, giving him a slight nod. He was good, but his car lacked agility. It couldn't quite shift as fast as mine, which was why I was in a different bracket than he was. There was more money on the line when it came to me, but that didn't really matter much.

Again, this was just something I did to get my heart pumping, to distract me from real problems—from reality. I didn't care about the money. Cash wasn't exactly hard to come by for me; forking out eight hundred dollars a weekend was like child's play. My father never even asked where my money went. There was an allotment on my card, but as long as I didn't go over it, he turned a blind eye.

Which was a problem all in itself.

Christian, on the other hand... If he knew I was here, doing this shit, he'd be royally fucking pissed. Which almost made it more fun.

I leaned back onto my Charger's leather seat as I peered out the rolled-down window to Brandon. "I'm always ready." I winked at Brandon's girl. She bit her plump lip and fluttered her eyelashes at me when he wasn't looking.

I chuckled. Girls here were thirsty. *So thirsty*. Every single one of them was dressed in revealing clothing, showing off their flat stomachs and perky tits, hoping that they'd get a piece of whomever won the race.

They were all the same.

Yawn.

Although, they *did* entertain me for a short while.

My eyes trailed a blonde girl as she walked over to the starting line. The tips of her hair were stained pink, which matched the color of her lips to a T. Once she flipped the strands over her shoulder, I knew that was my cue to get ready. My phone buzzed as I drummed my fingers along the steering wheel. I glanced down for a brief second, seeing that it was Eric asking where I was.

I quickly typed, **I'll be out soon, got some shit to do,** and I threw my phone in the backseat. Resting my back along the leather, I wiggled my fingers a few times before wrapping them around my steering wheel again. I revved the gas as I pulled up to the starting line next to a blue Charger much like mine.

I guess we'll see if this guy is as good as me.

"Are you boys ready?"

My lip curled at the blonde babe standing between the two cars. Adrenaline spiked my blood, and my heart went into triple speed, pounding against my ribcage. I basked in the control I felt sitting there, waiting for the go-ahead. My foot ached to smash the gas as I brought my RPMs up, waiting. My hand held the shift stick as if it were my own fucking dick, ready to go on a wild fucking ride.

"Get ready," the blonde girl shouted. I trailed my eyes down her bare legs, appreciating how short her shorts were despite the cool evening air. My blood pumped faster and faster as I scanned the crowd full of reckless teens all ready to watch the spinning wheels of our cars. "Get set." My teeth clenched together, my jaw as tight as a rubber band. "GO!"

My foot hit the gas, and I gunned it from the get-go. Dust flew all around me, so much that it was difficult to see, but I'd been on this road many times in the last few months. I knew where I was going. I was in control. I was the one making the rules here. I shifted a few times, going around the second curve, and then, I heard nothing. I had no clue if the other Charger was close to me or if he fucking drove into a tree. Being in this car gave me a sudden rush of exhilaration that soared through my body. My heart pumped with massive amounts of adrenaline which carried me further into an abyss, and that was exactly what I needed.

Distraction at its finest.

I passed the finish line as a deep breath escaped my mouth, my tires squealing as I fishtailed to stop myself from going any farther. I paused, sitting with my back against my seat, my pulse still thumping underneath my skin, as I waited for the other Charger to catch up to me.

Fucking pussy.

I knew I'd beat him.

He probably didn't even know how to handle a car like that.

My phone dinged from the backseat just as my opponent

came into view. I pushed my arm out the window and held up a number one to him. *Better luck next time, bud.*

A few guys with their cameras still out sent the text back to the ringleader of the races, Frankie, some washed-up guy from Wellington Prep who apparently flunked out of college, to let him know I won the race.

A sense of pride washed over me, but it did nothing to fill the gap inside my chest that was rapidly splitting back open like a fresh cut to my skin. A few minutes of racing and the high was already gone. So much build up for it to just disappear within seconds afterward.

But those few minutes of feeling nothing, worrying about nothing, hiding nothing, were worth it. They were so fucking worth it.

As soon as I drove back to the starting line, I parked off to the side and climbed out of my car. My lips tipped at the electric-blue Charger, the guy inside probably feeling like a complete fucking fraud of a man for racing such a shitty race, but someone had to lose, and it wasn't going to be me, that was for sure.

"Good race, my man. Good fucking race!" Brandon came over and slapped me on the shoulder and brought me in for a stiff bro hug.

"It wasn't hard," I bemused as I pulled myself back. His girl was still staring at me with those fuck-me eyes, and I silently said, *Thanks, but no thanks.* I didn't share girls, even for a night.

My phone dinged again as I watched Frankie splitting money for the race. I got a cut if I won, so tonight I made some money, but it would likely just go right back into next weekend's race.

Reaching into my backseat, I pulled out my phone as one of Frankie's girls handed me my money. "Thanks, *babe.*" I winked as I brushed my finger over the inside of her wrist before swiping the dollar bills from her. She blushed as she put her other hand up to her mouth, softly biting her thumb in the process. *See, too easy.*

One of Brandon's friends piped up as I began looking at my texts. "You down for next weekend's race, too? They might move you up a bracket. What is that, like, four weeks in a row that you've won?"

I scanned my screen as he continued to go on about my racing.

Christian: You going to Eric's tonight? I'm with Hayley. We're going to watch a movie at the house before she goes back to Ann's, then I'll head out for a bit.

Ann = Hayley's ex-social-worker who she now lived with.

I swiped that text away and looked at the next.

Eric: Dope. Squad is here, except Christian since he is pussy-whipped by Hay.

I snickered as I gave the guy rambling about my racing a slight nod, pretending that I was listening to him.

The next text had me pausing for a beat.

Hayley: Did you end up checking on Piper last night? I saw you leave Eric's for a few shortly after she left.

I sighed, still irritated that I just couldn't help myself. It'd been months since she and Hayley were chased off the road by a bunch of felons who were after Hayley due to her father's fucked-up shit, yet I still felt a deep hole carve out in the bottom of my stomach at the thought of her or Piper being on their own.

I knew Hayley was fine. Christian was with her 99% of the time—which was precisely why he didn't catch on to what I was up to on Saturday nights. But Piper... She had no one watching out for her.

There was a strange and twisted part of me that felt like I

needed to be her knight in shining armor. I was certain it was a Powell thing, Christian and I always needing to save someone. I was sure a psychologist would say it was because we weren't able to save the most important woman in our lives a few years back, but I wasn't for sure.

I quickly texted Hayley back.

Me: Yes, I did.

What I failed to tell Hayley—or anyone, for that matter —was that I sat and watched Piper's house for way longer than I should have. Once she arrived at her house, she sat in her BMW for a few moments, almost as if she were trying to gain the courage to walk inside her house, which was conflicting, considering there was no one home. From what I'd learned over the last few months of being near Piper and observing her from afar was that she was pretty much on her own the majority of the time. Her parents traveled often—as did most of our parents. That was why we at English Prep were *at* English Prep. Most of our parents were loaded, and that was because they worked a shit-ton, usually out of town, like my own father. But Piper was alone all the time. Hayley was her best friend, and other than her cousin, Andrew, who went to the other prep school in the area, that was it.

It perplexed me, someone as nice as Piper having no one in their inner circle but one close friend. *Why was that?* I knew there was more to her than her sweet face and kind heart. I was certain she had secrets; fuck, I *knew* she had secrets. That night, so long ago, was far too hot to ever forget, but there was definitely something off about her. Piper was hiding something. That was completely obvious to me, because Piper was a mere mirror of myself.

Burying secrets was something we had in common.

My phone buzzed in my hand as I finally looked up to the guy still going on about next weekend's race. He was a drab looking guy, wearing a shirt with its collar stretched out, and his hair had an unhealthy shine to it, like he hadn't showered in days. My eyebrow hitched up as he stared at me with wide eyes, waiting for me to respond to whatever the hell he'd just said as I was zoning out, thinking of Piper...*again*. Brandon nudged him, his girl standing by his side, still giving me those sex-vixen eyes.

Another text came in, and I glanced down.

Hayley: Did anything seem off with her last night?

Then another text.

Hayley: Christian and I just pulled up at her house to ask if she wants to watch a movie with us because she isn't answering my texts and it's weird. No one is answering the door, all the lights are on in the house, and her car is parked in a really weird spot. She's not with you, is she?

I typed quickly.

Me: Why would she be with me?

She texted back within a second.

Hayley: Oh...no reason.

Hayley wasn't quite convinced that there was nothing going on between me and her best friend. Anytime Hayley and I were alone, she'd grill me, and my answer was the same every time. *No.*

I slipped my phone in my pocket and rubbed at my tight chest. The incessant ache was bothering me, but I pushed all thoughts of Piper away. *She's not your problem.*

"Alright." I stepped closer to Brandon and his friend. "What were you saying? Race next weekend? I'm in."

The guy looked from me to Brandon with a puzzling look on his face. "Huh? Oh, yeah. I'll be here for it." He quickly looked back at Brandon and asked, "What the hell is he doing here? I haven't seen him around here for a long fucking time."

"Who?" I asked, coming back into the conversation that I completely spaced out of.

Brandon's girlfriend spoke up this time. "His name is Tank."

I followed her line of sight, passing by large groups of people clustered together, waiting for the next race to happen. Cars were revving up in the background, ready to burn rubber. I locked onto Frankie as he stood back, gripping a wad of cash in his hand. The sun was beginning to set behind him, casting an orange glow along the trees that lined the dust-covered road. "What's important about this Tank guy?"

I watched the guy Frankie was raising his eyebrows to. He was short with long, dark hair tied into a man bun on the top of his head. He was wearing a t-shirt that came down to his mid-thigh, which did nothing to help his lack of height. I bet he drove a souped-up truck, too, just to balance out his short, angry-man syndrome.

"He's bad news, bro. We should head out. You never know what the fucker is going to do."

I continued to stare at him and Frankie, a small crowd gathering behind them, watching to see what would happen. Others were slowly making their way to their vehicles parked off behind the trees—in hiding in case someone decided to call the cops on the illegal racing we did.

And then, that was when I saw it—a blur of coppery red hair walking through the wooded forest.

No, it's not.

My gaze switched from the petite girl with her face hidden behind a curtain of hair to a guy that looked *awfully* familiar.

I squinted, feeling my heart climb angrily inside my chest. The ceaseless ache that was there moments ago was morphing into a gaping hole filled with a hefty amount of apprehension. I ping-ponged my gaze between the couple making their way toward Frankie and this Tank guy. Before I knew what was happening, my feet were dragging me closer and closer to the forming crowd.

I was dodging those who were not-so-casually going in the opposite direction so I could get a better look at the girl, and when I did, I saw red.

What the fuck was Piper doing here?

CHAPTER THREE

PIPER

MY BROTHER WASN'T ALWAYS like this. His dull and lifeless eyes used to be the same shade of sparkling green as mine. His hair wasn't tattered at the ends like he took a rusty razor to the strands. In fact, his auburn hair used to have an even healthier shine than our mother's. The scruff on his now-sunken face used to be shaved each and every day before school, which typically made us late every morning, but alas, he was bright, happy, and *healthy*. Now, he was a shell of who he used to be, and every time he came around, the memory of my big brother grew even more tainted.

I often tried to reminisce on the good times I had with him—the happier memories. The ones of us playing outside on our freshly landscaped lawn while our nanny cleaned up the house and made dinner before my parents came home from a long day at the office. That was another thing ripped away from me after Jason drug our family name through the mud. All the stealing, vandalism, suspensions from Wellington Prep, and then of course the drugs, caught up to my parents, and they shut him out, taking me along with them. They uprooted me and all that I knew from one rich community to the next, not caring that *I* was being affected in the worst of ways. I had to say goodbye to my friends and familiarity at Wellington Prep—even my ten-year nanny, Margie. "*She knew too much.*" Per my father's explanation. Then followed by my mom. "*You're too old for a nanny anyway, Piper.*" Now, some random woman came during the day while I was at school and prepared meals for the week, did laundry, and tidied up the house only to be gone by the time I came home.

It didn't really seem fair to me at the time, and it still didn't. I promised myself that I'd stop caring about Jason, that I'd keep our better memories locked away in a pretty, ribbon-tied jar inside my head and let everything else wash away, including him.

Yet, here I was.

Enabling.

I knew what an enabler was, and it went against that very promise I made a million times over again. I was going against everything my parents drove into my head since leaving Wellington Prep—my old life. They'd washed their hands of Jason, and they expected me to do the same. After all, Jason *did* tear apart our family—what little of it we had. A ginormous, black hole was left in its place after my parents threw him out onto the streets. My life was forever changed the day they found him cleaning out my father's safe for money that he owed someone. I cringed at the memory hitting me fast and hard. Sounds of flesh being pounded, lots of yelling, and fallen tears hitting the floor. Slowly, after that night, things started to change. Jason was gone. My parents buried themselves even more into work—I'm sure in an attempt to try and push away the thought of their son being a drug user. They left me alone to deal with everything in an empty house that felt even more alien than walking into English Prep for the first time.

Try being the new girl from your current school's biggest rival.

So yes, I should have been pissed at Jason and shut him out. That was what my parents expected of me, but here I was, making my way to some desolate corn field on the outskirts of Pike Valley with one of the shadiest guys I knew by my side. I almost laughed at the predicament I was in.

My phone continued to go off in the back pocket of my skinny jeans, and I was certain it was Hayley, wondering why I hadn't texted her back, but I needed to figure out a good excuse before doing so.

I hated lying to my best friend, but this was something I wasn't willing to tell anyone, because if I confided in someone,—even someone like Hayley, with a wicked past of her own—then it made it real, and I wasn't quite ready to face my decision of enabling my brother. *Again.*

My morals were being smashed with every blade of grass I stepped on.

My parents would kill me if they knew I was helping him.

I kind of wanted to kill me, too, because I wasn't sure what I was walking into.

Cole, my cousin Andrew's friend and the guy who decided to give me my first kiss when I was twelve only to tell everyone at Wellington Prep that he only kissed me because he felt sorry for me, paused and grabbed my wrist. He was bad news, and that was exactly why I asked him to come with me. Cole had no issues looking for trouble. In fact, he *loved* trouble, and I knew he'd be all in if I hinted at just that. But to be honest, I'd much rather do this alone. Only I couldn't, because soon after Jason and I came up with a plan to fix things, he snuck out the door, driving off in *my* car, leaving me a note while I took a shower.

He'll kill me if he sees me.
I have to hide out.
Here are the directions.

The only downside to asking Cole for his help was that I was almost certain he'd want something in return. He was a little too eager to give me a ride when I'd messaged him, and it was going to be difficult to get him to keep his mouth shut about this. If he told Andrew, and Andrew told my aunt and uncle, I'd be toast.

I snatched my wrist out of Cole's grasp. "What?"

"Do we know what we're walking into? I need some more detail, Piper, especially if I'm going to be fighting someone. You've given me nothing." Cole, with his dark eyes and naturally tanned skin looked out into a flock of people. "What the fuck is this?"

I bit my lip. "Um..." *Hell if I knew.*

He shot me a look, his brown eyes deepening. "You don't know? What the hell are we doing here, Piper? What? Is some guy fuckin' around on you, and you're trying to bust him?" A wicked grin formed on his face, and I took a step back. "Show me who. I'll make sure to land a kiss right on your lips in front of him, and then once that happens..." He brought his thumb up to his mouth and swiped it over his lip as if he were now ten times hotter because of the simple gesture. "You'd be hooked on this dick."

I scoffed and rolled my eyes, annoyed. Crossing my arms over my chest, I shot back, "I'd rather shave my head and walk around school naked than let you kiss me again." Yes, I was twelve when he first kissed me, but the after-effect was mortifying enough that it was still fresh in my head.

"Again?"

A gasp flew out of my mouth just as a gust of wind blew

over my shoulders. I quickly spun around, the tall grass brushing over my ankles. My mouth dropped. "What the hell are you doing here?" My words were rushed and sounded like I'd sucked a balloon full of helium. I was already on the verge of losing my footing and letting the nerves fill me with fear, walking side by side with Cole, ready to throw not even a fraction of the money owed at who I assumed to be my brother's drug dealer. And if you add that to Ollie looking at me with his usual light and casual expression gone and replaced with furrowed brows and hooded eyes... I was nearly swaying on my feet.

Ollie walked closer to me and Cole, and my heart felt like it had wings of a hummingbird. His eyes were set on Cole with a loathing inside of them that I'd never seen from him before. He looked a lot like his older brother at that moment. "The better question is..." He got even closer to me, so close I could smell his cologne, his blue eyes growing a shade darker. "What the hell are *you* doing here...with him?"

I was too baffled to answer him, too caught up in being so close to him—so close that I felt his body heat—to come up with a reasonable answer. I couldn't tell him the truth, and now, to make matters worse, I had to figure out a way to find this Tank guy without Ollie butting into my business. *Lovely*.

"I recognize you." Cole stepped closer to me, and now I felt like I was the red flag between two bulls. Ollie didn't take his eyes off mine; his tall stance loomed over me like a nightmare in a pitch-black room. I swallowed as Cole's arm brushed along mine. "Is this him, Piper?"

"Wh-what?" I asked, continuing to stare up into Ollie's eyes. His breath was coming out warm and heavy, brushing over my face. I felt Cole's hand slide around my bicep, and before I could do anything, he snatched me over to his body, leaned me back, and placed a wet kiss on my mouth. His tongue plunged into mine, and I froze. Bile was rising up in my throat, and I couldn't figure out if it was because I was getting kissed by Cole in front of Ollie, just getting kissed by Cole in general, or if it was because I was about to meet with a drug dealer who'd beaten my brother senseless and threatened to kill him the night before.

Cole's tongue swiped over mine once more before I finally unfroze and pushed him off. He went willingly with a smirk plastered to his face when he'd stood up straight. "What the hell, Cole?" I yelled, taking a step back from not only Cole, but also Ollie. *I need air.*

"You've got about two fucking seconds to get the fuck out of here before I rip that grin off your face." Ollie's voice was rough, as if he had reached down, grabbed a handful of gravel, and swallowed the pebbles before speaking.

Cole's smile grew even wider, his white teeth shining behind a glimmer of mischief. "Oh now, there there, little Powell brother...I'm just giving you some payback for that one night you and your psycho brother decided to crash Andrew's." Cole swung his gaze lazily from Ollie to me and then back to Ollie. "Do you remember that night? The night your brother nearly put me in the hospital for a rumor his ex-girlfriend made up?" Cole's face was becoming darker, a red tint forming on his neck and cheeks. "I should beat your fucking ass right now, *pussy.*"

Oh, for fuck's sake. I do not have time for this.

Ollie seemed calmer, but I could still sense anger boiling under his skin. "From what I just witnessed, it doesn't look like my brother beat you up for a rumor. I hear things about you, *Cole.* Oh, and..." Ollie chuckled, looking down at the grass below our feet for a moment. "I wouldn't be too keen on spreading that around. It makes *you* look like the pussy. I don't even think you got one hit in that night." Ollie's laughter filled the air, and for a moment, it made me pause as warmth washed over me, but then I looked past his body and saw a large crowd of people and remembered what I was doing.

Cole took a step closer to Ollie as I took another step away. "I'm not a fucking pussy. I was blind-sided. Pretty unfair, if you ask me. Your brother all but attacked me from behind."

My foot stepped to the left just as Ollie was about to say something back to Cole, but instead, his head flicked over to me at the last second. I jumped like I was caught doing something I shouldn't. "Where do you think you're going?"

A twinge of anger was meddling in with my anxiety as I squared my shoulders. "Away from this pissing contest."

"What the hell are you doing here, Piper?" Ollie's square jaw was tight as he waited for my answer. He stood half in front of Cole, like he wasn't sure if he should protect me from him or not. And to be honest, I wasn't sure either.

"I'd kind of like to know the same thing." Cole turned his body around and was now standing beside Ollie. Both of them were staring at me intently, like they were about to gang up on me.

This was such a terrible idea. I should have just paid for an Uber instead of asking Cole for a ride. The wad of cash I had in my pocket was burning a hole in my conscience, and if I didn't do something about it soon, I wasn't really sure what would happen. *What if I didn't help my brother? Was he being serious? They wouldn't kill him. Would they?* Cole and Ollie began arguing about me again as I stood and contemplated what to do next. My brother's sad face flashed behind my eyes, and unknowingly, I began walking past Ollie and Cole.

I had to do something to help my brother.

My conscience might be slightly ruined by enabling my brother, but it would be downright destroyed if I *didn't* help him.

CHAPTER FOUR

OLLIE

I WASN'T an angry person by nature. Anger wasn't one of those emotions I was so in tune with that it didn't even phase me when I felt it. No, I *knew* when I was angry because every single nerve ending in my body sparked with a raging flame. And I was on fucking fire when I saw Piper walking along the high grass, mainly because I was pissed she was in *my* secret hide-out. But then I saw who she was with, and I was pretty sure I turned into the raging devil himself.

I walked up to the pair of them, telling myself to stay calm because what I wanted to do was grab her by the arm and snatch her away. But I was a level-headed guy. I thought about my actions, and I wasn't sure what was worse: knowing you were doing the wrong thing and still going through with it, or blaming it on being blinded by irrational behavior and losing your self-control. Either way, when Cole kissed Piper, I thought I'd never be able to breathe again. The rational part of my brain that I was so keen on keeping alive disappeared. I wanted to kill him.

Maybe it was because I wasn't used to seeing Piper with anyone else because—let's be frank—I'd sent out a massive ban over her months ago. Any guy that sent even the slightest compliment her way had a loathing look coming from me. It wasn't fair, I knew that much. Piper wasn't mine to play around with, yet something inside of me grew twisted, and my thoughts became fuzzy and distorted where she was involved. I didn't act like myself. I was on edge, and I desperately tried to cover it up with this side of myself that I didn't like to visit often, but here I was, ready to rip Cole's head off for even breathing in her direction.

Speaking of... I moved my body over to the left to give Piper another *what-the-fuck-are-you-doing-with-him* look, and I was met with the line of trees and a fading sunset. I moved over to the right, around Cole still running his mouth, and she wasn't there either. I quickly spun around, and my arms dropped to my side.

God damnit.

"What the fuck did she say when she brought you out here?" I quickly turned around and faced Cole again.

His I-eat-crayons face was flabbergasted for a moment before he recovered, realizing that Piper slipped out from our presence the second he started running his chops again. "Fuck, nothing, really. I thought she wanted to fu—"

I growled, interrupting him. "I'm trying to help you out here. Don't finish that fucking sentence."

Cole looked as if he were about to start his shit up again, but he refrained, sighing. "She texted me for a ride. That was it, really. Very cryptic, that one."

A heavy sigh left me as I turned on my heel and started to follow after Piper. Her tight ass was swaying in her skinny jeans, and her copper hair was brushing back and forth along her shoulders. I didn't see her in skinny jeans often. It was usually her long, lean legs in her plaid skirt at school that I was used to, and I had to admit, this look was really workin' for her. Which was exactly why I was all but running to catch up to her. Every guy at the race was going to be falling over his own feet to get her attention, and I couldn't have that. Most of these guys were scum.

Piper didn't belong here.

Neither do I.

"You can leave," I said over my shoulder to Cole, who was plodding after me, not at all eager to get to Piper.

"And miss out on all the fun? No, thanks. Andrew will kill me if I let something happen to his cousin."

I spun around for a moment, feeling cagey. "And yet, you just kissed her against her will. You're a top-notch dude, Cole. I'm pretty fucking positive that Piper is safer with me than she is with you."

Cole's eyes narrowed right before he smiled. "I think Piper thinks she's safe all on her own. At least, right now she does." His line of sight went past me, and a deep pit hollowed out in my intestines. When I turned around, the grass moving beneath my feet, I panicked for a moment. Piper pushed back a curtain of her hair and straightened her spine, all but pushing her perky chest up like it was her armor. My nostrils flared, and I inhaled a hefty breath of the cool air as she leveled someone with a stare and reached into her back pocket. *What the hell was she doing?* Was Piper betting on someone in the race? For a moment, I thought I might have been dreaming, but I knew that wasn't true—otherwise, this dream would go in an entirely different direction.

My gaze swung from Piper's hand to the person she was handing money to, and I twitched in my spot.

The guy they referred to as Tank smiled at Piper like he was about to enjoy a nice, juicy steak, and I couldn't stop myself from feeling protective of her—*again*. One foot went in front of the other as I made my way through the formed crowd. Piper's voice grew louder with each step I took, and it hit me right in the chest when I recognized the fear skirting over her words. I'd heard fear in her voice before, and it was just as unpleasant now as it was a few months ago.

Just what did Piper get herself into, and how could I save her?

CHAPTER FIVE

PIPER

HAYLEY ONCE TOLD me that if you acted like you weren't scared, then you'd eventually believe it, along with everyone else. Her exact words were, "*If you pretend you're brave, then you will be. If you pretend something doesn't affect you, then it won't.*" So, that was what I was doing. I pushed away the fear dotting my vision and stopped the shaking of my hand as I held out three thousand dollars of cold cash, waiting for the guy that inevitably was the cause of my brother cowering in my bedroom the night before.

My first thought when I saw him was that he was grimy. Not like he hadn't showered—although, by the looks of his greasy hair, I wasn't sure he had in the last decade—but it was more his overall appearance and the look in his eye. It was filthy. He was a bad person. I sensed it right away. His smile slithered onto his face with unrivaled evil as he stared at me. His eyes didn't even glance down to the money in my hand. His gaze stayed glued to mine, and I had to fight the urge to look away.

"I was hoping we could work something out," I repeated, still holding the money in my hand. To be honest, I had no fucking clue what I was doing. I'd bailed my brother out of trouble before—lying to my parents, helping him through one of his lows of not using, hiding him in my closet when my parents were absolutely livid with him. But this went deeper. I was openly trying to pay a drug dealer for him. I wasn't just giving Jason money or lying for him. No, I was flat-out participating in some bad shit. I was crossing the line of falling into a darker part of our relationship, and I feared it would become a relationship where I'd keep on giving and he'd keep on taking. I'd crossed the line once before, a year ago, and I told myself I'd never do it again. But apparently, I was lying.

"Maybe we should talk privately?" I finally let my eyes drop from his, and I scanned our surrounding audience. Too many people were staring at me, and that thing that Hayley told me about not showing fear was slipping away. My hand began to shake, and my voice was wavering between hysterics.

Tank's head tilted a fraction as he ran his gaze down my body. I wore my skinny jeans and a low-cut black tank, even though it was a little chilly, because I wanted to look the part. I was taking a page out of my best friend's handbook. *Look the part, Piper. If you show them fear, they will descend on you like a flock of crows.* But at this point, I'd take being attacked by crows over standing in front of this guy.

Tank's eyes flared with something that I couldn't put my finger on. I heard a few people snickering behind me, and that was when I realized that what I'd just said sounded overly sexual and not at all what I'd meant. *Maybe we should talk privately... Jesus, Piper!*

I opened my mouth to backtrack, my forehead getting sticky with sweat. I shuffled on my feet, loose pebbles popping underneath my weight. "I—I didn't—"

"There you are," a familiar voice came up behind me, and then an arm was draped over my shoulder. "I told you to wait for me, Piper." Ollie leaned in a fraction and whispered along my ear softly, "*What the hell have you gotten yourself into?*"

"Piper?" Tank's head twitched again, and then it hit him. "You're here for Jason."

Ollie's arm felt heavy on my shoulders, his breath still warm in my ear, and I couldn't help but notice the tiny bit of courage it gave me. *Act confident.*

"I am." I stepped forward, letting Ollie's arm fall. Ollie gave me that little extra push, but this was something I needed to handle on my own. No one else needed to get involved in this. *I* shouldn't have even been involved in this.

"So..." Tank began to walk around the formed crowd, and I felt like we were in the pits about to spar. "You think you can give me..." He pushed his hand out and urged me to give him the cash. I reluctantly did so, not daring even a glance at Ollie. Tank took a few moments to count, and then a sinister chuckle left his mouth. "This doesn't even make a fucking dent in what Jason owes me."

My chest began to squeeze. My knees began to wobble. Sweat droplets fell down my back. "I know. I was hoping we could work something out."

"Oh, we can work something out, alright. I want my fucking money."

And just like that, I regretted my decision to help my brother. *What are you doing, Piper?* The crowd grew quiet as I stood still. I could feel myself panicking on the inside, but things were moving so quickly that I didn't have time to bask in my anxiety.

"I can get you the rest by the end of the month."

Tank threw his head back and cackled in the evening air. Not a single person in the crowd laughed or chuckled. Not even the two guys standing behind Tank that appeared to be his right-hand men.

He walked closer to me, a mere foot away from my face. I felt Ollie's presence come closer, too, and I hated that he was here, seeing this—but that was something I'd have to deal with later. Right now, I was about to make a deal with the devil.

"And just how are you going to get me the rest of the money?" Tank looked me up and down again, a wicked grin creeping onto his face. "Mommy and Daddy? Are they gonna fork over the cash? Are you going to give them a sob story and cry at their feet until they spoil their little princess?"

That was unlikely.

A voice sounded from beside me. "I'll get you the rest of the money." My heart lurched in my chest. The muscles in my neck screamed in pain as I whipped my head in Ollie's direction. His temples ticked along his sharp jawline as if he were grinding his teeth in between each word that tumbled out of his mouth. I could hear the nasty bite they left behind.

"Oh?" Tank shot a lethal glare to Ollie. "And how is that?"

"I'll race every weekend for you until the debt is paid. You can keep my winnings and continue betting on me."

"No." I didn't care that I honestly had no other legitimate plan in obtaining over fifteen thousand dollars for my brother's mistakes. I could figure that out later. There was no way Ollie was getting involved in this.

"Yes." Ollie didn't even look at me when speaking, which only heightened my anxiety. I should have been thankful he just offered to help me, but I wasn't. This was dangerous, and risky, and he was the last person I wanted knowing more of my secrets.

Tank's menacing laugh shot through the air. "Now, this is just getting interesting." He shuffled around the gravel, putting his back to us with tattoo-covered arms crossed in front of him. I shot an unwavering glare in Ollie's direction, but he still wouldn't look at me, and for some reason, that bothered me. *Is he disappointed in me?* Wait. Why did I care? And plus, what the hell was Ollie doing here in the first place?

My gaze raked around the crowd as it began to murmur and then out into the opening. A few cars sat side by side, one of those being Ollie's maroon Charger. What is this place? Did he say he'd race? I didn't think to ask my brother any details about where we were going to pay off his debt because I thought he'd be with me, and not to mention, I'd been too swept up in fear and nerves mixed around with guilt to even inquire more. *I should have asked for details!* I was making some seriously poor choices lately.

"You are *not* getting involved in this," I whispered under my breath, waiting for Tank to turn back around.

"Too late."

A steely glare fell onto both of our faces when we caught each other's eyes. Ollie stared at me, and I stared at him. *What are you thinking behind those blue eyes, Ollie?*

"Here's the deal." Tank turned around quickly and stalked over to us. I fought the urge to grab Ollie's hand and ignored the fact that I even had that urge. "You race right now, and if you win,"—he shrugged, a snake-like smile slithering on his face—"I'll consider it."

A mix of emotions rose up my throat. Anxiety clawed at my chest, threatening to burst. One part of my brain was begging me to accept this, to accept the help that Ollie was giving me, because I seriously had no other options, but the other part was yelling at me to stop this, to stop this before I drug another person into this fucked-up mess of things. I honestly couldn't decide which side was the rational one; both seemed like terrible paths to go down.

"No," I reiterated, taking my gaze off Ollie and placing it

on Tank's. "If you give me another week, I'll get you the rest of the money." *How, Piper? How are you going to come up with that much money?*

Tank growled. "Not many people talk back to me, sweetheart."

"Ignore her." Ollie stepped forward, blocking half of my body with his. He stood at least four inches taller than Tank, and if you paired that with his wide shoulders, he all but shouted *proceed with caution,* but Tank didn't move even a fraction. He laughed and looked out into the crowd.

"This is just adorable." He placed his hands on his hips and moved his head around Ollie to stare at me. "Here your boyfriend is, trying to help you, and there you are, trying to help Jason."

I ignored the part where he said that Ollie was my boyfriend, because that didn't really matter at a time like this. I straightened my shoulders again, reiterating Hayley's advice in my head, and very calmly said, "No one else needs to get involved in Jason's mess. I will get you the money next weekend. I'm good for my word."

Tank clicked his tongue. "Oh, I'm sure you are, but shit... Jason has fucked-up one too many fucking times." The calm and relaxed man in front of me started to change right before my eyes, and I was seconds from reaching out to Ollie and telling him that we needed to make a run for it. "This is your one and only fucking chance to get an advance on this fucking money. Take it." I gulped again, swallowing my thick spit. *It's fine, Piper. Just breathe.* "I'd let your boyfriend here race once and for all, because like I said, it's your only chance."

"Piper." Ollie didn't turn back to look at me. "I'm doing this whether you like it or not."

"I'd listen to him, sweetheart, because to be honest, he is your guardian angel. Or maybe he's Jason's?"

One of the guys that was standing close to Tank snickered, and I flicked my eyes up to him. He winked at me, and I shivered. Needing to know more, I asked, "What do you mean?" My voice was no more than a whisper in the wind.

Tank smiled and pulled out his phone. He messed around on it for a second, and Ollie glanced back at me, meeting my eyes briefly. I looked behind me, and Cole stood along the crowd with a wary expression on his face. When Cole looked concerned, that was when you knew you were in trouble.

Tank talked into the phone for a moment. "Pan the camera over to our pet." Then, with a conniving smile and sinister look in his eye, he shoved the phone in my face. It took a moment for my eyes to adjust, but when they did, my hand shot up to my mouth as I gasped. *Jason.* I almost yelled into the phone to ask if he was okay, but at the last second, Tank snatched it back.

"I'll hold off on my plan until your boyfriend races. Then, we talk."

He shoved his phone back in his pocket, and I couldn't help the words tumbling out of my mouth. "What plan?" I thought back to last night when Jason was huddled in the bathroom. The fear in his eyes was evident, but Jason was known to blow things out of proportion so that I'd be more likely to help him. But after talking with this guy for the last few minutes, I wasn't so sure Jason was exaggerating. And now, somehow, Jason was his pet?

The conniving smile was gone, the sinister look in his eye more evil than before, but he didn't answer me. He looked out into the crowd as if he didn't want to say it aloud.

"Well, what's the verdict, Princess? Are you going to let him race, or am I going to have to go through with it?"

My hand shot out, and I grabbed Ollie's wrist before he said anything; the feel of his skin on mine soothed my fear for a moment. "What's your plan?" I asked again.

"I wouldn't say it's so much my plan, but more of Jason's."

"What does that mean?" A swirl of wind rushed past me, and I felt like it took my breath along with it.

He shrugged, his voice lowering so only we could hear him. "Jason has a little bit of a drug problem. It'd be a shame if he overdosed."

"Wh-what?" I stuttered. Ollie's wrist flexed in my grasp, and it only made me hold on tighter. "What does that mean?"

Ollie was the one to speak. "It means I'm racing, Piper." His wrist fell from my hand as he shot me a look—one that sent an entirely new batch of fear down my spine.

I stood back and watched as he walked over to his Charger, the crowd following closely behind him. Suddenly, it felt like I'd stepped into an alternate reality, and I was almost one-hundred percent positive it wasn't going to be a good one.

CHAPTER SIX

OLLIE

MY HANDS SHOOK as my long strides took me back to my Charger. My phone buzzed in my jeans again, and I finally took it out and shut it off, gripping my phone with such force I was certain it was going to snap. I swallowed back the rage bubbling up inside of my chest like a shot of Fireball.

Being behind the wheel was exactly what I needed after that exchange. There were a million and one things running through my head—so much that I could barely focus on starting my engine. It all began with seeing Piper walk her sweet self through the tall grass with Cole, and from that moment on, I felt like a caged animal ready to rip people to shreds.

That was what being around Piper did to me.

She brought out something inside of me that was charged with jealousy, anger, and desire. I felt wild. A protective shield shot out of my very bones when I was near her. Maybe it was because she knew my secret. Maybe this was my way of protecting that little bit of myself that I gave to her so long ago. I wasn't sure. Either way, I hated the feeling of unsteadiness that it gave me.

Who the fuck was Jason? I turned my Charger on, feeling the rumble settle in my blood. *Why was Piper so dead set on paying his dues? Why was she protecting another guy?* I pulled up to the starting line, eyeing her standing beside Cole with her arms wrapped around her middle. *What was she thinking coming out here with him?* I revved the gas a few times, waiting for my opponent to pull up beside me. I had no clue who I was racing, but it didn't matter. This was something I had to do. The second I slid up beside Piper and took a stance with her was the second all rationality flew out of my head. Sometimes it scared me how defensive I became around her. I felt tethered to her in more ways than one. She was the one person I had confided in, and even if it was on the sly, she was there. She was my anchor. She helped keep me afloat that night. In a way, I owed her. *Maybe that was why I couldn't stop.*

The other car pulled up beside me as the crowd began to pull back, giving us space. *Fuck, I really had to take this one seriously.* The need to win had been instilled in me from a very young age. My dad had drilled it into my brother's and my heads. Of course, Christian, being the hothead of us both, always won when we'd play football in the backyard, but that was not to say I didn't *let* him win—something I was sure he'd argue until he was blue in the face. Nonetheless, winning was usually the only option for a Powell. *But are you even—* I growled out loud, stopping the thought before it consumed me. "Pay the fuck attention, Ollie."

My gaze wandered over to the other guy racing. He was driving a Chevy Camaro, and it looked expensive. The cherry-red color gleamed, even with the sun fading into dusk, and the tread on the tires had my confidence wavering for a moment. There was a tap on my window, and when I looked over, I saw Brandon staring at me with apprehension. I hurriedly rolled the window down.

He glanced at the Camaro before giving me a look. "He has a supercharger and nitrous."

My heart slammed. "Great."

Brandon flicked his eyes to the Camaro rumbling beside me. I darted my gaze to Piper who was biting her nail on the side of the road. Something awakened inside of me. *I'll win, Piper. Watch me.*

"I've got this," I said, eerily calm. My limbs relaxed as I wrapped my fingers around the stick shift.

"I've watched him race before. He has a fast car, which is why he's in the next bracket, but he loses control easily. Stay steady and do your thing. That's the only thing that'll help you now."

I nodded and began to roll my window up, but his hand shot out as he gripped the glass.

"You're going down a dangerous path, my man. You know that, right? Tank is bad fucking news."

I turned my head away and looked out at the dirt road. "No backing down now."

He chuckled. "Spoken in true Ollie form. The most confident son of a bitch I know." My mouth tipped upward but quickly fell when he asked, "Is that your girl?"

I followed Brandon's line of sight to Piper, and my heart sped up even more. I swallowed, taking my eyes off her. The unparalleled anxiety I felt from just seeing her quaking little body caused me to rev my Charger again.

"Not yet," I finally answered.

Brandon grinned and shook his head. "She looks worried."

"She shouldn't be. She knows me. She knows I don't like to lose."

"Oh, she's perfectly right to be worried. I don't know what type of business she's got with Tank, but the dude is bad fucking news, Ol. Tread lightly. Don't make a deal with him. You'll be signing your own death wish."

Too late, bro. The second I saw Piper involved, I'd already signed over my rights.

"Alright, boys." The blonde chick from earlier walked up beside the passenger side of my Charger and the driver's side of the Camaro. "Get ready."

I rolled the window up, watching Brandon retreat back toward his girl and Piper. My eye caught hers once, and I hoped she could read what I was trying to say. *I've got this, Pipe. Relax.*

She nodded her head slightly, so slightly that I barely noticed when she did. She knew I wouldn't lose, not with her involved.

I took a moment to breathe, my chest expanding and falling calmly. My back rested along the leather of my seat, and I felt the world shut out. The only thing I saw was the dirt road in front of me and the face of a girl that made my heart beat a little faster. The only thing I could hear was my engine rumbling with life. The only thing I could feel was the power of my car and the drive to win.

"Go!"

I sped away quickly, so quickly my back flew into the seat even harder than usual. Dust flew all around me and drowned out the rest of the crowd. Piper crept into my head, but I pushed her away, knowing I needed to focus in order to win. My car wasn't as fast as the supercharger, but I'd win. I'd win because I had to.

The sight of the red Camaro skirted my peripheral vision as I rounded the curve along the side of the forest, and I pushed the gas harder, knowing I needed to shift to gain more momentum. *You have to win, Ollie.* Brandon's words replayed in my head. *He's bad fucking news, Ol.*

The adrenaline in my veins was pumping so hard my

fingers prickled with heat on top of the steering wheel. I felt high on the rush, and it only pushed me further.

"Not today, bud." I shifted again as I came around the next curve, seeing the finish line up ahead. We were side by side, his car gaining traction faster than mine due to the upgrade he had. *Fucking hell.* I urged my Charger to go faster. My blood was pumping hard, my heart racing with so much speed I was certain I was going to have a heart attack.

Just then, as I heard a screeching, I got the push I needed to gun it. The Camaro disappeared from my vision, and I trudged on, speeding past the finish line quicker than I'd ever done before.

I fishtailed as I hit the brakes, coming to an abrupt stop before diving down into the trees.

My head snapped up to the rearview, my entire body running on the fumes of exhilaration. The dust was thick and heavy, but as I glanced around my windows, solace started to settle in.

The cool air and smell of unsettled dirt wafted around me as I climbed out of my Charger. My eyes adjusted as dust began to clear out and a grin etched itself onto my face as I spotted that cherry-red Camaro head-first in the middle of a line of trees. The driver was out behind it, pacing back and forth with his hands placed on his head. He appeared to be fine, but his car...not so much.

I got lucky.

I knew deep down I wouldn't have won if he didn't break traction and lose control. His car was faster, but thankfully, I was better at driving.

The universe was on my side this time. Maybe it was a nice little gesture, given the current circumstances I was facing.

After I tipped my chin to my opponent, I climbed back into my car and rounded back to the starting line.

I won this one, but that didn't mean the night was over by a longshot. As I climbed out of my seat, I spotted Piper instantly. Tank was standing entirely too close to her, and she looked ready to bolt. Her naturally pink-tinted cheeks were a ghastly white, and her copper-colored hair did nothing but enhance that. Brandon was right; I *was* about to sign a death wish, but first things first—who the fuck was Jason?

CHAPTER SEVEN

PIPER

OLLIE SLOWLY WALKED over to where I was standing, and chills rained down my spine. Relief pooled in my heart, and my eyes welled up. The entire time he was racing, I was trembling. My legs shook, and my heart was beating so fast I felt like I couldn't breathe. I should have pulled him out of his Charger and drug him back to his house, demanding he stay out of this. But one look from Tank eyeing me with malice had me shook. It was like he had me pinned to my spot. I didn't even want to blink, too afraid I'd show all my cards and he'd know just how afraid I was.

I kept trying to reiterate Hayley's words in my head, thinking back to a few months ago when we were in a situation that had both of our stress levels rising to their full capacity. Showing fear did nothing but heighten the anxiety and worry, but I was truly afraid.

I was afraid the first time I saw my brother high.

I was afraid the first time my parents threw him out.

I was afraid the first time he came back, beaten to a pulp, begging for my help.

And I was even more afraid last night when I'd been met with the same bloody and bruised Jason that I'd grown accustomed to seeing. But this time, he didn't just have disappointment in his eyes—he had fear.

He was terrified.

I wanted to believe he was being dramatic. But now I knew he wasn't.

What exactly did Tank mean? Was he going to kill my brother and make it look like an overdose?

My hand shot up to my mouth again. My throat felt constricted, like a snake was squeezing the air out of it the more I thought about my brother on Tank's phone. My brother was definitely messed up with his head lolled back like he was too drunk or high to even hold it upright. There was graffiti on the wall behind him, and his arms were hanging by his sides as he sat slumped in a chair. *Why was this happening?* I breathed through my nose to keep myself from doubling over and puking.

"Well, color me fucking surprised. You won."

I was brought back to reality when Tank spoke up beside me. I jumped an inch closer to Cole—the lesser of two evils surrounding me at the moment.

Ollie didn't take his gaze off mine. His blue eyes were shadowed by the evening sky and his heavy brow line. "I did," he finally answered, walking closer and standing directly in front of me. My heart was still racing, but having him near and seeing him safe after speeding down a dirt road had a smidge of my anxiety lessening.

Tank made the exchange quick, and I couldn't even fathom looking in his direction. He disgusted me. The conniving smile he gave me a few moments ago when Ollie took off in his car made my skin crawl. I knew he was a bad person. I'd been around bad people before, but I was almost certain he was evil down to his very core. There wasn't an ounce of goodness in him. Or maybe there was because, after all, he was making a deal to prolong whatever his plan was with Jason if I paid back what he owed.

"Keep the money." Tank handed the three thousand dollars I gave to him earlier to Ollie, and my head whipped over to their exchange. *What?* "Put a turbo in your car. You race for me every Saturday until I make back the money that Jason"—Tank's gaze settled on me for a beat—"shoved into his veins. Then, we will revisit the idea of you continuing to work for me."

Before I knew what I was doing, I blurted, "No way!"

Tank leveled me with a look that made me take a step back. *Piper, what the hell are you doing?* A burning anger had the reasonable Piper—the one who let people walk all over her— speaking up. I suddenly felt a wave of protectiveness wash over me, and to my surprise, it was for Ollie instead of my brother, which was maddening because I was certain that Jason was facing life or death over this. "I will have twenty thousand by Saturday. There is no need to drag anyone else into Jason's mess."

Tank threw his head back and laughed into the night sky like a wolf howling at the moon. The crowd that had formed around us grew quiet, waiting to see what would happen next. "Let me say this once, and only once." Tank's amusement was long gone, and in its place was something that resembled a monster. "Your boyfriend will race for me until I have the money paid back. I don't give a fuck..." He stepped closer to me, and Ollie reached out and grabbed my arm, pulling me over to his side in a flash. Tank tipped his chin and continued. "I don't give a fuck if I get the money from your boyfriend racing or from you draining your precious trust fund that I'm sure your parents set up for you, Princess. I will get my money, and if I don't..." He leveled me with a look. "Well...let's just say... if someone steals from me, it's the last fucking thing they do. You got it?"

My mouth was suddenly sewn shut. I kept the anger and resentment and fear all bottled up inside of me before I said something that blew up in my face.

Ollie's voice calmed me for a moment, but the words did not. "I'll be here Saturday. I'll race for you until the money is paid back."

The crowd whispered, but I didn't dare take my eyes off Tank.

I watched him smile with approval, showing off his yellowing teeth, and then he backed away, heading for another guy who seemed to be watching from the sidelines.

Ollie's grip on my arm never lessened. He pulled me with him, like a child being dragged away by a parent, all the way to his Charger, my shoes dragging in the loose dirt.

Once I finally grew the ability to speak again, I asked, "What are you doing?"

He shook his head once as he opened the passenger door. "Surely you didn't think we'd just go our separate ways and show up at school on Monday, acting like this never happened, did you?"

I opened my mouth, and then I slammed it closed again. *What the hell did I get us into?* The panic in my body started to make itself known, and my eyes began to water. *Do not cry in front of him. Do not. Do not fucking cry.*

"Get in," he demanded. His voice was nowhere near the teasing tone I was used to.

I held onto the top of the door and took a deep breath. "You're not racing for him next weekend. I won't let you."

He let out a deep chuckle, looking out into the distance.

His straight and perfect nose was the only thing I could focus on. "Get the fuck in the car, Piper."

"Don't treat me like that." The weeping girl inside of me was suddenly gone. I was angry. Everything I'd felt in the last day and a half suddenly turned to raging frustration. I wanted to lash out. I wanted to scream. I wanted to bang my fists on something.

"Like what?" His blue eyes locked onto mine, and suddenly, his face was inches away.

"Like I'm a child who just got in trouble."

His breath fanned over my face, and I had to fight the urge to inhale. A rush of heat cut through me, but I stayed still. "Get in the car."

"Make me."

Ollie's lip twitched as his eyes narrowed. "Do you really want me to? Because trust me, Piper..." His lips came closer, and I held my breath. "I can *absolutely* make you."

The pair of us stayed still, our faces too close for comfort. I stayed locked onto his eyes, but I wanted to trace my gaze over every curve of his features until they erased the way Tank had made me feel. I wanted Ollie's hot lips on mine. I wanted to feel the richness of them all over my body. Ollie had made my problems disappear before, and it seemed my body remembered.

And it wanted him to do it again.

"Get in." Ollie took a step back, and a rush of air flew out of my mouth, interrupting my inappropriate thoughts.

Embarrassed, I climbed into the passenger seat, and he slammed the door. I sat and waited, watching him talk to the guy Tank sought out after the race. The entire time, I was trying to come up with a plan to fix things—to make things better.

And sadly, I came up with nothing.

But one thing I knew: I couldn't let Ollie fix this problem.

Jason had already brought down too many people with this destructiveness.

He wasn't going to do that to Ollie, too. Not if I had anything to do with it.

I just needed some time to think. There *was* a way around this. I was certain of it.

CHAPTER EIGHT

OLLIE

PIPER and I didn't speak at all the entire drive to her house. Not a single syllable was shared. I didn't want to speak. My mind was spiraling out of control. The severity of the night had come crashing down on my shoulders as soon as I got on the freeway. My gaze stayed transfixed on the blurring yellow lines on the road, trying to focus on those instead of Piper, but I wanted to look at her. I wanted to place my heavy gaze on her until she broke and spilled everything.

She sat in the passenger seat, twiddling her fingers together in a nervous habit. There was usually a hefty amount of tension between the two of us, even more so when we were alone, but tonight it was off the charts. Although, it didn't feel like her tension was directed entirely at me. There was something bigger weighing on her mind, and I was going to find out what it was.

When we pulled up to her house, all the lights were on, just like Hayley had described, and her car was parked off near the mailbox. I held my phone in my hand and scanned my earlier texts, shooting Eric and Christian the same one, telling them I was on my way to the cabin. I had to cover my tracks—or else there'd be an even bigger mess on my hands.

Parkway Drive was streaming through my speakers when I placed my phone back down in the cup holder. I watched the thought cross Piper's face as her hand shot out to the door handle.

"Don't even fucking think about it, Piper."

She rolled her eyes and dropped her hand to her lap, not daring to look at me.

"Who's Jason?"

"Ollie..." Her red tendrils of hair swayed as she shook her head. "You are not getting involved in this. Don't worry about who Jason is. I have this handled."

Why won't she tell me who Jason is?

That familiar feeling of jealousy was sliding up my back and resting on my shoulders. "Who the fuck is Jason?" *Shit, calm down.* I cleared my throat and leveled my breathing. "Whoever he is, he must mean something big to you for you to get mixed in with that type of trouble."

My mind drifted back to that night so long ago that we shared in secret—so much a secret that she wouldn't even admit it aloud. *"I did something bad tonight."* Yes, she fucking did. Goody-Two-Shoes Piper turned into a desperate minx that night. She was an oxymoron. An angelic sin. A good girl turned bad. And it was so hot that I had a hard time seeing her as anything but.

"I'm not the good girl everyone thinks I am, Ollie."

I scoffed, leaning back in my seat a little more. "Oh, trust me. I know."

Piper eyed me out of the corner of her eye, knowing very well what I was referring to, but again, she wouldn't admit it.

Silence encased the car, the pair of us sitting in the dark

with only the glowing interior lights of my dash as our guidance. "Who is Jason?"

Piper finally looked my way for a brief second, just long enough to say, "Stop. Please," before looking out the window. "I will handle this. Don't worry about racing on Saturday. I'll get the money."

"From where? Do you have twenty thousand just laying around? I know our families are wealthy and all, and we're pretty fucking privileged, but even I don't have that much in my bank account. Do you?"

Her mouth opened then closed. She wrapped her arms around her torso, and for a moment, my chest ached. *Why won't she let me help her?* I knew there was an unhealthy bout of anger and tension around us. There were times I tormented her, flirted incessantly with her, and then turned around and flirted with another girl. I'd get under her skin on purpose because I loved it. I loved watching her react. I'd always kept Piper close but not close enough to where I could have her. We shared something together. She knew something about me that no one else did—of course I had to keep her close. *Keep your friends close, but your enemies closer.* From the moment I watched her enter English Prep our junior year, we'd been like this. At each other's throats. The recognition and shock in her eyes when her gaze transfixed on me that day told me that she recognized me, too.

Piper's voice was hardly above a whisper. "No, my parents watch my spending closely. Even if I did have that much in my bank account, they'd freak if I spent that much money."

A puff of air left my mouth. "So, then what's your plan? Because from where I'm sitting, you have no other options except to let me race on your behalf."

"Ollie." She shot me a glare. Her pouty lips flattened in a frown. "Let it go." Her hand was on the door handle again, and my heart jumped.

"Face it, Piper. You need my help. Just say it."

She wavered for a second, her hand pausing on the shiny handle. Her chest rose and fell softly as she deliberated. Then, her red locks shook with her head. "I don't want you involved. You're not racing for him. He's bad news." I was about to argue, but her head snapped to mine. "Wait a second. Why were you even there in the first place?" The flawless skin around her green eyes crinkled. "Is that what you do on Saturday nights? When Christian is with Hayley? Do you...race?"

My pulse buzzed in my ears. My fingers wrapped around my steering wheel as I twisted myself out from under her scrutinizing stare.

She reiterated, "Why the hell are you out there racing, Ollie?"

And I countered, "Who is Jason?"

"Why are you out there racing with those people? You shouldn't be involved with them."

I ignored her, asking again, "Who is Jason, and why are you so keen on helping him if you know these people are *bad news?* Must mean he's bad news too."

Piper shut her eyes tightly, her thick eyelashes fanning over her cheeks. "You really expect me to tell you my secrets, but you won't tell me yours?"

Something inside me changed. A smirk crept along my face as I looked her in the eye. "A secret for a secret?"

Even in the dark, I could see Piper's face turn a shade of pink. Her cheeks were dotted with freckles outlined by the burning feeling of embarrassment. *That's right, a secret for a secret. Ring any bells?*

"Are you really going to play this game, Ollie?"

I shrugged, leaning back in my leather seat and propping my arm on the center console. "You're the one playing games, Piper. If you won't let me help you, then fine."

Piper was right. I was playing a game. But I didn't like to lose. She knew that.

"Fine?" she asked. "That's it?"

"Yup," I answered, forcing my face to stay neutral. I reached for my phone and started up a new text to Hayley.

Piper's voice grew higher. "What are you doing?"

I stayed casual, shrugging. "Just texting Hayley."

"What? Why?" Her words came out rushed, and my heart sped up.

"I'm going to fill her in. If you won't let me help, you'll let her help."

Her gasp had my finger pausing over the keyboard. My pulse matched the bass of the song filtering through my speakers.

"I'll tell."

I looked at Piper out of the corner of my eye, pausing. "What?"

"I'll tell your secret." Her words were like ice in my veins.

Everything in my body froze. My hand was no longer moving over my phone screen. My breathing was drawn out, as if I couldn't quite catch an even breath. The beating inside my chest pounded slow and hard as calculated anger flew through my veins.

I slid my gaze over to Piper, and she was leveling me with an equally horrified expression, as if she couldn't believe she was stooping so low. "You wouldn't," I said under my breath.

I watched as Piper gulped, and she nodded her head slowly. "I will."

My nostrils flared as I tried to rein myself back in. "So, there it is."

Her eyebrows drew together in a mask of confusion.

"You're finally going to admit it."

Piper stayed silent. So, I continued on.

"I want to hear you say it."

"Say what?"

"Tell me you know it was me that night."

Piper and I stared at one another, her green eyes laced with so much emotion I couldn't pinpoint exactly what she was feeling. The one thing I did know was that she was simmering with something big.

"Admit it, Piper. If you're going to stoop to that level, at least have the decency to admit it to my face."

Piper teetered her pink lip back and forth between her teeth. My car was charged with so much rising energy that I was certain one of us would explode soon.

Anger was beginning to lace the surface of my feelings, and I was trying desperately to reel it in before I said something I regretted, but the thought of Piper spilling my darkest secret had me second-guessing the nature of our relationship. *Maybe she really does hate me.*

I licked my lips before prodding her even further. "Do you remember how I made you feel that night?"

Because fuck, I did.

The room was dark, not even a sliver of moon shone through the window. I could barely see anything in front of me, but that was okay. I didn't need to see the girl standing here to know who she was.

I spotted her the second I walked into this party. How no one noticed me, I'll never know, as I didn't even go to this school. But alas, I was here, and when she came into my sight, I was stuck to my spot against the wall. She had a bright and pretty face, free of too much makeup, and her hair was the color of a fallen leaf in the middle of autumn. On the outside, she looked sweet and innocent, but her body language was telling me something different. And now that we were alone in this room together, I sensed it was something along the lines of anger.

"So, a secret for a secret?" I whispered around the softness of her

ear. Her lithe body quaked, and I smirked. "I told you mine. Now you tell me yours."

I heard her lips part. "I did something."

My hand pushed her hair back from resting along her shoulder, my dick pulsing in my jeans. "You did? What was that?"

Her chest rose and fell swiftly, her head falling to the side, giving me access to her neck. My mouth was a breath away as she answered.

"I did something bad. Really, really bad."

I paused, keeping myself from sucking on her skin. Damn, she smelled fucking good. Too good. *"And did it feel good to be bad? I get the sense that you're a good girl."* Which was exactly why I was trying to give her an out.

She gulped. "It did in the moment."

I didn't say anything. I knew I should have told her to leave, that if she was a good girl, maybe she shouldn't be in a room at a Wellington Prep party with a guy she didn't know, but I couldn't bring myself to say it. So, I just stood there, my hands wrapped around her jean-clad waist, my mouth hovering over her neck.

Somehow, she took a step closer to me, and now her tits were rubbing on my chest. Fuck.

"I wanna be bad again."

Fuck me. My dick throbbed, begging to be free from my boxers. *"Are you sure you wanna be bad? If you're a good girl, maybe you shouldn't be in this room with me."*

"Are you saying you're a bad boy?"

I chuckled against her ear. "Depends on who you ask."

Her soft breath hit my cheek as she turned her head. "I'm asking you."

"What do you think?" My heart was flying throughout my chest. I hated having small talk with a girl, except for right now. I felt lighter after spilling my secret to her. I told this girl something I hadn't told a single fucking soul, and for some reason, that made me feel insanely comfortable with her. She asked why I was alone in this room, and I came right out and told her. A secret for a secret.

"I think you're a good guy, because you've yet to kiss me or act on that hard-on you're sporting."

My eyes glanced down to my dick rubbing against her, even though I couldn't see shit.

"But..." She swallowed, and my head came back up. "Do you think you can be a bad boy right now? Because even though I'm a good girl, I really wanna be bad...with you."

The shift of Piper moving in my passenger seat had me coming back to reality. I poked her again.

"Do you remember the way my lips felt on that spot behind your ear? Or how about the way your body fit so perfectly in my hands? Your soft skin rubbing on my rough calluses. Do you remember that, Piper?"

She was breathing faster, focusing her attention on anything but me. "Knock it off, Ollie."

I knew I was pushing her buttons, making her sweat in the passenger seat of my car. My chest was heaving with a hunger for her. Even as Piper threatened to take away the one thing I held under lock and key, I still found myself craving her. I enjoyed watching her squirm.

"Admit it, Piper. Say it out loud. If you're going to black-mail me, you might as well play dirty."

The way her lips felt on mine that night was forever branded into my brain. We were sloppy and desperate. Lips on lips, skin on skin. Piper and I were forever different after that night. I never thought I'd see her again.

And yet, here we were, stuck inside a car together with her basically blackmailing me.

"You forced me into playing dirty, Ollie. If you would just leave this alone, everything would be fine."

My voice was low, hoarse. "*Admit it, Piper.*"

Her hand rested on the door handle as my pulse thick-ened. I wasn't even sure why I wanted her to admit it. I knew it was her that night, and she knew it was me. It didn't matter if it was said aloud, and yet, I wanted to hear it.

The cool air sliced through the car when she opened her door. It was a welcome break in the hot-and-heavy feeling, but I wasn't letting her off the hook. "Fucking admit it, Piper." My own voice surprised me. It was rough and demanding, laced with anger.

At the last second, with her leg hanging out the door, Piper snapped her head over to me. Our eyes locked. "I'll admit it if you stay out of this and keep your mouth shut. This is my thing. My business. I don't want anyone to know."

My chest actually ached as the word tumbled out. "Fine." *No. Not fine.*

Piper's tongue quickly darted out to lick her lips before the words flew out of her mouth. "I know it was you at the Wellington Prep party. I remember every minute of how it felt with your hands on my body. But that also means I know who you *truly* are, Ollie. And I swear to God, I'll tell Christian everything if you don't stay out of this. I'll tell him you've been racing, too."

I felt the muscles in my face go lax as she stepped all the way out of my Charger and slammed the door so hard it made me clench my teeth. Disappointment washed over me. I thought I would have been happier to hear her admit it. I thought a feeling of euphoria would have rained down on my shoulders. I thought it would have given me back the feeling of control, but that was not what I felt at all.

Piper was being blatantly ruthless.

She didn't want my help with whatever the hell she got herself mixed in, and maybe it was time I listened to her. After all, she just threw me a curve ball.

"I'll tell your secret."

Fine, Piper. You fucking win.

CHAPTER NINE

PIPER

TWENTY SECONDS.

I was giving myself twenty seconds to breathe before I had to put on a brave face in front of my friends and act like everything was A-okay. How I went from being at Eric's party on Friday with them, to seeing my brother bloody on the bathroom floor, to some sketched-out race in the boonies with Cole and Ollie by my side, to school on a crisp Monday morning, I had no idea.

I scanned the entrance of English Prep as I sat in my driver's seat while students zipped through the parking lot to park their high-end cars before the first bell rang. It was chaotic on the outside of my car, but if I just sat inside and stared at the wrought-iron doors and lush greenery covering the stone on the school, I'd feel safe.

Calm.

The outside of my car depicted what I'd felt all day yesterday: chaos. I wasn't sure when it'd happened, but I was in way too deep with my brother's shit. The urge to run and tell my parents was strong, almost deafening, but I knew they wouldn't do anything. It was on the tip of my tongue when they FaceTimed me last night. My father continued to ask if everything was alright, and after the third time, I *almost* gave in. But then, Tank's words sounded in the back of my head, and I lied again. The sad thing was that I couldn't even blame my parents for not wanting to help Jason. He had screwed my parents over more times than I could count. He'd screwed over everyone. Even me. If you looked up the word *selfish* in the dictionary, Jason's face would be beside it.

But yet, here I was, stuck in the deep end, waving my arms frantically, all while my brother was tied like a chain around my ankles, dragging me under the water each and every time he messed up and begged for me to save him. He knew I'd help him, because it was what I did. I tried my hardest to fix people. It was a fault of mine. I recognized it, but for some reason, I couldn't stop doing it. I wanted to fix Jason so badly. I wanted things to go back to normal.

A sigh left my mouth as I opened my car door and stepped out, lugging my backpack behind me. The early morning breeze floated around and caused goosebumps to rise on the skin peeking between my knee-high socks and the hem of my plaid skirt. I scanned the courtyard, noting that Hayley wasn't here yet, and neither was Ollie—not that I was keeping track.

My stomach burned each and every time he crossed my mind yesterday. Things got heated between us Saturday night, and when he'd sped away from my house, I felt sick.

I was certain he truly hated me for what I'd said. I'd blackmailed him. I threw something in his face that I shouldn't have, but it was the only way to make him stay out of it.

Whatever. Leave it be. I had other things to worry about, like what Jason was doing and where he was. I gulped, thinking back to the image of him on Tank's phone. It bothered me not knowing how he came to be in Tank's possession. Did he go somewhere voluntarily? Did someone take him from the house? When Ollie and I pulled up Saturday night, my car was back. And although it was parked in a weird spot, with the keys dangling from the ignition, it appeared normal. So, my thought was that someone had come to the house to get Jason. *That means they know where you live.* I hated to think what would have happened to Jason if I didn't show up at the races, all but begging Tank to give an extension on his debt.

My hand wrapped around my hollowed-out stomach as I walked through the threshold of English Prep. *All I want is to be a normal fucking teenager.*

As soon as I was in front of my locker, my anxiety lessened some. Being in the halls of English Prep felt familiar and comforting. A year ago, I had felt like an animal that had escaped from the zoo while walking these halls. English Prep was vastly different from Wellington Prep. From the stone walls to the hundreds of years of old history, English Prep felt like more of a monarch. The school was ruled by tetrarchs of wealthy breeding—the Powells being one of them. Christian was the King of English Prep—that was his actual nickname, as ridiculous as it sounded—and Ollie was right there beside him. I cowered in the shadows my first few months at my new school, trying desperately to blend in. But being thrusted into a group of royal-like trust-fund babies with their glossy salon hair, flawless skin, and the most pristine uniforms was daunting as I looked anything *but*. I had a pressed uniform, sure, and an expensive car, but I was the new girl with the red hair and freckles from the opposing school, and if you paired that with the feeling of absolute isolation and a sense of not belonging, I didn't even come close to fitting in.

Madeline tormented me, and the guys snickered when I'd walk past. And don't even get me started on the first time I laid eyes on Ollie. My heart lurched; my stomach twisted. Recognition hit me square in the face, but he casually passed over me like I was nothing. As if he didn't take my virginity at a Wellington Prep party. He did so well acting like he didn't know who I was that I actually started second-guessing that it was him—my dirty little secret.

Then, of course, as time went on and I spent more time around him due to Hayley, I realized he was faking it the entire time.

Ollie knew exactly who I was, and I knew exactly who he was.

The only beneficial part of being a student at English Prep was that no one knew my history. My last name wasn't tainted here—and it still wasn't—although now, Ollie had gotten a little glimpse on Saturday night. He had now gone through yet another tunnel of secrets I held close.

I slammed my locker shut with a scream, the books I held in my hand tumbling down onto the checkered floor.

"Jeez! Sorry, Piper. Why are you so jumpy?"

My hand was still covering my chest as I looked into Hayley's eyes. I couldn't quite catch my breath. "Oh my God! You scared me."

My hands shook as I bent down to grab my things. Hayley bent down and helped, too. "I said hi as I walked up. Christian did, too, when he passed to get to his locker." My eyes darted down the hall as I placed the last book in my arms. I spotted Ollie instantly as he stood beside his brother and Eric, along with a few other guys from the football team. His hands were wrapped around the straps of his backpack, and I swore I could see their grip harden as we locked eyes.

I almost inhaled a breath as he narrowed his eyes. He tilted his head to the side, his light hair moving effortlessly atop his head. His look was questioning at best. *Problem?* his eyes read.

My walls went up. *No problems here. Everything is fine.*

He shook his head disapprovingly and turned his back, shutting me out.

"What's going on with you?"

"What?" I straightened my spine and adjusted my books so they were level in my arms. Hayley leaned back onto my locker and kicked her foot up behind her.

"You're acting...unlike yourself."

I rolled my eyes playfully, pulling down my metaphorical mask. "You know I'm clumsy. I drop my books one time, and you automatically think I'm being jumpy. Everything is fine." I laughed it off.

She eyed me cautiously but let it go. "So, what exactly were you doing again on Saturday when I came by? You never said."

Quickly remembering what I'd made up in my head to cover myself on Saturday. "Oh, someone from the soup kitchen needed my help. Her dog got out, and she needed someone to watch her kids so she could go find it." *Stupid excuse, but whatever.*

Hayley nodded as we walked over to her locker, which of course was only a few down from where the kings of the school were standing. I kept my back to Ollie. "Oh, so did she find her dog?"

I nodded. "Yep, all is well."

My face was tight with all the fakeness I was forcing out. All I wanted to do was pull Hayley aside and blurt out where I actually was, but this was my thing. Hayley had been through enough bad shit in her life to last several lifetimes. There was absolutely no way in hell I was dragging my best friend into this mess. She needed a break. Hayley was happy and doing well. She was safe, and that wasn't something that came easily for her.

"That's good. I want a pet one day." She sighed, reaching

into her locker. "Anyway, do you still want to do a girls' night this weekend?" She spun around with a cheerful smile after shutting her locker, the color of life bright in her cheeks. "Would it be okay if we did it at Ann's? I know she's older than us and has a career and all of that, but she's kinda cool, and she'd probably love to hang and watch movies all night with us." She shrugged, looking down at her books for a second, bashfully. "And I think it would make her feel good that I was inviting a friend over for the night. She keeps stressing that her house is now my house and that she is technically no longer my social worker, so..."

I smiled. "Of course, Hayley. I've always liked Ann, even when you hated her."

She laughed, and I followed suit, forgetting for a moment that Ollie was only a few feet away with his back turned to me.

Hayley smiled before looking past my shoulder. "Did you hear that, Christian? Piper and I are having a girls' night this weekend, so no interruptions."

"Fuckkk. I forgot. When is it again?"

She rolled her eyes, a smirk on her face. "I don't know. Saturday?" She looked at me for confirmation.

"Saturday?" Ollie's casual tone hit my ears, and I froze.

Hayley raised her eyebrows at me. "Is Saturday good for you?"

Then, before I even had a chance to speak, Ollie came into my line of sight. He moved beside Hayley and smirked at me, but it wasn't playful by any means. His chiseled jaw was set firm as his lip curled upward. His blue eyes squinted, waiting for my answer. Ollie was mad at me, and that didn't sit well.

I felt my face getting hot. "Yep, that works. I'll see you at lunch. I have to go to the bathroom."

I quickly walked past my group of friends and acted casual

as I found the door for the bathroom. The second I was inside, my eyes grew blurry. *What did I get myself into?* I took a deep breath. *And why do I even care that Ollie is upset with me? I'm supposed to hate him!* Short gasps of air were clawing to get out of my chest, and I tried to do anything but think of the reality of the situation. *Take a deep breath, Piper. Stop crying.*

"Move."

My head snapped up, and I was met with blonde hair and a catty expression. Madeline's perfect, dainty nose was upturned in my direction, and I wanted to lash out. I wanted to smack her so I could put forth all the emotion that was trying to escape into her. Instead, I took another calming breath and squared my shoulders, staring her dead in the eye. A year ago, I would have instantly backed down and moved out of her way. But now? No. Madeline was mean and callous, but I wasn't afraid of her anymore. I mean, just two nights ago, I was face to face with a guy who said he was basically going to murder my brother, so this was nothing.

Plus, Madeline was a pariah now. Christian made that very clear the second Madeline did him dirty. She had no upper hand. Hayley took her place as queen in the school, and Madeline suffered every day.

"You don't scare me, Madeline. *You* move."

"I should scare you, Piper."

A laugh was seconds from coming out of my mouth, but Madeline's expression changed from angry to conniving in three seconds flat, and it had me wavering.

She flipped her long hair behind her shoulder as the first bell rang above our heads. "So, are you switching back and forth between them or...?"

What? My eyebrows folded.

"Which is better? Cole? Or Ollie?"

My heartbeat thumped in my ears. "What?"

The only reason she would say something like that was if she...

"I saw you with them at the races."

My mouth fell open as the bathroom door swung behind me.

"Piper?" Hayley paused with the door half open, allowing everyone to see into the girl's bathroom. "Are you—" Hayley paused. "What the hell are you doing, Madeline? Still trying to torment people? Do we need to revisit the conversation we had the last time we were in this bathroom?"

Madeline's eyes darted for a moment before they landed on Hayley briefly, then she looked at me. One of her mascara-clad eyes closed in a wink before she pushed past me and stood in front of Hayley standing half in front of the door. "I was just complimenting Piper on her taste in men." She glanced back at me once more before sighing happily. "Too-dles, girls."

Then, she left, and Hayley stared after her, dumbfounded. "What the hell was that about?"

I pulled my books closer to my chest. "Just Madeline being Madeline." Hayley and I exited the bathroom, walking toward our classes before the tardy bell rang. I had to force myself to take even breaths with every step.

We stopped in front of Hayley's class, Christian standing by the door, waiting for her. He gave me a tip of his chin and walked inside. I made myself keep my eyes on Hayley and not inside the classroom where I knew Ollie was. "What were you doing? Looking for me?" I asked.

"Oh, yeah, Ollie said you looked like you were about to cry, so I came to check on you. You're okay, right?"

I brushed it off quickly, laughing. "I'm fine! I wasn't crying." *Lie.*

"I didn't think so, but Ollie was so sure you were crying that he actually bet me. He's so dumb sometimes."

I swallowed, inching my way toward my class before I was late. "Why did he say I was crying?"

She shrugged, looking confused. "He made up a stupid excuse, saying that he made you cry with his good looks...that some girls just couldn't handle them." She chuckled. "But I could tell he was lying. He seriously thought you were crying."

I rolled my eyes, pretending I wasn't angry beyond belief. He *knew* I was panicking, and he sent her in there for what? So I'd spill and tell her? Or did he send her in there because he was actually concerned that I was upset? Either way, I was mad. I swore, Ollie could make me smile in one breath, and in the next, he could make me so incredibly angry. It was infuriating!

But two could play that game.

Before going into my class, I shouted to Hayley from across the hall, "Tell Ollie I said his looks have nothing on Cole."

Her face blanched. "Cole? Like, the Cole Christian beat up a few months ago?"

I nodded. "Just tell him...and tell him I said to fuck off while he's at it."

Hayley let out a small laugh and shook her head before turning around and walking into her class. Over her shoulder, she shouted, "You two are exhausting."

She had no idea.

CHAPTER TEN

OLLIE

THE COLOR YELLOW was always meant to be welcoming—
bright, happy, all things golden—but it had been my least
favorite color for several years now. I scanned the four
yellow walls in my parents' bedroom as I sat with my back
against the door. This room used to be my favorite room
in the house. It hadn't changed at all. After my mom
passed, no one dared to enter it, let alone *change* it. Christian could barely even walk past the door without bending
over at the stomach with pain. The large king bed still sat
in the middle, untouched. I wasn't even sure if my dad
slept in it when he was home—which wasn't often—but it
looked like it hadn't been slept on once in the last five
years.

It felt like razors were in my throat when I swallowed,
looking at my mom's vanity—the vanity that changed me
entirely. My mother's perfume still sat with the lid beside it,
and if I tried hard enough, I bet I could smell her flowery
scent. The brush that laid next to it still had her blonde

strands running throughout, and her makeup was still spilled all over the place.

My eyes dipped to the now fully closed drawer that ran underneath the top, the one that was ajar a year ago. I still regret the day I pulled it open and started digging.

That moment defined everything in my life after, and it was a moment I had been replaying in my head every single hour on the dot after my argument with Piper.

I'll tell your secret.

I grew angrier with each passing day. Yesterday, I tried to catch her in a lie in front of Hayley, and I knew I was toying with her, crossing over that invisible line of keeping my mouth shut like she wanted, but fuck, did I want to break her. I wanted to break her down until she told Hayley what was going on, *or* until she told me everything and let me help her. I was half ready to tell Christian what I'd found a year ago just so Piper couldn't dangle it over my head and keep me at arm's length, but I stopped myself at the last second.

She told you to stay out of it.

I knew what it was like wanting people to stay out of your business. It was why I was racing in the first place. I wanted to do my own shit and shut everything and everyone out. Sometimes it made me wonder if that was how my mom felt when she got wrapped up in drugs. Was she trying to escape something? Was she trying to deal with shit on her own instead of relying on my dad?

But he's not your dad, Ollie.

My head dropped between my knees as I ran my hands through my hair. It was a hard pill to swallow. I'd known for a year now that Daniel Powell wasn't my father, and yet, every time I'd said it, it cut fucking deep.

I wasn't a Powell—not by blood, at least—and I struggled with that every single day since I'd found my birth certificate tucked away in my mother's vanity like it was in hiding.

My father and I got along fine. I mean, he wasn't home much, so we rarely talked, and Christian and I had pretty much fended for ourselves for the last five years, but my father didn't act like I was the bastard child that I actually was. He pretty much treated Christian and me the same. He gave us an allotted amount in our bank account each month, checked in with our grades occasionally, and boom, that was the extent of it. He didn't treat me like shit or favor Christian. He was just *Dad*. Except he wasn't my fucking dad.

And I had no idea if he knew that. He wasn't on my birth certificate. The only name listed was my mother's. So, where was he when she was giving birth? With Christian? My brother and I were only eleven months apart—Irish twins— and it was truly hard to fathom that my mom went out and got pregnant only two months after Christian was born. It didn't make any sense.

But what did make sense was when I looked into the mirror or at a picture with Christian and me side by side, we looked nothing alike. We shared the same firm jaw, but that was it. He looked like Dad, and I didn't.

Since I was young, I'd been hearing how strong the Powell genes were, and yet, I didn't have a single feature. How could my dad not see that? Did he just chalk it up to me taking after my mom? Or did he know and pretended like he didn't?

When I'd first found the birth certificate, I knew there was more to my mother than Christian and I thought. And just a few months ago, we learned how our mother truly died. Apparently, there were a lot of buried lies and lurking secrets.

Our mother had an ugly past, one that Christian and I had only touched the tip of.

And maybe it didn't matter. Maybe my dad knew I wasn't his biological son. Christian probably wouldn't look at me any differently, but would it fuck up the memory of our mother even further? Would he and Dad butt heads again?

A growl escaped my chest as I slowly raised my head.

The funny thing was that even though Piper pretended she didn't know my secret and acted like she didn't know who I was that night at the party a year ago, it was comforting that she *did* know. She grounded me. It felt like I had someone in my corner, someone to share all the little secrets with, but now that she threw it in my face and threatened to tell, I felt more alone than ever.

Part of me didn't believe she'd tell Christian, knowing very well that it was too personal of a secret to fuck around with, but that was a gamble in itself. Piper was proving she wasn't who I thought she was.

Yet, I still had my phone pulled out to text Brandon.

The veins on the back of my hand popped as I held my phone tight and typed.

Me: Yeah, I still want the turbo. Tell me when and where and I'll drop the Charger off.

I paused, swallowing back the anxiety.

Me: And I want to know everything there is to know about this Tank fucker.

I pushed my phone into my jeans as I stood up, giving the vanity one last look, and walked out of my parents' bedroom like nothing had ever happened.

That was what I did.

I shoved all the secrets down and went about my day like they didn't even matter.

And maybe they didn't.

The next day at school, Eric and I pulled up and hopped out of his car with Christian staring at us from across the parking lot. He was clearly confused.

"Where's your car?" he asked the second I walked up to him, leaning back on his own Charger. A few guys were standing around, shooting the shit, discussing what parties they were going to this weekend, which was pointless because we all knew they'd be at Eric's, like always.

I shrugged, fixing my navy tie. "Wanted to get some work done. It's in the shop."

"What kind of work?"

This was the thing with Christian. We were eleven months apart, but he had this underlying need to act like he owned me. Granted, I'd acted more recklessly than he ever had, partied harder than he had, and had been late more times than I could count, but for the last few months, I'd fixed my shit. Instead of burying myself between English Prep's finest legs and drowning in booze, I'd started channeling my need for release into something else that allowed me to fly under the radar. I wasn't as heedless as he liked to think anymore.

Instead of not being interested in anything but partying and having fun and escaping all the pent-up shit inside, I was now calculated in where I threw my aggression.

Christian could back off, and I could still do my own thing without him breathing down my neck.

"Just some tuning, brother. Chill." I continued fixing my tie so Headmaster Walton wouldn't have an aneurysm when he saw me walk into school as Christian continued to lean on his Charger and stare at me.

"Why didn't you ask me to take you to school?"

I sliced my eyes to his. "Why the fifth degree? And you weren't home when I got up. Still sneakin' into Hay's room at night?" I grinned, and he looked away.

"Speak of the devil." Hayley pulled up in *her* Charger that Christian and I talked her into getting after she got the money from her father's will. She refused at first, saying it was too cutesy to get a matching car like her boyfriend, but the Powell brothers could be quite convincing. Plus, after she went 0-60 in three seconds flat, she was a goner. *Hayley would love the races.*

I chuckled silently. Christian would have a fucking heart attack if Hayley popped up at the races with me. Not because he'd think I liked her like that—Hayley was like a sister to me —but more so because he was overly protective of her, and the races weren't exactly the safest place to be. Hayley didn't need much protection, though, unlike Piper.

My gaze caught her pulling into her spot, and it seemed like everything else faded away. I didn't hear Hayley as she walked up, talking to Christian before wrapping her arms around his torso. I didn't hear what Eric had mumbled before he stormed off after locking eyes on Madeline. I had tunnel vision when it came to Piper climbing out of her BMW. She looked tired—her hair thrown in a ponytail on the top of her head, swaying as she walked up to our group. Her arms were wrapped around her tiny frame, and the dark circles under her eyes were a deep purple against her pale, creamy skin.

It had me forgetting that she blackmailed me as an achy feeling settled in my bones.

I continued to watch her as she briefly talked to Hayley and Christian, pretending everything was okay—as if she weren't living a double life. I hated that I wanted to dig further into it. Not only did I want to know who Jason was, but I wanted to know how the hell it was all related to Tank.

He was a bad guy. A scumbag. He was one-parking-ticket-away-from-going-to-jail bad. After Brandon had met me at the shop to drop off my Charger yesterday, he gave me the rundown.

Tank got kicked out of Oak Hill—the high school that most of the middle class and poor attended—a few years ago, in the middle of his senior year. Since then, he'd been to jail three times for possession of drugs, assault, and petty theft. He had a lengthy record and was—according to Brandon—completely fucking crazy. Brandon reiterated that making a deal with Tank was a lot like making a deal with the devil—*he'll fuck you over if you even blink wrong*. He ran with a bad crowd, and if people weren't afraid of him, that meant they were just as shady.

So, I couldn't, for the life of me, figure out how Piper got mixed in with him. Almost every Friday, she was at Eric's, unless her parents were in town for what seemed like their monthly check-in. And then on Saturdays, she usually hung out with Hayley or occasionally went to her cousin Andrew's.

Andrew went to Wellington Prep, and even though he was a fuck-boy like Cole, who went to Wellington Prep, too, I didn't see those guys getting mixed in with Tank's crowd, but I wasn't sure.

Regardless, as I stood back and observed Piper, it completely took me by surprise that she'd somehow be roped into a mess like this. Then again, she did tell me she did something bad a year ago—not that we went into many details before smashing, but I couldn't help but wonder if the two situations were related.

There were too many unanswered questions and variables for it to make sense to me.

Piper gasped as she looked at her phone. "Oh, shit. I told Mrs. Dewinkle I'd help her prep for today's student council meeting."

Hayley let out a light laugh. "You're not even on the student council, Piper."

Piper sighed as she started to walk toward the doors to

the school. "I know. But she was frazzled after class yesterday, and I said I'd help her."

"You're too nice, Pipe. You help everyone."

"It's one of my faults." She smiled shyly at Hayley before turning around and walking through the threshold of English Prep, ignoring me all together.

My brow crinkled. *That's not a fault, Piper.*

But it was true. Piper did help everyone. She was kind and genuine, even if she did give me shit the majority of the time. Piper could dish out all the kindness and help there was, but when it came to someone else wanting to help her, she refused. Why was that?

CHAPTER ELEVEN

PIPER

THE HALLS of English Prep were quiet, as if I were the only person in the building. All of my peers were still outside, waiting for the first bell to ring, chatting with their group of friends, the guys adjusting their navy ties, and the girls pulling their skirts down so Headmaster Walton didn't turn red in the face when he saw a little too much leg.

After Mrs. Dewinkle thanked me for helping her prep the student council packets for their meeting today, I was free to go back outside with everyone, but the peace and quiet with a fresh mind was just what I needed this morning.

I had four days to figure out how I was going to come up with the money for Tank. Four days to basically pull a wad of cash out of a magician's hat. Four days to keep Ollie away and to get my brother out of this mess.

I rested my head against my locker, the metal cooling my warm skin. *Think, Piper. Just think.*

The first bell rang above my head, and I sighed, pushing myself off the lockers. Soon, everyone would be coming inside and getting on with their day, their only worry being the Spanish mid-term that brought students to their knees every year. Yet, my biggest worry was coming up with a large amount of money to pay off my brother's drug dealer and keeping my story straight so my friends wouldn't know. *Sweet.*

Just as I was about to unlock my locker, I realized that my bookbag was still in my car. *Get yourself together, Piper.*

On the way, I passed by Hayley. "I left my bag in my car. I'll see you at lunch!"

She nodded as Christian pulled her in close. I kept my eyes straight ahead, ignoring the fact that I knew Ollie wasn't far behind and that he was probably eyeing me with suspicion. As soon as I was through the doors and had rounded the bend along the side of English Prep, there was a harsh tug on my white blouse, and I flew backwards. "Umph."

My body flung on top of the sidewalk, and I tumbled backwards, landing on the grass, banging the side of my head off the ornate stone siding. My mouth gaped as I sat up straight, my hand reaching above my ear and locating my source of pain.

"Hiya, Piper."

A girl who looked a little older than me—or maybe she wasn't; maybe she was just that run-down—stared at me from up above. I hurriedly tried to scramble to my feet, hearing a loud rip as I moved. I glanced backwards and was met with two long legs standing close to me with one foot on the hem of my plaid skirt. *Nice. Now my fucking skirt is ripped.*

"What is this?" I asked, staying on the lush grass, pinned down by an obnoxiously large foot on my skirt. *If Headmaster Walton thinks there's too much skin showing in a regularly hemmed skirt, he's going to faint when he sees a giant rip down the back of mine.*

"Let her up." Slowly, the foot holding me down by my

uniformed skirt moved, and I slowly stood up. I brushed my hands down the plaid fabric and bit back agitation.

"Who are you?"

The girl standing in front of me twisted her ratty, dark hair with her finger, the chipped red nail polish catching my eye. Neither she nor the other girl was wearing an English Prep uniform. I didn't recognize either of them. "Tank sent us."

I swallowed my thick spit and tried to stay calm, although my body was shaking. "Tank sent you? For what?" I could feel the panic sourcing through my veins, an anxious tremble starting in the tips of my fingers. This wasn't the first time I'd been face to face with someone over my brother's shit.

Once, at Wellington Prep, right before my parents tore me away, a girl came up to me and pulled my hair right in front of the entire cafeteria. I screamed out as she demanded my brother pay hers. I remembered looking her dead in the face, the entire cafeteria silent as we sparred off, and telling her that I didn't pay for my brother's mistakes and she shouldn't be doing her brother's business either. Eventually, a teacher came and took her to the office, and Andrew rushed to my side to make sure I was okay. But I wasn't. I wasn't okay at all.

I still wasn't.

The girl behind me walked over to her friend like a sneaky cat, and she smiled deviously, as if she knew something I didn't. "Tank just wanted to let you know that he has his eye on you and to not get any bright ideas."

My arms crossed over my chest in defense. "Like what? Going to the cops?" My throat constricted as I swallowed back my breakfast. A cool breeze wafted around my bare legs and up my ripped skirt. I fought the need to shiver. I'd have been lying if I said I didn't consider going to the cops over this. The image of my brother on Tank's phone frightened me, and I kept going back to it anytime my thoughts relaxed. But what were the cops going to do? Jason was just as likely to get in trouble as Tank was, and the last thing my parents needed was for Jason to go to jail. It would just make things worse.

The girl with the dark, stringy hair instantly got in my face and forced my body up against the side of the building. The rough stone scraped my skin, but I didn't move a muscle along my face. I wasn't going to show her I was in pain.

Her breath reeked of stale cigarettes, and my nose upturned in the opposite direction. "If you go to the cops, it'll be the last fucking thing you or your brother do."

Slowly, I brought my gaze down and leveled her with a stare. "Is that a threat?"

Her hand reached up, and she grabbed onto my ponytail. My heart sped up, but I kept my gaze neutral. *Do not act afraid. You've been in this position before.* I fought the urge to yell out as she pulled my hair, my chin flying upward. "That's absolutely a threat. Jason is already on thin ice, Princess. And so are you."

A heavy breath flew through my nose as the final bell rang. I couldn't even focus on the fact that I was late for first period. Not a single person was in sight; everyone was securely tucked inside their classrooms. And here I was, being handled by a bunch of girls who scared me more than I'd like to admit.

"So, what? Tank sent you to do his dirty work? A simple text would have sufficed. There's no need for this. He'll get his money."

The girl tugged on my ponytail again, and a small yelp escaped me. Miss Big Foot cackled like a wicked witch behind her.

"Sky, that's enough."

My eyes moved over to the right where I saw Madeline

slowly approaching. She looked from me to Sky and then to the other girl. "Her teacher is going to wonder where she is. The first bell has rung. I think you've made your point."

Sky snickered at Madeline and then looked at me again, her grip on my hair getting tighter. "Is that so? Do you get it? Don't fuck over my man, Princess."

So, this was Tank's girlfriend? What guy sends his girlfriend to scare an innocent girl into paying her brother's debt? And how did Madeline know her?

Sky tugged on my hair again and got closer to my face. I pressed my back even harder against the stone as a burning pain sliced through my shirt.

"I get it," I bit out, and she finally let go of me. My body flew forward so the stone would stop digging in, and Sky and her friend turned on their heel and headed for the parking lot. Sky called out over her shoulder, "Thanks for pointing her out, Madeline. And I'll see you on Saturday, Red. Tell your boyfriend to get ready to race."

I waited until they were long gone to breathe out a sigh of relief. Madeline continued to stand beside me as she watched them leave too, not moving or saying a thing, as if this were a completely normal day.

"Lovely friends you have there, Madeline." I felt behind me to determine how bad the rip was in my skirt. "What? Did you feel the need to get new friends after Christian ran your name through the dirt?" Anger had me spewing at the mouth just with the sight of her face. "Are you that twisted inside that you think bullying me is going to get you a spot back at his table?" Madeline's cheeks grew pink when she finally took a second to look at me. "Newsflash, Madeline: you got yourself booted from the hierarchy here at English Prep, and I had nothing to do with it. So, for you to follow me around and stick your nose in my business is petty." My face felt hot, and my stomach was bubbling with a fierce need to hit something. I was even more pissed that my skirt was ripped so badly my underwear was showing.

"You have no idea what you're even talking about." Madeline flung her platinum hair over her shoulder and walked back into school, and I was left standing on the side of English Prep with my skirt *literally* flapping in the wind.

Great.

CHAPTER TWELVE

OLLIE

"Fuckin' yessss," Jace—who was more of an acquaintance of mine—yelled out as Mr. Calhoun slapped the paper down on his desk. "A *fucking* plus."

"Yes, yes, I get you're very excited." Mr. Calhoun continued to walk around the classroom, handing out tests. "And while I appreciate all words in the English language, the word *fuck* isn't exactly appropriate, so watch it."

I'd always liked Mr. Calhoun, and he was a damn good teacher—not too stuffy, a little lax on the rules, but still taught English so well that I actually paid attention and didn't feel the need to sleep. I wasn't going to lie; I slept through a lot of my classes. And if I didn't get stellar grades, my teachers would have been pissed. But it was hard to yell at me when I still continued to get As in their classes, and not to mention, I was their favorite student. I could get away with basically anything. Next year was going to be a breeze, although, a lousy breeze because ninety percent of my friends—Christian included—

would be away at college, and I'd be stuck here for one more year. Why my mother held me back one year, even though I was technically old enough to be in the same grade as Christian, was beyond me, and unfortunately, I couldn't ask her why.

"Great work, Hayley. As always." I grinned as Hayley smiled at Mr. Calhoun when he handed her paper back and as Christian tried to hide his scowl at him giving Hayley yet another glowing compliment. He was such an overbearing, protective hot-head.

My phone vibrated as Mr. Calhoun laid the white paper down on my desk. "You too, Oliver. This was a great paper. I enjoyed reading your view on such a delicate topic."

"Thanks, Mr. Calhoun. I did my best to impress, as always." I heard a few girls giggle, and I smirked, but just as the smirk came on my face, it quickly disappeared.

The text on my phone had me pausing.

Madeline: Outside, right wing of school. Go now.

Me: Is this a booty text? I don't do my brother's leftovers, especially not at 8 in the morning. Sorry.

I glanced at Christian, and he was too busy talking to Hayley as I waited for a reply. What the fuck was Madeline doing? Why she would think I'd ever touch her pussy was beyond me.

Madeline: Fuck you, Ollie. It's about Piper.

I shot out of my chair immediately, my knees banging the wooden desk as I climbed out.

"Mr. Powell? Is there a problem?"

Christian stood up, too, blindsided by my sudden need to jump out of my desk. "Ollie? What's wrong?"

I cleared my throat. "Sorry, Mr. Calhoun. I just remembered I left my book in my car."

My eyes averted from him as I lied, and I caught Eric's gaze. His dark brow was crinkled, and he shook his head slightly. *Oh fuck.* "I mean, in Eric's car." *Christian now knows I'm lying.* "Do you mind if I go grab it?"

Mr. Calhoun sighed. "Be quick."

Eric tossed me his keys at the last second, going with my story as the lies flew out of my mouth. Christian slowly sat down in his desk and adjusted his tie around his neck, as if it were suffocating him. He stared at me all the way to the classroom door, but I kept my face steady. *Everything is just dandy, big bro.*

As soon as I was through the door, I quickly made my way to the doors of English Prep, passing by the front office as casually as possible. As soon as the daylight greeted me, I rushed to the side of the school, and that was where I saw Piper pacing back and forth on the sidewalk. Her head snapped up, her ponytail from earlier now loose with strands of copper-colored hair floating around her face.

"What are you doing here?" she demanded, wide-eyed.

"What happened?" I walked a little closer to her as I glanced around. No one else was near. The parking lot, which was several yards away, was silent and unmoving. I didn't see Madeline, either.

Piper appeared nervous. Her hand shot to her mouth, and she nibbled on her thumb nail. The closer I got to her, the more my anger with her faded away. She looked so delicate and innocent standing there. It made me forget that she had so many secrets closed away behind her pretty lips.

"Why aren't you in class, Piper?" I was surprised at how soft my voice came out. I was a wolf approaching a lamb, treading nice and easy because I didn't want to scare her away. I wanted her to let me help instead of clamming up and shoving me away.

Why can't you just leave her be, Ollie?

Piper's shoulders dropped slightly before she took both

hands and put them on her face. She disappeared into her palms, and I almost reached out to her. *Is she crying? Jesus.*

Suddenly, her hands dropped, and she leveled me with an intense stare. "I'm not in class because my skirt ripped, and I can't drive home to change because I left my stupid keys in Mrs. Dewinkle's classroom."

Her skirt ripped? My eyes dipped down to the blue fabric to see if I could get a glimpse of the hidden goods, but I hastily brought them back up to her. "You don't have an extra in your locker or something?"

"Ugh. No. I lent it to Hayley a while back when Madeline stole her clothes that one day." *Ah yes, I remember that.* Piper rolled her eyes. "I forgot to put it back in there when she gave it back."

My brow furrowed. "Why is your skirt ripped?" I looked around the area again. "And why are you on the side of English Prep when you should be in class? I didn't peg you for a rule breaker."

Piper only stared at me. She didn't roll her eyes or give me a sassy response like in the past. She just stared, her green eyes glassy, as if they were part of the sea. "Piper? Does this have something to do with *Jason*?"

Her eyes clenched tight, and that was when I really took the time to take her in. Her hair was messy, the perky pony-tail now sad and limp. Her usual pink cheeks were pale, and the bags under her eyes almost seemed worse than when I saw her a little while ago. "Piper, tell me who Jason is. Tell me why you're involved with a known drug dealer who's been to jail several times. Tell me what's going on."

"Why can't you just stay out of this?" Her eyes opened, and the spark was back. Piper was back. "I have everything handled, Ollie. Why are you even out here?" she growled. "Ugh! Just go back to class!"

"Madeline texted me. Said you needed help."

She scoffed, crossing her arms over her white blouse. "Madeline? What is her deal with me? Oh, and by the way, she knows you race on Saturdays. She was there."

What? Fucking Madeline.

I stalked closer to Piper, and she immediately raised her chin and met me with a look that somehow held both fear and strength. "Stop fucking around. What's going on, Piper?" I held her attention for a moment before I took my hands and threw them around her waist, flipping her around at the last second. Her breath caught, and mine did, too, as I scanned the tear in her skirt. The wind picked up just at the right moment, and the plaid material swayed with the breeze. Her panties were a dusty blue, and they looked as soft as silk. I swallowed back a hot lump in my throat. "Why is your skirt torn?"

Piper growled again and swung her body around and hit me with a glare. Her arms flew upward as she shouted, "Because Tank sent his girlfriend to warn me not to go to the cops about our deal and to tell you to get ready for Saturday. They wanted to scare me." Her breathing was labored as she seethed at me. Looking from the outside in, someone would think we were ready to brawl. She was simmering with anger, angling her delicate chin in my face, and I was towering over her with furrowed brows and a look that could kill.

Her voice grew higher as she continued to shout at me from down below. "Since you can't take a hint, I'll tell you something that'll hopefully resonate with you and make you back the hell off." I kept my face steady, my brows still a shadow over my eyes. "Jason is my brother! And I'm going to do whatever I can to get him out of this mess without anyone butting in! So just stop butting in!"

I pulled back instantly, almost as if she had punched me in the stomach. *She has a brother?*

As if she could read my thoughts—which I wouldn't put

that past her; she and I had an unusual connection to one another—she nodded. "Yep. I have a brother. And now you know the whole secret, Ollie. You got a small taste of it a year ago, locked away in that dark room together, and now you get to gulp it down. So just stay out of it!"

I was stunned. Unable to speak. I couldn't wrap my head around the fact that she had a brother. Who? How old was he? And what type of person was he to let his sister pay back money he owed to a guy like Tank?

I allowed myself five seconds to take in the information, and then I piled it away in my back pocket for later. Piper was on the verge of tears, and I wasn't sure if it was because she was angry with me, upset about her brother, or if it was the fear of some chick coming to scare her this morning. Maybe it was all of the above. Regardless, this wasn't the time for me to ask questions or prod her more. She was crazy if she thought I was letting her handle this on her own, though. Blackmail or not, I wasn't backing down where she was involved. She should have known that by now.

"Go to the girls' locker room and stay there until I get back."

Piper looked up from staring at the grass. "What? Where are you going? And I can't just skip class!"

"I have it handled, Piper. Does your house have a code to get in? What is it? I'll grab you a skirt and come back and bring it to you. I'll handle Headmaster Walton."

Piper looked ready to argue, and I tilted my head, silently telling her that it wasn't going to work. Reluctantly, she obliged. "Top drawer of my dresser. I'll text you the code. The cleaning lady might be there, but just tell her I sent you. Call me if she doesn't believe you."

"Okay, go." I nodded my head to the side door of English Prep and turned around to head to the front to butter up Headmaster Walton with a believable story about why I needed to leave English Prep for a few. You couldn't typically sign yourself out of school without a parent, but he loved Christian and me, and so did Ms. Boyd. This would be a breeze.

Before Piper disappeared inside the school, I called out to her, "You know this conversation isn't over, right?"

She paused with her back to me, her ripped skirt still swaying with the breeze, but then she trudged herself through the doors without even sparing me a glance.

This wasn't over, and she knew it.

CHAPTER THIRTEEN

PIPER

TWENTY THOUSAND DOLLARS. Those three words had been on repeat in my head since Saturday night. That, and the encounter with Sky earlier today. My life had done a total 360 in the last few years, so it shouldn't have been a surprise that I barely recognized myself in the mirror anymore. My life used to revolve around the occasional family dinner that my parents would deem necessary after weeks of being away at work, leaving Jason and me with our nanny who, in a poor attempt, would try to make us feel loved by playing Scrabble with us each weekend. It worked for a little while. But as soon as Jason got a little older and he became distant, that was when I started to change. I became independent. Jason shut me out, my parents were gone more than ever, and soon, everything was flipped upside down. And here I was, a new person. I morphed into a girl that lied to everyone she cared about and contemplated breaking into her father's safe to save someone who probably didn't even deserve it.

My eyes traced over my reflection in the side of our spotless, stainless steel fridge as I stood there eating my organic, microwaved dinner that our housekeeper stocked the freezer with a few days prior. Sure, I had the same bright-green eyes and red hair. My nose was still lined with a few faint freckles, but the girl inside was vastly different than who she was a year ago.

Everything fell apart the second my parents tore me away from Wellington Prep. It was like they had a vendetta against that side of Pike Valley, as if Wellington Prep was the reason for my brother's mistakes—not theirs. Not the fact that, instead of getting my brother help, they just turned a blind eye and buried themselves even further into their careers, acting like everything was okay—all just to keep their appearances clean and pristine. That was why they tore me away from my old school in the first place. Jason had ruined our name. Painted them as bad parents. It was why I'd kept it a secret for so long—that was what I was taught to do.

I turned away from my reflection with frustration as Ollie's face popped into my head. *Ollie knew.* The shock that rippled onto his face earlier was blatantly apparent. I told him who Jason was. My secret was no longer a secret. And maybe it never should have been, but the mere thought that someone was getting a peek into my life made me uncomfortable. All I wanted was to fix my brother's shit discreetly and go about my business, pretending that my life was normal. I only had a few more months until college. Once I got to college, everything would be better—at least that was what I had been telling myself since last year. I'd be several hundred miles away. I wouldn't have to worry if Jason was going to pop up randomly one day, asking for my help. I wouldn't have to feel guilty, either. *Sorry, I'm four hours away from home. I can't come get you.*

Who was I kidding? I'd still feel guilty.

Placing my dinner on the counter, I pulled out a piece of

paper and flung my damp hair over my shoulder. The clock on the stove read 8:58. My homework was done for the evening, I had already showered, and my linguine was half-eaten. This seemed like the perfect time to come up with a list of ways I could somehow make twenty thousand dollars within a few days *without* Ollie's help.

My stomach continued to twist as my thoughts drifted toward him, and then it dropped completely when there was a knock on the front door.

I gasped as the piece of paper flew out of my hands and floated to the floor.

The first person to come to mind was Tank. He was like a bad dream that lurked in the dark shadows inside my bedroom before I fell asleep, reminding me that bad things were on the verge of unleashing. He'd already sent his girlfriend to scare me at school; I wouldn't put it past him to send someone to my house, too. I tried taking a deep breath as I walked through the long hallway to get to my front door. I eyed the alarm on the far wall, noting that it said *Armed*. At least I did one right thing today.

My calves stretched as I reached up on my tiptoes to peek out the peephole.

"Open the door, Piper."

My breath caught as I saw Ollie standing with his back against the side railing of the porch with a black hat backwards on his head, looking as casually hot as he always did. My feet fell flat to the hardwood with a slap. *What is he doing here?!* I brought my hands up to my damp hair and ran my fingers through the wet strands. *Wait. Who cares what I look like?!* I was pretty sure Ollie had seen me look much worse.

The heavy door creaked as I slowly swung it open, half hiding behind it. "Ollie, go home."

A throaty chuckle left him as he flew past me, the door opening even wider. The beeping of the alarm was ringing in the background as I stood with my mouth gaping. Why I was surprised that Ollie just rushed into my house like he owned the place was beside me. It *was* Ollie, after all.

"You gonna get that?" Ollie nodded his head to the beeping coming from the side of the wall as I stared at him. He shook his head and gave me a chaste eye roll as he stalked over to it and punched in the numbers. At that moment, I knew I shouldn't have given him the alarm code earlier in the day, but he *did* grab me a new skirt from my house and handled Headmaster Walton, *so...*

"Ollie, what are you doing here?" Ollie stood back along the wall with his eyebrows raised to the brim of his hat. His mouth was slowly creeping into a smirk, and I felt my face flame.

"What?"

His head tilted to the right slightly as his fist came up to rest on his chin. "Are you...?" He scanned me from the top of my head all the way to the tips of my toes, and I tried my hardest not to shift on my feet. I hated more than anything that Ollie's stare did things to my body. His look heated me up from the inside out. "Piper, are you wearing my shirt?"

"Wh—?" I snapped my head down and almost died right then. Looking back up at me was the face of a bulldog on a navy shirt with big block letters that said ENGLISH PREP in white. *Oh my God, I should have burned this shirt!* "I..."

The sound of my gulp echoed in the empty foyer as Ollie continued to stare at me from across the hallway. My ears felt hot, and my face was surely one match away from actually erupting into flames.

"I can't believe you're wearing my shirt. You little thief." He shook his head lightly. "Did you steal it that night you and Hayley stayed at my house?"

I totally did. Hayley and I stayed at Christian and Ollie's

the night she was attacked after one of the football games. It was a comfy shirt; of course I took it with me.

Speak, Piper. Deny, deny, deny.

Ollie pushed off from the wall, looking more smug than I'd ever seen him. "You did. You stole my shirt." He sighed. "Naughty, naughty Piper. I knew you weren't a good girl."

My eyes narrowed, and I could tell by the instant spark in his eye that he enjoyed the rise he was getting out of me. "Well..." He chuckled, glancing away for a moment. "I kind of already knew you weren't one of the *good* girls."

I crossed my arms over the stupid shirt, ignoring that little snide remark. "What do you want, Ollie? Or did you come here just to feed your egotistical personality?"

He stared at me, still from across the hallway, wearing a dark-gray t-shirt and jeans with a smile that could dazzle me right off my feet if I let it.

A troubling thought seemed to flash across his face as his smile fell, and it surprised me at how much it bothered me to see him *not* smiling. I looked away quickly, annoyed.

Ollie's voice was softer now, less playful. "I just came to check on you."

I flashed him a look. "You're lying. You want to know more about Jason."

He shook his head, looking down at the floor for a second. "That's not true. You know I'm not a liar, Piper. I came to check on you. It bothers me that someone came to the school to mess with you—especially on Christian's and my watch."

I snickered. "On your guys' watch? What are you? The bodyguards of English Prep?"

Ollie's naturally cheerful personality was replaced with something fierce. The planes on his face were drawn tight. "When it comes to you and Hayley, yeah, pretty much. I do remember, not too long ago, when you both were run off the road in what seemed to be a high-speed chase. Oh, and again, when Hayley was actually *taken*." My heart thudded in my chest at the thought, but it burned with heat as I thought of Ollie feeling protective over me. I wanted to close the vulnerable part of myself off so I could bask in the warmth of his protectiveness, but I quickly shut that down.

I hated that I was like this. That I so desperately wanted to be alone. *Invisible*. Letting someone in was very difficult for me, and I recognized that. I guess it was the lack of love and attention my parents gave me growing up. Or maybe it was because Jason kind of just left me hanging—by myself. Regardless of the reason, I thrived in my independence. I didn't need anyone's help. There was no way I was getting close enough to Ollie so he could just leave me, too.

"I'm fine," I finally answered, not daring to look him in the eye, too fearful he'd see right through the wall I threw up.

Ollie ignored me as he pushed off the wall, more than likely frustrated with my fake answer, and headed for the kitchen. "Alone again?" he asked over his shoulder. I watched as he took long strides down the hall, and again as he sat down at the kitchen island, waiting for me to follow.

"I'm always alone," I mumbled, walking around the counter to stare at him. The island was a nice barrier between the pair of us—made me feel a little more grounded. There was just something about being alone with Ollie that stirred things up inside, things that I'd rather push away.

Ollie leaned back and crossed his arms over his chest, tightening that steely jaw. "Precisely why I'm here. Do your parents ever come home?"

I shrugged as I stood back along the cabinets lining the kitchen. "Sometimes on the weekends. Just depends on their schedules."

"And what about Jason?"

I swallowed to keep myself from cringing. I knew we'd

have to touch on this subject eventually. "He's not allowed to be here."

Ollie raised one eyebrow as he leaned his long arms on the bar top. "Not allowed?"

I shook my head. "No. My parents kicked him out a little while ago and banned him from ever coming back to the house." The secrets were coming out of my mouth effortlessly, and I was surprised at how good it felt. If I even mumbled Jason's name to my parents, they'd instantly shut the conversation down. Jason was a no-talk zone with them— or anyone, really. He was cut out of our lives, *forgotten*. So, this actually felt good. Wrong, but good. "He stole from them the last time he was here, and when you add that to everything he'd ever done wrong...my parents were done. That was where they drew the line."

I looked away from Ollie's intense stare as I got sucked into the things I'd managed to bury over the years. A little bit of guilt started to seep in. I always felt the need to defend him. "My brother wasn't always like this. He used to be good. Normal. We were best friends once." A shaky sigh left my mouth as I pushed my back even further into the cabinets. "But he got in with the wrong crowd, and well...here we are."

I heard Ollie shift, but I kept my gaze trained to the floor. "Yes...here we are, raising twenty G's to pay back a drug dealer."

My stomach dipped, and I stood up straight, placing my attention on him. "There is no *we,* Ollie. You aren't getting involved. These people—"

He interrupted me, throwing his hands out. "Are bad fucking news, which is why I'm so intent on helping you. I don't like that you're near these people."

I didn't like that he was near them either. "Why were you even racing that night?" I crossed my arms over *his* shirt as I walked closer to him. He peeked up at me through his thick eyelashes, the blue in his eyes sucking me in like a storm over the ocean. He shrugged but kept his mouth in a straight line, not answering me.

Our eyes were locked and loaded. I gave him a look that said I wasn't backing down, and he gave me one right back.

"Why were you racing?"

He clicked his tongue and gave me a half smile. "I was bored?"

I narrowed my gaze. "I told you about Jason...the least you can do is tell me the truth."

Ollie looked away, his chest puffing out with a deep breath. I knew he was thinking of changing the subject or skirting around the real reason, but that wasn't going to work. I wanted to know why he was racing.

An idea hit me after a few seconds of watching him nervously crack his knuckles. A sly smile had my lips moving. "A secret for a secret?"

Those blue eyes flew to mine, and he cocked an eyebrow. After sighing again, he adjusted the backwards hat on his head, giving me a glimpse of his light hair before relaxing back in his seat.

"Don't you ever just need an escape?"

My mouth fell into a frown at the sound of his voice. For a moment, I forgot that I pretended to hate him. We were almost face to face, the kitchen island no longer in between us. The barrier had suddenly vanished. It was always like this with us. Things got stirred up between us within a moment's notice. The chemistry pulsed. Our emotions ran high. I blamed it on that night at Andrew's. Like some twisted spell was cast over us in that room, forever tethering us together. He was raw that night, spilling his secrets to a complete stranger, and looking at him now, I got the sense that he felt the exact same way. As if nothing had changed in the last year we'd pretended to be at odds with one another. The secret he held close still ate away at him.

I could always tell when the thought would cross his mind, whether it was someone mentioning how he and Christian didn't look alike, or when Eric would compare Ollie's chipperness to Christian's broodiness. Each and every time, I'd watch Ollie's behavior. His smile wouldn't reach his eyes, his laugh wouldn't echo throughout the room, and above all else, he'd look *lost*.

"Is that why you're here tonight?" My voice came out like a lullaby. Soft and welcoming. The air quickly changed between us, and for once, I wasn't trying to hide behind my masked hatred or basking in an old grudge. There was a weird pull in my heart that ached with the need to rid him of his problems. Strangely enough, I wanted to pull him in instead of push him away.

He cleared his throat, and I quickly snapped back to reality, shaking off the warm and fuzzy feeling I was getting. "I'm here because I was worried about you and because we need to figure things out. I don't like not being in control."

I began to shake my head to protest, but he slapped his hand on the counter. "I'm fucking racing regardless, Piper. Go ahead and say you'll tell Christian he's not my real brother."

All of a sudden, the tall chair scraped the floor as Ollie stood up. My arms quickly uncrossed and fell from my chest as he crept toward me. I began walking backwards to the cabinets, trying desperately to put some space between us. Ollie was tall, much taller than me, and with the look of desperate determination in his eye, it felt like he grew ten more inches. The heavy tension was back as he pinned me to my spot and almost spat the words, "Tell me you'll blackmail me and tell my dirty little secret. I don't care."

I could never. I was bluffing the other night, fueled by the intense need to cover up my problems, and he knew it.

Ollie was within spitting distance, erasing almost all of the space between us. If I reached my hand out even a fraction, I'd be touching his rising chest. My head continued to tilt upward as he came closer to me, caging me in with his heavy presence. In this moment, I very quickly learned there was more than just one side to Ollie. There was the light and fluffy Ollie, the one who teased and joked and smiled so brightly he lit up an entire room. And then there was this one, the fiercely protective, determined beyond belief, and intimidating Ollie. It was a little bit like getting a glimpse of his older brother. They may not have shared a father, but they sure shared something. His determination was unwavering. He wasn't going to take no for an answer.

I felt his seething hot breath on my face as he towered over me. My heart thumped hard, and my vision was a tunnel to his mouth as the words continued to tumble out. "You can pretend all you want that you're dark inside, Piper, that you'd take something so fucking personal and skew it to benefit yourself, but you and I both know that's a lie." I held my breath as Ollie's hand cupped my chin. "You're too good. You're sweet. *Caring*. You wouldn't do that because you know it would hurt Christian and me both. You don't destroy others, Piper. You *help* others."

I said nothing as he continued to hold my chin. The blues in his eyes sucked me in, and I felt myself becoming submissive. My body wanted to sink into him. I wanted to dive in deep. Ollie was the water, and I was completely on fire.

Ollie's eyes searched mine as he asked, "Have you ever noticed that the broken ones are always the ones who help others?"

It felt like a knife was being thrusted into my chest.

"No," I answered breathlessly, barely keeping my legs from giving out.

His grip on my chin tightened. "That's because *you're* the

broken one, Piper. You're too busy helping everyone else to realize you're the one that needs help."

The knife twisted with his words.

"I'm not broken." A lump began to form in my throat at the validity of his words. *I'm not broken.*

"You are, Piper. Don't you realize it? You instantly stepped in and helped Hayley the first day she arrived at English Prep, and you continued to do so even though it put your own life at risk." I tried to shake my head, but Ollie's grip wouldn't let me. He shook his head, that stupid backwards baseball hat staying perfectly perched on top. "You're helping your brother even though I'm certain he doesn't deserve it. And I wonder how many times you've helped him in the past."

Too many.

"And yet, you can't see that you're the one that needs a little help. You can't do this on your own."

I clenched my teeth together. *I know I need help. I just don't want it.* "Well...you're helping me, so what does that make you?"

Ollie and I stared at one another for far too long. The moment between us was full of crackling electricity. We were covered with an impenetrable blanket. *"Broken,"* he said, clenching his jaw. "It means I'm a little broken, too. And that's how I know you won't tell Christian. That's not you, so stop pretending it is."

I finally tore my chin away from him, and his hand fell swiftly from my face. I breathed in a heavy breath, like I was starved for oxygen. "You don't know me, Ollie."

He slowly walked away from me, and I wouldn't dare look at him, because he was right. He was right about everything, and I *hated* it. I hated it so much.

This was exactly why I didn't want him involved. Ollie saw right through me. He saw me, and now he was seeing all my flaws and just how messed up I truly was. How messed up my family was.

I was lying to my parents and my best friend. I was going down a rocky path, trying to save someone that wouldn't even save themself.

"I do know you, Piper." Ollie's voice was distant, and I couldn't shake the feeling it left me with even after the front door closed behind him.

I felt seen, and that scared me, because for once, it didn't feel wrong.

CHAPTER FOURTEEN

OLLIE

THE VISION of Piper wearing my shirt was all I saw. From the moment I woke up in the morning to the second I closed my eyes at night, I saw her. The smooth, toned legs hanging out from below the hem had me sweating even in a cold shower. And don't even get me started on being in close proximity to her. It took everything I had inside of the teenaged horny part of me not to creep my knee in between her legs as I had her pinned against the tall, kitchen cabinets the other night. Her sweet breath fanned over my face, and her hurt, doe-like eyes sucked me in so far I didn't think I'd ever be able to crawl out.

Piper had me in her grip. The hurt that flashed behind her green eyes...I felt that. In the past, I've teased her incessantly. I've flirted, only to turn around and leave her. I've pushed her away, only to pull her in at the last second. It was just how we were. But the other night, both of our shields were down, and I didn't know if she noticed it, but I was at her mercy. I wasn't playing. I wasn't trying to make her uncomfortable. My body was acting on its own.

Piper had me at her mercy.

She needed saving, whether she wanted to admit that or not, and I was going to be the one to do it.

"What the fuck is going on with you?" I glanced to my left and saw my brother standing beside Eric, both of them staring at me.

"What?" I asked as I pulled myself back to reality. I quickly scanned the room and realized that Eric's cabin was full of most of my classmates. *When the fuck did they get here?*

Christian straightened his shoulders. "You've been sitting in that same spot for over twenty minutes, lost in thought. Are you high? I thought you quit smoking."

I shook my head. "I'm not high. I did stop smoking. I was just thinking, I guess."

Eric raised his eyebrow. He'd been onto me since the day I made up that stupid shit about my book being left in his car when he and I both knew very well that it was a lie. I had to turn around later that day and make up another excuse when Christian asked why I'd never come back to class. He texted me four times before he all but demanded I tell him what was going on during lunch. I was lying to him more and more lately, and I wasn't sure what was worse—lying to him over and over again about the little shit or keeping something big from him. If I just told him the truth about Dad, I'd probably never have to lie again. I wouldn't have to avoid my dad at all costs, and I wouldn't feel the need to race to escape anything. It would all be out in the open.

But then, what would that lead to?

I wasn't sure where that would put the three of us. Things were good with my dad and Christian. I didn't want to fuck it up.

Christian dipped his head in low. "Thinking about what? You okay?"

My lip tipped. "Bro, I'm fine. Why does everything have to have an underlying cause? I was just thinking about who I wanted to fuck tonight."

Now that wasn't really a lie, was it? I mean, Piper *was* on my mind seconds ago, and it seemed she was the only girl I wanted.

Eric stayed off to the side, still eyeing me incredulously. He wasn't buying my shit at all. He didn't believe a thing I'd said when I told him I was *tuning* my Charger for shits and giggles. Earlier, he'd dropped me off at the shop to pick it up, and when he'd heard my turbo whistling, his head damn near snapped off his neck. Brandon talked me into getting new injectors and some head studs along with the turbo, so underneath my Charger's hood was a whole fucking party.

Piper and I hadn't discussed the races since the other night at her house. I kept my eyes trained away from her face at school. I was afraid we'd get in another staring match and raise even more questions from Hayley and Christian.

Speaking of those two, Christian was pulled out of my space as Hayley entered the party. She wrapped her arms around him and tucked her face into the crook of his neck. "Leave your brother alone, Christian. He's fine."

I grinned. Hayley always had my back.

Standing up, I gazed around the room, trying to land on the only person I truly wanted to see. Some girls in the corner all smiled wide when I passed over them, and I winked in an attempt to appear normal.

"Where's Piper?" I asked as Hayley came out from my brother's grasp.

Nonchalantly, she answered, "Oh, she stopped at Andrew's to talk to Cole."

My heart thudded to the floor. *What the fuck? Alone? Again? With him?*

I knew I should have threatened him further the other night. Before Piper and I had left the races, I shot him a glare and told him to lose her fucking number. He was bad news, and I didn't trust him.

My pulse drummed beneath my skin as I started to head for the door.

"Where are you going?" Christian called out, but I didn't answer.

Just as I was pulling my keys out of my pocket, I collided with something small. My hand shot out to steady the person in front of me, and when my palm felt the soft skin underneath me, I instantly knew who it was.

"Piper?"

Her vivid green eyes were wide with shock. "Jeez! What?"

My head snapped over to Hayley as she stood back beside Christian with her arched eyebrow raised high. The grin on her face had me grinding my teeth. I knew what she was doing. She knew something was going on between her best friend and me, and she was trying to catch us in it. Hayley wasn't as easily swayed like my brother was. She wanted a reaction out of me, and she knew she'd get it by awakening the jealous beast inside me.

Christian snickered as he looked from me to his girl-friend, then he shook his head and dragged Hayley away by the hand.

Piper looked from my face down to her arm where my hand still rested. "Why are you still holding my arm?"

My hand dropped immediately as I looked away. I felt trapped. On edge. I wasn't exactly nervous to race tomorrow, but I was definitely worried about Piper being involved. I felt like things were slipping out of my control.

I slowly slipped my keys back into my pocket and began

walking past her. Before I got too far, I whispered in her ear, "We need to talk. Find me later." And then I headed straight for the keg.

Some malty beer should help calm my worries—at least for tonight.

Piper was becoming a staple in my head more and more as time went on. Especially now that I knew she was mixed up in some bad shit. My worries were at an all-time high, and if I let her overtake every part of my brain, that meant there was room for mistakes, and I had my own secret to worry about, too.

CHAPTER FIFTEEN

PIPER

THE DECK RAILING was smooth along my palms as I held onto the edge, looking out below as my friends gathered around the bonfire that Eric so excitedly shouted about moments before. The fire roared to life in hues of orange and red as he poured gasoline over it, everyone yelling in their loud drunken manners.

Ollie was standing back, observing Eric throw some type of paper into the fire and periodically watching his brother and Hayley stare at one another with that intense connection they'd always had. Even from above, I could tell Ollie was struggling with whatever he was thinking about. The glow of flames danced along his high cheekbones and along the side of his jaw. His light hair was disheveled on top, as if he had run his hand through it before coming outside.

Ollie was attractive—and not in the way that most of these guys were. He was painstakingly beautiful. His smooth face, his deep-blue eyes, his smile that literally lit up a room. Whereas his brother was broody and dangerously hot with a smirk, Ollie was more of the glowing, made-straight-from-heaven, flawless type of beautiful.

He made my heart skip a beat. Whenever he shined that flirty smile my way, my stomach would dip low, even more so when I tried to ignore it. But the other night, in my kitchen, was different. He wasn't his usual charming self, and I couldn't get it out of my head. Sleep never came after he'd left. I kept tossing and turning in bed, wondering what would have happened if I had inched just a fraction closer to his body, how my body would have reacted if I had felt his lips on mine again.

It was a distant memory, but I would never forget the way kissing Ollie felt.

His kiss ruined me. I knew, after that night, I'd compare every kiss after to his.

I wondered if he remembered how it felt to kiss me. Was I like all the other girls he'd kissed? Or was I different, too?

Almost as if he heard me, he swung his attention up to the deck, and he landed on me. Half of his face was shadowed by the midnight sky, but the other half was glowing.

He slowly looked away, but before I knew it, he was making his way up the hill and over to the deck stairs.

No one else was up here besides me. Everyone was down around the fire or locked away in a bedroom somewhere, fooling around just like Ollie and I had done a year prior at Andrew's.

"Hey."

I kept my attention on the bonfire, almost too nervous to look Ollie in the face. Things had shifted between us after he came to my house. The truth was spewed, and I still wasn't sure what to do with it. Ollie read me like I was his favorite book, and all I wanted to do was rip out every single page.

"Hey," I said back, ignoring that pesky little dip in my belly.

Nothing was said between us for a little while. I watched the party down below, and Ollie stood back along the side of the cabin, staying a safe distance away from me. Maybe he felt the shift between us, too.

I was the first to break the silence. I slowly turned around and leaned against the railing. I covered my hands with the sleeves of my chunky sweater. "Are you sure you want to do this?"

It was hard to see Ollie as shadows from the night covered his body. I could only make out his silhouette, and that comforted me slightly. At least with his face in the dark, he couldn't strip me bare with his eyes again. "Do what, exactly?"

I felt every word that left Ollie's mouth cover my skin. His voice was tight, like he was angry about something.

I cleared my throat, pressing myself further into the deck railing. A couple of shouts and laughs came from down below, but I ignored those and focused on Ollie's shadow. "Racing. Racing for Tank. Paying my brother's debt. Helping me."

Ollie emerged from his shadow, and his light eyes found me in an instant. "Of course I'm sure."

I hated how at ease I felt with his words. I looked away. "I feel guilty."

There I went again. Being completely open to him. Uncovering feelings I tried to hide. It was his eyes. They somehow pulled me in even when I was trying to run away.

When I looked up again, Ollie was closer. Almost too close. "Guilty about what? Because I'd be racing tomorrow regardless of this little thing with Tank."

There was a gaping hole opening up in my stomach. I felt sick knowing I brought him into this mess with Tank—racing or not. "Yeah, but now you're racing to pay off a drug dealer. I brought you into that. Now money is involved. And not to mention, he's sketchy."

Ollie scoffed. "You know the money doesn't matter to me. If I had enough in my account right now to pay him off outright, I would in a fucking heartbeat. This is the second-best choice. Now at least I'm racing for a real purpose."

I felt myself starting to relax. My shield always came down around him. There was no fooling Ollie Powell. When he saw you, he *saw* you. That was why I always had to be on my toes when he was near. It was why I'd always kept him at a distance, acted like I despised him. If he got too close, he'd see me, and that was exactly what happened the night of the race. He got close, and now look at us. "You didn't have a purpose the first time you raced?" I asked, trying desperately to shift the attention off me.

Ollie shook his head as he came and stood beside me. I was still facing the cabin, but he looked out to the bonfire, his strong jaw the only thing I could see when I peered up at him. He shrugged. "I guess I did, in a way, but it was purely selfish. One could say I was using racing to hide."

My brows furrowed as I continued to stare at the sharp angle. "Hide from what?"

That was when he decided to look over at me. His stare almost paralyzed me. It was intense and heavy. I had to bite back a gulp as my eyes bounced back and forth between his. "My dad. Christian. Whenever I'm alone with the both of them, I feel trapped. A little out of control." Our stare held for a second, maybe two, but it felt like an eternity had passed. "I'm just...a little lost, I guess." It was dark outside, the distant stars our only light, but I could still see the defeat on his face. I opened my mouth to say something, anything, but Ollie quickly looked away. He didn't say a word, but I could tell he was done talking about the subject. He closed that wound almost as soon as it opened up. "Whatever. That's not what I wanted to talk about."

I decided to let it go for now. "What did you want to talk about?"

Ollie flipped around and leaned back on the deck railing. "We need to be more careful. Hayley keeps questioning us, and that's partly my fault." He paused a second, thinking. "I really don't want Christian to know I'm racing."

"Because?" I asked.

He brought his arms to cross in front of his chest. "Because that'll just lead to more questions, and inevitably, I'll get tripped up on my lies, and shit will spill." I nodded alongside him because I knew all about keeping my lies straight. "And you don't want Hayley to know about this, either, right?"

I answered quickly. "I don't want anyone to know about it, but yes, Hayley finally has some normal in her life. I want to keep it that way."

"Me too, so you need to act the part."

I pulled back. "Excuse me?"

Ollie pushed off the railing and flipped around, resting his arms along the worn wood. "Right now, it looks like you and I are plotting something, and if Hayley or Christian look up here, seeing us getting along, it'll raise questions. So, you need to act like you hate me."

I scoffed as I put distance between us.

"I mean"—he grinned—"we all know you *can't* truly hate me, but you can try."

And there was the Ollie I knew. The arrogant, cocky, and sometimes funny Ollie.

I tried to keep my smile away. "Oh, I can hate you alright."

Ollie let out a deep chuckle that floated right over my skin. He flipped the hood of his navy bulldog sweatshirt up before giving me a sly smile. "Is that what you tell yourself so you can forget about that night?"

Oh, not this again!

"Ollie, shut up."

His grin matched mine, and I tried so hard to fight it. Usually, I was much better at this. I could shove away my feelings and really dig into that small piece of me that wanted to hate him, but I was struggling right now. It may have been the grin, or the hood of his sweatshirt that made him look a little bit like a bad boy. Either way, Ollie was making my heart feel a little fluttery tonight—even more so than normal.

"But seriously..." Ollie's grin began to fade. The shadows surrounding his features began to darken with the fire dying down. "I don't want you at the races tomorrow."

"What?" I yelled, completely taken aback.

Ollie's jaw ticked as he dipped his head down to mine. "Shhh!" I grabbed onto the railing so I didn't sway on my feet with him so close to my face. I zeroed right in on his lips. "I don't want you there, Piper."

Is he serious? "Well, I don't really care. I'm coming." I kept my voice hushed. "I have to! Tank is expecting me."

Plus, what if Jason is there? I can at least make sure my brother is okay.

"I'll deal with Tank. I took on the responsibility to work out a deal with him in exchange for paying off what your brother owes. This has nothing to do with you anymore."

Anger flashed throughout. I felt my face get hot. I almost stomped my foot. "This has everything to do with me!" I lowered my voice as I glanced down at our friends. Thankfully, they were all still gathered around the fire. "Jason is *my* brother! How can you say this has nothing to do with me?"

Ollie's voice was soft but stern. "You're not going."

"I am!"

"Piper, goddamnit!" Ollie's face was an inch away from mine, and here we were again, sparring off. At least, now, if Hayley and Christian were to look up at us, they'd see that everything was as it seemed. We were still at each other's throats, but damnit, I just couldn't help but stare at his mouth. "I don't want you there because I'll fucking worry about you the entire time! I won't be able to focus."

I stepped back a hair. "Ollie, I'll be fine. I'll bring Co—"

"I swear to God, if you say you'll bring Cole to keep you safe, I will lose my shit."

My mouth smashed shut as Ollie towered over me. His jaw was clenched tightly, the small muscles dancing along his temples. "Piper, let me handle this for you. Okay? I've got it under control. It's no different than any other Saturday night. I'll race, I'll leave, and I'll come here. Except, this time, I won't be leaving with any money. Which is fucking fine by me."

I wanted to protest. I wanted to stomp my foot and throw my arms up like a child, but it would have done no good.

Ollie was set in his ways, determination present in his icy tone. He said he'd be worried about me if I went, but didn't he understand that I was worried about *him?*

In the end, I finally submitted. "Fine."

His cheek lifted, and he backed away slowly, lowering that stupid hood on his head, thinking he'd won.

But he didn't. I'd be at the race; he just wouldn't know it.

CHAPTER SIXTEEN

OLLIE

I READ the sign hanging crookedly above my head, *Pike Valley Soup Kitchen,* and I realized right away that I'd been here before. To the naked eye—or to my naive, ten-year-old self—it looked like my mom was trying to teach Christian and me a lesson by bringing us here. Teaching us to volunteer our time to feed the poor. Teaching us the importance of giving to others. But now that I was standing here, I knew that wasn't the case.

My mom came here to buy drugs.

The exchange would happen on an early Saturday morning, right here at this exact soup kitchen. My mom dragged Christian and me here once a month to *help feed the poor.* We hated coming. She'd drag us out of our warm beds at eight in the morning on the third Saturday of every month, and we'd hand out food to all sorts of people while she disappeared. I hadn't thought anything of it at the time, always buying into her sweet lies, but as I stood here, looking down the alleyway behind the building that was lined with homeless people, I knew. I'd watched the exchange. I saw her with my own two eyes; I was just too young to understand.

But now that my naivety was gone, it stung. The memory was ruthless, taking my breath away as it came. I tried my hardest to remember the good memories of my mother, her bright smile, the blonde strands of her hair that stood out under the golden sun, but lately, I was having a really fucking hard time holding onto those memories. It seemed all the good memories were being overshadowed by the bad ones.

"What are you doing here?" Piper asked, clearly agitated. I quickly turned on my heel and locked onto her heart-shaped face. Piper's face was a mask of confusion but still as pretty as the day I first laid eyes on her. The bright-pink cheeks under the glow of the morning sun. The shine of her hair all but blinding me. Her green eyes were narrowed. "Hellooo? What the heck are you doing here?"

Oh, right. I cleared my throat, tearing my eyes away for a moment. "Ya know..." I brushed off the memory of my mom and put on my best smile. "I just felt the need to feed the homeless."

The gravel under Piper's white Converse crunched. *Hayley must have talked her into buying those.* "That's a lie. I've been volunteering here for the last year and a half. I've never ever seen you before. What are you doing here?"

I eyed more people jumping into the line wrapping around the building—most with crying babies, some other randos, a few in wheelchairs that looked as if they'd seen better days. "I'm serious. I'm here to help."

Piper raised an eyebrow and crossed her arms. "Ollie."

I fought the need to roll my eyes. "Fine. I just felt like you needed another friendly reminder not to show up tonight."

What Piper failed to realize last night was that I could

read her like a fucking book. Her sudden agreement after I told her not to come to the races raised some serious red flags. She didn't back down easily, and I saw the motive right behind her eyes.

"I already told you I wasn't coming."

I laughed. "And I'm honestly surprised you thought I bought that."

A small puff of air flew out of her mouth as she stormed past me, all but ignoring that I was right. I chuckled the entire way down the alleyway, following after her. The tightness in my chest from walking down the narrow path to the side doors was hard to miss, but as soon as we were inside, the tightness lessened.

"Did you really think I bought it?" I asked, swooping in behind her, shooting my words down her neck.

Piper jerked out of the way, flipping her red hair over her shoulder. "You should have. I'm having a girls' night with Hayley. Go ahead! Text and ask her!" I stood back and watched as Piper began pulling her hair up into a bun on top of her head. She hastily walked over to a tall cabinet, smiling briskly at the other volunteers who were eyeing me suspiciously, and pulled out something from a small box. She was back in front of me within a second, holding out a net.

"What's this?" I asked, taking it from her hand.

She rolled her eyes, clearly not pleased. "It's a hairnet. If you're going to hound me, you might as well do it while passing out food. Put it on."

Piper didn't give me a chance to argue; she turned on her heel and walked away, leaving me standing in a room with a bunch of strangers.

I sighed, slipping the stupid net onto my head. *I don't remember having to wear this years ago.*

After walking down the hall and entering a giant room full

of people, I spotted Piper. My heart came to a sudden stop because she was simply glowing. She looked adorable, scooping out mashed potatoes with a giant ladle into Styrofoam containers. Her cheeks were flushed, and her smile was wide. Something in my heart tugged, and before I knew it, I was standing right beside her.

"Well," she said, glancing at me between patrons, "grab a ladle and help."

My tongue darted out to lick my lips as I followed her instructions like a lost puppy. Piper could have just told me to cut my arm off, and I probably would have done it.

After filling several rounds of Styrofoam containers, not speaking to one another, things began to slow. The people coming in were few and far between, and when I glanced up at the clock hanging across the room, my jaw fell.

"Jesus, fuck. It's 11:30?"

Piper laughed. "Times flies when you're having fun." She stepped back and pulled the hairnet off her head.

I did the same, shoving it in the back pocket of my jeans. "I mean, I wouldn't really consider this fun, but time did fly." I shrugged. "I really just came to give you a little in-person reminder to not come tonight, but somehow you roped me into feeding the homeless."

She rolled her eyes again but not before I caught the tiny glimpse of a smile. "I told you; I'm not coming. In fact..." Piper pulled out her cell phone, walking back to the far wall, away from the food line. I followed after her, my eyes tracing her backside in the faded jeans she was wearing. "You can read the text between Hayley and me about our girls' night tonight."

I leaned my shoulder on the wall, waiting patiently as she scanned her phone. Panic set in when her mouth fell open and she flicked those vivid green eyes in my direction. "Did you..." Piper was stunned. Her mouth was hanging open as she looked down to her phone and then back to me.

Pushing off the wall, I asked, "Did I what?"

"Did you threaten Cole?!" Piper's voice was rising with anger, and I snapped my mouth shut. *Shit.* "Ollie!"

"What?" I asked innocently. "Did he say I threatened him?" *He couldn't even keep his mouth shut. Bad seed, that one.*

Her fingers flew over her phone before she gave me a glare. "I'm going to kill you. He told Andrew!"

I played stupid. "He told Andrew that I threatened him?"

Somehow, a million emotions flew over her soft features within one quick second. "He told Andrew about me being at the races!" Her eyes clenched, and she dropped her head. "Fuck!"

"Who cares if your cousin knows?" I asked.

Her jade eyes were somehow even greener when they flew open. "He'll tell his parents, and then they'll tell mine."

Ah, yes. Didn't think about that. I wasn't going to let that happen, though. "Relax, I'll talk to him."

"You will not!" she seethed. "You'll probably just threaten him, too!"

"Now, listen. The only thing I told Cole was to lose your number. He's a shady guy, Piper. I don't fucking trust him. Do you?"

She threw her arms up, clenching her phone in her hand. Her voice was hushed as she looked around at the line picking back up. "Of course I don't trust him!"

"Then, can you blame me for wanting to protect you?"

Piper's lithe body was quaking with anger, her cheeks so flushed it started to creep down her neck. I had to bite my tongue to keep my gaze trained on her eyes. "Ugh!" she finally ended up saying. She turned on her heel and stormed off to the mashed potatoes again.

I did the same, following after her.

We both stayed silent when we put our hairnets back on and began dishing out more food to the line that was picking up. I wasn't sure of what to say. I liked pushing her buttons, but for some reason, I felt myself pulling back. I might have felt a little bad.

"I'll talk to Andrew, okay?" I whispered, nodding my head at a man who looked to be around one hundred years old.

"Do not talk to Andrew. I'll fix this."

More silence passed between us. She put up a good front, though, smiling and laughing with the homeless, but anytime she would catch my eye, she would scowl.

I sighed and continued handing out mashed potatoes, trying to find a way around the anger she was throwing my way. I should have welcomed the familiar feeling, but instead of it feeling like a comfort, it felt...heavy. "So," I started, dipping my ladle into the container, "do you just volunteer here for fun, or...?"

Piper glanced at me for a millisecond before reluctantly giving in. "I've been volunteering since I started at English Prep. Headmaster Walton said volunteering would look good on college applications."

"Aren't your college applications already in?" I asked, glancing up at her every few seconds.

"Yep."

"Then, why are you still volunteering?"

Piper paused, her hand stilling on the ladle. "I guess because I don't have anything else to do. It's something I look forward to. And"—she shrugged—"I like helping people."

Piper was definitely the type of girl you brought home to your parents at the end of the day. Nice, sweet, caring. It really irked me that her parents were never home.

"I've actually been here before."

She looked over at me, a crease evident on her forehead. "What? Like, to volunteer?"

I lifted a shoulder. "I guess you could say that."

"What exactly does that mean?"

I nodded my head at an older male as he shoved his shaking Styrofoam container in my direction. "My mom used to bring Christian and me here before she passed. One Saturday a month, we'd hand out food or whatever."

"Really?" Piper reached under the lip of the metal container no longer holding mashed potatoes and lifted it up, her arms straining with the weight. I quickly put my ladle down and grabbed it.

"Refill? Where?"

She nodded back toward the kitchen, her lips slightly parted. I quickly took it back and found the other metal container full of mashed potatoes and came back, placing it down. Piper switched spots with me, her shoulder brushing over my chest.

As soon as we were back in our rightful spots, continuing to fill people's containers, she asked, "What made you guys stop coming?"

I swallowed back a lump, feeling the tightness in my chest return. "Well," I started, clearing my throat, "I kind of just forgot about this place after my mom died, and..." *Do you really want to go there with her, Ol?*

Piper's soft voice floated all around me, almost luring me to tell her all the things I kept buried. "And what?"

I focused on the half-lumpy cloud of mashed potatoes resting on the end of my ladle. "And when I got here this morning, and the memory started to come back to me, I realized that my mom wasn't exactly here to volunteer."

The line had started to pitter out again, so I placed the spoon down. I dropped my head and counted the worn tiles beneath my feet. My chest stopped rising when I felt a small palm slide into mine. My eyes moved to Piper's hand clasping mine, and that was when I let the vile memory spill.

"I remembered the alley—the one we walked down to get to the side door." I swallowed back another rough lump before continuing, focusing on her palm against mine. "I remembered seeing my mom down the alley once, soon after she dropped Christian and me off inside to pass out whatever it was, and I'm almost certain she was getting drugs." A sarcastic chuckle left my mouth. "She brought us here once a month under the impression that we were giving to the needy, when really she was here to meet her drug dealer."

A light gasp sounded from beside me, and I instantly regretted telling her. I hated pity, but didn't everyone?

And there was no denying the amount of hate filling my head at the memory resurfacing. I fought the urge to rip off my hairnet and turn around, leaving Piper alone so I could be away from this place, but her hand in mine tightened, reminding me that she was here, and I wasn't alone...not really.

I hadn't thought about it until now, but Piper and I had something in common. Maybe it was why we were so drawn to one another. She loved someone who had an addiction, and I did, too. It was hard loving someone, knowing they didn't love you the same. An addict would always choose you second...and their vice first. I learned that the hard way.

Piper's hand tightened in mine again, and I glanced up, ready to swallow that pity whole, but she wasn't looking at me.

"Oh my God," she whispered, finally letting go of my hand.

"What?" I asked, confused.

Her head turned to mine for a second before she angled it toward the door. "It's Sky."

I followed her line of sight to a girl who looked as if she hadn't brushed her hair in weeks. "Sky?"

Piper turned to me with a hushed voice. "Sky, as in Tank's girlfriend. The one who—"

My voice turned steely. "The one who came to the school the other day?"

"Yes!" she whisper-shouted.

A woman who reeked of cigarettes stood in front of Piper and me, thrusting her Styrofoam container in our faces. Piper scooped up a bundle and placed it down, hearing the container crack under the weight.

"Don't even think about it!" Piper urged, giving me a side-eye.

"What?" I asked innocently.

She rolled her eyes. "You've already threatened Cole. Leave this one to me. The last thing we need is you threatening the drug dealer's girlfriend."

I cracked my neck, watching the girl in the far corner grab a Styrofoam container and climb into line for free food. Piper was right. Threatening a chick wasn't really on my list of things to do. I'd never even had the thought before, but if Sky wanted to throw bows at Piper, a little word wouldn't hurt.

"Trust me, Ollie," Piper said, dragging me out of my thoughts. "Being on this side of the table versus the side she's on is enough to put her in her place."

I scoffed. "I doubt that."

She shrugged. "I'm all about giving people a break. She's mean, but what good is going to come of it from me telling her so or you threatening her? She knows that she's mean. It's because she's unhappy. I mean, she *is* dating Tank."

I chuckled. "Touche, Piper. Touche."

She smiled at me before dipping the spoon back in the mashed potatoes as another person came up.

I felt a strange string in my chest, pulling at the muscle inside, as her smile lingered.

Piper was *definitely* the type of girl you brought home at the end of the day. There was no question about it.

And it was really hard to believe that she had a drug addict for a brother and parents who didn't seem to give two fucks about her.

This girl deserved more.

After I left the food bank, reiterating to Piper—*again*—that I didn't want her at the races, I went home and, basically, sat and watched the clock. With each slow and painful tick forward, the anticipation grew. Soon, the sun would be setting, and I'd be on my way to flying down a dirt road with a couple hundred people gathered around, all with wide eyes, hoping they had bet on the right person.

The right person = me.

I walked through the front door of my house, feeling even more excited to race after practicing with the turbo one last time. I wanted to make sure I was ready, and since Brandon talked me into getting a turbo, injectors, *and* new head studs, I needed to get a feel for my Charger with all the extra power. I was good at driving; I always had been. And racing for the last few months only strengthened that trait.

I stopped at the threshold of my house as the unwelcomed thought filtered through. *Was my real dad a good driver?* It was thoughts like that that made my skin crawl. Guilt threatened to suffocate me from every angle. I felt like complete fucking shit every time I let myself wonder about my real dad. Who he was.

What he was like.

If he had a family.

If I had any other siblings.

That last one especially fucked me up.

I never wanted to replace Christian, and even having the mere thought of adding another sibling into my life made me almost double over.

This was exactly why I needed to race tonight. I needed to get out of my own head. Take a breather. Feel nothing but the rumble of my engine and the leather on my steering wheel.

As I all but ran through the hallway heading upstairs to change to get ready for the race, I faltered at the sound of his voice.

"Son?"

I paused with my back toward him. Fuck. *What was he doing home?*

Slowly, I spun around. My chest began to feel tight again, but I put on my mask and acted nonchalant. "Hey, what are you doing home?"

My dad leaned against the far wall closest to the kitchen. His dress shirt was rolled to his forearms, and his dark hair was laying in a disheveled mess on the top of his head.

I looked nothing like my father. I always thought I took after my mother. I mean, we both shared the same light hair and light-blue eyes, but now that I knew my dad wasn't *actually* my dad, I wondered if I took after my mom, after all. Maybe it was my real father I took after.

I kept an even face as another guilty thought entered my head. My father shrugged. "I had a couple of days in between trips. Thought I'd spend some time with you boys tomorrow. I assume you both are busy tonight."

I grinned. "Well, you know what they say, *Saturdays are for the boys.*"

My father chuckled before turning sincere. "Did you do something to your Charger? It sounded different when you pulled up."

Again, I kept my face steady. "Nah, just some tuning to make her run smoother."

I couldn't decide if he bought it or not, but nonetheless, he changed the subject. "So, tomorrow? Text your brother and tell him I want to have lunch with you boys, maybe even dinner, too. I never know what mood I'll catch Christian in, so it's up to you to make sure he gets word."

He raised his eyebrows at me, waiting for me to agree. My dad and Christian had a rocky relationship just months prior. But after the Hayley situation, and how my father actually stepped up for once and helped Christian out, they'd stopped arguing so much, and he'd actually put in some effort—like spending the next day and a half at home and having dinner with us.

He never used to do that—even when Mom was alive.

And that was part of the reason why I didn't know if I could ever tell Christian the truth. It would open up that fresh wound that was finally beginning to heal.

I stared at my father for a few more seconds, a question right on the tip of my tongue that I *knew* I needed to keep in. My heart was ruthlessly beating against my rib cage, almost begging me to poke the bear.

My mouth opened, but I closed it. I began to turn away, my pulse drumming underneath my skin. *Just let it go, Ollie.* But then I snapped my attention back over to him, his furrowed brow meeting me halfway. "Dad?"

"Is everything okay?"

"What did you do the day you found out Mom was pregnant with me?"

My gaze was set directly on him. I was waiting for the tick of his eye. The flinch of his features. But there was nothing. Instead, his gaze stayed level with mine as he stared.

"Why do you ask?"

I shrugged, trying to hide my disappointment in not

being able to read him. He was as bad as Christian. They did *not* wear their emotions on their sleeves. They were both stoic, for lack of a better word. If I wanted information out of Christian, I had to dig it out of him. It was going to be the same way with my father.

"Just curious." *Fuck, make something up. That's a sketch answer.* "I was just thinking about how close Christian and I are in age and wondered how you felt about it. I just wondered if you and Mom were happy we were so close in age."

My father's eyes darted away for a brief second. *There it is.* "I was glad because I knew you two would be best friends. Having a brother is a tight bond you can't get anywhere else. Don't ever forget that, Ollie."

My dad answered with so much confidence that it actually threw me off. It wasn't what I was expecting. I felt unsteady on my feet as I slowly nodded in agreement and even as I climbed the steps to my room.

His answer bothered me the entire ride to the races, too. I had no idea why my father had answered with so much conviction when he didn't even have any siblings. *"Having a brother is a tight bond you can't get anywhere else. Don't forget that, Ollie."* How did he know that? Why was he so sure of his answer? It was a weird response and not one I was ready for. The only thing it did was confuse me more. I had hoped he would have given me some type of clue as to if he knew he wasn't my father, but no. I got nothing except more fucking questions.

I tried to steady my breath as I pulled up to the races, parking my Charger off to the side near the starting line. There were several heats to be run, and I would likely be one of the last since I'd moved up a bracket, thanks to being in business with Tank.

As I walked along the dirt road, gravel crunching underneath my shoes, I spotted Brandon.

I tipped my chin as he came around and gave me a bro-pat. "What's up? You ready for this?"

I relaxed back onto his truck bed. "It's no different from any other night. I am ready to play around with that turbo, though."

Brandon's face lit up, and that was when I noticed his girl wasn't with him.

"Where's your girl tonight?"

Brandon gave me a side glance. "I told her to stay put. Word has it that Tank will be here since *someone* had some business with him." He flicked his eyebrow up, the shiny hoop hanging off it catching the setting sun. "And I didn't want her around him."

I nodded. "Good call."

I was glad I told Piper to stay away tonight. There was no fucking way I'd be able to concentrate if I knew she was here on the sidelines with Tank looming in the darkness. I understood that the business deal technically wasn't with me and Tank, but more so Piper and Tank, but I couldn't handle the thought of her being here in this environment.

The races were no place for a girl like Piper.

I'd handle her shit with pride.

She had nothing to worry about.

Brandon was talking to a few other guys about the turbo in my Charger when I looked up ahead at Daniel who was cupping his hands around his mouth, calling for the next race.

There were two more sets until I raced, and I could almost feel the anticipation tingling in my fingertips. I had texted Piper an hour prior—*again*, to remind her to stay home and that I'd let her know how much we had left to owe after it was over.

I glanced around at everyone watching, hoping the

majority of them bet for me and forked money over into the pool.

Not only did Tank keep 50% of the entire money pool, but he was also keeping my share tonight, too. And the better the race, the more people bet and participated. So basically, Tank was coming out on top tonight because of me, and that money would go straight into what Jason owed him.

A little bit of unease settled in my bones as the race began. The two cars zipped past me as I reminded myself that I needed to figure out some unanswered questions tonight.

Tank obviously couldn't be trusted, as he wasn't a straight-laced guy by any means, but I needed his word that after the debt was paid off, Jason was free to go, and Piper was no longer even a thought in his tiny, birdseed-sized brain.

I didn't give a shit if he wanted me to keep racing to gain him more money. Whatever. That was not what I was worried about.

Piper was who I was worried about.

She needed to stay far, far away from this shit.

Brandon nudged my shoulder as I was deep in thought. "Bro, isn't that your girl?"

My blood ran cold. I didn't have a girl, and I'd never even been seen with anyone at the races except for a quick kiss on the cheek by an admirer, so I instantly knew who he was talking about.

My vision blurred when I spotted that beautiful copper-colored hair half hiding behind...*what in the actual fuck?*

Eric's gaze was dead set on me as he had his hand wrapped around Piper's wrist like she was a toddler being dragged to the car after running the aisles in a grocery store. Piper looked pissed. Her pouty mouth was set in an angry frown. But Eric appeared mighty pleased with himself for holding Piper's wrist and for finding out what I was up to.

I growled like a fucking barbarian as I began stalking toward them.

Not only did I have to get my head straight to win this race, but now I had to explain myself to Eric *and* worry about Piper.

Racing, which was my only outlet, was now becoming more of a chore.

Which really fucking sucked.

CHAPTER SEVENTEEN

PIPER

OLLIE WAS all but stomping toward Eric and me, and for a moment, I thought about running away, which was pointless because he'd already seen me, and Eric, who was now my number one enemy, wouldn't let go of my freaking wrist.

"You should have listened to me!" I half-whispered to Eric. "We could have hid, and Ollie would have never known either of us were here."

Eric sliced his dark eyes over to me. "I want him to know I'm here, and by the looks of him, he isn't happy that *you're* here. How interesting."

I scowled. "What's interesting is how you even found out about tonight. What? Were you following Madeline?"

His eyes flared, and I knew I was right. I raised an eyebrow. "Oh yes, Eric. I know your secret."

Ollie decided to saunter up right then, and we dropped the subject. Eric didn't need to worry. I wasn't there to expose his infatuation with Madeline. I was mad he snagged my wrist and acted like he was my father, though.

As soon as Ollie was in front of us, he seethed. "I told you to stay home." His heavy brow line shadowed his eyes, and I felt a swift kick to my stomach. My breath caught as he peered down at me. "You shouldn't fucking be here! This is an important race, and now I'm going to be worrying about you near Tank." He shook his head as Eric's hand loosened a little around my wrist. Ollie pinched the bridge of his nose before snapping his attention to Eric. "And what the hell are you doing here?"

Just then, Eric squeezed my arm gently as a warning. He didn't need to give one, though; his secrets weren't mine to tell. "I knew you were lying through your fucking teeth about tuning your car. Christian is going to be livid when he finds out you've been racing down here."

Ollie's stare darkened, and a fire erupted. *My God, he's hot when he's mad.* Butterflies swarmed my belly. "Christian isn't going to find out. Do you hear me? This has nothing to do with him, and you're going to keep your mouth shut."

Eric slowly raised his hands as a smirk covered his face. I swore these boys and their smirks could make panties drop everywhere. They were dangerous. Ollie, Eric, Christian. They, all three, had the ability to make good girls turn bad.

"Relax, Ol. I'm not here to fight. Just want to make sure you're good. You're my bro. Christian's my bro. I have both of your backs."

Ollie seemed to relax for a moment, but it wasn't long before his back grew stiff. Someone yelled his name and was waving him back to where his parked Charger was. Nerves waved across my shoulders and settled right on top. The thought of Ollie flying down the gravel road at a high speed made my stomach hurt. Guilt was sliding down my spine, and fear was clouding my vision.

He didn't even look in my direction—too angry with me, I'm sure. Ollie and I were so hot and cold. We were either angry with one another, or our guards were down, and we were sharing something on an entirely different level. And I had no idea what that even meant.

"Keep her off the sidelines and out of people's sight. She shouldn't be here."

Eric nodded. "I got you." His hand wrapped around my wrist again.

Ollie focused on Eric's hand on my arm. "Just...keep her safe." Then, he turned on his heel and began jogging back to his Charger.

My heart was lodged in my throat. *He's fine, Piper. He knows what he's doing.*

But did he?

I could feel myself spiraling out of control. *What did I get us into?*

Eric's thumb rubbed along the inside of my wrist. "Relax, Piper. I've got you. No one will mess with you."

I craned my neck up to Eric, my hair tumbling down my back and out of my face. "I'm not worried about someone messing with me, Eric. I'm worried for him." I nodded my head in Ollie's direction, and his eyes flared.

"What kind of shit did you guys get yourselves into?"

I only shook my head, unable to answer as I watched Ollie's long legs climbing into his Charger. His window was rolled down, and when he pulled up to the starting line, he glanced my way once, and it was enough to make me regret every bit of my acceptance in letting him race for Tank.

One could have argued that I didn't have much of a choice, but that wasn't the truth.

I didn't have to let Ollie in, but deep down, it felt really, *really* good knowing I had him to lean on.

I was so messed up. Jumbled. Nothing seemed right anymore.

One thing I did know: I had to figure out how to get the

rest of the money for Tank before Ollie got too much deeper in this.

I had to keep him safe.

And somehow keep Jason safe, too.

Eric didn't wait for me to explain what I'd gotten Ollie and myself into. Instead, he pulled me by my wrist, and we ended up near the starting line, away from the thickening crowd. I heard murmurs from people as we snuck by, talking about who'd win the race and who they'd bet against. The majority of the people said they bet for Ollie to win because someone let it leak that he'd done some upgrading to his Charger.

I only hoped that he knew what he was doing, because the suspense was wrapping around my throat and suffocating me.

I scanned the crowd as the cars revved their engines, ready to take off whenever the girl wearing the short, make-you-take-a-double-look shorts walked in between the two cars to wave her flag.

My heart stopped as I spotted Tank with his stupid man-bun several yards away. Sky was standing to his right, but when my eyes shifted to the left, I froze.

Jason.

There was my brother, casually standing beside Tank as if nothing at all was wrong. I raised up on my tiptoes to get a better look, but Eric pulled me down by my arm.

"Stay out of sight, Piper."

I gave Eric a dirty look before trying to get a better glance at my brother when I heard the two cars taking off at a rapid speed. My heart fell to the ground along with my stomach, and my hand flew up to my mouth. *Oh my God.*

The back of Ollie's maroon Charger zipped down the dirt road, and people flocked to the billowing dust to get a better look.

Black dots crowded my vision as I tried to catch my breath. *Ollie.* The only thing I could envision was Ollie's car being wrapped around a tree, or it coming to a sudden stop and flipping with him inside.

The distant roar of the two engines faded into the background, and I continued to force out choppy breaths. Small puffs of air escaped me when I felt two hands on my shoulders. I peeked up and saw Eric hovering over me. "Breathe, Piper. He's going to be fine, but not if you pass out right here. Take a damn breath!"

I gasped as I watched the worry fade from Eric's eyes. "There you go. Just breathe. He'll be back soon."

My eyes shifted past Eric, and I searched for my brother. Another wheeze escaped me, and oxygen seemed to come in a little easier knowing my brother was here and that he appeared to be okay.

"What the hell are you doing here?"

Eric's hands dropped from my shoulders as he settled in on Madeline's voice from behind me.

I didn't dare take my eyes off the direction of the rising dust and crowd of people. I kept my attention on Tank and my brother, waiting patiently for Ollie's Charger to reappear.

"What the fuck, Madeline? Why the hell are you hanging around here?"

Madeline's tone was packed full of heat "I don't know. Probably the same reason you are!"

I tuned the two of them out as Eric rounded my body and walked over to her. I could hear my heartbeat in my own ears, but as soon as the sound of a roaring engine filtered in, everything else faded. My throat squeezed with anticipation; my heart fluttered against my ribcage. The one and only time I'd felt relief like this was when I'd seen Hayley again after she had been taken by the men from her father's past.

A small yelp left my mouth as Ollie's Charger got closer,

and before I knew what I was doing, my legs were pulling me into the sea of people. *Ollie.* My legs were picking up their pace as I pushed past people I didn't even know, my hands coming out and moving them aside so I could get closer to him.

Ollie.

I heard Eric calling after me, and I was certain he was hot on my heels, but I didn't care. The only thing I was worried about was wrapping my arms around Ollie, because the fear of him dying in a car crash was still fresh in my mind. The anxiety that I'd pushed away all week was catching up to me.

My hair swished around my face as I continued getting closer, and when I saw his long legs climb out of his Charger, I almost wept right there. The sun was setting, and the moon was coming up, but when his eyes landed on me, I swore I could still see the shine in them. *He's fine, Piper.* But my body acted on its own. I rushed past the last person, and before I knew it, my arms were around his torso, and my head was pushed against his chest.

I was gasping, all but wheezing for air, almost to the point of hyperventilating.

"Piper?" Ollie's hands immediately wrapped around my upper arms, but I only clung on harder. "Piper? What happened?"

"Jesus, fuck, Piper! You're fast." Eric sounded out of breath, but I pushed my head even further into Ollie's chest. He smelled like Ollie. Woodsy, but calming. Comforting. The sound of his heart beating had mine calming. The guilt was still there, lingering right over my shoulders, but he was okay, and that made me feel entirely too happy.

What does this mean?

"What the hell happened?" Ollie asked as his strong arms wrapped around my body. "She's fucking trembling." *I am?* Ollie's voice dipped lower. "Was it Tank?"

Eric was closer, too. "No, bro. She kind of flipped when you started down the lane. I had to tell her to relax, and as soon as she saw your car, she fucking took off running. She's fast as fuck."

"Piper?" Ollie's voice was soft, almost like a light touch to my skin. "What's going on?"

I slowly took my head off his chest and met his eye. He took in my face, and his blush-colored lips parted. "You're crying."

I am? I swallowed and unclenched his t-shirt that I had unknowingly bunched up in my hand. My face was sticky and wet when I touched it. "Oh."

"What's going on?"

I gulped, trying to swallow down my emotions. "I-I don't like this." I knew there was a crowd around us, but for some reason, it felt like it was only Ollie and me standing in the middle of a dirt road underneath the darkened sky. "I'm going to fix this. I'm going to get you out of this. You shouldn't be here racing like this."

He began to shake his head when a hush came over everyone's murmurs.

"Tsk. Tsk." My body stilled as I recognized the voice.

"You won me a helluva lot of money tonight, boy."

I watched as Ollie's Adam's apple bobbed up and down. The sides of his temples flexed. "I told you I would."

"Get these people out of here," Tank barked to one of his friends before coming over and grinning down at me. My eyes searched around him frantically, trying to find Jason, but he was no longer in sight, and that made me feel even more nervous.

Soon, the only people left standing around were Tank, two of his friends, Eric—who refused to leave—and Ollie and me.

Ollie's large hand was suddenly clasped in mine, and my

entire arm sparked when our palms touched. I still felt twisted with nerves, though.

"Where's Jason?" My voice was shaky, but having Ollie near gave me a boost of confidence. The fear from watching him race was slowly dissipating, and now that I was looking Tank head-on, I felt the fiery girl inside awaken.

Tank shrugged, grinning with his stained teeth. "I sent him on an errand with his... handler."

My stomach ached. *His handler?*

"I want to talk about terms." Ollie squeezed my hand as he squared his shoulders. "How much of tonight is actually going onto what Jason owes?"

Tank stared at Ollie for a moment before tipping his chin back. "I'll know more after Derek counts the winnings for tonight." He nodded to a guy several yards away, standing around everyone who'd watched the race, passing out money. I recognized him from last week. "Once I've made back what Jason owes me, and fucktard himself is out of my hair, we'll talk more about you racing for me for good." A sneaky grin found its way onto his face. "Or doing some more business for me."

Absolutely fucking not. My mouth opened, but Ollie's hand almost broke mine with its force, so I quickly slammed my lips closed.

"Sure thing," he answered, completely indifferent about the situation. "I just want to make sure that these races are going toward our end goal."

Tank's beady eyes sliced over to mine, and I was suddenly thankful that it was dark out and he couldn't see the pure disgust that lingered within. "Don't worry. Your princess's fears will vanish after a few more races, I'm sure. Twenty K isn't that hard to come by when you race that well. Although, I'll be sad to let Jason go, as he's quite the little helper these days."

Helper? What did that mean?

Ollie nodded. "Alright, good shit. I just want to make sure we're clear on terms if I'm burning gas like that."

"Not a worry, brother. Not a fuckin' worry." Tank walked over to us, and I held my breath. He nodded his head over to the guy counting out money. "Let's take a walk and see how much money we made, yeah?"

Ollie's hand left mine as he glanced down. A warning flashed along his features before he turned to Eric. "Make sure she gets home."

Then, he walked away with Tank by his side, and it left a sickly feeling in my stomach.

Eric stepped up beside me, and we watched Ollie walk with Tank. The ends of my nerves were singed. I suddenly felt exhausted, and I couldn't stand to watch Ollie be friendly with Tank any longer, so I turned on my heel and began walking to where I had parked my car. The night was far from over for me. I needed to be alone to recharge. "Eric," I called over my shoulder as we walked along the high grass. "I'm going right to Hayley's. You don't need to follow me."

"Well, excuse the fuck out of me, but I don't know if I trust you right now. What the hell is going on?"

I stopped right along the side of my car as I glanced over to the crowd past Eric. "It's a long story."

He snickered under his breath, running his hand through his dark hair. "I've got time."

"Are you sure you've got time? I just saw Madeline climbing on the back of some dude's motorcycle." And as if on cue, a motorcycle started up in the distance. *Thank you, God.*

Eric quickly spun around and searched desperately for the noise. "For fuck's sake."

"Go, Eric. I'm going to Hayley's."

Eric looked me dead in the eye when he glanced back at

me. "Don't make me regret not following you home, Piper. Right to fucking Hayley's, alright?"

"Okay, okay. Now, go. And don't worry," I shouted as he was rushing away. "My lips are sealed—as long as yours are."

He gave me one dip of his chin and then jogged away.

Now, I just had to wait in my car until I saw Tank leave.

Then, I could get on with my plan.

CHAPTER EIGHTEEN

OLLIE

IT WAS funny how quickly anger could take over your body. One minute, you're laughing, and the next, your blood pressure is rising to an unsteady level. I told Piper to stay home from the races, and I really thought she was going to listen.

But I was wrong.

The second I found her, it was as if my finger was hovering over the trigger of a gun loaded with protectiveness as the bullet. It was ready to be unleashed at a moment's notice. I was certain her absence from the races would have helped me focus, but I might have been wrong. I had raced even better knowing she was there watching. I had pushed my foot down on the pedal in hopes that I'd get back to her quicker—that I'd get back to her before Tank ran his devilish eyes down her body.

Tank pocketed six thousand extra tonight from the bets on me, so that meant we owed fourteen more. There was no doubt that the next two or three races would cover the rest of the money, but then I had to figure out how to get out from under his thumb. I went along with his little scheme of having me work for him, or continuing to race, but that was all for show. I knew pissing him off or challenging him in any way whatsoever would be a bad move. There was a time and place to show dominance to a guy like him, and this wasn't it.

Tank liked to be in control. He liked people fearing him and obeying him.

I wasn't that guy, but for now, I'd pretend.

Slamming the door to my Charger, I lazily walked up to the cabin. It didn't look to be a banger tonight; only a few cars were there—Eric's, Christian's, and Jace's.

My phone lit up as I glanced at the screen, waiting for Piper to text me back, letting me know she made it to Hayley's, which is where Eric had said she went.

A dull ache nestled into my stomach with each second that passed and she hadn't texted back, but I took a calming breath and put on a front as I walked through the threshold of the cabin.

The lights were dim as everyone sat in the living room. There was some movie playing on the screen and a box of pizza on the counter.

Christian was the first to look up, and he immediately pressed pause on the remote. Then, all eyes were on me. *I swear to God, if Eric told him...*

"Brother."

"What up?" I answered, keeping my face relaxed.

Christian tipped his chin to Jace and Max, and they hurriedly got up and went out onto the deck, leaving Eric, Christian, and me in the room.

My nostrils flared at Eric when Christian looked away. He shrugged innocently.

"Did you get Piper pregnant?"

I sputtered as I choked on a piece of pizza. "What?!"

Christian's stare hardened. "Dad thinks you got someone

knocked up, and Hayley is convinced you and Piper are fucking."

I walked farther into the living room. "Why the fuck does Dad think I got someone pregnant?"

Christian leaned forward, placing his elbows on his knees. Eric sat back, observing us with an amused expression on his face. I scowled. *Oh, fuck off.*

"He said you came home and asked a loaded question, but when he tried to poke you for more information, you shut down and left shortly after." He shook his head. "What did you ask?"

I clenched my jaw, grinding my molars back and forth. My hands squeezed the back of the couch so hard my knuckles ached. "First off, Piper and I are not fucking."

Eric snickered, and I envisioned myself picking up a chair and throwing it at him—which, to be honest, was way out of character for me, but never say never when a certain redhead was involved.

"And—" Just before I could make up something to feed to my brother about asking shit I shouldn't have been asking, the door barged open.

Hayley shoved through, and the second she saw me, she placed her hands on her hips. "What the hell is going on with my best friend?"

My pulse immediately quickened. "What are you talking about? I thought she was with you tonight."

Hayley shrieked. "No! And she gave me a bullshit excuse last week when we were supposed to hang, and she texted a little while ago and made up another excuse. She isn't home, either. Her parents are, but Piper isn't. Something is going on, and..." Hayley's voice dropped, and she all but glared at me. "I *know* you know what's going on! Did you break her heart, Ollie?"

Christian interjected. "They're not smashing. I just asked him."

I stood frozen as I stared at Hayley. *If Piper isn't with her, then where the fuck is she?*

My gaze went right to Eric, but just as I opened my mouth, my phone vibrated.

Piper: Ollie. I messed up.

My fingers flew over my phone's screen as Hayley came over and read the text.

"Ollie. What is going on?"

I ignored her and texted back.

Me: where are u?

Piper: I'm at Tank's and I'm stuck inside. He doesn't know I'm here.

My heart clunked to the floor. Just then, another text came through.

Piper: I'm scared.

My entire body went into overdrive. I blocked everything out. I knew Hayley was asking me questions, and I knew Christian was trying to calm her down, but the only thing I could concentrate on was getting to Piper.

Me: Tell me where. I'm coming.

Fuck. Fuck. *Fuck*. My chest felt like it was split open, and I was scrambling to put myself back together so I could focus on getting to Piper. I needed to calm down. My feet drug me across the wooden floor of the cabin. Back and forth. Back and forth.

"Ollie!" My head snapped at Hayley yelling at me with frantically desperate eyes. "Please tell me it isn't Tank, the high-school-dropout-turned-drug-dealer Tank."

My legs stopped moving. I froze. "You know who Tank is?"

My phone buzzed, and Hayley and I both ignored Christian who was asking questions.

Piper: pike valley trailer park.

Hayley's neck of the woods.

Hayley's voice dropped. "Yes, I know exactly who Tank is. You can explain on the way. Let's go. Now."

Hayley grabbed onto Christian's hand, and I followed them out the door with Eric trailing after us.

Christian glanced over his shoulder and gave me a look. He knew exactly what I was feeling in this moment, and let me tell you, it wasn't fucking good.

CHAPTER NINETEEN

PIPER

MY LEGS SHOOK as I stood inside the ceramic tub that had black mold growing in the corners. It smelled like a dirty basement with a touch of Irish Spring. I glanced at the ceiling of the bathroom, and there was mold growing on it, too. Sneaking into Tank's trailer was a poor decision on my end, but it wasn't difficult by any means. When I'd followed him home after the races, I parked at the front entrance of the trailer park, crept toward his trailer on foot, and waited until I saw him leave again. It didn't take long. He was back out the door and onto his motorcycle, flying on top of the make-shift, loose-gravel-covered road. I held my breath as he whizzed past me crouched down by a nearby dumpster. It smelled terrible, but not as terrible as the moldy bathroom I was currently hiding out in. I had snuck in through the sliding glass door on the back end of the trailer after snooping to make sure no one was hanging out in the living room.

It was pitch black inside, except for the glow of a phone

or tablet on the table, so I tip-toed inside, ready to look in the bedrooms for my brother, when the front door began to swing open. I panicked, my heart flying throughout my chest as I rushed down the narrow hallway and into the first door I found.

It latched softly as I tried my hardest to be quiet, which wasn't hard. I'd always been a quiet person. I was meant to blend in. I'd been doing it all my life. *Play nice with the other rich kids. Act like you belong. Be quiet. Don't make a fuss. Stop crying.* My parents wanted nothing more than to fit in with their superiors, to make the same amount of money, to have the brightest children wearing their expensive prep school uniforms following in their footsteps. Only, Jason ruined their plan. Thus, why I was stuck in a rundown trailer's bathroom, holding my breath until I found a way out.

I sunk down into the tub, my eyes well-adjusted to the dark bathroom. There was a tiny sliver of moonlight casting a bluish hue from the tiny window above the toilet, which allowed me to take in the size of the area.

There wasn't much room inside the bathroom, other than a few feet between the front of the tub and the wall. There was a tiny vanity beside the toilet and a chipped, oval mirror leaning on the wall above it.

My first thought was to climb out of the window and go back to my car without finding Jason. Tank was back. I could hear his booming voice through the thin-as-paper walls, as well as several other muffled voices, all of which were hard to identify due to the now blaring music. So, leaving was my best option. But the window was jammed, and the ends of my fingernails were now bleeding from trying to pry it open. Through the pain, I'd texted Ollie, desperate for him to help.

I knew he'd be pissed that I was here. He was already angry that I'd shown up at the races. But I had no other choice. Ollie was the only one who knew about Jason—my fucked-up brother who I kept saving over and over again.

The ache settled deep within my chest as I dropped my head to my jean-clad knees, waiting for the text from Ollie.

I hoped he had a plan to get me out of here.

I messed up. I messed up so bad, and I kept messing up.

At this point, I wasn't even sure I deserved Ollie's help, and I knew, very well, that Jason didn't.

My head snapped up as the bathroom door creaked open and the light blared on. I looked to my left, meeting the hanging, brown-stained shower curtain as a shadow passed by it. *Oh my God.*

Small, steady puffs of air fell from my lips as I tried to stay calm. *Relax. They're just going to the bathroom.*

My spine was as stiff as a board as I leaned forward, out of sight. There was a small gap between the shower curtain and the shower wall, and all it would take is one glance to the left as someone was using the toilet to see me crouched in the tub all wide-eyed with fear.

My lips smashed together to keep my breathing silent, but when I looked down at my shirt, I could see the rapid rising and falling of my chest. Staying calm was becoming harder and harder. Nerves were eating away at my sanity. *What if they're about to take a shower? What the hell am I going to do if they spot me? What if it's Tank?*

A creak echoed throughout the tiny room, and my ears strained to figure out what it was.

Slowly, I leaned my body back until I could see between the small gap of the shower curtain, and I held my breath, watching.

The guy was squatting, his head hanging low as he dug through the bottom of the vanity. I watched as he found something hidden in the very back. He was still squatting, half hidden behind the vanity doors, as he placed the top of a bottle of some sort on the vanity top. When he stood up, his back was turned to me, but I continued to stare. My stomach churned as I waited.

Next came the shampoo bottle that he had unscrewed the lid from, placing it on the counter, and then came a small plastic baggy.

When the guy turned slightly, I slapped my hand over my mouth. My eyes grew wide.

Jason.

I recognized the color of his hair with his back to me— the same coppery color as mine, although his was unkempt and wild looking. My mouth opened to blurt his name, but my heart began to sink as I clamped it shut and bit my tongue, watching.

A metallic taste filled my mouth.

The sound of a plastic bag rustled, and I dropped my gaze from the side of his face to his hands. White powder.

No.

I willed my eyes to stop filling with moisture as he poured some of the dust onto the vanity top. With his back still toward me, I watched as he bent down over the substance.

No. Stop.

I could feel my heart shattering in my chest. This wasn't supposed to happen. Jason wasn't supposed to be like this. It wasn't part of the plan. He should have been in college, getting stellar grades and hanging out with the popular crowd. Instead, he was stuck in a disgusting trailer on the wrong side of town, snorting drugs up his nose while his little sister was crouched in a bathtub, watching from afar, contemplating her recent decisions.

I really had no choice as of late. Ollie was involved. Tank knew me and Ollie both, and if we backed out, not only was Jason going to get the brunt of it, but so were we.

I clenched my eyes shut as he bent forward to snort the

powder. I felt hollow. But the longer I sat in that bathroom, the quicker anger replaced sadness. He had promised me. He had promised he was done. Why did I always believe him? He continued to prove me wrong, and each time, the disappointment swallowed me entirely.

I hurt. *It* hurt.

I rubbed at my chest and pushed away any ounce of sadness I had. I hastily stood up and pushed the shower curtain out of my way, the rings on top screeching on the bar above my head.

Jason's head flew toward mine, his nose a mere millimeter away from the white power.

"What the fuck!"

I was too angry to say anything. I just stood, standing in the disgusting tub, my hand still on the mildewing shower curtain.

Jason's mouth dropped. "Piper? What the hell are you doing in here?"

I barely recognized my own voice. "I snuck in here to come see if you were okay, to tell you that everything was going to be fine and that I was figuring out a way to pay off Tank, but look at you!" My voice rose toward the end of my sentence, and I shot my eyes to the bathroom door. I hurriedly stepped out of the tub and ran the few feet over to the door and locked it. Music was still blaring throughout the trailer, so I felt confident that no one heard me yell. "You're in here using? At a party? Having a grand ol' time?"

My brother stuttered, "I...I..."

"You what?" My phone buzzed, and I glanced down.

Ollie: Almost there. Hayley is with me. She knows where Tank lives. Tell me how to get you out.

My stomach fell out from beneath me. A hot coat of embarrassment and shame covered my body, but I shook it off. I didn't have time to worry about who knew about Jason and my life. I needed to get the hell out of this trailer before someone other than Jason found me.

Me: I'm in the bathroom on the back side of the trailer. The window is jammed. Try to stick something under to pry it open.

I looked back at Jason, ignoring the texts I had from my parents who were demanding I come home since they were here for one night and one night only. I dropped my head, trying to push my guilt away. It was almost suffocating. "Jason, I'm done." My voice trembled, breaking with every word. "After the money is paid back, and I get my boy—" I paused, clearing my throat. "I mean...my friend. After I get my friend out of this stupid mess I drug him into to save your ass, I'm done. I can't keep doing this." Jason stood in the same spot, his lips sealed shut. "I can't keep saving you if you won't even save yourself."

His bloodshot eyes had my own eyes watering, but I knew I needed to keep my shit together. Otherwise, he'd use it against me. Jason might have been drunk, or maybe even high, but he was smart—one of the smartest in his class, actually. And if he knew I was hurting, he would turn it around and use it to his advantage. He'd done it before, and he'd do it again if I gave him a chance.

"You sound like Dad."

It felt like he took a knife and carved an X on my forehead. He felt betrayed by me. Telling me I sounded like our father was brutal, because we both held resentment when it came to our parents.

"Jason—" I jumped as a loud bang sounded on the bathroom door. Flesh pounding against the wooden door had my heart climbing to my throat and staying there.

"Fuck." Jason scrambled to grab the little plastic baggy, scooping the unused powder back into it.

Someone yelled from the other side of the door. "Jason,

get your pussy bitch out here and make us some fuckin' food. You might be a cool guy, but you're still my bitch...until your hot-as-fuck sister pays back that money."

Our eyes met, and I knew instantly that the drugs he'd just unscrewed from an empty shampoo bottle weren't really his for the taking. The questions were nonstop. Did he steal them and hide them? Surely, Tank wouldn't have let Jason in here alone when he knew there were drugs in here. What drug addict could be trusted being alone in a room with drugs?

"I'm coming, bro!" he yelled back through the door. He quickly put the baggy back into the empty shampoo bottle and placed it underneath the sink.

My phone vibrated a few times as I continued to watch Jason move with agility. I ground my teeth back and forth, trying to will away the tears. I barely recognized my brother standing in front of me.

I'd never felt so alone in my entire life.

"You need help," I whispered as he stood back up.

Jason's eyes found mine, and they were empty. So empty it was like I was looking right through him.

When he walked over to the door, he dropped his head and paused. My phone vibrated again, but I continued to stare at him, feeling sad. I just felt sad. He finally whispered, "I know. I fucking know."

My phone vibrated again; I finally looked down.

Ollie: Hayley is about to cause a diversion. Eric and I are gonna pry the window open. Get ready.

"I'll try to keep people from coming back here. Hurry up and get out before Tank finds you. He's cool with me right now, and he's happy he's makin' money off your friend, but he can turn vicious in a fucking second. Trust me, Piper. He's fucking dangerous. That's why I'm still here. That's why I haven't tried to leave. Not until he gets his money."

My voice came out low. "My friends are here. They're about to pry open the window because it's stuck. I'll be gone soon."

He nodded, and I could see the muscles along his jaw clenching. He shared the same jaw as my father, and watching it twitch like that brought back many, many memories of my father holding in his temper. "I'm sorry, Piper. I'm so fucking sorry. I'll fix this. I will."

I climbed on top of the toilet as I heard pounding on the front door of the trailer, knowing it was probably the diversion from my best friend. Before Jason left the bathroom, I said over my shoulder, "I hope so, because if not, I'm done until you find it in you to help yourself."

He said nothing as the light switched off, and the door opened and closed behind him.

Ollie had seconds to pry this window open and help me climb out, or I'd likely be caught red-handed.

And for some reason, I didn't even care if I got caught.

A numbness fell over me the second I watched Jason dip his head down to the counter, seconds away from snorting something, and I wasn't sure if anything could bring me back.

CHAPTER TWENTY

OLLIE

MY HEART RATE climbed to an unhealthy speed as I stood behind a rundown trailer, staring at the window on the backside. There was a chill in the air, and I wasn't sure if it was from the cool temperature or if it was from fear.

It was a shaky feeling, and it had my heart pounding. Usually, spontaneity was my thing. I was the guy who everyone dared to do stupid shit because I liked the thrill, but this was different. Piper was involved, and she was scared.

My girl was scared, and that had me flexing my knuckles. *My girl?* Yes. My girl. She felt like mine, even if she truly wasn't, and I wanted to pound her brother's face in simply because he was the reason she was here in the first place.

"It's go time. Tank is on the porch, talking with Hayley about her mom." Eric's voice was low as he came back into sight.

I immediately went to the window and stood up on the cinder blocks Eric and I had found a few yards away and had stacked below. It was hard to make out anything, but I could see the glow of Piper's phone. My fingers tried to pry the shitty window open, but I was certain it hadn't been opened in years, because it wasn't budging at all.

"It's fucking stuck."

"Let me try." I moved over, and Eric took his pocket knife and began sliding the blade underneath the ledge. My stomach coiled like a bunch of snakes as I watched his blade bend.

Feeling agitated, I whipped out my phone and shot Piper a text.

Me: Grab a towel and wrap it around your fist snug and hit the window as hard as you can. You're going to have to break it, and in order to be quiet, the glass has to fall out and not in.

Eric stepped back and waited beside me. A cold sweat broke out along my forehead the longer she stood on the other side of that window.

"You alright?"

Was I alright? No, I was not fucking alright.

I answered harshly. "No."

"Relax, bro. I'll walk right through that fucking party and grab her if I have to."

An unhealthy amount of jealousy surged through my body. *That's my job.*

I shook my head. This was what Piper did to me. The girl snuck inside my head and ran circles. She messed with my heart, and the sad thing was, I didn't even think she knew she was doing it.

My phone went off, and Eric and I both looked down.

Piper: There aren't any towels in here!
Me: Use your shirt.

"Don't even think about looking at her tits when she climbs out."

Eric chuckled. "Relax. What's yours is yours. I know the bro code."

My eyes strained to listen to Tank and Hayley. Christian was probably losing his shit knowing Hayley and Tank used to live close to one another. The trailer park was probably the worst thing I'd ever seen in terms of homes. I thought Hayley's last foster home was shitty, but now I knew that it was an upgrade from where she grew up.

My head snapped up as glass came tumbling out of the window. I gritted my teeth, hoping Tank didn't hear from his barely standing front porch. Eric and I quickly got to the window, and I stood up on the blocks, reaching in after snatching my own shirt off my back and wrapping it around my hand to brush away the remaining jagged glass. My hands immediately found her rib cage. "I got you," I whispered, pulling her out inch by inch. The window was small, but so was Piper. My large hands cupped her body, and a sense of relief shot right into my chest. Having her body in my hands did something to me. Something shifted and locked into place.

I would go to hell and back for her.

Her shaky hands grabbed onto my shoulders as her hair swung in between us. As soon as her legs were out the window, I heard her hiss.

"You okay? What happened? Did you get cut?"

Her voice was monotonous. "I'm fine."

She wasn't fine.

Once I placed her down onto the ground, I kept one of my hands on her warm skin and placed the other under her chin. The moon and stars shined above us, and when I tipped her head back, I saw the glassy waves. Piper was definitely not fine.

"What happened?"

"Not now, fucking go!" Eric came out of nowhere. I forgot

he was even here. I saw the light in the bathroom click on, and I snatched Piper's hand and rushed us around the side of the trailer. I pushed her body back into the metal siding and caged her in, shielding her from whatever came our way. We were closer to Hayley and Tank now but stuck on the side between the other shitty trailer propped a few feet away. Either way we went, we were fucked.

"You are not fine, Piper," I whispered softly, keeping her tiny body caged in. Our bare bodies were inches from one another, but I didn't dare move. In case anyone came around the side, I wanted to make sure she wasn't seen. Eric was a few feet away, also pinned to the side of the trailer, waiting for the go-ahead to run to our cars.

Piper didn't say anything to me, but I could sense the tension rolling off her body. She was as tight as a rubber band, ready to snap in half. Slowly, her head dropped into my shoulder, and within seconds, I felt something wet hit my bare chest.

Piper was crying, and it tore me in half.

It felt like someone had taken a knife to my skin.

"Did someone do something to you in there?"

I'd kill every fucking one of them. My temper had raised my body temperature so high I actually started to sweat. *Is this what it felt like to be Christian?* I was the level-headed one, but right now, I was ready to kill.

Piper's head shook back and forth slowly as her shoulders trembled. She was breaking. Piper was breaking, and there wasn't a thing I could do about it with us hiding like this.

My eyes raked around our surroundings, and I took the first out I could find. My hand clamped onto Piper's, and I made a run for it. I whipped us around, and we were behind the next-door trailer within a second. The ground was hard against my shoes, and the pounding of my feet matched the muscle behind my chest. I caught Eric's eye, and he silently questioned me, but I kept going, dragging Piper behind with me.

For a second, we paused, Piper's palm nestled right next to mine. I waited a beat, making sure there wasn't any commotion or following footsteps, and I pulled her with me, jogging behind the trailers, climbing through the tall, unkempt grass, and finally making our way past the dumpsters to get to the front of the trailer park.

If I'd paid attention earlier and glanced at the broken, flickering Pike Valley Trailer Park sign, I might have taken it as an indication that this would be a shitty night. It was ominous looking. A warning of sorts.

Breaking glass, running through a fucking forest of small lawns that hadn't seen a lawn mower in months, and Piper's tears. All those things combined were a recipe for a shitty fucking time.

I liked adrenaline rushes, but not when Piper was involved.

Not when I could see the wet streaks on her cheeks glistening with the blue hue of the trailer park sign.

I was certain we only had a few minutes before Hayley, Christian, and Eric walked up, but I was going to take advantage of it.

"Tell me what happened."

Piper tucked her hair behind her ears, and suddenly, she didn't look like the girl that I had mouthed off to in the past. Her clever comebacks and devious smiles in my direction had always showcased her fighting spirit, but right now, it was nowhere to be found. She looked sad. Lifeless. Broken.

"I'm okay," she finally answered, her voice small.

"You're crying."

Piper's face twisted. Her eyelashes fluttered closed for a moment before she reached up and dabbed her cheeks as if she couldn't believe she was truly crying.

"Oh." Her hands fell quickly as she cast her eyes to the ground.

I took a step closer to her, the gravel crunching underneath my shoe. "Don't do that. Don't hide from me."

She said nothing as crickets chirped in the background. The buzz from the flickering light sparked the air with a tension even heavier than what she was carrying.

"I'm learning that you hide from everyone." Piper slowly raised her chin, and we locked eyes. "Does anyone know the real you, Piper?"

I could hear footsteps getting closer. Twigs breaking and small rocks crunching. But Piper and I were at an impasse, and I wouldn't back down. I needed her to see that I was here...and I was seeing her.

Her tongue darted out to lick her bottom lip. I dipped my eyes down, seizing the emotional hold we had on one another, and felt myself pause. Her shirt was clenched in her one hand from breaking the window, which meant she had nothing on but her bra.

My mouth went dry, and I worked my jaw back and forth. It wasn't the time to let lust overtake, but I let it anyway. I wanted to pull her in and kiss her. I wanted to wrap my hands around her waist and let our bare bodies touch. I wanted to tip her head back and kiss away her tears and drink up every last secret she held close to her heart.

"There you are!"

Piper jumped back from me and scrambled to throw her shirt over her body, covering up that dainty piece of fabric she called a bra. I cleared my throat and locked eyes onto Christian. A shadow hid half of his face, but I could tell he had several questions on the tip of his tongue. On the way over, I gave them a brief run-down of what we were walking into, but nothing of true substance. Only that Piper had a brother, she was in trouble, and we needed to get her out of

Tank's trailer as soon as possible. They knew nothing about the situation or my racing.

Those were *our* secrets. I felt overly protective of them and somewhat closer to her knowing we shared something away from the rest of our privileged world.

Hayley rushed over to Piper and threw her arms around her slender shoulders. "Are you okay?"

Piper nodded her head. "I'm okay. I'm sorry."

"Why are you sorry?" Hayley pulled back, and her eyebrows cast an even darker shadow along her face. "You never have to be sorry for relying on us, Piper."

Piper's eyes shifted to mine momentarily before resting back on her best friend. "I know. It's just... There's a lot I need to tell you." She tucked a strand of hair behind her ear again. "But I need to get home right now. My parents are going to flip if I don't get home. I told them I was on my way a long time ago."

Hayley nodded. "Go! We will catch up tomorrow. Just as long as you're safe."

Piper forced a smile at all of us and slowly trudged over to her car. Once she got in and started to pull away, never once looking at the four of us, Hayley turned and faced me. "What the hell happened in there? She seems..."

Everything inside of me was wound tight. "Empty."

Hayley nodded, placing her hands on her hips. "You two have a lot of explaining to do." She let her arms fall to her sides. "But for now, let's just go back to Eric's and give her some time."

Eric was the first to walk over to my Charger. "And let's not forget we just broke a fuckin' window in that trailer. We need to get going. Now."

Christian cracked his neck. "Yeah, it'd be a shame if that fuck came at us..."

Hayley started to climb in the back of my car. "You don't want to pick a fight with a guy like Tank, Christian."

"I'm not scared. I was giving him one more sly glance in your direction before I knocked his teeth in."

She rolled her eyes, ready to retaliate, but I interjected as I began pulling onto the highway. "I'll drop you guys off at Eric's."

"Where are you going?" Christian asked.

Hayley's head popped in between Eric and me up front. "Ollie. Her parents are home, and they're pretty strict. I've met them once, and that was plenty. You can't just walk through the front door like usual."

I shrugged, flipping on my blinker. "Who said I'm walking through the front door?"

For a moment, she stayed quiet, but then she began shaking her head. "No. You cannot climb into her window! Her room is on the third floor! It's not like Pete's house when your brother climbed in and out of my window every night."

Christian snickered. "I still climb through your window."

Hayley turned back. "And it's on the first floor now. Not the second. Piper's room is way up high, and also"—she turned back to me—"she probably wants to be alone."

There was a ding in my chest, and I almost reached out and rubbed it. "Being alone is the last thing she needs right now, Hayley. Piper's always alone."

"That's—"

"True," I finished her sentence. "It's true. Her parents are never home, and even when she's hanging with you or the group, she's alone. She has secrets. And we just walked right into one."

Hayley slowly sunk back into the backseat with Christian and didn't say anything until we got to Eric's.

When I parked the car, silence filled the car until she finally said, "You're right."

I nodded. "I know I am."

We all sat in my Charger, letting the beat from my music ring out around us.

Hayley took a deep breath before placing her hand on the door handle. "Go make sure my best friend is okay, and then tomorrow, after lunch with your dad, we'll all meet and figure out what the hell is going on. Piper doesn't need to be alone, and I should know that better than anyone."

I watched in the rearview mirror as Christian grabbed onto her hand. Hayley smiled softly at him, and they climbed out. My brother shot back through the door before shutting it. "Don't think I forgot about what you said to Dad earlier. I know when something is eating at you, Ollie, and I will beat it out of you if I have to.

"I'd like to see you try," I answered back, playing it cool, but deep down, I was sweating like a motherfucker. *Why couldn't I have kept my mouth shut with my dad?*

Hayley pulled Christian farther toward the cabin, and I waited for Eric to climb out. He kept his eyes forward, looking out the windshield. "Do you know what you're doing, bro?"

No.

"Of course. I always have a plan. Don't worry about it. Just keep—"

His lip curled. "Just keep my mouth shut. I got it."

I dipped my head, and as soon as he slammed the door, I threw my Charger into reverse and headed right toward Piper.

There was no way in hell I'd be able to get her sad eyes out of my head tonight. There wasn't enough alcohol in the world to drown that out. So, going to her was inevitable.

CHAPTER TWENTY-ONE

PIPER

WHAT MADE PARENTS *GOOD* PARENTS? The question was certainly subjective, but it was one that I couldn't quite answer. Were you good parents if you simply provided shelter and food for your child? Or did it go further than that? Did it make you good parents if you read bedtime stories to your child every night and put bandages on their scraped knees? I really wasn't sure.

I didn't consider my parents to be bad parents, but I didn't consider them to be good ones, either. They provided me with a house to live in, clothes to wear, a car to drive, and I had a housekeeper who stocked my fridge weekly—although, I never really saw her. They put money into my account, and even though they watched my spending incessantly, they still gave me an allowance nonetheless, so they weren't *bad* parents. They just weren't the loving kind. They never had been. Maybe that was why I had such a hard time letting other people in.

But Ollie.

He was finding his way in more and more lately, and I liked it.

When his hands wrapped around my body as he pulled me out of Tank's trailer, I felt safe. I felt okay. Like I wasn't alone. Seeing his face after being crammed in a bathtub, hiding, was like holding onto a lifeline. I didn't know when it had happened, but my feelings of annoyance and anger toward Ollie had changed to something else entirely. I *liked* how I felt when he looked at me. I *liked* how I felt when he was worried about me. But then, of course, I got in my car, and everything came rushing back to me—the slimy feeling I had talking to my brother, the shame that went through me seeing Hayley looking so wounded that I hadn't told her I had a brother and that I was struggling with something. I felt like a terrible person who kept trying to save someone who wasn't even worth saving.

God, that made me feel even worse.

"So, yes, brunch tomorrow with your father and me before our flight? We'd like to talk to you about your college acceptance letters."

I stared at my mother as I sat lost in thought. Her long fingers drummed over the counter as she waited for my approval. Her red hair was tied into a loose bun at the nape of her neck, resting right above a dainty gold necklace my father had given her for their fifteenth anniversary.

"My college acceptance letters aren't even in yet, Mom."

She rolled her eyes. "Well, we already know you've been accepted to Stanford. Marcus called to let me know weeks ago."

"What?" I squeaked, jumping up from the chair.

She waved me off. "Oh yes, you know our friend Marcus Kellens. He's on the admissions board. Once he saw your name, he immediately put it in the acceptance pile."

Disappointment came crashing down. "So, I cheated my way into a good school? Because you're friends with Marcus?"

"Of course not." My father walked in and began rummaging through the fridge for something. His shirt was unbuttoned at the top, and his dark-brown hair was rustled on his head, probably from running his hands through it during the conference call he was just on. "You're accepted because of your hard work and dedication—something you obviously got from me." He glanced at my mom and smirked. She rolled her eyes.

I always found it funny how my parents could work so well together in a business sense, but when it came to family dynamics, they lacked severely. I wondered if it was how they were raised. I had only met my grandparents a handful of times before they'd passed. Jason and I were younger, so I didn't remember much from the meetings, but I knew they weren't anything spectacular. There were no *baking-cookies-with-Grandma* memories in my childhood. There were no *baking-cookies-with-Mom* memories in my childhood, either.

"Your father is right about one thing: you are dedicated and a hard worker. We are so proud of you, Piper." Her hand reached out and grabbed onto mine, and I was shocked. My eyes glanced down. *When was the last time we had even touched?* "Thank you for making the *right* choices."

And there it was. That achy feeling I always got when my parents came around. It didn't matter the situation or where we were, there would always be an underlying insult thrown at Jason buried underneath a compliment for me. *Thank you for making the right choices.* If only they knew I was showing up at illegal street races and sneaking into trailers during my spare time.

My throat was tight as I removed my hand from my mother's. I gave both of my parents a brief goodnight before all but running up the stairs and down the hall.

Once I was safely tucked behind my bedroom door, I rested my head against it and took a steady breath. There were times that I'd wished with all my might that my parents would come home from their business trip so I wouldn't be alone. But now, as I grew older and the resentment grew bigger, I found myself wishing that they'd just stay away.

Not only did I not know Jason anymore, I didn't know my parents either. Our family was broken into puzzle pieces that no longer fit together.

I continued to rest my head against my door, willing my thoughts to stop for just a second. The night was young, but I felt like I'd lived an entire lifetime from the moment I woke up to now. I was mentally exhausted.

Just as I pushed off from my bedroom door, I heard a small ding from the balcony. I spun around and looked past the glow of my bedside lamp and zeroed in on something glowing outside.

What is that?

Another ding.

My feet padded over the soft carpet, and as I got closer to the door, my heart jumped like I'd been shocked. The glowing was waving back and forth, and when my eyes adjusted, I almost fell backwards.

The door swung open, and the cool night air wafted around me. "Ollie! What the hell are you doing on my balcony?! How did you even get up here?"

Panic rushed to my chest as I grabbed his hand and hurriedly pulled him inside. I shut the door quickly and ran over to my bedroom door and locked it.

When I spun back around, Ollie was casually sitting on my bed with his cheek lifted. My stomach fluttered. Something inside of me sparked from seeing Ollie in my bedroom.

I crossed my arms over my black tank, playing it off.

"What is it with you Powell boys? Climbing into girls' bedrooms whenever you feel like it."

Ollie's deft fingers ran through his light hair, making it even more unruly. It was a good look for him. *Way too good.* "I needed to make sure you were okay."

I wanted to cave into him so badly that I felt it in my very core. Something softened inside of me, and that vulnerable feeling that I kept pushing away was creeping back as I stared at him from across my bedroom. He was sitting perfectly still on my white comforter, wearing the same dark T-shirt he had on earlier. His blue eyes were drinking me in, watching my every move. His face was relaxed, not a trace of playfulness on his features. He appeared cautious—probably waiting for me to lose it again, like a few hours ago.

My eyes dropped quickly, feeling embarrassed about earlier. I walked over to my desk and opened up my calculus book. "Ollie," I started, flipping through the pages for the lesson I needed to study. "I am perfectly fine. Thank you for helping me earlier, but things are okay now." I shot him a soft glance, and he was now leaning forward on the side of my bed, his arms resting lazily over his legs with a look on his face that made me shift on my feet. It was the *I-can-see-right-through-you* look that made me want to hide.

"Why do you do that?" he asked.

I glanced back at my book, focusing on the numbers so hard they started to blur. "Do what?"

"Why do you hide from me? Pretend you're okay when I know damn well you're not?" There was a bite to his voice, and I popped my head up, staring at the wall above my desk. "Do you thrive on being alone? Do you like not having anyone in your corner? It has to get lonely, right?"

A protective shield of anger was falling down in between us. My nostrils flared as I straightened my spine. I suddenly wanted the old Ollie back. It was a defense mechanism, I was sure, because the old Ollie who teased me and flirted only to turn around and flirt with someone else didn't do this. He didn't spit the truth at me. He didn't make me feel so *seen*.

My hair was a blur of red in front of my face as I spun around in my chair. "I could ask you the same question."

His gaze never left me, but it did narrow. "I do have someone in my corner."

"Who? Did you finally tell Christian about your dad?" He had my full attention now, and just like that, my anger had vanished. I tucked my hair behind my ear and waited with hopeful eyes.

"Nah." He smirked. "I've got you."

An exasperated sigh left me. "Just because I'm the only person who knows your dad isn't really your dad, doesn't mean I'm in any way helping you, Ollie. I'm not in your corner."

His jaw ticked before he asked, "Why do you think I'm here, Piper?"

"I don't know. To check on me, which is pointless because I. Am. Fine." My words came out sharp and fast, like knives being thrown at the wall. I could feel myself closing up again, becoming angry at myself for doing just that.

Part of me relished in the fact that Ollie was in my bedroom. That he cared enough about me to climb up a tree and jump onto my balcony to make sure I was okay.

But the other part of me was panicking that he saw me. The real me.

"You're not fine. And neither am I. I'm here because I don't want to be alone either, Piper. Do you know how fucking hard it is to go home to an empty house, knowing there are secrets buried all over the place? Do you know how much it kills me to wonder if I have another sibling out there? How much guilt it causes me to even have that thought? I have to bite my tongue every time I look at my father, knowing he likely knows that I'm not his son. And the worst part is that I *want* to know who my real dad is. What does that say about me?" Ollie was up on his feet now, pacing back and forth in my bedroom. "My life is good. I mean, yeah, I lost my mom, and that shit digs deeper than deep, but at least my dad is starting to come around. He asks about my grades, where I want to go to college; he's making an effort to have dinner with Christian and me on the weekends. And here I am, wondering about my *real* dad. I should just be happy with what I've got." He ran his hand through his hair and tugged on the ends. "I feel guilty. Confused."

I stood up and rested my back along my desk, watching him unfold. "Why do you feel guilty, Ollie? You shouldn't feel guilty."

He shot me a long glance, the edge of his jaw profound in the soft glow of my room. "Do your parents ask you those types of questions? Do they ask where you want to go to college? Do they care? Why are they okay with you being home alone all the time?" I went to stop him, but he continued on. "Do they know that you're in line to become valedictorian?" *How does he even know that?* "Do they ask about Jason? Do they even ask about you?" He shook his head angrily. "My dad isn't the best, but he's better than your parents. That's why I feel guilty. I should just be thankful I have him. I shouldn't be digging into the past, but I can't seem to stop."

It was like a slap to the face with every question he asked, but seeing Ollie all worked up had me ignoring every single one. I felt selfish. I was so focused on my own shit with Jason and Tank that I forgot Ollie had his own shit, too. He was good at downplaying it, putting his focus on something else to hide, but Ollie needed someone.

"Hey," I whispered, walking over and taking his wrists in

my hands. He paused, his eyes latching onto mine. "Take a breath."

"No," he answered sharply. "I don't like this. I don't like feeling like shit is spiraling out of control. I don't like seeing you sad. I don't like knowing you're alone all the time, and I hate that you push me away. You push everyone away. I see you, Piper. I've seen you for months."

"I see you too, Ollie," I whispered, gazing up into his eyes. I felt like he was sucking my soul into his. We had a connection, and we'd had that connection since the Wellington Prep party. Sharing secrets connected you with someone. I saw that now. "You're doing the same, Ollie. You've pushed everyone away so you don't have to deal with your own stuff. You're trying so hard to help me so you don't help yourself."

He turned away, but my nails dug into his wrists. "You've pushed everyone away, and I've done the same."

His Adam's apple bobbed up and down as his arms slowly relaxed in my grip. Our eyes locked again, and I could see the way his walls were crumbling. Just like mine. The more time I spent with Ollie, the weaker they grew. "Then maybe we should just stop."

My voice was soft as I took a step closer to him, our body heat melding together. "Okay."

His hands moved to my waist, my grip on his wrists never lessening. "Okay then," he whispered. His lips slowly fell apart with the words, and I couldn't take my eyes off them. A hot wave started from the top of my head and melted all the way down my body.

I watched his mouth move. "Let's make a deal."

I blinked, hoping my eyes weren't betraying me as I looked back to his. "What kind of deal?"

His grip on my waist tightened, and the feeling it gave me didn't go unnoticed. "You fill Christian and Hayley in tomorrow and let us come up with a plan to get us both, *and*

Jason, out from under this mess with Tank, and I'll tell Christian what I've been hiding." I began to nod my head. *Sounds reasonable.* "But I need you to do something for me first."

Anything.

"What?"

His gaze was fiery. His pupils dilated as he took his hand off my waist, mine falling from his wrist with the motion. His touch was soft as he tipped my head back. "Tell me what happened in that trailer, because I'm going fucking crazy not knowing why you were crying."

The words *I'm fine* were on the tip of my tongue, but I stopped myself and let myself cave. "My brother came in the bathroom when I was hiding."

His jaw clenched. "And?"

"And I..." Tears formed, but I blinked them away. Ollie could tell; his eyes bounced back and forth between mine as his mouth fell into a frown. "I saw him come pretty damn close to snorting something." I swallowed a lump, trying to look away, but Ollie held my chin straight and shook his head.

"Don't do that. Eyes on me." My chin wobbled under his grasp. "I yelled at him right before he went to snort whatever it was. I was so angry. And then hurt." I sniffed, feeling the burn from holding back my tears. "I told him once we paid the money and I got *you* out of this mess, I was done with him. For good. Unless he got help."

My chin continued to wobble, and I tried my hardest to hide it. Watching my brother drop his head down to the sink made me sick. I flinched at the visual.

"I hate that you're hurt right now," Ollie whispered, his hand leaving my waist and cupping the side of my head. He brought my forehead to his chest, and that was when I felt the moisture coating my cheeks. Ollie's fingers wove throughout my hair as a sob erupted from deep within my chest. *Oh my God, I'm breaking right in front of him.*

"Shh." I tried to focus on Ollie's beating heart to calm my own, but it was no use. I let the gate open; I let myself fall apart, and there was no going back.

Ollie rubbed circles on my back as he pulled me over to my bed. He lay down, never letting go of me, and I instantly curled into his side. "I'm sorry," I managed to choke out while squeezing my arms around his torso. His hand stilled on my back as I continued. "I'm sorry you're involved in this mess. I'm sorry you have to see me like this. And I'm sorry I threatened to tell Christian your secret."

"Stop it."

I shook my head. "I promise I'll make this right. I'll get you out of this mess with racing."

"Piper, fucking quit it. I'm a big boy. I can take care of myself." I sniffled. "And I'll take care of you, too." I stilled in his arms as my silent tears continued to fall onto his shirt. I wanted to argue with him and tell him that he didn't need to take care of me, that I was fine on my own, but I couldn't find it in me to say the words, because deep down, I wanted him to take care of me.

I could survive on my own, but I didn't want to.

CHAPTER TWENTY-TWO

OLLIE

THE SOUND of plastic bags and Styrofoam containers being bent open did nothing to take my mind off last night.

It hadn't been a usual Saturday night in the slightest. I could still smell Piper's sweet scent on my shirt. Her warm body was curled next to mine all night with her pretty hair framing her peaceful face. Piper was cute. I loved the shape of her small nose and the freckles that lined the top of it. The way her pink lips parted as slumber took over and the small moan that escaped her mouth when she curled into me at three in the morning.

"Why are you smiling like that and not touching your food?"

Something hit me in the head, and I threw Christian a glare. "Did you just throw a fucking French fry at me?"

My dad cleared his throat. "Don't curse in front of a lady."

I gave my dad a glare, too, and heard Hayley giggle. "You like Hayley better than you like us," I joked, giving her a grin. She blushed and shook her head. She was always a little shy in front of my dad, and I had no idea why. Christian thought it was cute. I wondered if Piper would be the same way.

"What *are* you thinking about over there, Ollie?" Hayley raised an eyebrow as she stuffed a French fry into her mouth.

"I bet I know." Christian grinned.

"Do you have a girlfriend?" my dad asked, truly interested.

"No," I quickly answered.

"Pretty much," Christian mumbled, and I shot him another glare. *Shut the fuck up.*

Hayley smashed her lips together as my dad drummed his fingers on the table, eyeing me with curiosity. "Are you taking this mystery girl who *isn't* your girlfriend to the winter formal?

"How do you know about the winter formal?" Christian asked, mid-bite of his hamburger.

My dad pulled back before he coughed uncomfortably. It was a little surreal sitting there talking to him about normal, mundane, high school things. Usually, whenever my dad and Christian were around one another, it was like an airing of WWE but without the actual wrestling. I was usually the one stuck in the middle, trying to keep the peace, but things were calm now. Better. Which was exactly why I was keeping my mouth shut about the birth certificate—for now, at least. No need to disrupt the calm waters with my massive fucking tsunami at lunch.

"I read about it in my parent newsletter."

I choked on a pickle. "Your what?"

"My newsletter. I signed up for the English Prep parent newsletter a little while back."

My brother's mouth opened a little as he stared at my dad in disbelief. Hayley, always wanting things to stay calm, smiled. "I think that's great. I didn't even know they had a parent newsletter. But"—she glanced at me with a twinkle in her eye—"*are* you taking Piper?"

Shit. I'd forgotten all about the winter formal, and I knew no one had asked Piper to go because I had banned every guy in the school from doing so. It wasn't long ago that I stood in the locker room after our last football game and told them all I'd fuck their mom if they continued to talk about the "hot redhead" that was hanging around Hayley.

I wouldn't actually fuck any of their moms, but I was known to be a little on the crazy side. I'd followed through on enough dares and threats to back up my street cred.

"When is it again?" I asked.

Hayley's eyes lit up. "Satur...day." Her voice dropped at the end, and I no longer felt hungry. Shit. *Saturday.* The races.

A hush fell over the table as soon as the word left her mouth. I wouldn't be able to take Piper, and I instantly felt like shit, knowing she wouldn't have a date because I had banned everyone from asking her. I was such a *jealous* fuck.

"What just happened?" My dad bent his head down, his cool, gray eyes moving between the three of us.

Hayley quickly intervened. "Oh, Ollie is probably feeling a little bad for not asking Piper when it's less than a week away." She turned to me. "Don't worry. Piper and I will go get dresses this week. Just make sure you ask her so she knows she actually has a date."

I nodded and mouthed the words, *"Thank you,"* as soon as my dad looked away.

I went ahead and added *winter formal* to my list of things we needed to convene about at Eric's cabin later.

Shortly after the awkward conversation about the formal, Hayley and Christian began cleaning up before we all headed to Eric's. Christian was dropping Hayley off at her car so she could head to Piper's so they could drive together to Eric's. Piper and Hayley needed to talk, apparently, so they were catching up on the drive over.

As soon as they left and I gathered my keys, my dad came

and stood in the archway, leaning against the wall with his arms crossed over his dress shirt. His forearms were flexing back and forth from below his rolled-up cuffs as if he were nervous and trying to gain the confidence to ask me something.

That immediately set off alarm bells in my head. My father and I got along for the most part. We didn't butt heads like he and my brother, and I was certain it was because we were nothing alike. Christian was an exact replica of my father—thus why they constantly argued. But my father and me? We didn't even share the same physical features, and now I knew why.

"Need somethin'?" I asked, glancing at him from my phone. There wasn't a damn thing on my phone at the moment, but I needed something to hold my attention before I lost a hold on my sanity and blurted out something that gave him an indication that I *knew*.

My father reached up and rubbed his five o'clock shadow, the scruff echoing within the tall ceilings of our entryway. "Is everything okay with you?"

Don't panic. Don't look away.

I kept my eyes steady on his. "Yeah, why?"

He tilted his head, squinting his one eye. "You seem distant. Far away. You're not your happy, loud, annoying-the-hell-out-of-your-brother self."

The need to shift on my feet was hard to ignore. But I kept them planted to the floor. "I'm good."

"Are you upset your brother is going off to college next year without you? And most of your friends? Is that why you were asking about you two being so close in age yesterday?"

No. I quickly averted my eyes and knew that was an instant mistake. The secret was planted inside my head like a seed the second I'd found the birth certificate. Tiny sprouts formed the more I thought about all the differences my dad and I had, and when it clicked, the roots continued to grow and spread until it was the only thing I could think about. It consumed me. The desire to hear it from him. The confirmation I needed. The questions I wanted answered. Standing here, looking at my father with his quizzical eye, was too much.

But then my phone vibrated.

Unknown: We need to talk

I glanced at my father again and then back down to my phone.

Me: Who is this?

Unknown: Who tf you think? Meet me here and we can discuss what we need to do this weekend.

I recognized the pin that was sent. It was Tank's trailer, the one I was at the night before, rescuing Piper. It felt like I had been hit in the back with a baseball bat. My back went rigid for a moment before I shook my arms out and slipped my phone in my pocket. I grabbed my black hat off the banister of the stairs and placed it backwards on my head.

"Everything is just dandy, Dad. I gotta go." Before stepping out the door, I glanced back at him, and his mouth was in a straight line. I knew I was raising more questions with being standoffish. I knew he was likely concerned, or maybe he was sweating a little, wondering if I'd found out his secret —I wasn't sure—but I turned back and said, "Later," before closing the door and walking to my car.

First stop: Tank's.

Second stop: Eric's.

Hopefully, the first didn't interfere with the second. Walking into Tank's trailer alone was probably a step in the wrong direction, but what choice did I have?

CHAPTER TWENTY-THREE

PIPER

MY LIP STUNG from biting it so many times. The pastries I'd had for brunch with my parents tasted great in the moment, but now they were threatening to come back up as Hayley and I drove to Eric's cabin.

I didn't know what to say. I didn't know where to start. Did I start at the beginning? Did I just come out and tell her I was sorry? Because I was. I didn't like hiding things from her, and when I sat down and thought about it, it wasn't fair in the least. I knew all about Hayley's past. I'd been with her through some scary stuff. We'd been chased off the road together—that definitely formed a bond between two people, right?

As soon as Hayley had parked on the cobblestone lot in front of the cabin, I did everything I could to calm myself down. I took in the stone pillars and focused on the different sized rocks, counting each one until I felt I was ready to talk. I turned the music down, and Hayley smiled at me patiently.

And I knew, right then, that I needed to tell her. So I spilled *everything*.

It probably only took ten minutes to fill her in on Jason and the drama within the walls of my house, but it felt like it took eons. I was drained, but strangely, I felt lighter.

Hayley pulled her dark hair into a high ponytail before unbuckling her seatbelt. "Is this why you were so open to my shit? My past?"

I shrugged, biting my sore lip again. I was back to staring at the stone pillars. "I guess. I...I don't know why I didn't tell you." I quickly shook my head. "Wait, yes I do." When Hayley and I met each other's gazes, I felt a tug in my heart. I had felt sorry for her life, the stuff she had gone through, and I knew she hated that. She didn't want pity, but I had felt it anyway. Hayley didn't deserve the shit she went through. There was so much negativity already in her life, so why would I have poured even more onto her?

Hayley sat up a little taller, bringing her legs up to sit cross-legged. "So, why?"

"Well, the first reason is because you had way too much going on in your own life to take on my family drama. I mean, why would I let all of that out when you *just* got into a stable living environment?" The more I explained to Hayley, the lighter I felt. The bricks stacked on my shoulders fell off one by one. "I didn't want to bombard you with it. And my parents have driven it into my head to never talk about what happens behind closed doors." I wrung my hands together in my lap. "They even took me out of Wellington Prep and moved us to the other side of town, thrusting us into yet another rich society just so we could hide the mess in our family. They completely shut Jason out of our lives. There aren't even family photos of him hanging up in the house anymore."

Not only did I feel angry about that, I felt hurt, too. I

knew Jason was making mistakes. I knew he was in way too deep, but if the thought of him being shunned from our family hurt me, I couldn't even imagine how it felt for him. *Or maybe he didn't care at all.* Did addicts have feelings? Or did everything and everyone they'd ever cared about slowly dissipate, and their worries morphed into where the next party was? Or when they'd be able to get high again?

Slowly, I brought my head over and rested it along the window. I had the urge to bang it off of it a few times to get the thoughts to stop. "I told Jason last night that I was done with him when Ollie and I finished cleaning up his mess." I turned to look at Hayley who was fiddling with the locket around her neck. "I have to figure out how to get Ollie out of this mess. This is all my fault, Hayley."

Hayley frowned as she reached over and put her small hand on my leg. She gave it a squeeze. "*We* will figure it out. Not you. You're not in this alone, okay?"

Just then, Christian walked out of the cabin and leaned along one of the stone pillars. Hayley's cheeks turned pink as she smiled through the windshield before turning back to me. "I love you; Christian loves you; Ollie loves you; and I'm pretty sure Eric does, too, even though he's even grumpier than Christian now." A light laugh fell between us. "And I know *very* well there is something more going on with you and Ollie."

I desperately tried to catch the butterflies flying in my stomach. "Why do you say that?"

Hayley was fighting a smile, the apples of her cheeks twitching. "You're going to be pissed when I tell you what he did."

The butterflies stopped abruptly. "What did he do?"

"He may or may not have banned every guy from asking you to the winter formal."

My mouth fell. "Wait. The winter formal?"

Hayley let out a loud laugh, plopping her legs back down. "Winter formal? Remember, this weekend? Aren't you on the committee?"

Shit. This time, I really did hit my head off the window. "Damnit! I have shit to make for that. Decorations. And I don't have a dress." *Oh my God.* See! This was how I knew I was in way too deep with Jason's shit! I was leading a double life. High school was still on the horizon. College acceptance letters would be coming soon. Those things hadn't crossed my mind in a while.

I sighed. "I don't even have a date!"

Hayley was quick to add, "Yeah! Because of Ollie."

"Wait." I flung myself up from resting along the glass. "He did what?" *I'm going to kill him.* "Ugh!" I opened my door and stepped outside onto the uneven pebbles.

Hayley was giggling as she followed me up the stairs. She was loving this. She secretly liked seeing Ollie get under my skin. I was pretty sure everyone did.

Christian pushed off the stone pillar and placed his arm over Hayley's shoulder. "Everything okay? Are you ready for the gang to help?"

I was fuming underneath my skin. I couldn't believe Ollie had banned everyone from asking me to the dance. Not only was I annoyed with Ollie for doing that, I was almost irritated that a twisted part of me *liked* knowing he didn't want me going with anyone else. Why was it like this with us?

One minute, I wanted to punch him and push him away, and the next, I was basking in his touch and pulling him in close.

Hayley snickered under her breath as she filled Christian in. "I just told Piper that Ollie banned everyone from taking her to winter formal."

Christian chuckled. "And he's too much of a pussy to ask you himself."

Or maybe he just doesn't want to go with me. I bit my tongue as I roughly started throwing my hair up in a ponytail. I didn't have time to think about if Ollie liked me like that. Jason was stuck in a cockroach-infested trailer, Ollie was racing for Tank, we had over ten thousand dollars to pay back before Tank would let my brother go, I had to figure out a way to get Ollie out from Tank's slimy grip, *and* I had seven million things to do for winter formal. Oh! And a stupid, five-page paper to write on the fucking Great Depression.

And don't think I didn't see the irony in writing about the Great Depression. My life was pretty fucking depressing at the moment.

My head slowly twisted toward the incoming car. *Hmph.*

When Ollie stepped out of his Charger with his black baseball hat on backwards, wearing an English Prep bulldog shirt—much like the one I had stolen from him—my stomach flipped. Every time I saw that glowing smile of his, it did something to me. He was good-looking. So good-looking that I always found my breath catching when he was near, but that didn't stop me from rushing down the front steps to get to him, and it didn't stop me from smacking him upside the head, either.

"Whoa, what the hell, Piper!" He caught his hat as it flung off his head.

"You are such a pig, Oliver Powell! What? You can't stand to see another guy take me to the winter formal?"

He tried his hardest to wipe the grin off his face, but it stuck, staring at me, taunting me. But the only thing it did was piss me off further, because my knees wobbled a bit.

"I don't want to hear a single word out of your mouth right now. Get inside so we can figure this bullshit out with you racing like you're trying out to be on the *Fast and the Furious* cast. I need to get home and get started on the other part of my life where I have papers to write and decorations to make!" I stepped aside to let him walk up to the cabin. Eric was outside now, and everyone but me had smiles on their faces. Even my best friend.

"Oh! And you need to do your homework, too!" I shouted as Ollie began walking past me. "I know you're smart enough to be in senior-level classes, but you can't get away with not doing your homework...not if you want to keep those scholarships promised to you next year."

A deep chuckle hit my ears as I stared at his back. He looked over his shoulder, raising an eyebrow. "You just can't help but care about me, huh?"

"I do not care about you!" *I do.* Even more now because he kept swooping in, saving the day.

I rushed past him, still trying to keep a tight grasp on my anger that was washing away, when he snuck a hand around my waist. A gasp caught in my throat when his palm connected to my hip. His minty breath hit that tender spot right below my ear. "Say it like you mean it, Piper."

My mouth was suddenly glued shut. All eyes were on me, and yet, I couldn't say a single thing. Ollie chuckled again as I pushed his hand off me.

There. Now I can breathe.

I stormed past all my friends and went right to the kitchen and flung myself onto a barstool.

It was time to get my head on straight and focus on the bigger picture. So what, Ollie gave me butterflies. So what, he made my heart stop. So what, he held me last night while I cried. And so what, everyone knew what I was hiding.

I couldn't focus on that. Not right now.

CHAPTER TWENTY-FOUR

OLLIE

SINKING DOWN ONTO THE BARSTOOL, a smile overtook my face. I couldn't help it. Seeing Piper all riled up, a glint in her eye as she stewed in her annoyance for me, made the world seem right again. Like it was spinning the proper way on its axis. Like global warming was nonexistent, and we'd have sunshine-filled days for the rest of eternity. Piper had fought this connection we'd had since day one, and I proved to her today that the fighting was over.

Yes, she was annoyed with me.

Yes, she smacked me on the head.

Yes, she was sitting with her arms crossed over her perky chest as it heaved up and down. *But...* She didn't deny it. She didn't deny that she cared about me, and suddenly, the future didn't seem so dull anymore. My problems seemed to fade. Fuck Tank, and fuck having a different dad than my brother.

Piper cared about me.

"So, are we gonna figure this shit out, or are we all gonna sit in here and explode from the rising tension you two have compiled up together?" Eric lazily leaned back onto the counter, picking at the label on his beer. I glanced at the clock. *2:43.* I watched as he tipped back the bottle and chugged it like it was water. *What the hell was going on with him?* I pushed back my concern for later, after my own shit was handled.

"Can someone fill me in?" Christian leaned forward on the bar top and propped his elbows up. "Right now, all I know is that my girl dragged me to the place she grew up, and we had a lengthy conversation with a fucking shit-bag about her mom, and I'm still feeling the after-effects of anger." He turned to me and Piper. "How the hell are you two involved with that guy?"

Christian leveled me with a glare, and I held it. I loved my older brother, and I knew in the past I'd given him absolutely no reason to think I could handle shit on my own, but he had no fucking idea. He was going to be pretty pissed when he found out I'd been racing. He was going to demand answers, wondering how I'd gotten roped into all of this.

My eyes shot to Piper for a moment. Her long hair was pulled into a ponytail, her face free of any makeup and, ironically, clear of flaws. She was the prettiest thing I'd ever seen, and I never thought girls were *pretty*. They were hot, bangin', fuckable. *Baddies.* I didn't use words like *pretty* to describe a girl. But fuck me, Piper was pretty.

"Ollie!" My eyes flung to her. "Pay attention."

I cleared my throat. "My bad. What?"

Christian repeated himself. "Ollie. What the *fuck* is going on?"

My breath seized to come. *Did I tell him the truth?* Did I tell him I'd been racing for months, and I stumbled upon little miss Piper and all her baggage, and that was how I got roped into this? He'd surely understand why I was helping her. After all, it wasn't too long ago that the five of us sat around our kitchen table, assembled our group, and tried to come up with ways to help Hayley with her shit, but this was going to open up so many questions. Questions I wasn't ready to answer.

"It's my fault."

I paused, flicking my eyes to Piper. Her voice was so strong. So sure of herself. It was hard to believe the night before she was curled in my arms, crying.

A light cough came from her as she cleared her throat. "I asked Ollie to go with me to meet Tank so I could hash out a deal in order to pay him back. That's when Ollie offered to race for him. Tank bets on the races, and he gets a certain percentage of the money pool—even more so if he bets and wins."

My girl. Coming in clutch. I almost wanted to raise my fist with triumph.

Christian's eyes were in slits. "Pay him back? For what?"

Hayley was biting her lip, looking from Piper to me. I wasn't sure if Piper had told her the truth. Or maybe they didn't even get to that part. Piper's secrets went deep. Just like mine.

"My brother."

Christian's face flattened. "You have a brother?"

"Exactly my reaction," I said, still a little confused by the revelation. The girl was constantly alone. There weren't even photos up in her house of him—or anyone, really.

"Yes. And he's into some bad shit. Like dealing for Tank. Except, my brother didn't deal the last batch of drugs—or batches, if it's any correlation to the amount of money he owes. If I'm guessing correctly, my brother kept all the drugs for himself, thus not being able to pay up."

"And if there's one thing I know about Tank," Hayley whispered, "it's you don't fuck with his money. My mom made that mistake once."

An eerie feeling came over the group. Even Eric stood up a little taller.

Piper swiveled on her barstool, now facing Hayley. "Did he do something to you?"

Hayley pulled the hair tie from her hair, letting her dark hair down. "No! You know I don't take shit from people. But my mom had to repay him..."

Piper quickly got up and wrapped her arms around Hayley, resting her head on hers. "I'm sorry I brought you into this."

A tug in my chest had me looking away. *God damnit, Piper was too sweet.*

"Do not apologize to me. You almost died because of me."

Piper giggled. "We're kind of a fucked-up batch."

Hayley shrugged. "Makes life exciting."

Oh, yes. Real fucking exciting. I love when my heart almost stops beating at the sound of their screams. The night they were run off the road was still alive and well in my brain. I'd never felt fear like that. *Ever.*

"I think there is an obvious solution to this problem."

The four of us swung our gazes to Eric. He was still casually leaning along the counter, now holding an empty beer bottle.

"What's that?" I asked, resting my arms along the counter.

"Piper. Aren't you rich? I've seen your house. And your car. Why can't you just pay him off?"

"It's over ten thousand dollars," Piper announced, her head dropping with defeat. "It was twenty."

Christian cursed under his breath. "Twenty? Fuck. How much drugs did he use?"

Piper's face turned pink, and I shot him a glare.

"Okay." Eric threw his bottle in the trash, a clank of glass hitting glass echoing throughout the cabin. "So? You don't have that much money? Don't your parents give you money?"

Piper looked uncomfortable, and I almost took the reins from her. Seeing her fold into itself drove a knife into my gut. It bothered me. My blood was spiked with an overpowering need to protect her from everything in the world—even Eric's invading questions.

"No. She doesn't have—"

Piper quickly interrupted me, so I let her finish. "My parents watch my money very closely. After my brother started to spend all his and steal from them, they took total control. They're afraid I'll turn out like him, too."

Eric met her eye, and after a few seconds, he nodded. "Okay, well..." He switched his attention to me and Christian. "What about you two? How much do you guys have? Your dad watches your money, I know, but maybe if we compile it all. And Hayley? You just got a shit-ton from your dad, right?" He shrugged. "I don't have much. Family drama. Daddy-o is icing me out. And no, I don't want to fucking talk about it. But I'll give what I can."

"No." Piper shot up quickly. "I need to find another way. I can't take my friends' money, and I can't keep having Ollie race for this psycho. Maybe..." Piper looked down at her shoes. "Maybe I'll just say fuck it. Jason can figure it out on his own."

As if she and I were connected, I could feel her pain like it was my own. And if I could, I'd take it all away in a heart-beat. I knew, deep down, she didn't want to give up on her brother, and who knew what Tank would do if I all of a sudden stopped racing? *Fuck.* I began to reach out to Piper, not caring that we weren't alone, but the wobble in Hayley's voice had us all pausing.

"I—I don't have much to give."

We all stared at her, and Christian turned his body completely and had her caged in. "What do you mean?"

Her head dropped, her dark hair almost shielding her. She was cowering, and Hayley didn't cower.

Piper's voice was hesitant. "What's going on Hay? Is everything okay?"

The gulp from Hayley was loud enough for all of us to hear. "I don't have much money left."

"How do you not have any money left? You put back some for college in case you didn't get a scholarship, and you bought your car, but you still had plenty." Christian's voice was unsteady. I'm sure no one else noticed. But I did. I knew my brother. I knew when he was seeing red. "Did someone take money from you? Threaten you?"

Hayley's brown locks flew past her face as she snapped her head up. "No!"

"So?" Christian's ears were turning red, and I was certain mine were, too. We didn't take kindly to people fucking with what was ours—another Powell trait, I was sure.

Hayley held her breath, smashing her lips together. Piper inched closer and delicately placed her hand on her shoulder for support. "I paid for my mom to go to rehab."

My heart jolted. *Oh, shit.* Christian's nostrils flared as his fists clenched. I sat back, waiting for steam to come out of his ears. That was one major difference between my brother and me. I could hold my anger in, level out my temper, and think rationally. Christian could not.

"You...what?"

Hayley's eyes were like glass. Unshed tears were on the brink of her dark eyelashes. "I was going to tell you."

Christian shot up from his barstool and stormed out of the cabin kitchen. Hayley rolled her eyes, sighing, and reluctantly followed after him.

Piper slowly came and sat back down as Hayley and Christian argued in the other room, loud enough for us to hear.

Piper dropped her head to the counter. "This is all my fault."

I leaned back and crossed my arms over my chest. I didn't see how any of this was Piper's fault.

"None of this is your fault."

A sarcastic chuckle tumbled out of her lips as she sat back up. "How is none of this my fault?"

"What exactly is your fault? Me racing?" I shook my head roughly. "Nope. I was racing way before you showed up. Hayley and Christian fighting right now? Not your fault, either. It has nothing to do with you, really. And Eric and me sitting in here with you, trying to get a hold of this problem? That's just what friends do."

Eric nodded silently.

All three of us snapped our heads to the other room as Hayley's voice rose. *"I didn't want you to try and talk me out of it! It was my decision and my decision alone. I didn't think you'd understand!"*

I cringed when Christian's tone grew even harsher. *"How could I not understand, Hayley? Fuck. If given the chance to get my mom clean, I would have done the same. Don't you remember that my mom died as an addict?"*

My entire body went cold. My chest cracked open, and my heart fell onto the floor for everyone to see.

Christian spoke again, his voice less harsh but still loud enough for us to hear. *"I get it, Hayley. I think your mom is a piece of shit and she deserves nothing from you, but babe, I get it. You have to start trusting me. You don't have to be alone anymore. Why can't I make you understand that?"*

A tremble of pain skittered over my skin, like the whisper of a ghost. Goosebumps broke out along my arms. There it was—that reminder of my mom that I often pushed away so I didn't have to feel its effects. It was one of the reasons I began to bury myself in girls and partying, only to move onto racing in the end.

That scar on my heart was as open to the world as a wound on my very skin, but the other scar—knowing my father wasn't my real father—was buried deep under the skin. Both scars always snuck up on me and hit me at the worst of times.

"Is that why you're so understanding of all of this? Why you're so adamant about helping me?"

Piper's voice was like a light in the dark. The softness of her words helped soothe the hurt that was cutting me deep. "Is it because you get it? Is it because, if given the opportunity, you'd do the same? You'd try to save someone you love?"

I followed Eric's body as he quietly left the kitchen, leaving me and Piper alone. I was thankful, because I needed to be alone for this, I thought.

I turned toward her. Her green eyes were locked and loaded on mine, ready to swallow up all my deepest, darkest secrets—and there was no one else I'd rather share them with.

Piper.

She and I.

Me and her.

We understood each other.

A small thud sounded as she hopped down from her barstool. Her feet padded over to me, and before I knew it, she was easing her way in between my legs and reaching her arms around my body. I stilled, not knowing what to do other than to submit to her. I wasn't sure if there was ever a time that we had *truly* hugged each other. We'd touched each other before, of course. Just last night, she curled next to my body. I'd even had her naked body in my hands once, but this was different. This was something deeper.

Piper's warm breath coasted over my skin. "Is that why

you're helping? Is that why you're racing for Tank? Is that why you're helping me pay him back?"

My voice sounded like I'd swallowed glass. It was almost painful to talk. "No." Piper pulled back quickly, her face faltering. "I'm helping because it's *you,* Piper." Didn't she understand I'd do anything for her? Couldn't she see that she was the first person I looked for when I walked into a room? Didn't she feel this?

Her head shook back and forth, small strands of her hair falling from her ponytail. "But this is my problem." Her eyes clenched shut, and suddenly, I was back to feeling cold. I wanted her eyes on me. The connection between us was beginning to be what I lived for. "I need to find a way to get you out of this. I hate that you're involved. I hate that I'm involved."

"Hey." My voice was almost merciless. I needed her to understand what I was saying. As soon as she locked onto me, I drove my eyes into hers as I wrapped my hands around her face. "This may have started with you, but I can promise you that it'll end with me. Tank will have no fucking part in your life, or mine, soon. You got it?"

Piper's eyes bounced back and forth between mine, and right before Christian and Hayley walked back in the room, hand in hand, she gave me one short nod.

Whether Piper believed me or not, I knew I was good for my word.

This would end.

There would be no more of Piper breaking into trailers; there would be no more of me racing. Tank had no idea...but I was coming for him.

CHAPTER TWENTY-FIVE

PIPER

MY BODY FELT FUNNY. My head was fuzzy. My blood felt spiked with something potent. There was too much going on, too many emotions over the last day and a half. I was all over the place. Ollie and I kept teetering over the line we had drawn so long ago, and it was doing weird things to my head. I kept peeking at him, my cheeks flaming every time he caught me.

"Well, so now we know that we can't just pay this guy outright, so we need to exhaust our other possibilities." Eric rested his elbows on the counter and dropped his head. "So, you owe over 10k, and then once that's paid back, he'll just let your brother go? What? Does he have him chained up? Or is your brother just a complete pussy and afraid to leave?"

"He must have something on him. I'm not sure. I know my brother is afraid of him, though." Ollie didn't bother looking up. He kept his head straight in line with the cabinets that stood on the back kitchen wall. I wasn't going to lie;

having him sit beside me as I continued talking about Jason made me feel a little better.

"I don't know how my brother ended up in Tank's trailer in the first place. I don't know if someone lured him there. I don't know if Tank threatened him. But..." My pulse thudded painfully loud in my ears. "He also threatened that he'd feed my brother drugs and blame it on an overdose if he didn't get his money back."

Christian hissed, and Ollie stayed still. He didn't even blink.

"Who the fuck is this punk?" Christian's hand slapped against the bar top.

"He's probably bluffing," Eric said, not worried at all.

Then Hayley interrupted, "Doubt it. He's a fucked-up guy. I've heard stories. I don't even know how the police haven't put him away for good." *Which was exactly why Ollie needed to get away from him, too.*

Hayley scoffed. "Oh wait, I know why he hasn't been put away... It's because the system is completely unreliable—at least where I come from it is."

Silence encased the room, all five of us sorting through our thoughts. But then Eric's chuckle cut through and cut the silence in half. "Does anyone else think it's funny that we're a bunch of rich, privileged kids who can't even pay off a drug dealer? Why did our families choose now to rein in our spending? It's fucked."

I shrugged. "I've never really had free range."

Ollie cleared his throat. "I spent most of what I had saved on the turbo to race."

Christian pointed at him. "I fucking knew you put that in there for a reason." He used air quotes. "'*Just a tune up,*' my ass."

That smug grin worked its way onto Ollie's face, and I

found myself staring, lips parted and all. Once he flashed his blue eyes over to me, I quickly turned my head.

"Okay, so." Hayley got up from the barstool and began pacing the kitchen, her Converse slapping the floor with each step. "There are a few ways to make fast cash. The first thing we need to worry about is paying back Tank. The next will be to distance ourselves from him—especially you." She gestured to Ollie, but he didn't say a word.

I opened my mouth to include what Tank had said—that he was wanting to work something out with Ollie after the money was paid back, but the clipped shake of Ollie's head in my direction had me waiting. I quickly looked around to see if anyone noticed. Christian and Eric were looking at Hayley, not paying Ollie a bit of attention. My eyes crinkled. *Why?* Why didn't he want me to say anything?

He lowered his gaze and chucked an eyebrow up. He shook his head again.

Fine.

Hayley dove deep into her knowledge of fast cash-making —something she had probably learned when she was in foster care.

"First, there's drug selling. Obviously not the best choice, especially in this situation." Eric snorted as she continued. "There's an underground fight club that I've been to a time or two, but it's sketch, and it'll raise questions when one of you has bruises. Headmaster Walton won't let that fly."

I shot up from my seat. "No one is fighting to pay back *my* brother's debt. No way." I could hardly fathom the thought of Ollie, Christian, or Eric throwing punches and possibly getting hurt for me or Jason.

Christian rolled his eyes. "As if anyone could get a hit on one of us."

"Truth," Ollie said as he leaned back in his seat.

He and his brother pounded knuckles, and Hayley laughed. The Powell boys. So smug.

"Then, there are the street races, but you're already doing that. So, it's out of the running. The only other way is possibly charging admission."

"Charging admission?" I placed my hands in my back pockets, rocking back on the heels of my feet. "For...?"

Hayley grinned. "Parties. It was done *all* the time at Oakland High. Gabe always begged me to go with him, said he'd pay my way in."

Christian popped his knuckles, and I understood why. *Gabe.* Disgusting pig.

"We can't do that," I started. "People already know Eric's cabin is the place to be. What are they gonna think when we charge them to get in?"

Ollie clicked his tongue as he nudged Christian. "Let's do it at our house. People will fucking go crazy if they get to see the inside of our house. A party at the Powell house? Everyone will be there. Fuck-boys and all."

"Have you ever had a party at your house?" I asked, looking back and forth between them.

"Never," Ollie answered. "You and Hayley are the only two girls that have ever been there. And not a lot of guys have been, either. Except for Eric and Taylor."

Christian rubbed along his jaw. "It could work. When? We have to make sure Dad won't be home."

Eric popped up. "How about after the winter formal? Make it an after-party. Get some underclassmen to take admission, charge all the rich fucks $20 to get in. I'll supply kegs. I've got a guy who owes me."

The five of us waited and thought for a moment. I did the math in my head. There were easily two hundred people that would come. Predominantly, the senior class and most of the juniors—that *was* Ollie's class, after all, even if it didn't seem like it since he was in the majority of our classes.

This was *much* safer than anything else Hayley laid out on the table. If we raised $4,000 at the party, plus another night of racing, we'd be almost to the end of the debt. Then, this would be behind us. Jason would be free to, *hopefully,* get the help he needed, I could focus on normal high-school things like my college acceptance letters and hanging out with Hayley, and the best part—Ollie would be away from Tank. That was, as long as I could get it through his thick skull to stop racing.

"Let's do it," I announced. Certainty had my chest blooming like a flower. *Yes. This will work.*

"Ollie and I will come by after the races and set up while you guys are at winter formal."

Ollie's neck moved so fast in my direction I heard it pop. "Fuck no. You are going to winter formal, and you're not coming to the races again. I told you yesterday I didn't want you there, and you came anyway, and I ended up pulling you out of Tank's fucking trailer afterwards. No."

God. Was that just last night?

My face instantly grew warm as I shot him a glare. "You aren't the boss of me, Ollie. And not to mention..." I walked over to him and shoved a finger into his chest. "*You* banned everyone from taking me to winter formal!"

I forgot I was supposed to be mad at him for that. But lately, it was hard to be anything but grateful since he kept being Mr. Nice Guy and saving the day. It was becoming harder and harder to stay on the other side of that line, especially when I kept getting a glimpse of the true Ollie. He was no longer hiding behind the secret winks and agitating remarks or flirting with girls across the room and staring at me while he did it. Ollie was letting me in, and I secretly loved it.

Ollie grabbed my finger and clutched it within his palm. Skin on skin contact shot sparks to my fingertips. "You're going to the winter formal. You"—his grip grew firmer—"Are. Not. Going. To. The. Races."

"Ugh!" I ripped my finger out of his grasp, feeling myself becoming submissive again. We were so hot and cold. Ollie and I were either stuck together like a magnet to metal, or we were two ends of a battery. On or off. There was no in between.

Ollie's cheeks were becoming red with hidden anger. His bossy side came out in full force. "Eric will take you to the winter formal, right?"

My face fell. *Was he serious? No.*

Eric shrugged. "I'm cool with it."

I'm cool with it. Yes. That was what *every* girl wanted to hear from their date.

"He's *cool* with it?" I shot Ollie a look. "What are you? My handler? Not only do I find out you banned guys from asking me out, but now you're forcing me to go to the dance with your best friend? You're acting like you're my father or something. Picking my dates out for me now?"

Eric mumbled under his breath. "*Why am I always in the middle of this shit?*"

Hayley and Christian silently laughed.

"Hey, someone's gotta do the job. Your parents couldn't care less."

"Oh, don't act like you care or like you're protecting me by warding off other guys. You're just making Eric take me so you can make sure I don't show at the races again."

Why was I being so difficult about this? That pesky guilty feeling was creeping in again. Ollie and I had gone head to head many times in the past. And sure, he banned other guys from taking me to the dance. *But*...look at him. He'd been there for me when I needed him. Maybe this was just his way of keeping me safe.

"As interesting as this drama-fest is..." Eric waltzed past us to go lie on the couch in the den area. "Let me know when y'all are finished and what time I should pick ya up, Pipe. There's no way you're going to the races. I'm with Ollie on this one. You simply cannot be trusted."

My mouth dropped. "What! Why?"

Eric's dark head of hair popped up for a moment. "You know why." Then, he flopped back down on the couch and started looking at his phone.

I did know why. I lied last night and told him I saw Madeline climbing on the back of some guy's motorcycle, knowing *very* well it would make him bolt. Madeline was not, in fact, on someone's motorcycle.

It did, however, prove that Eric was keeping secrets of his own.

I heard Ollie sigh from beside me, and I peered up at him. He inched his head to the door. "Come on, I'll drive you home, and you can continue yelling at me the entire way. It'll be loads of fun." His cheek lifted as he stood up and walked out the door. My mouth was still set in a firm line when I glanced at Hayley leaning back into Christian's arms. They were both grinning like fools.

Everyone thought this was amusing.

I did not.

CHAPTER TWENTY-SIX

OLLIE

LOOK AT HER. All hot and bothered. Her cheeks were a rosy color of pink, and her eyes appeared feline, like she had morphed into a sneaky cat who was ready to give me cat-scratch fever. I paused, watching her stomp down the cobblestone drive. *I'd gladly welcome Piper's nails digging into my back.*

The door of my Charger swung open, and Piper angrily got in. She used too much force putting her seatbelt on, and the only thing it did was make me laugh.

I *loved* seeing her like this. I *loved* getting a rise out of her. It excited me that she was all worked up again.

I quickly backed out of Eric's drive and headed toward my house. Piper had no idea we were making a pit stop, but she'd soon find out.

The whistle of my turbo filled the air as I went around the bend in the road. Piper refused to look in my direction, so I laid it all out for her.

"Listen, I'm sorry."

Her head snapped over to me, her hair whizzing past her face. "You are not!"

I shrugged slyly. "I mean, I am in a way. I was being selfish when I told the team to back off, and you didn't deserve that. But you're right. I'm more *not* sorry than I am."

She crossed her arms over her chest, and my eyes dipped down. I swore, the inside of my Charger grew ten times hotter with my eyes on her.

Piper appeared to be letting her resolve fall, though. Her arms were crossed, sure, but her chest wasn't rushing with hidden anger. She glanced out the side window, and I almost begged her to put her attention back on me. I wanted to feel the way I felt when her eyes found mine. But she was refusing to look, because if she did, she knew I'd see right through her facade. The guise she used was a poor attempt at concealing what she really felt.

I stared out the windshield, smiling on the inside. "You like it."

Piper's leg stopped bouncing, and when I looked back at her, I could see her eye peeking at me from the corner.

"You like the thought of me not wanting someone else to take you to the formal. You like that I wanted you to myself."

Her neck started to get red, and it was all the confirmation I needed to keep going. My hand tightened on the steering wheel, and I threatened my dick to stop getting hard.

But fuck, did I want Piper in the worst of ways. And it was true. I *did* want her all to myself.

Piper's demeanor changed fast. She was now staring at me, leaning a little bit closer to the center console. "Is that why you did it? So you could keep me all to yourself? Or is this just another twisted way to pick on me?"

My nostrils flared, and I had the urge to whip the car over

to the brim and tell her every last thing that was going through my head. *Of course I wanted her to myself.*

"This isn't me picking on you."

"Isn't that what you do, though? Get off on picking on me and getting me all riled up? You've only been doing it for months now. Flirting with girls and winking at me behind their backs." She huffed and pulled herself away. "What are we? In elementary school? Picking on your crush."

Oh, this was much more than a crush.

I swore under my breath as we began pulling through my gated neighborhood. The whistle of my turbo lessened as I crept past the large homes.

"What are we doing here? I thought you were taking me home."

As soon as I pulled up into the empty garage, I put my Charger in park. "I need your help with something."

She glanced around the garage. "Okay. What?"

"Come on. I'll take you home right after so you can work on your paper."

I climbed out of my Charger and waited for her to follow, knowing she would. I glanced at the time on my phone. My father was long gone now, and hopefully, Christian wasn't coming home soon. But that was why I had Piper with me.

She could keep watch as I dug a little deeper into my parents' past, hopefully finding out something that would answer the questions constantly floating around in my head.

It was easy to get lost in Piper's problems, and it was easy to bury myself in things that served as a distraction: girls, partying, *racing*. But I knew the time would soon come that I had to face my brother and dad. There would be many more slip-ups, and I couldn't keep shit locked away forever. I did, however, need to get my head on straight. I needed to collect myself. I needed answers.

"What are we doing, Ollie?" Piper's whisper floated

throughout the hallway as she followed me past my bedroom and Christian's.

I spun around quickly, startling her. "I'm taking you to bed; what does it look like?"

Her rosy lips parted instantaneously with the widening of her eyes. She tripped over her words. "You're... Wh- wha...what?"

Oh shit. Was she down for that?

I snatched the hat off my head and ran my hand through my hair, tugging on the ends slightly to keep me level-headed. "I'm kidding."

Her face flamed, and I had to turn around so I wouldn't change my mind. *Jesus Christ.*

"I knew that."

I couldn't fight the lift of my cheek as I threw my hat back on. I cleared my throat before saying, "I need you to keep watch."

We stopped in front of the very last door at the end of the hall, and silence encased us.

"What am I keeping watch for? What are you doing?"

Well... Here goes nothing.

"I need to go through my parents' things, and I don't want Christian to come home and see me. It'll raise questions that I'm not ready to answer."

Piper's eyes ping-ponged between mine. My pulse mimicked the little drummer boy's drum. *Thump. Thump. Thump.* I bet if she looked hard enough, she could see it thumping along the side of my neck. Nerves started to eat away at me. I suddenly felt vulnerable, which, in the end, only made me feel weak.

"Why aren't you ready?"

I blinked. "What?"

"You've been keeping this secret for how long?" Her eyes darted away momentarily. "Since that night."

That night.

Images and lost feelings came crashing through my head as I dipped my gaze down her body—tight jeans; loose, off-the-shoulder shirt; tiny glimpse of her lacy bra strap visible. I swallowed back the urge to palm her hips and pull her body into mine.

"I'm just not ready. You should know that better than anyone."

Piper took a step toward me, and my vulnerability increased. I took a step back. Everything in my body grew tight. I didn't like this. The roles were reversed. Piper somehow was driving into me, causing my resolve to fall without even touching me. Her rosy lips beckoned for me to spill every last secret I had.

And fuck me. I wanted to tell her everything.

I wanted her to be my clutch. My anchor. I just wanted her.

"What do you think will happen?" She took another step closer, and I clenched my jaw. "What are you afraid of?" I felt suffocated. Like her hands were around my neck, ready to squeeze.

My mouth was sealed shut. Nothing would come out. *What do you think will happen?* Fuck. *Bro, just say something so you can move past this conversation.*

My hands began to shake by my sides. I wasn't sure what would happen. I didn't know how Christian would react when he found out. Would our father lie? Would he and Christian go at it again once we knew the whole story? Where exactly *was* my real father?

Piper's voice grounded me. "You know Christian loves you no matter what, right? You're his brother regardless. It doesn't matter if you have different fathers."

My stomach burned as if I'd gotten kicked. I placed my hand on the door jamb to keep myself steady.

I didn't want to talk about this anymore. I didn't want to look up and see Piper's doe-like eyes staring back at me. I didn't want her words of encouragement or her comfort. She saw me. I was split wide-open for her to see. I couldn't hide behind a witty comeback or a sly smile.

"Whatever," I mumbled, quickly unlatching the door to my parents' room to escape. "Knock twice if you hear Christian come home. This won't take long." Then, I slammed the door shut, pressing my back along the wood.

It felt good to be alone and away from Piper's prying eyes, but at the same time, it felt lonely.

I cursed under my breath and counted to ten, staring at the ceiling.

Being in this room always made me a little edgy. I used to come in here for comfort, to feel closer to my mom, to feel less alone when Dad was gone and Christian was closing himself off, but now it just made me tick.

I zeroed in on the untouched vanity. Everything was still the same as it was the last time I was in here, which wasn't much of a surprise. As my feet carried me over to the dainty piece of furniture, something foreign came over me, and I froze, my hand outstretched toward the little drawer that had changed my outlook on everything.

Fear.

I was afraid.

Piper was right. *I was afraid.*

I cracked my neck as I pushed down the need to call out her name. The clank of the drawer opening did nothing to soothe me, and when I looked down and saw the cream-colored paper missing, my stomach fell to the floor.

Frantically, I pushed away the untouched makeup and lipsticks, looking for the paper that I knew was there.

What the hell?

I heard a noise and inclined my head toward the door. I

stopped moving, my fingers still well inside the drawer, like I'd been caught with my hand in the cookie jar. But when I didn't hear another noise, I went back to searching.

Where the fuck is it?

It wasn't there.

My birth certificate wasn't there.

I snapped my neck over to the door again when I heard a louder, more frantic knock. *Shit.*

Slamming the drawer shut with frustration, I whipped the bedroom door open to find Piper's wide eyes.

"What? Is someone—"

Her hand wrapped around my wrist as she pulled me toward her. I slammed the door in the process, and when she backed herself along the wall, she looked up at me and said, "Quick. Kiss me."

She didn't have to tell me twice.

My lips were on hers within a second, and everything I was feeling moments ago—the anxiety, the fear—it was completely gone. I grabbed her waist as I assaulted her lips with mine, our hot breath mingling and swirling as I moved my tongue over hers. A fire erupted inside of me, and there was no putting it out. I palmed the backside of her ass as a whimper escaped her mouth, and before I knew it, her legs were wrapped around me, and her hands were knocking my hat to the floor.

This. Fucking yes.

Her lips on mine.

This was sealing that loud but invisible connection we had.

It was just her and me, and I didn't fucking care about anything else.

Fuck Tank. Fuck racing. Fuck the missing birth certificate.

Her tongue moved over mine, and I wanted more.

"Whoa."

Piper pulled back as her legs clenched my torso like a vise grip. She wiggled to get down, but I gave her a look. *Not a fucking chance.*

The sound of a slow clap had us breaking our stare. We were met with Christian's lazy grin and Hayley's amused eyes.

"It's about fucking time." Christian clapped again, and Hayley smiled wide, glancing down to Piper's legs wrapped around my body.

Piper wiggled again, and I finally obliged.

"This isn't what it looks like," Piper answered, all but pushing me away.

Christian chuckled and shook his head. "Riiight."

I reached down to grab my hat and secretly glanced at the bedroom door, making sure it was shut. *There's no way he knew you were in there. Chill.*

"I...um..." Piper began slowly walking away from me. "I probably need to get home to do my homework and start on decorations."

"I'll take you," Hayley said, realizing that Piper was definitely ready to bolt.

I flashed her a warning look. *This isn't over.*

Piper's tongue dipped out of her mouth as she licked her bottom lip. My blood surged as she turned around and began walking down the hall to reach the stairs.

I had to give it to her—Piper was quick on her feet. Using a kiss as a distraction so Christian wasn't wondering what we were doing standing outside of our parents' bedroom was good thinking.

But that kiss was so much more.

That kiss sealed the tear in our connection we'd found a year prior.

The real meaning behind the kiss lay in the depths of secrets, and I was definitely ready to unravel them.

CHAPTER TWENTY-SEVEN

PIPER

As I sat at the lunch table, I wondered where my allegiance laid. I kept catching Ollie's eye, feeling that tug in my chest, and I knew, without a doubt, that I stood on the same side as he did. Yesterday, I covered for him. I lied to Hayley, *again*, when she'd asked me about the kiss she and Christian walked in on. That meant my allegiance laid with him, right? You were supposed to tell your best friend everything, but here I was, covering up for Ollie and hiding more secrets. The bad part about it? I didn't even feel bad. I just hoped Hayley would understand in the long run. After all, she knew what it was like to love someone.

My fork fell out of my hand, crashing to the tiled floor as the thought slipped through. I couldn't even pick it up. I was too stunned to do so. *Love? You're not even in a relationship!*

"Pipe," Hayley said, bending to pick up my fork. "Are you good? Your hand is shaking."

I clasped my hands together, panicking. "What? Yes! I'm fine. What were you saying?"

Hayley eyed me suspiciously but thankfully dropped it. "I asked if you wanted to go get dresses tomorrow after school?"

I blinked. *Dresses. Oh, right.* "Um."

"The answer is yes, she'd love to get a dress with you tomorrow, because Piper is, in fact, going to the winter formal with Eric."

The urge to shoot Ollie a dirty look had the hair on my arms standing erect, but I wouldn't dare look at him. I *couldn't* look at him. The second I did, my face would flame. He'd know exactly what I was thinking. I swore he could read my mind sometimes. There was no way I was risking that, not after having the thought I just had. And not to mention, this morning, I peeked up from my trig book, skimming my eyes over his forearm that was peeking out from beneath his rolled cuff, and my face instantly flamed. Then, at the last second, he turned in his seat and caught me staring. I almost fell out of my desk.

Trying my best to ignore Ollie, I answered Hayley. "Sure. Can we go around five? I'm gonna work on some more decorations tomorrow after school."

"Yeah, do you need help?"

I picked at the food on my tray, giving her a nod. "We can use all the help we can get."

I wasn't in charge of the winter formal, but somehow, I was the only person taking it seriously. There were a few cheerleaders who were on the committee that said they'd stop by to help after practice today, but it was hard to tell how much help they'd actually be.

"I can help, too." I could tell that Ollie was smiling just by the way his voice sounded.

I kept my eyes down low and tried to keep my heart from sprinting right out of my body. "No, thanks. We've got it."

"Oh, now, come on." Even his voice was becoming hard to listen to. I kept thinking about the kiss. It was packed full of heat. Ollie's kiss came from the center of the universe. It gave life. "I said I was sorry."

Hayley could sense my agitation, so she spoke up for me. "You banned every guy from taking her to winter formal. Saying sorry was just the tip of the iceberg, Ollie. You're gonna have to do better."

"What do you think the kiss was for?"

I couldn't help it; my eyes instantly flashed to meet his. He did that on purpose. He wanted me to look at him and knew the only way I would was if he pushed my buttons hard enough.

The entire lunch table hushed except for one of the football players. "Wait, you guys hooked up?"

A few cheerleaders that Eric was entertaining gasped.

"We did not hook up," I said very flatly, attempting to shut down the rumor mill before it even started. I shot up out of my seat quickly, snatching my tray in the process. "I'm going to work on decorations. I'll see you later, Hayley."

I left the cafeteria, my legs trembling with anger. I wasn't sure if I was angry with Ollie for telling everyone we kissed, or if I was angry with myself for liking it.

Either way, I was angry.

By the end of the school day, I felt a little better about what had happened yesterday with Ollie and his need to gloat about it at lunch. I took out my frustrations on snowflakes for the formal, and sure, they were cut like shards of glass and looked more like weapons than actual snowflakes, but whatever.

It made me feel a little bit better.

I tied my hair up in a ponytail and took off the little navy bow that was hung around my neck per uniform requirements and got to work. I gave the two nerdy boys the job of hanging the banner at the end of the auditorium so they'd do something other than stare at me with stars in their eyes as I waited for the group of Madeline's ex-friends, aka the cheerleaders, to see if they could make better-looking snowflakes than the ones I'd made.

Glitter coated my fingers, and blue and white paint was splattered on my shoes, but it was sort of therapeutic being lost in a creative lull that didn't involve fast cars, drugs, money, or the *kiss*.

"Hey."

My paintbrush stopped stroking the cardboard cut-out of an ice-covered tree. I stared at Ollie's shoes and tried to appear unbothered. "What are you doing here, Ollie?"

"I'm here to help, obviously." The cheer in his voice had a small smile trying to work its way onto my face. *There* was the Ollie everyone was used to. The happy one. The light one. The one who acted like he didn't have a care in the world.

I put the paintbrush back in the silver paint container and wiped my hands down my skirt as I slowly stood up to stare at him. The lift of his lip and hooded eyes made my heart stop momentarily. My mouth opened, but nothing came out. Why couldn't I seem to stay mad at him? Why wasn't he annoying me? Was it the kiss? It was. It was the kiss.

"Go away, Ollie." I cringed internally. Even *I* didn't believe my words.

He chuckled. "Oh, you can do better than that, Piper."

I placed my hands on my hips, telling myself to stay angry with him. "You're a jerk for what you said at lunch. Telling everyone we kissed."

Ollie ignored me as he began taking his uniform blazer off. My eyes followed his every move. He threw it to the side and loosened his tie, then he began to unbutton the top of his shirt. I felt my mouth go dry, and yet, I couldn't stop myself from staring. Next, he rolled the cuffs of his shirt up to his elbows, and I was instantly sweating.

In the past, I'd done an exceptional job at keeping my feelings to myself. I'd blocked out the night I spent with him like it was nothing. Whenever I was close to him, feeling his body heat clamber off him in the back of Christian's car, or when I'd catch his wink at Eric's cabin, I'd play it cool. I'd roll my eyes and brush it off. *Nothing to see here.*

But yesterday had changed things. My mind was muddled. My hands itched to pull him in close—not even to kiss him, but to just *feel* him. The chemistry. Our connection. I wanted it.

My heart drummed. My blood trickled through my veins. The auditorium began to blur as I continued to stare.

When I reached his blue eyes, and they latched onto mine, I sucked in a small breath. I dove into their blue depths and found myself stalling. Ollie and I did a lot of staring at each other, but it was because we knew. There was something different about us.

Ollie erased the space between us, and his breath grazed my skin. His whisper floated over all my sensitive spots. "Did that kiss do to you what it did to me?"

I could hear my heartbeat in my ears. I traced the outline of his lips, and I was seconds from pulling him in by his collar when I heard a girl's voice. *"Hey, Ollie."*

Ollie growled, his eyes narrowing, clearly annoyed with the interruption. But me? I was thankful. It helped me get myself together. I was becoming swept away by Ollie, and that scared me.

Ollie ignored the cheerleaders and kept his head dipped down low. "What are you thinking? I see it in your eyes." His mouth was set in a straight line as he tried to read me. "I see the fear. I see the retreat."

My mouth opened, and I stuttered, "I'm...I'm...thinking I need you to hang these up over there."

I quickly backed away and bent down to catch my breath as I pulled up some deranged-looking snowflakes.

He was clearly confused as he took in their appearance, but nonetheless, his large hand wrapped around the snowflakes, and he began walking over to the auditorium entrance and started climbing the ladder.

His eyebrows raised in question as he held one up, asking if it was where I wanted.

I gave him a nod and turned around, kicking myself for acting so stupid around him.

It's just Ollie, get a grip!

CHAPTER TWENTY-EIGHT

OLLIE

I WASN'T GOING to lie. I missed football. I missed the feeling of grass underneath my cleats, and I missed the way the pigskin felt in my hands as I caught the ball, dashing to the end zone. In fact, I almost tried out for the baseball team just so I had something to do with my time until summer conditioning came around, but I was glad I hadn't.

If I'd taken up baseball, I wouldn't have been standing in the middle of the auditorium, helping Piper with these stupid winter formal decorations.

I supposed the old adage was correct: everything *did* happen for a reason.

"Why are you attacking it like that?"

Piper's head popped up. She was fucking adorable. "Huh?"

I smirked. "You're painting that tree with so much aggression your bristles are fraying."

Piper looked down at the paintbrush in her hand, and her mouth fell open. "Oh. Oops."

Leisurely, I walked over and gently took the paintbrush from her. "Here, let me."

A shimmering blue color shined underneath the lights of the auditorium as I stroked the paint on lightly. Piper took a step back, and instead of sighing with frustration like she'd been doing for the past half-hour, she actually looked relieved. Her body slumped down along the wall as she watched me.

My eyes danced around the auditorium. A few guys were standing back, looking at the banner I'd made them rehang because it was crooked the first time they'd hung it. Then, a few cheerleaders that I may or may not have hooked up with a while back were wrapping some see-through material around round tables, and then I was back on Piper.

She had her plump bottom lip tucked in between her teeth, and her legs were crossed at the ankles. I scanned the bare skin between her knee-high stockings and her skirt and forced myself to look away.

"So?" I asked, still painting. "How am I doin', boss?"

Piper's lip plopped out of her mouth with a pop, and I was honestly very impressed with my self-control. I wanted her. I was like a lion on the prowl, my blood pressure rising when I'd thought back to yesterday. Her lips on mine. Her legs around my hips. My hands digging into her skin.

Hot. It was so fucking hot.

"Why are you here helping?"

Stroke. Stroke. Stroke. *Why was painting feeling dirty all of a sudden?*

"Just wanted to help out. Give back to the school, ya know?"

Piper shot me an incredulous look, but I ignored it, going back to painting.

"So, what did you find yesterday?"

Playing stupid, I asked, "Yesterday? What was yesterday?"

I waited a second, and just before she tried to answer, I said, "You mean before you begged me to kiss you?"

Piper sucked in a breath and sat up a little taller. The fire in her eyes was evident, but instead of saying something snarky back, she stopped herself. I watched her entire body language change. She wasn't putting up her metaphorical fists to fight with me; she was backing down.

I was confused at first, and a little let down, until I realized what she was doing.

Her face softened. "Don't do that with me, Ollie."

I played it off, getting more than enough paint on my brush. "Do what?"

"Try to change the subject so we don't have to discuss your problems."

The grip on my paintbrush grew harder. "Why not? Your annoyance with me is a far better topic to discuss." I glanced up at her, and her features were relaxed. Patient. I could feel the control slipping. "I know what we can talk about. Let's talk about your hatred for me. That used to be your favorite topic."

"I don't hate you, and you know it."

"You just don't like people knowing I kissed you."

Piper ignored me. "So? What did you find?"

I held back a sigh as I placed the paintbrush down. I walked over to her and slid down along the side of the wall beside her. Her legs were still crossed at the ankles, her hands in her lap, folded nicely together. She was waiting. And for some reason, instead of feeling trapped and anxious, I felt open. I wanted to tell her.

"I found nothing."

Her lip jutted out again. "Nothing? What does that mean?"

I shrugged. "The birth certificate I found a year ago—the

one that *clearly* did not have my father's name on it—was missing. Gone. As if it'd never even existed."

But it did. I would never forget the feeling of that piece of paper in my hand. It felt heavy. I'd never forget the dense, empty feeling it gave me.

"So..." She looked away, thinking. "That means..."

"That means someone else took it."

She snapped those green eyes over to me. "Do you think it was Christian?"

I chuckled. "Fuck no." I glanced back out into the auditorium. A few sets of lingering eyes were on us. One of them was Clementine, a girl I definitely remembered hooking up with at Eric's. "You know Christian can't control his anger well. He would have confronted my dad by now, and I would have heard about it from one of them. Or at least sensed it." I ran my hand through my hair, feeling tired. "I'm sure it was my dad. I kind of hinted that I knew something the other day. A minor slip-up from me."

"So...now what?"

Fuck if I knew. My head fell back against the wall, and I angled my chin up to the tall ceiling.

I felt the softest brush of skin on my arm and dropped my gaze. Piper's hand was covering my forearm. I couldn't bring myself to look at her face. "We'll figure this out, Ollie. Let's get through my Tank problem, and then we will tackle this. It'll be okay."

The realness in Piper's voice sucked me right in.

This girl made my world go around, and she had no fucking idea.

To be honest, I wasn't sure I'd had any idea until recently.

"You mean our problem," I said, looking up from her hand.

Her brow crinkled, but her palm on my arm didn't move.

"It's *our* problem," I urged. "Not yours. I'm in this with you, Pipe."

I could tell she was getting ready to argue with me, so I grabbed her hand on my arm and squeezed. "Say it." Her lips smashed together as I repeated the words. "*Our problem.*"

She scanned my face but kept her lips pressed firmly together. "Say it, or I'll take that paint can and dump it on your head." I inclined my head over to the paint.

She rolled her eyes, following my line of sight. "You would not."

Oh, she knew very well I would.

"Try me."

That was the wrong thing to say to a girl like her. Piper liked a challenge. Or so I thought. Regardless, when she didn't say anything, I shot up to my feet. She did the same.

"Don't you dare, Oliver Powell."

Exhilaration had my feet moving to the paint can. I smiled cunningly over my shoulder, and her pretty lips tugged upward.

When I reached the paint, she hissed. "Ollie..."

Instead of grabbing the paint can, I grabbed the brush, blue paint dripping down to the cardboard cut-out below. "Say it." I took a step toward her, and she smiled excitedly, taking a step back.

Her eyes were playful, and I was here for it. I thought I liked when she shot me a glare and spat something at me. I thought I liked the fire in her eyes when she rolled them in my direction, but this was so much better.

Piper was smiling at me. I wanted to bottle it up and keep it forever.

"Piperrr," I sang out. "Say the words: *It's our problem.*"

"It's my problem; you're just being very chivalrous."

We were having a stare-off. Her back pressed along the wall, my legs moving slowly like I was on the prowl. There could have been a thousand people in the auditorium with us, and I wouldn't have known the difference.

"That's it," I said, and her twinkling eyes grew wide. My strides were three times hers, so I took one long step and swiped the paintbrush over her cheek.

Her mouth fell open as a squeal came out. "Ollie!" She tried to run away, but I wrapped my arm around her upper body, and her back fell into my chest with a thud. Her hands came up and wrapped around my forearm, and I whispered into her ear, "Say it." She wiggled so much I ended up getting more paint on her.

Her laugh echoed throughout the room, and I swore I felt my heart grow. *What the fuck was she doing to me?*

She fought me for a few more seconds as I swiped another bit of paint on her forehead.

"Fine! Fine!" she shouted, still laughing. "It's our problem!"

I didn't want to let go of her, but in the end, my arm dropped. She spun around quickly, her hair a chaotic mess in front of her face. A laugh erupted from my mouth as I took in the streaks of grayish-blue paint on her cheeks. Her smile was captivating, her eyes bright with humor. "I can't believe you painted me!"

I raised my eyebrows. "You know very well I'm a man of my word, Piper. I said I would."

She tried to hide her smile as she reached up and smeared the paint from her face. "So..." She eyed me closely. "Since it's '*our*' problem..." She used air quotes around the word 'our' that I completely ignored. "Does that mean I can come to the races on Saturday?"

A loud laugh came out of my mouth. "Nice try."

She cursed under her breath. "You're acting like you're my father."

I shrugged innocently. "Like I said, someone has to."

She rolled her eyes and huffed. "Fine."

That was easy.

Before I knew what she was doing, the paintbrush was ripped from my hands, and something cold was coating my face. Her laughter floated around me, and I couldn't even be mad.

I loved this side of her.

I liked making Piper smile, and I thought it was the best distraction yet.

CHAPTER TWENTY-NINE

PIPER

"So…" Hayley walked down the aisles of the dress store, scrunching her face at every other gown she looked at. "How did you rope Ollie into helping with the decorations yesterday—and today?" She paused. "Actually, how did you get most of the football team to help?"

I laughed, running my hands down a blue dress that would likely look amazing on her. "He came on his own and rallied all those guys." I smiled. "I'm glad, too. Mostly everything is done with their help and yours. Thanks again for helping today. I know it's not your thing."

Hayley rolled her eyes. "Ann and Headmaster Walton cornered me the other day during school hours to tell me that I needed to do more 'teen-agey' things, especially now that I was in a safer environment."

I laughed. "I'm sure you loved that conversation." I pulled a dusty-blue strappy dress off the hanger. "But it's true."

"What is?"

"You do need to do more teen-agey things. You missed out on a lot."

Hayley's shoulders fell. "I know, but we've all got our issues. No one's childhood is perfect, right?"

Oh, she was right, alright.

"How are you doing with the whole Jason thing? I'm still concerned that you're involved with Tank. Christian is, too. He's worried about Ollie."

I stilled. Every part of me wanted to spill every last dark secret to my best friend. Every single one of them. But I couldn't because they weren't my secrets. "You're breaking our agreement."

Hayley's hand paused on a dress. "What agreement?"

"The agreement of not talking about Jason, or the races, or you paying for your mom to go to rehab."

Hayley's dark brows knitted together. "We didn't agree to that."

I laughed. "Worth a shot."

Hayley's laugh was light as she turned around and looked at a few more dresses. Just when I thought she was going to drop it, she intoned, "Piper?"

I took my gaze off the pretty purple dress that I was holding and took in her expression. Hayley's features were drawn into a frown, her bright eyes crinkled around the edges. "Do you remember that time in your car when I was being super stand-offish, and you looked me in the eye and said, *'This is what best friends do. We tell each other everything and then dissect it together'?*"

I swallowed my guilt. "Yes."

Hayley erased the few feet that stood between us and rested her hands on my shoulders. "I'm here for you, okay? I get what it's like to hold things in. It gets..." She slowly dropped her hands after giving my shoulders a light squeeze. "It gets lonely."

But these weren't my secrets to tell.

I gave her a soft smile, and she continued walking down the aisle, pulling out a few more dresses. I wanted to say something, but the words were stuck. I was too busy shoving down my guilt to come up with anything good to say.

My hands stilled on the soft fabric of a rose-colored dress when she yelled over her shoulder, "Also... I know there's something more going on with you and Ollie."

My entire body grew warm.

"Don't try to deny it; I just want you to know I'm here when you're ready to talk." Hayley smiled as I nodded in relief. I wasn't necessarily about to deny something going on with Ollie and me; I just wasn't sure what exactly to say. Thankfully, though, with Hayley, I didn't usually have to say anything. She understood me, and I understood her. She knew that I'd come to her when I was ready.

The rest of the shopping trip went smoother after our conversation. Hayley and I stopped talking about the serious things, and we just had fun. Something I thought we both needed. It all felt very *normal,* which wasn't something we had often.

"Christian is going to pass out when he sees you." I cocked my head to the side, running my gaze down Hayley's body once more. She was wearing a navy-blue dress that hit mid-thigh. The bodice was lacy and cut very low in the front. "Then, he's going to wake up and demand you take that scrap of fabric off. Mark my words. That's exactly what he'll say."

Hayley threw her head back and laughed. "He knows very well he can't boss me around."

"But he'll still try." Hayley and I continued to laugh until my laughter was cut short. A familiar voice hit my ears. *"Just grab it, and let's git."*

Sky. I'd recognize that voice anywhere. The twang and

wrong usage of the English language was evident from my first run-in with her, and it was just the same now.

"Alright, I'm gonna change," Hayley said, doing one more turn in the mirror.

I mumbled, "Okay," and silently retreated backwards, trying to get out of the way before Sky saw me.

But then I heard her twang again. "Hayley fucking Smith. Is that you?"

I could see Hayley from where I was standing. Her eyes widened for a split second before the recognition hit her. "Skylar. Wow. It's been a while. How are you?"

How are you?

"I'm finally out of the system, so better than when you ran around with my group. I heard you were up with the rich folk now." Sky's hair was still a tangly mess, and the dark circles under her thick, black-lined eyes were almost haunting. But according to Hayley, the system did that to you. It'd eat you alive until you were of age, and then it threw you back out to the wolves.

Maybe that was why she hung around Tank.

Hayley shrugged. "I go to English Prep, but it's not because I'm rich."

I still stood back to the side, hoping Sky wouldn't look my way. It wasn't that I was afraid of her—well, okay, that wasn't true. I still got a little twitchy walking to my car after school, as if she'd show up out of thin air again and pull me back by my uniform blouse. But right now, it was more that I didn't want to have to tell Hayley about my little run-in with her. That was just another thing to add to the "Things I've Kept from Hayley" list.

Sky blew a bubble with her pink gum. *What was she even doing in here?* "English Prep? No shit? I was just there a couple of weeks ago."

Hayley looked confused. "Why?"

"Oh, I was there delivering a message from my man to this little rich redhead bitch who owes him money. She looked like she was going to shit herself." Sky laughed, and it pissed me off.

I stepped out from behind the dressing room door. "She's referring to me."

Hayley's confusion quickly turned to anger. If there was one thing I knew about my best friend, it was that she loved fiercely. She didn't cling to people often, but when she did, she clung for life.

Sky's mouth turned into a snarl when she saw me standing there with my dress draped over my arm. "You again?"

I bit the inside of my cheek as I walked over to Hayley. "Come to try and scare me again?"

"Depends if your little boyfriend knows how to follow directions."

I hid my confusion.

"Directions for what?" Hayley asked.

My spine straightened as I kept my gaze on the girl in front of me. I almost felt bad for her. What a shitty life she must have had to end up with Tank.

"As long as Jason comes out unscathed and you leave us the fuck alone after this is done, everything will be fine." I hardly recognized my voice as the words came out. I sounded confident and angry. And I was. A wave of protectiveness came over me when she mentioned Ollie.

Sky's dull eyes sparked when my voice rose. Even Hayley glanced over, clearly astounded by my outburst.

Another voice sounded from behind me. "Wow. So she *does* have a backbone."

I spun around quickly and found Madeline standing with several red dresses hanging over her arm. Her platinum hair fell in luscious waves, framing her perfect face. It was a shame she was so callous as she truly was pretty.

"A bigger backbone than you, some would say." Hayley's tone was neutral, but I knew deep down she was holding back a snarl. She and Madeline didn't get along, but did anyone get along with her?

"It seems we hit a sweet spot with this one." Sky casually walked past me, her unkempt hair brushing my arm because of how close she was. I didn't move a muscle. She was trying to intimidate me, but it wouldn't work. I was too riled up.

Madeline raised a perfectly arched eyebrow when Sky came to stand beside her. *Why is she hanging out with Sky?* Something didn't add up with her. She was always appearing in places she didn't belong and clearly hanging out with a bad group of people.

"Sky, tread lightly," Hayley warned.

"Oh, so it is true, then. You *are* with the rich folk."

Madeline stayed quiet, and it surprised me. Did Sky not know that her new BFF was rich also?

Madeline and I locked eyes as Hayley and Sky did. Something unreadable crossed Madeline's features, and she immediately dropped her gaze. "Come on, Sky. Let's just go."

Sky huffed, moving her stare from Hayley. When she sliced her gaze to me, I got goosebumps. "You better hope your little boyfriend keeps his word."

Panic was settling into my belly. *What word?*

I kept my mouth shut and my face unmoving as she twisted around and walked toward the door. Madeline was turning on her heel to do the same, but I stopped her at the last second. "What did you get yourself into?"

Hayley's arms crossed over her dress, waiting for her to answer.

For a moment, Madeline looked like she wanted to confide in us. Her pink lips fell, and her light-blue eyes dropped to the floor. But then she snapped to attention as Sky yelled for her.

I watched her push past the vulnerability as her words cut through the air. "None of your fucking business."

Then, she dropped the dresses to the ground in a lumpy pile, and the bell chimed as she and Sky left the shop.

It only took Hayley half a second to look at me.

"You have some explaining to do."

And it seemed Ollie did, too.

CHAPTER THIRTY

OLLIE

THE TRAILERS that lined Pike Valley Trailer Park were something out of a horror film. It was hard to believe that people lived in conditions like that. The first one on the right was yellow and drab with a few broken pieces of siding hanging loose off the side. The next one was just as bad. It was gray in color, but I was pretty sure it hadn't started out as that shade, and it had several broken windows with cardboard duct-taped over them. They were all like this—run-down, dirty, and full of filthy people who were barely surviving.

It made my skin crawl thinking back to when Piper was stuck inside Tank's bathroom. The second I stepped foot in his trailer the other day, it was like cold water being dumped on my head. Chills ran over my flesh. A place like that wasn't a place for her. She was too clean, too delicate.

While I was there, I couldn't even stomach looking in Jason's direction. After all, he was the reason Piper was in the trailer in the first place. When Tank asked me to sit down beside Jason, it took everything in me not to reach over and punch his crooked nose.

But I knew I had to keep my cool. I needed to act unbothered by the entire situation.

Sure, Tank, ol' buddy, ol' pal, I'll throw the race on Saturday so you can cheat more people out of their money. I'm on your side, bro.

Men like Tank were weak. They liked to scare people into following their command so they could have some sort of control in their lives. But those who followed others purely out of fear weren't true followers.

Plus, couldn't Tank sense that I wasn't a follower? I was a leader, and soon, he'd understand that.

The clock on my dash read 4:05, and just like every day this past week, Tank left his house and climbed onto his shitty motorcycle and sped down the gravel lot, pebbles flying in every direction as he zoomed away.

I had approximately forty minutes to get this over with.

As I climbed out of my Charger, hidden just behind a few older, broken-down vehicles, I felt the warmth from the sun on my back. The nice thing about out town in the winter was that it was still somewhat warm during the day, but cooler in the evening. I cracked my knuckles as I walked past a few dying plants in broken and chipped pots and jogged up the rickety porch stairs. The door to the trailer creaked loudly as I opened it, and it slammed with a thud the second I was through the threshold.

The inside of the trailer was filled with stale smoke; a hint of weed lingered there, too.

I found Jason immediately, sitting on the couch, slumped back, relaxing in a stretched-out T-shirt and ripped jeans. His brownish-red hair was long, covering his ears. He'd definitely seen better days.

"Out," I said to the other people in the room, keeping my

fists closed by my sides. Intimidation wasn't my strong suit—
at least not compared to my brother.

Unless, of course, Piper was involved.

Piper caused me to morph into something else entirely.
My blood spiked with adrenaline, and if I had to use my
height and strength—*thank you, football conditioning*—to pound
the hell out of the few other people in the room just to get
Jason alone, I would.

"Who the fuck are you?" The guy standing in the corner
of the room jumped to his feet.

I was hoping I didn't read the situation wrong the other
day when I was here, and he wasn't packing a gun or something. Although, I was sure there were weapons somewhere
around this filthy shithole.

The other guy sitting beside Jason sat up a little taller,
answering the question. "He's the one that was here a few
days ago, talking with Tank about the race on Saturday. He's
makin' him *good fucking money* right now..." He chuckled,
flicking his hair-cut-to-the-scalp head to Jason who was now
unmoving as he stared at me. "Because of this idiot."

"Get out," I demanded again.

The smile dropped from the man's face. "Who the fuck
are you to come in here uninvited and demand we leave? We
have orders to stay right the fuck here with this pansy bitch."

Ah, right. Jason is their little pet.

My feet carried me farther into the room. I knew I was
potentially outnumbered, but confidence was the key in this
situation. I laid it right out for them. "Here's how this is
gonna work. You two are going to go outside for a few
minutes so I can talk with Jason." I paused as the guy
standing in the corner crept around the couch and headed for
me. I easily had a foot of height over him and could probably
take him down easily. "Or...I can get my guy who's currently
waiting down the street to come arrest you two fucks on drug

possession. I know very well that you *both* have drugs in your system, and you"—I smirked at the one sitting beside Jason with his shoulders tight around his neck with fear—"are currently holding a little baggy of something in your jeans pocket. Am I right?"

His face turned white. *Bingo.*

"You're bluffing, and you have three seconds to get your little rich fuck-boy ass outta here before we call Tank, and he can deal with you himself."

"I'm bluffing?" I shook my head and chuckled as I pulled my phone out of my pocket and dialed Eric. I put it on speaker for everyone to hear.

He picked up within a second. "You need me to come? I can have backup here within a minute or two."

These two had no idea who I was talking to. Eric did a damn good job at pretending he was an officer, though. "Possibly."

"Roger that. Give me the go-ahead and I'll be there in a second. I have no issues taking them down to the station."

My eyebrows tugged upward as I watched the guy standing throw his arms up. "Fine." He angled his chin to his friend. "We'll be outside for five minutes. That's all you have."

When they brushed past me, I made sure to add, "And if you tell Tank I was here, I swear to God, you both will be in jail. Don't underestimate the power of people owing me favors. Cops can be dirty, too, you know?"

That was the truth, although *I* didn't necessarily have any cops on hand to use in a situation like this. I couldn't even get Jim, our family PI, to step foot in this. Not after Christian snuck behind our father's back and used him to investigate Hayley's father a few months back.

"We got you."

And my conquest was done. It seemed Tank's "friends" weren't actually friends. They'd likely throw him under the bus if it meant saving their own ass. But again, there was no loyalty when you forced people to follow you with fear.

As soon as they were both outside, I quickly lasered onto Jason. My fists ached to punch him across the jaw. My legs twitched to kick him in the stomach, especially as he sat and stared at me from his laid-back position on the couch.

"How do you feel about letting your sister fight your battles for you?" My voice was laced with something unrecognizable. My words were short, slicing through the dim room.

Jason slowly sat up and dropped his head down low. His arms came out and rested along his knees. "I hope you have a plan, because Tank is never going to let you go, man."

I walked closer to him, wanting him to hear me loud and clear. "And yet, you let your sister walk right into his fucking hands. What were you thinking, letting her take on the responsibility of paying back *your* debt? What is wrong with you?" I was full-on seething. The muscles along my chest were straining. My fist squeezed so hard that my nails dug into my skin. But I just kept thinking about the pain on her face when she talked about him. The fear in her voice. "Do you understand how dangerous this is for her? Do you not understand that she is absolutely destroyed by what you've become? Do you enjoy knowing she cried her fucking eyes out the night she almost watched you snort that shit up your nose in that tiny fucking bathroom down the hall?"

Jason's head shoved away from me as if he were trying to get away from my words. I half-expected him to cover his ears. But I didn't care if this wasn't what he wanted to hear. I kept going because he needed a little dose of reality.

"You're a selfish prick for bringing her into this. She's broken, and each time you run to her and drag her into your shit, she's flooded with guilt. So much that she has a hard time keeping afloat. Your sister is drowning."

Jason's voice was strained. "Fuck, I know!" He threw his arms out. "I fucking get it."

I got closer to him but quickly took a step back because I couldn't trust myself not to knee him in the face. "But do you?"

His empty gaze found mine. "Yeah, you wanna talk about guilt? I can't even keep myself clean for more than a day." He scoffed, dragging his attention around the room. "It's not like it's easy being around these guys—especially since I know all their hiding spots."

That could come in handy.

"So, are you going to do something about it, then?"

"Wh-what?" Jason looked confused. "Do you have a plan?"

Did I have a plan? Of course I had a fucking plan.

"Are you ready to fix this, Jason? Are you ready to stop taking from Piper and start *giving*? Because from where I'm standing, you owe her a lot more than just getting yourself clean."

Jason straightened his shoulders, hope in his eyes. "Tell me what to do, and I'll do it. I want to take Tank down just as badly as you do—if not worse, because I know shit. He's fucking crazy."

I knew time was quickly running out, so I hurriedly got on with the more important part of the conversation. *The plan.* If Jason wanted to fix his mistakes, he was going to have to start somewhere.

As soon as I exited the trailer, the two guys from before were standing outside, smoking a joint. They tipped their chin at me as I walked by, and I hoped that meant they were going to keep their mouths shut. I couldn't bank on that for sure, but I didn't really have another choice.

Once I got back into my Charger and started up my engine, I checked my phone that had been buzzing since I'd last called Eric.

Eric: I assume this means you don't need me to throw on my old cop costume from last Halloween?

Eric: Kegs are all set for Saturday. Word is that the entire school will be coming to your house for the party. My vote is we up the price.

Christian: You owe me a car wash and breakfast in bed all next week. I just covered for you with Dad. He said you've been dodging his calls since he left. He asked if something was going on. I assume you're avoiding him because you're preoccupied with Piper's drama. Correct?

I swallowed back my guilt. That was definitely not why I was avoiding my father, but for now, one problem at a time.

First up: Tank.

Second up: Figure out what was going on between Piper and me—if there was anything.

Third up: Confront my father.

CHAPTER THIRTY-ONE

PIPER

THE GLITTERY MAROON dress hugged my torso, and I wiggled to break free. It wasn't that it was an uncomfortable dress; it was just that I didn't necessarily want to be wearing it.

The winter formal seemed so stupid at a time like this. Every time I glanced at the clock, my nerves intensified. The only thing I could think about was Ollie and how he was at the races—*alone*. My heart had sped up a little each time I had caught his eye this week. I hadn't been alone with him since he helped me with decorations on Monday, but I could feel him watching me during class. And during lunch. Butterflies swarmed my stomach, and I was pretty sure I'd formed an ulcer from all the uncertainty going on in my life.

I hated that he was racing tonight.

I hated that he wasn't taking me to the dance.

And I hated that he wasn't going to see me in this dress, because I totally picked the color to match his Charger. Yes, I was that pathetic.

"You girls look stunning!" Ann walked into Hayley's

bedroom and beamed at us. I'd always liked Ann, even when she was just Hayley's social worker. I had a hunch that Hayley did, too. They shared a special relationship, and I kind of envied it, which wasn't really fair since Hayley hadn't had a real motherly figure in a very long time—if ever.

I did, sort of.

My parents didn't even know the winter formal was tonight. They had no idea I'd slaved over decorations the past few days or that I was even on the committee. Maybe part of it was my fault. They had called and checked in with me last night, but I eluded talking about anything with real substance in my life. They didn't ask, and I didn't tell. It was as simple as that.

"Thanks, Ann." Hayley smiled shyly as she looked at herself in the mirror once more. She ended up getting the navy-blue dress that cut at her mid-thigh. I'd already bet her an iced coffee that Christian would demand she take it off.

"Yeah, thanks, Ann," I repeated, looking down at my dress again.

It definitely was a pretty dress, hugging my body like a glove until it reached the curve of my hips. Then the bottom part fell gracefully to the floor, landing at my sparkly gray heels. The best part about the dress was the slit in the front that went dangerously high. The dress was almost a reflection of me: mostly innocent with just a glimpse of sin. I wasn't as innocent as some people thought—like my parents.

Speaking of the pair... "Where are your parents? I told Hayley they could come by and take photos if they wanted!" Ann walked over to me and fixed a piece of my hair. "This maroon color looks so beautiful on you, Piper."

I smiled, ignoring the drop of my stomach. "Oh, um..." I felt embarrassed, and I hated that. I had decent parents; they just weren't present.

Hayley swooped in and saved me. "Her parents work a

lot." She bent down to strap her heel around her ankle. "They're on a business trip, right, Piper?"

"Yes, I think they're in Prague until later next week." I was able to hide my disappointment, although I was certain Ann could see right through me.

She watched me closely, her mouth splitting to say something, but the doorbell rang, and she sighed. "Must be the boys. I'll go get it."

Hayley and I exchanged glances, and she gave me a crescent-like smile. I didn't need to say thank you because she already knew how I felt.

Soon, Hayley and I left her bedroom and walked down the short hall to meet Eric and Christian. The pull in my stomach pulled even tighter with each clank of my heels against the hardwood. *I should be with Ollie right now.*

I glanced down at my phone, hoping I'd have a text that read along the lines of, *Come watch me race.* But there was nothing on the screen besides an old photo of my brother and me.

I wondered briefly what Jason was doing and if he was at the races, watching Ollie win back the money *he* owed.

"You boys look quite dapper!" Ann's cheerful voice rang out into the foyer, and Hayley snorted.

Then, came the brooding voice of her boyfriend. "Hayley, you said your dress wasn't short!"

I held back a giggle as I watched the pair of them spout off. "It's not that short! I thought you'd like it."

Ann was standing back with her hand over her mouth, as if she were truly enjoying seeing them argue back and forth. Eric came to stand beside me, and the three of us waited until Christian ate his words and basically groveled at Hayley's feet. "You look amazing, Hay. Of course I like it. I just don't like to share."

"No one is getting anything from me, Christian. Relax."

"I can't relax when you look like that."

Eric glanced down at me and gave me his famous bad-boy grin. "You look pretty good for a fake date."

I rolled my eyes. "Shut up." Then I paused, feeling bad. "But thanks. So do you."

A deep chuckle tumbled from his mouth, breaking the ice, and before I knew it, we were all posing and smiling for Ann and her one thousand photos.

Once we said our goodbyes and Hayley climbed into Christian's Charger, I climbed into Eric's Range Rover, and we were all on our way to the formal.

My leg bounced the entire time, and I was certain the dark nail polish Hayley painted onto my nails was chipped from my incessant chewing.

Eric's palm gently landed on my bare thigh as we stopped at a red light. "Piper. You're shaking my entire fucking car."

I stopped my leg, staring down at his splayed-out hand. "Oh. Sorry."

"Alright, spill," he demanded as he removed his hand and pressed the gas.

I inhaled a deep breath. "This feels wrong, Eric."

He glanced at me for a moment. "What does?"

"Going to a stupid dance when Ollie is missing out because he's racing for something my brother did."

He shook his head, his dark hair unmoving on his head. "Not happening."

My bare shoulders fell with disappointment. I played stupid. "What?"

"You are not talking me into driving you to the races. Ollie has it handled."

I looked out the window at the blurring cars. "It still doesn't feel right. I should be there."

"For what? For every scumbag to check you out and for Ollie to feel stressed about you being on the sidelines alone?"

He clicked his tongue. "That'll just fuck him up, Piper. Leave it be."

I ignored Eric and crossed my arms over my chest, still staring out the window. Ollie might have felt uneasy if I were on the sidelines alone, but what about me? I felt uneasy knowing he was there alone, too.

Didn't he understand that I was worried about him? Didn't anyone understand that? This was exactly why I didn't want him involved in the first place. It was just one more person I had to worry about, because whether I liked it or not, I cared about Ollie.

And I should have been there. I should have been there for him, just like he'd been there for me.

One way or another, I'd get to the races tonight. I just had to figure out a way.

CHAPTER THIRTY-TWO

OLLIE

I wasn't nervous to race tonight. In fact, I was as relaxed as ever. Piper wasn't here; she was safe with Eric. And also, I didn't even have to try to win tonight. I had to race to lose. *Fun.* Sure, it kind of sucked for my street cred, but soon, I'd be done racing, and it wouldn't even matter.

Tank was standing a few hundred feet away with his arm draped heavily over his girlfriend's shoulders, and for a moment, I envisioned myself running his body over with my car. Jason was standing right beside him, being the good little pet that he was, and I hoped to God he'd keep his word until next weekend when shit hit the fan.

My fingers flexed over the steering wheel as I waited for my turn. I was racing a guy named Jaxon tonight, and if Tank hadn't asked me to throw the race—so he'd make more money, of course—I'd easily beat him. My car was faster; I could tell just by listening to his idle. Mostly everyone was betting on me to win, except for this douchebag's friends and girlfriend, but since I was throwing the race per Tank's request, and he was betting *against* me, he was about to make fucking bank.

Part of me wanted to be defiant and win anyway, because what a fucking cheat. *But* in order to keep my cards aligned to make sure things went the way I needed them to down the road, I had to stay on his good side. Being on Tank's good side meant he was on my good side. Our relationship was mutual at this point, at least in his eyes, and he wanted nothing more than to keep it that way, because he thought I was going to continue racing for him well after Jason's debt was paid off.

Little did he know, I had no intention of doing that. Tank was someone that needed to be knocked down a few notches, and I would gladly be the one to do so.

I checked my phone for the hundredth time, wishing more than anything I was the one being tagged in photos on social media at the winter formal. Not because I wanted to go, but because I knew Piper was there without me.

The gentleman side of me wanted her to have a good time, but the selfish side of me was sweating from jealousy.

As soon as my car creeped up to the starting line, I scanned the crowd. Usually, I looked forward to racing. I craved the escape it gave me, but now I felt agitated and bored. I was ready to get this over with so I could see Piper at the party later.

My phone vibrated as my Charger rumbled, and I all but dropped the phone when I saw Eric's name flashing.

I quickly answered. "Hello?"

"She fucking stole my Range Rover!"

My foot hovered over the clutch. "What?"

Eric shouted, "Fucking Piper! I have no idea what we're going to do with her. She's out of control!"

I couldn't help the laugh that echoed throughout my car. "She stole your car?"

"Yes! Fucking keep up! She's probably already at the races even though I told her not to go. I swear, your girl is worse than a toddler."

I wanted to be mad, but I wasn't in the slightest. An excited thrill went surging through my blood. It was the same feeling I got when I'd catch her staring at me from across the room, or when she'd try to hide a half smile from me.

I hung up on Eric, throwing my phone in the center console, and scanned the crowd again. I wiggled my jaw and drummed my fingers along the leather steering wheel. *Where are you, Piper?*

Just as the thought entered my head, I found her.

The smile etching itself on my face was too hard to ignore. There was Piper, standing back behind the crowd of people, wearing her winter formal dress. She stuck out like a sore thumb, but she was by far the prettiest sore thumb I'd ever seen.

Our eyes locked almost immediately. She was already watching me, probably knowing very well that I'd be searching the crowd for her.

I rolled my window down, the rumbling car engines filling the space. We kept a hold of each other's eyes, and when I let my grin free, she smiled coyly.

Well, what are you waiting for?

Piper read my thoughts, because before I knew it, she was pushing past people and heading straight for me—winter formal dress and all.

This race was about to get a whole lot better, even if I was about to lose.

CHAPTER THIRTY-THREE

PIPER

THE SECOND I got into his car, his cologne flooded my senses. I almost closed my eyes to savor the woodsy smell. I suddenly felt very calm being next to him. The nerves I'd felt while driving to the races intensified as I walked through the tall grass, and when I found Ollie staring at me, I almost retreated backwards—at least, until he grinned.

It was almost like he knew I'd show up, and if I wasn't mistaken, he was glad.

We both stayed silent for a few seconds, neither one of us wanting to admit the truth. I wanted to be with him tonight, and he wanted to be with me. Why was that so hard for us to admit?

"So what, you wanted to be my good luck charm tonight or something?"

I gasped as I came to the realization that I was sitting in the passenger seat of his Charger, seconds before he was due to race down a gravel road. How did that slip my mind? How did everything slip my mind when I was with him?

I waited for the fear to come as I gazed out the windshield, noting everyone standing around, ready for the next race to start, but it never came.

Racing with Ollie should have scared me. I had all but fainted the last time I watched him speed down the gravel road, but here I was, buckling my seatbelt, with him in the driver's seat—like it was him and me against the world.

I spotted Jason a few yards down, standing beside Tank. He looked like he always did: run-down, tired, a little messy. It made me sick to see him.

"So?" Ollie repeated. I turned away from my brother and found Ollie's patient stare.

"I'm honestly surprised you're not angry with me and throwing me out of your car right this second."

We both heard the clapping from the crowd as the last race must have ended, but neither of us broke our gaze.

"Why are you here, Piper?"

"Because—"

"Nope. Do not say because it's your problem. We've been down that road before." Ollie leaned over the center console, invading my space. "Tell me the truth. Why are you here? Why are you here in my car, about to race down this gravel road like you aren't scared out of your mind?"

I licked my lips and turned my body even more toward his. I felt the slit of my dress open, the cool air conditioner blowing over the bare skin on my thigh. "Oddly enough, I don't feel scared at all."

"No?" he asked.

I felt the car moving forward a bit, knowing it was almost his turn to race. Shaking my head, my eyes dipped down to his perfect lips. The ones that had been on mine almost a week ago. Heat coated my skin. The tension in the car was charged with electricity, and I swore, if anyone were to stick their hand through the window, they would have been electrified on the spot.

I had no idea when things changed between us, but somewhere along the way of us being on the same team, I let my guard down.

"No," I finally whispered. "I don't feel scared when I'm with you, Ollie. Not even a little bit."

His Adam's apple bobbed as he traced along the side of my face and down my chest. His lips parted, and I felt the flame in my core burn brighter. It was like he was trailing a finger over my most sensitive spots, except he wasn't touching me at all.

"Did you pick out that dress knowing I'd see you in it one way or another tonight?" He kept his attention on my thigh peeking out between the purple fabric.

I gulped, my heart hiccupping in my chest. "No."

His face twitched. "Liar."

I glanced at his mouth again, but he quickly looked away and pulled himself back over to the driver's side, looking straight ahead. "I'm throwing the race tonight."

I rushed out. "What? Why?"

Ollie kept his attention in front of him, and I felt the thunder of his Charger's power. We were seconds from racing. "Tank asked me to come over last week to discuss a plan. He's betting against me, whereas everyone else is betting on me because they know I have the turbo. I'll lose, and Tank will get a shit-ton of money."

My jaw fell. I watched as a girl who was wearing a short dress came in between the two cars. She had a bra in her hand, which I was assuming was her version of a flag.

Ollie cracked his neck, preparing for the race, as I stared at the side of his smooth jaw. "I mean, it's a good thing. The more money he gets, the closer we are to paying back what Jason owes. But..."

The nervous jitters were back. "But what?"

"But he's shady, and this just proves it. He's using me to cheat, and I don't like that."

There was a ping in my chest, and I knew exactly what it was. *Guilt.* There it was. The guilt that came crashing down on my shoulders as I sat in the passenger seat of Ollie's Charger as he continued to get wrapped up in shit he should have never even stepped foot in. Ollie had all kinds of things going for him—a promised football scholarship being one of them—and I'd drug him into *this*.

"Ollie," I whispered, watching the girl in front of us as she raised her hands above her head. "I don't know how I'm ever going to repay you for this."

He revved his Charger and so did the guy beside us.

Right before the girl dropped her arms and we took off speeding down the road, Ollie whispered, "Piper, you repay me by breathing. Now, shut up and enjoy the ride."

And that was exactly what I did.

CHAPTER THIRTY-FOUR

OLLIE

"OH MY GOD, OLLIE!" Piper shouted as I came to a sudden stop. Her glossy red hair fell out from her loose bun, framing her face. Her cheeks were flushed, her green eyes wild with excitement. "That was so much fun!"

There was a sudden surge of energy inside my car, and I was certain it had to do with her and nothing to do with flying down a gravel road.

I had almost won the race by accident, getting too lost in Piper's excitement, before I remembered the plan.

"See?" I threw a shoulder up. "Don't knock it before you try it. Why do you think I've been doing this for so long?"

Piper sunk back into the seat, her bare leg playing peek-a-boo with the cut in her dress. I tore my eyes away at the last second. "You can't fool me, Oliver Powell. I know very well you've been racing for a reason much deeper than the fact that it's fun." She sighed happily, resting her head against the seat before turning to look at me. "It really is fun, though. Will you teach me how to drive like this?"

I barked out a laugh as I rounded the bend in the road, heading toward the beginning. "Fuck no."

She pouted, and it was the cutest thing I'd ever seen. "Why?"

"Because it's dangerous." The roll of her eyes caused me to smirk. "I'm sorry, but someone has to look out for you."

"I'm a big girl, Ollie."

I laughed again. "Says the girl who gets stuck in shitty trailers and needs me to come rescue her. Oh yes, you've got it all handled."

She rolled her lips together to keep herself from smiling. Instead, she cleared her throat. "So, um, now what? Do we just leave?"

I found Tank standing by Brandon with a sneaky smile on his face because he'd won the bet. Everyone around him had slumped shoulders, and some people were even throwing their hands up. *Maybe I should get out of here.* People were going to be pissed that they bet on me and I lost. A lot of them were probably suspecting something since Tank was collecting a lot of money right now.

Piper pushed forward and squinted. "Why does my brother disappear after every race? He did that last time we were here, too."

I wasn't sure, but I was glad. Jason and I had an agreement, but I couldn't be certain that we wouldn't tip off Tank with a shared look. We had to act as we always did when he was around, which was us not acknowledging each other at all.

A text on my phone came through, and Piper and I both read it.

Tank: Head out, people are curious why you lost.

"Yeah, no shit," I muttered.

Piper scoffed. "He's not the smartest guy, is he?"

I snickered as I began turning my car around. "Nope, and that'll work in our favor, babe."

Her head snapped to mine, and I froze. *Did I just call her babe? And not in a way that was teasing?*

I did.

And it felt good

"So, um..." She twiddled her dainty hands in her lap. "Do you want to drop me off at Eric's Range Rover? And I'll follow you to your house for the party?"

Okay, so we're just gonna slide right over that. Noted.

"Yeah, that's cool."

My chest felt tight again, and the words I wanted to say weren't coming out of my mouth. I was stuck in a sort of hell that I wasn't used to. I was nervous. My heart drummed in my chest, and I was pretty sure I was sweating. I glanced at Piper's bare leg again, and my dick instantly got hard.

I wanted to pull her body over to mine and kiss her senseless. I wanted to lose myself in her. I wanted to rip apart her dress and savor every part of that creamy skin she kept teasing me with, and if it were anyone else, I'd have done just that. I'd lay the charm on thick, and within seconds, I'd be pulling that dress down, but this was a different territory. This was Piper.

Feelings were involved.

I cared about her. This wasn't a fling, and I didn't know how to handle that. I didn't even know if she felt the same way. Piper was like looking at a road map but having no sense of direction. I couldn't read her like most girls.

Maybe this was one-sided?

"Ollie?"

I jumped, and she looked confused.

Fuck. Was this one-sided?

"Sorry. Yeah, let's go."

Once I dropped her off at Eric's Range Rover, I was

suddenly glad she was out of my car. I felt like I could breathe again. I had a twenty-minute drive to clear my head.

I pushed away everything that had been weighing down on me. Even Piper.

Tonight, I'd be Ollie. The one everyone was used to.

The one who didn't give a shit if a girl was into him.

Because I was beginning to think that Piper didn't feel for me what I felt for her.

And that stung.

CHAPTER THIRTY-FIVE

PIPER

THERE HE WAS.

Oliver Powell—the guy who everyone was instantly drawn to. Ollie was the center of the universe, and everyone else were the dainty little stars, scattered all around him, lost without his guidance. A group of our classmates was standing beside him, totally engrossed in his story. A few girls blushed when he smiled, and the jealousy inside of me was slithering out like a snake, ready to constrict every last one of them.

I huffed and wrapped my arms around my torso. My back was resting along the banister, and I was ready to go upstairs just to escape the show in front of me.

I was confused and irritable. When Ollie and I were alone, everything felt right. My worries faded; my uncertainties disappeared. A lightness around us formed. I almost felt like I could float when I was with him. But when we were apart, in a group of people or at school, that was when things became unclear. They were muddy. It was kind of scary to think about. Ollie silenced the bad, and that was a heavy thought.

My heart came to a screeching halt as I watched Ollie dip his head down to Clementine, a girl I knew he had frequented many times in the past. She used to brag about it in the library during study hall, not quite loud enough to draw the attention of English Prep's cranky librarian but loud enough so everyone around her could hear. It used to infuriate me, and seeing her whisper something in his ear did just the same. I quickly pushed off the stairs and shot her a dirty look.

Holy shit. Relax, Piper.

My breaths were coming in fast and hot, jealousy being the main component.

Run.

I turned on my heel, knowing very well I needed to take a breather, when I smacked right into someone. My hand shot up to my head as it thudded off a hard chest.

Eric's brows were furrowed with confusion, and when he saw it was me, they furrowed even deeper. "Where are you going now?"

Eric was angry with me, and I couldn't even blame him. I stole his car and left him at the winter formal with Hayley and Christian. But he was preoccupied with watching Madeline the entire time, so I didn't feel *that* bad.

"Look," I started, staring down at my Converse. "I'm sorry I took your Range Rover. Here." I reached into the back of my jeans that I had changed into the second I got here and pulled out his keys, handing them to him.

Eric's hands clamped down on them as I placed them into his palm. His voice was deep. "Why don't you just tell him?"

I played dumb. "Tell who what?"

He tilted his head, his dark hair falling slightly over his forehead. "Why don't you just tell Ollie you want him? For

fuck's sake, you left the winter formal and stole my car just to
be at the races with him."

I opened my month to argue, peeking up at him through
my eyelashes. Eric was standing on the first step, so he was
even taller than usual.

"Don't blame it on needing to see your brother or needing
to be there for any other reason. You and I both know you
went to the races because you couldn't stand the fact that he
was there without you. You went solely to be with him.
Didn't you?"

I mean, yeah. He was right. I wasn't going to admit it,
though.

Eric stood up taller and looked out into the party over my
head.

"Just tell him. It's annoying watching you two dance
around one another."

My hands found my hips. "Well, it's annoying to watch
you dance around Madeline."

His eyes flared to mine, and I knew I'd hit a chord. I
pushed past him and the truth that he so clearly stated and
climbed the stairs, huffing.

Ollie and Christian had banned everyone from coming
upstairs. But I was hoping I was an exception.

Once I reached the top stair, I found the door at the end
of the hall—Ollie and Christian's parents' room. I shifted my
gaze to the wall beside it, the wall that Ollie had pressed me
against when he kissed me last week.

A hot wave fanned over my body, but I quickly grew cold,
wondering if Ollie would bring Clem up here later. In the
past, I'd brush it off. Ollie being with another girl wasn't
unusual. But now, it felt like my heart was going to break in
half at the thought.

My hand wrapped around the doorknob to his room. I'd
never been inside Ollie's room before. I only knew it was his

from the night Hayley and I stayed here a few months back.

But I needed a moment to breathe. I needed a dark, quiet room to gather myself in, and since Ollie seemed to be the only thing that could calm me these days, his room was going to have to do the trick.

There was no way I was going back down to that party to drag him away in a jealous rage.

That wasn't me, even if my heart was begging me to do just that.

CHAPTER THIRTY-SIX

OLLIE

MY EYES FOLLOWED her tight jeans all the way up the steps. *One step, two steps, three.* She paused at the landing for a moment, contemplating something as she pushed her hair behind her shoulder.

A group of people surrounded me, listening to Taylor tell his side of the story about the championship football game we'd won a couple of months ago.

Once Piper was out of sight, I looked to Hayley and Christian who were lounging on the couch together. Hayley gave me a look, as if she were asking me why I wasn't following her best friend upstairs. Christian acted like his usual self, nonchalant and like he didn't give a fuck, but I saw the slight flick of his chin toward the stairs.

The beat of the music lessened as I pushed past the group of people and made my way up the stairs. There were a shit-ton of people here. Majority of the upperclassmen. I knew we were making a good chunk of change from charging people to come in. It felt sneaky and dirty, but for some reason, everyone all but dropped to their knees for an invite to the Powell house. I wasn't sure if it was because they thought this after-party was going to be wild since we'd charged money and hyped it up, *or* if it was because they just truly wanted to see our house. Maybe they just wanted a peek into our lives. Christian and I were both pretty private, but our lives weren't that interesting. Unless, of course, you were into daddy issues.

My limbs felt stiff as I continued to jog up the stairs. On the drive home from the races, I'd told myself to have fun tonight. I didn't want the stress of the races or Tank's bullshit lingering over my back. I didn't even want to be bothered with my unresolved feelings for Piper, but here I was, chasing after her.

Once I got upstairs, my gaze shifted to each door that lined the hallway. I had no idea where she was, but my best bet was the guest room.

Although...

I smirked when I opened *my* bedroom door. *I knew it.*

There she was.

Piper flew up off my bed, her hair blowing behind her face. Her green eyes were wide with surprise. She shouted at me, clearly embarrassed. "What are you doing in here?"

The door latched behind me. The orange glow of the lamp on my desk brought out all the shadows along her face that I couldn't help but look at.

"Better question is, what are *you* doing in here?" I walked a little farther into my bedroom and sat down on the chair by my desk. I spun around and leaned back, crossing my arms over my black T-shirt. "We said no one was allowed upstairs."

Piper's gaze dropped to the floor. Her feet were dangling off the edge, and she looked so damn cute and innocent. The only thing that would make this better was if her pants were off and she was wearing my T-shirt.

I stared at her mouth when she looked up again.

"I just needed a second to collect myself. It's been a long...day."

I scoffed. "It's been a long few weeks."

A puff of air left her as she flopped back onto my bed with a whoosh. For the first time ever, I was actually glad to be away from a party. I didn't care that there was a keg downstairs. I didn't care that Clementine *and* Casey both whispered dirty nothings in my ear. I didn't care that my friends were playing a game of pong in the kitchen. What I cared about was lying on my bed, and the only person I wanted beside me was her.

So, that was what I did.

Piper tensed as I dipped down on the other side and lay the same way she was, both of our backs flat against the mattress, staring at the white ceiling painted with our silhouettes. Our hands were millimeters away from touching, and it was daunting. I actually had to fight the temptation of interlacing our fingers.

"We've come a long way," I whispered, still staring at the ceiling. I felt the shift of Piper's head, and I knew she was looking at me. I swallowed. Being this close to her sparked something inside of me. Anticipation and exhilaration. She was such a tease, but innocently so.

"We really have." Her soft breath floated across the bed and hit the side of my face.

My chest heaved. The dip in my core did not go unnoticed.

Silence passed between us, and I couldn't help but wonder if she was thinking the same thing I was. The air was crackling; I could feel the zing of electricity through our hushed words. I loved these quiet, small moments with her—the two of us shut away from everything and everyone.

The soft sound of her moving her head back to look at

the ceiling caused me to look out of the corner of my eye. I was mesmerized by the slow rise and fall of her chest.

"Have you decided what you're going to say to your dad? Or when?"

I clenched my eyes tight and felt myself slipping into that territory I didn't like to get into. "I don't want to talk about that. Not right now."

Another hushed moment passed, the low thump of music our only melody. I slowly shifted so I could see her again. I traced over her delicate profile as she continued looking straight. The high cheek bones, the long eyelashes, her dainty nose. The curve of her lips that I wanted to run my tongue over.

I moved back to my rightful position, taking my eyes off her. "Have you decided what you're going to do once Tank is paid off? Where that'll leave you and your brother?"

Piper sucked in a sharp breath. The slow rhythm of her breathing sped up. I wanted to rest my hand over her chest to let her know I was here, but when I felt her move, I turned, and our gazes locked. "I also don't want to talk about it. Not right now."

"We're quite the pair, you and I." I grinned and took pride in the fact that she was fighting her own smile. "Shoving away our problems. Hiding out upstairs during a party."

"This isn't the first time we've done this." She said it so softly I almost didn't hear, but her whispers were like a beckoning call to me. I clung to them hard.

The memory drifted back, and I had glimpses of that night again. The dark room, her soft curves, the slow in and out movement, the sloppy lustful kisses that I would never forget.

Groaning, I sat up in bed, pushing away the memory. I shifted some, putting much needed space between us as I rested along the headboard.

I wanted nothing more than to relive that night.

But this moment right here was nothing like the past. We had been able to let our boundaries down that night because there was nothing on the table but hidden secrets in a dark room. We weren't invested. We didn't care about each other. Feelings weren't involved.

But now, they were. I could feel it, and she could feel it. There was something between us. Leaning over and kissing her had the potential to blow up in our faces. There was a frightening connection between the two of us, and it'd only grow stronger if we crossed into that territory.

"Do you remember that night?" she asked quietly.

My jaw clenched as I pushed my back further into the headboard. *Stupid question, Piper. Of course I remember that night.*

She whispered under her breath, "I told you something that night."

I looked at her out of the corner of my eye again, too afraid that if I saw her longing eyes, I'd throw caution to the wind and take her right there, not caring about the consequences. I cleared my throat. "I remember. You told me you did something bad, and you came upstairs to escape the party. For a moment of silence." There was nothing about that night that I could forget.

Piper shifted a little closer to me, and I held my breath. Our jeans rubbed together, denim scratching against denim. "And you told me you had just found out that your dad wasn't really your dad."

I huffed. "Just two teenaged strangers telling secrets in a dark room at a banger." All of my nerves were at a standstill. A year of rising tensions rested between Piper and me, and I was certain we were seconds from exploding. The entire house was going to go up in flames if I didn't get out of this room as soon as possible. But I couldn't. I couldn't leave with her looking at me the way she was. Her pupils were dilated, and the apples of her cheeks were tinted. Her soft lips did nothing to deter me from staying in my room with her.

"Did you know it was me that night? When we had sex? Did you know?" I asked, curious.

Piper nodded, and my eyes went back to her mouth. I watched the words fall out. "I did. And then I recognized you the first day I started at English Prep."

Something felt heavy inside my chest. "And you still never told anyone about my dad?"

Her head shook back and forth.

"Not even when I pretended like I didn't know you?"

My heart grew so large in my chest I thought it might split my ribs open. Piper knew my deepest, darkest secret, and she didn't tell a single soul, not even when I'd made her stumble over her words or caused her to sway on her feet from flirting. If there was one thing I loved most about her, it was her gentle heart. Her loyalty. Her need to help others. She protected me and my secret well before she even truly knew me.

"Your secrets aren't mine to tell, Ollie. And even though, in the beginning of all of this, when I said I'd tell Christian, I knew deep down I never would. I couldn't do that to you."

I pinched the bridge of my nose before pushing down a rising lump in my throat. "You're a good person, Piper. You have a heart of pure fucking gold." I paused before meeting her face. "I really hate that it's broken."

She quickly looked back to the ceiling, keeping her features calm. "It's not broken."

"It is. The broken ones are always the ones who help others. That's you."

Silence fell between us like a brick wall as she gathered her thoughts. I felt unsettled. My words were true, but part of me wished I'd never said them.

Piper slowly rose from the bed, and I waited for her to

leave the room. I was certain I'd upset her, but instead of her swinging her legs over the side of the bed and walking back down to the party, she turned toward me leaning against the headboard. "Then mend me."

I stilled. "What?"

She was staring at my mouth, and I grew hot. *Don't tempt me, Piper.*

"You were the one who said I was broken." She scooted closer, and the bed dipped. Her hand wrapped around my bicep, her warm palm on my searing skin. There was a single lock of her copper hair that fell onto her face. "So mend me."

Fuck.

I wanted to be a gentleman. I wanted to tell her no, because I knew, deep down, fucking her wasn't going to fix things, but at the same time, I knew it would put a Band-Aid on her heart, and if that was all I could give her right now, then so be it.

Whatever she wanted, I'd give to her. Even if it tore my own heart out in the process.

It happened fast. My hands were on her body, her hair spilling out all around her as I pushed her flat to her back.

Piper gasped as I towered over her. One of my knees wedged in between hers. "You really want to do this?"

I bounced my eyes back and forth between hers as my chest constricted. *Please say yes.* Piper kept a hold of my stare, and her pretty lips parted. "Yes. Let's be us again...the us that no one else knows."

And just like that, every single coherent thought left my head. Even if this was only a trip down memory lane, I didn't care.

Piper and I were like putting gasoline on a flame.

There was no putting us out.

Not tonight.

CHAPTER THIRTY-SEVEN

PIPER

MY LEGS TREMBLED as Ollie shot up from the bed. The beating of my heart drummed so wildly it drowned out the low music from the party. His long legs carried him over to his bedroom door, and for a moment, I thought I'd made a fool out of myself. I thought I'd read the situation all wrong, but when I heard the click of the lock, I clenched my thighs together.

Ollie's sharp jaw was pointing toward me, his pretty blue eyes burning all the places he touched. My chest was heaving as shivers skittered down my back.

This was it. Ollie and me, again.

And there was absolutely no way I was denying this feeling. Something was different between us. Like we were tethered by a fraying thread of twine. I wasn't sure if it would hold, but for tonight, we weren't pulling in opposite directions. It wasn't pulled taut with tension. Tonight, we were on the same side. There was no question about it.

I lay still on the bed as Ollie appeared at my feet. I felt

small on his king-sized bed, his dark comforter soft underneath my body. The small lamp on his desk made the room glow in warmth. There were shadows underneath his firm jaw, on his high cheekbones and straight nose. He ripped his shirt off, and I felt my jaw fall slightly. Peaks and valleys of muscles lined his torso, and I couldn't stop staring.

Last time we did this, we were fumbling in the dark. I'd felt his hard muscles and traced over the lines with trembling fingers, but now that he was standing right in front of me, I was certain I'd never seen anything so beautiful.

"Take your clothes off."

I sucked in a breath at the sound of his demanding tone, but I loved it all the same. I gingerly sat up and reached under the hem of my shirt and flung it off. Ollie watched my every move with each tracing line of his eye, and I swore it made things ten times hotter.

I liked this. I liked watching him fall to his knees with lust. His chest was moving quickly, the veins in his forearms bulging as he clenched his fists together.

You like this, Ollie? 'Cause so do I.

The button of my jeans sprang free, and his hooded eyes widened. I shimmied off the bed and pulled the tight material down my legs, kicking my pants across the room.

A black lacy bralette and a skimpy pair of underwear were the only things left on my body, and for some reason, I wasn't timid in the slightest. The last time we'd done this, it was too dark to see anything, which was good, because I was nervous. I had been way out of my comfort zone but so desperate to rebel that I had pushed away all doubts and uncertainty until afterwards.

But tonight, the nerves were gone. The only thing I felt was excitement.

A hiss between his teeth had me smirking. His nostrils flared as he stomped toward me. His warm hands went around my hips, and I swore they seared my very skin. For a moment, we just stared at each other. My chest pressed along his, his fingers digging into my hips. I gulped as he took his hand and angled my chin up. "I'm going to ask you one more time, Piper. Are you sure about this?"

It only took half a second for me to nod and the other half for him to kiss me. His tongue slid in and moved over mine languidly, and I fought back a moan. Ollie was a damn good kisser. Warm, soft lips and a slow, calculated tongue that dipped in my mouth, making warm tingles float over my skin.

But soon, our slow and sensual kiss turned into a starving thirst that neither of us could quench. Our teeth clanked, and my lip was tugged by his bite as he quickly backed me up against his closet door. My legs involuntarily spread open as his knee slid in between them. Our kisses were rushed and raw, his hand pulling on my hair as I opened myself up to him. The heat between our bodies was enough to melt anyone who came near.

His hardness hit my belly, and I panted, pulling away for a moment. The softness of Ollie's baby blues was gone, and in its place was an untamed need that I was clawing to get at. His dark pupils were dilated with lust, and I simply felt wild. There was a part of me that craved to be timid and self-conscious, but when Ollie kept hold of my stare and crept his hand past my hip, gripping the inside of my thigh, I bit so hard on my bottom lip that it bled.

"Open those legs for me, babe."

A rush of breath fell out from my mouth, and I fluttered my eyes shut. His palm was rough along my soft skin as he very slowly traced a line from the inside of my knee to my most sensitive spot.

A growl from him had me withering against the wall, my legs opening even wider.

I felt the cool air brush over me as he moved my panties

to the side, and I had to force my legs straight to keep my knees from buckling. I was shivering.

When his finger slowly dipped inside of me, my eyes flew open.

Ollie was watching me, his eyes lustful and dangerous. His free hand came up, and he gripped my face as he dipped his mouth onto mine again. His kisses mixed with the swirl of his finger had me losing my breath. I couldn't breathe or think clear thoughts. The line I had drawn between us over the last year was completely invisible now, and I didn't care in the slightest. Hate blurred with love, and I wasn't sure where I stood anymore. The only thing I cared about was riding his hand.

"Ollie," I managed to croak out.

His knee pushed my legs even further apart, and I threw my head back. His hand slipped from my face and rested along my neck.

"That's it, baby. Right there." He seemed to find my sweet spot, and I moaned. "Let go for me."

And I did.

My body exploded, and I all but collapsed in his arms. He caught me quickly, scooped up my legs, and wrapped them around his waist. They felt like Jell-O as he laid me on the bed.

Ollie's hair was a rustled mess, the light strands sticking up in the hottest way possible. His tongue darted out and licked his swollen lips as he stared down at me with a look that had me burning up all the same.

"Fuck me," I whispered, surprising myself.

His eyes flared as his hands wrapped around my legs. "Only if you promise you'll say those words to me again, preferably in the near future."

Was that even a question?

I slowly sat up in his bed and kept his stare in line with

mine. I reached my shaky fingers behind my back and unclasped my bra, letting the straps fall down one by one against my shoulders. "Fuck me, Ollie. Fuck me like I'm the only girl you *want* to fuck."

In an instant, Ollie was completely naked and pulling a condom over himself. He was hovering over me with a look that I'll likely take to my grave. "Don't you see, Piper?" His mouth was a breath away from mine. "You"—he pulled my panties down my legs and tossed them to the side—"are"—he began to slide into me, and I arched my back—"the only"— he was one thrust in, and I lost my ability to focus on anything other than him—"the only girl I fucking see."

His thrusts were slow at first, but as soon as I began moving below him and our lips fused, they were hard and fast. His name fell off my lips through a muffle of moans as I found another release, and just as I thought it couldn't get any better, he flipped me around mid-thrust and took me in a completely different way.

His hand trailed over my spine slowly as he paused for a minute, and I felt myself tighten almost instantly. *This is way too good.* If I wasn't careful, I could completely lose myself in all things Ollie. This might ruin me for life.

My body was spent, but it was winding up again as Ollie moved over me. "Fuck, Piper," he moaned as I began crumbling. His hand found my breast, and all it took was one handful and his body stilled. His head dropped to my back, and his heavy breathing coated my skin like a warm blanket. He placed a soft kiss to my spine, and I felt something I'd never ever felt before.

Ollie was all sunshine and smiles around a group of people. He was chivalrous and a true flirt. But behind closed doors, he was dark and raw and unforgiving in every single way, and I loved every single second of it.

CHAPTER THIRTY-EIGHT

OLLIE

NEVER IN MY life had I acted so feral. I was wild with lust and desire at the sight of Piper opening herself up to me, and I took every single part of her. Her creamy skin and fuck-me eyes. Pair those with her dirty mouth, and I could fuck her every day for the rest of my life, and it still wouldn't be enough.

Nothing else mattered now that I had her like this. I had her completely. It wasn't a secret locked away in a dark room, disguised as a one-night stand. This was unforgettable. We did it, and we *knew* it. This wasn't something you brushed under the rug. This wasn't something you came back from.

Piper was mine.

And I hoped she knew it.

Once I pulled out of her and wiped the sweat off my brow, I got dressed and threw her one of my T-shirts. She sat up in my bed, her hair tumbling down her chest, hiding those perky breasts that were in my hands a second ago, and pulled the shirt over her head.

I smirked as I walked over to her, standing at the foot of the bed. "Don't steal this one, okay?"

Her head tipped down as she took in the English Prep shirt. "I make no promises."

I chuckled as I climbed onto the bed. Piper tried to sit up straight, but I wrapped my arm around her and pulled her in close. Her warm body snuggled up to me as she fit in the crook of my arm. The bareness of her leg hooked over mine, and for the first time in months—maybe even all year—I felt at peace.

Calm.

Serene.

Like all was right in my world again.

We lay in silence for a little while until our breathing evened out. I listened to the music downstairs and the muffled laughter from the party.

"Do you think next weekend will be the last race?" she asked.

Yes.

"Depends on how much we make tonight from the party. Tank texted and said he'd profited over 5k from the races. So, I think so."

Piper peered up at me, her hair brushing along my arm. "I was thinking, if we need to make more money, I can ask Andrew to have a party like this. I'd help him, of course. We can make it a themed party. He's the equivalent to Christian and you, but at Wellington Prep. He could charge $1,000 and people would still probably pay it." She shrugged. "He'd be down for it. He felt kind of bad after I explained the situation when you threatened Cole."

I held back a snarl. "There's no way you're going to a Wellington Prep party to be around Cole. Not without me."

She laughed against my chest. "What, we have sex and now I'm yours? How very caveman of you."

"I don't trust Cole."

The vision of him kissing her still bothered me. It felt like tiny shards of glass sprinkling my skin.

"No one trusts Cole. But he wouldn't hurt me. He knows Andrew would rip his head off. They have a weird relationship."

Still don't trust him. "It doesn't matter. Next weekend will likely be the last race."

Her head tilted toward mine, but I didn't look down. "And then what?"

"What do you mean?"

The air between us changed. It grew from warm to cold. "Well...what do you plan on doing about Tank? You're going to stop racing, right?"

"Right." I knew I was being elusive, but that was how it had to be, for now.

She seemed to relax, snuggling closer to me. "Good, but... how? Tank said..."

A bout of anxiety hit me deep in my stomach, but I brushed it off. I looked down at her green eyes. They were like sea glass, and it felt like they were cutting me with their eagerness for the truth.

"Don't worry, Piper. I have everything figured out. Let's just get this shit paid and your brother out of trouble. Then, I'll worry about Tank and..." My eyes darted away. "And other things."

Her voice was soft. "Other things like telling Christian about the issues with your dad?"

"Yeah. That."

She nodded against my chest. I hoped she couldn't hear the rapid increase of my heart beating.

"Can I ask you something?"

Her soft tone lingered. "Sure."

"A year ago, you said you did something bad. What was it?"

It'd been bothering me for a while now. After I found out more about her, and Jason, I'd wondered what she was referring to that night so long ago. What exactly did she do?

Piper's body stilled, so I joked to lighten the mood. "Oh, come on, I thought you and I were into the whole sharing-secrets thing?"

A soft breath brushed over my chest. "You'll never look at me the same."

I clicked my tongue as I shook my head. "I can assure you I will. I like all of you, Piper. The good and bad, the broken and whole."

Her pink lip twitched as she shot me a look. It didn't last long, though. The small smile faded just before she buried her head into me again. "I did two things that night. Two things my parents would totally disapprove of, which is probably why I did them in the first place."

I said nothing as she sorted out her thoughts. Instead, I twirled a piece of her hair around my finger and waited.

"It was right after they told me I was being taken out of Wellington Prep and would be attending English Prep. I was so angry. I was angry for a lot of reasons, but the fact that they were running from Jason's mistakes lit a fire inside of me. They had already kicked him out of the house, shunned him from the family, and then that? I was livid."

My head moved up and down. "I get that."

"They forbid me to ever see him again. They told me to call the police if he even stepped foot on our property."

Damn.

She gulped, and I felt the slight tremble of her body. I pulled her in even closer, wanting to take away her fear. "Hey," I stopped her. "You don't have to tell me."

She shook her head. "I want to."

Those three words settled right into my chest. *She wanted to tell me.*

"My brother actually ended up reaching out to me that night. I was going to Andrew's because he was having a party, and I couldn't stand to be in the house with my parents. So, I snuck out, and that was when I got a call from an unknown number. It was Jason." Piper's voice was so low I could barely hear it over the music from downstairs. "He'd been beaten up —again. I don't even remember why. Maybe he stole something. Or owed money." She shrugged. "I ended up going to him, and I helped him get cleaned up. He was in an alley, kind of close to Pike Valley Trailer Park, actually." A sad laugh erupted from her. "I still remember the smell of the spoiled milk in the dumpster nearby. Seeing my brother that beat up and high at the same time wrecked me. I got him in my car and drove him to his friend's house. He didn't hang with the best crowd, but Alec was better than the rest. He got him inside, and we cleaned him up. But then his friend told me he knew who was responsible."

"He told you who beat Jason up?"

Piper nodded against me again, her body buzzing with anxiety. "Yeah. Tank isn't the first mess I've tried to clean up for Jason."

Both anger and apprehension were sprouting in my chest, but I kept my body relaxed and appeared unfazed. I didn't want her to stop talking. My thumb began to stroke her arm.

"So, I went to his place. He didn't live far from the alley. And maybe he didn't deserve what I did. Jason probably deserved what he got, but..."

"But what? What did you do?"

Her voice shook. "I took a baseball bat and shattered every window on his car. I was like a wild freaking animal."

I stopped breathing for a moment. "You...what?"

The words came out fast. "Yeah, and he came out, and I

ran back to my car and sped away. I was certain I'd get in trouble. That the cops would find me. But I was so mad that he'd hurt Jason and frustrated with what my family had become. It felt so good to let go. It felt good to be bad."

I stayed quiet for a few minutes, digesting what I'd heard. It was hard to imagine her acting like that, but I understood it. She was hurt. And angry. Sometimes, we just snapped.

My thumb continued to graze her arm. "It was a good distraction, yeah?"

"Yeah, and then..."

My thumb stopped. "And then what?"

Piper pushed up off my chest, and I suddenly felt my breath go with her. I watched her sigh as her eyes locked onto mine. "That's not all."

My shoulders grew tense. Piper was nervous. She couldn't hold my gaze for more than a few seconds, her swollen bottom lip tucked between her teeth. Reaching forward, I swiped it out from them and held her face. "You can tell me anything. You know that, right?"

She took a deep breath. "I also lost my virginity that night."

My hand instantly dropped from her chin. I felt my eyebrows come together in a bundle. I blinked once, trying to sort out what she'd just said.

The only thing that came out of my mouth was, "What?"

Her hands wrung together in a bunch as she sat perched on her knees, atop my bed. My t-shirt hung loosely on her body. "I...I lost my virginity that night."

Breath seized in my chest. I almost couldn't talk. "So..." I tried to reel in my confusion. "So, you're telling me that you fucked someone that night...and then fucked me after?"

This doesn't sound like the Piper I know.

An intense bout of jealousy surged through my veins to the point that I jumped up from my bed. I wanted to punch something. I was angry. So angry. I wasn't sure I'd ever been so angry, and I really had absolutely no right.

"What!" Piper jumped up, too, and rushed over to me. Her soft hands landed on my skin and kept me in place. "No! It was you!"

I tipped my head backwards and stared at the ceiling, grinding my teeth. *What the fuck is going on?*

"You—" I cleared my throat, still staring at the ceiling. "You mean to tell me I took your virginity that night?" *For fuck's sake.* "Please tell me I'm wrong."

I mean, I wasn't going to lie; there was a fleeting second where I felt proud knowing I was the one to take her virginity, and it was much better than the alternative, but no. There was no fucking way.

Her hands slowly dropped from my arms, and I gave her my full attention. Her cheeks were blazing pink, the freckles outlining her nose even more evident. The red waves of her hair cascaded down past her shoulders as she barely nodded.

"*No,*" I said.

No. Fuck.

There were so many things that were wrong with this. So many things.

"You're mad."

"Yes, I'm mad!" I shouted.

She flinched, and I instantly reached out to her. I cupped my hands on her slender shoulders. She peeked up at me. "I'm not mad at you." Her face flickered with uncertainty. "I'm mad at myself. Piper, that sex was…" I gulped the air, looking away for a moment to collect myself. "That was rough sex. Hot and fast. That's not how your first time should have been! You deserved so much better. God, I probably hurt you."

Fuck. I felt like a complete fucking dick. I acted like I didn't even know her the day she walked into English Prep.

My hand came up, and I rubbed it down my face. "Fuck, I am so sorry."

Her mouth dropped. "You're sorry?"

I paced my room. "Yeah, I'm fucking sorry! I would have never fucked you that night if I knew it was your first time."

I continued to pace but stopped abruptly when she started to giggle. Her cheeks were still red. "Why are you laughing?"

She giggled a few more times and ran her fingers through her hair before smiling. *My God, she is beautiful.*

I didn't see that smile often. Not the real one. Things had been so serious lately. And emotional. And draining.

But this? This was something I could get used to.

Her hands fell down to her sides, and suddenly, I forgot about everything we were discussing when I truly took her in. She was standing there, smiling, with nothing but my t-shirt on.

She took my fucking breath away.

"Ollie." Her voice brought me back. "You are such a good guy." Her smile fell a little as her eyes glossed over. "I know I didn't know your mom, but she would have been so proud of the man you turned out to be."

We stayed locked on one another, and I felt so fucking much. My heart was roaring, and the only thing I wanted to do was pull her into me.

And I wasn't sure if I'd ever let her go.

CHAPTER THIRTY-NINE

PIPER

OLLIE'S ARMS felt like chains of protection. The beating of his heart sounded like a lullaby made just for me. The smell of his t-shirt was my favorite scent. Everything felt beautiful when I was with him.

"Can we just stay up here all night? Away from the party and everyone's watchful eyes?" My muffled words made him laugh with his arms locked around me.

His chin wobbled on top of my head. "There's honestly nowhere else I'd rather be right now."

Once he dropped his arms from my body, he pulled me over to his bed. We snuggled in under the covers, and I was back in my spot right in the crook of his arm. "I never thought I'd see the day where Ollie Powell didn't want to party."

His deep chuckle vibrated his chest along my cheek. "Neither did I, but I also never thought I'd take a girl's virginity, but here we are."

My face flamed. I never ever expected to tell him that

little tidbit, but there was something about Ollie that had me spilling all of my secrets, one by one. It was as if he had the password to my diary. A few weeks ago, I would have hated that, but now, I loved it.

It felt good to be real with him. To show him all of me.

"You know I'm going to be making up for that, right?"

"Make up for what?"

"For taking your virginity. For being so...feral."

I busted up laughing. "Feral?"

He pulled me away and drove his blue eyes into mine. "That was some serious sex. We were..."

"Passionate," I finished for him.

He half nodded. "It's hard to wrap my head around the idea that it was your first time. Are you sure?"

I gave him a look and playfully smacked him. "Of course I'm sure. I think I'd know."

He thought for a moment as I snuggled back up to my spot. I wondered for a moment if Hayley was wondering where I was, but chances were, she already knew.

She'd been rooting for Ollie and me since the beginning.

Ollie cleared his throat. "So, how many people has it been since?"

Embarrassment washed over me. *This conversation, really?*

"It's only been you."

I wasn't sure what I expected from him. Would he laugh? Be surprised? Not surprised? Maybe I wasn't good at sex? Maybe he could tell.

"Not possible."

"What? Yes, it is! It's not like I've had many dates—someone made sure of that." I raised an eyebrow, and he looked away, ashamed.

"There's no way you've only had sex twice. You're..." His voice was hoarse. "You're...your body..."

Where was he going with this? I suddenly got nervous. "Did I not do it right?"

He barked out a loud laugh, and I smiled instantly. "I fucking love you, Piper." His laughter quickly faded, and his face was nothing less than mortified. "I mean...I..."

I was holding back my own laugh as I pulled up again and crawled over his legs. The playfulness in his eyes disappeared, and he froze. His jaw was taut with tension. I could tell he was smashing his teeth together and his muscles ticked. My hands found the curve of his cheekbones. "Relax, I know you didn't really mean that you loved me like that." A sly grin curved on my face as I dipped my mouth to his. My lips hovered over his. "Not yet, anyway."

I expected him to laugh and say something jokingly back to me. But instead, his palms grabbed my waist, and he pulled me closer. A breathy sound came from me when he rubbed me over his hardness. Then, his lips were on mine. They moved slowly, but the kiss was deep. His fingers dug into my skin as mine found his hair.

I moaned as he moved me up and down over his sweatpants. He pulled away for a second. "You and I...we're going to do this whole thing right after next weekend."

"What thing?" Our lips were almost touching.

"You and me. In a relationship. Dates. Holding hands at school. Prom. You and me...you got that?"

His voice was soft but rough in all the right places. I swore I could feel his words gracing my skin.

"I got it."

Then, our lips were back on one another, ceasing the conversation.

The distant sound of vibrating woke me from a slumber. My body ached as I shifted my legs on top of Ollie's and peeled my eyes open. I instantly shut them again as the lamp on his desk almost blinded me. I felt Ollie move, too, and when I was finally able to peek out from under my eyelids, I saw him reading his phone with squinty eyes. He looked sleepy, and it made me smile.

What time was it?

I no longer heard the music thumping from downstairs, and it sounded quieter. But that didn't mean much when it came to an English Prep party. I was certain people were still here.

"Oh, fuck." Ollie snapped up, and I fell backwards onto the pillow.

"What?" I slowly eased up and rubbed my eyes before looking at his text. It was a group text between him, Christian, and their dad.

Dad: Nothing better be broken, and you boys better have that house spotless for Ms. Porter on Monday.

Ollie mumbled, "How the fuck does he know we had a party?"

Another text came in from Christian.

Christian: Have no idea what you're talking about.

Dad: The hell you do. I just saw you go to your room with Hayley. And I assume Ollie is in his room with her friend.

I almost choked on my spit. "Um...does your dad have cameras?"

Ollie pulled back, offended. "There's no fucking way. I'd know if there were cam—"

Another text.

Christian: Are you fucking spying on us?

His dad texted back immediately.

Dad: Cameras in the house. I installed them after Hayley was taken. I wanted to make sure you all were safe.

I felt Ollie tighten beside me. "Oh shit."

My hand fell to his arm. "What's wrong?" Ollie's face turned white. The muscles along his cheeks were tight. "Ollie? Are you okay?"

He turned his head to mine, and the look in his eye had my own heart beating fast. He looked afraid. Or sad. Maybe both.

"He knows."

My voice was softer. "He knows? He knows what?"

"He knows I know, Piper. That's why my birth certificate was missing. I go in their room all the time. I don't usually snoop like the day I had you come keep watch, but I go in there and sit." He dropped his head. "It helps me feel closer to my mom. At peace."

How was it that I could actually feel his sadness? His sadness became mine, and I was bleeding out watching him. His broad shoulders were caved in; his head was low. His breathing was choppy as I pushed his phone out of his hand and made him lie down.

Ollie was lying on his back, and I did the same, falling softly onto the pillow behind my head. I intertwined my fingers with his and held his hand tight. "Then, that means it's time to face the truth, Ollie."

He sounded pained. "I don't know if I want to know the truth."

We both stared at the ceiling above our heads. "I think you do want to know the truth; you just don't want to face the outcome." I squeezed his hand. "I'll be here, though. You won't be alone."

He squeezed back. "This is going to open up a lot of shit.

Christian is going to flip out, knowing there are more secrets buried about our mom."

"Buried secrets are never a good thing, Ollie. I think we can both attest to this."

I felt him look at me, so I did the same. He shrugged. "They're not all bad. I mean, secrets brought us together, right?"

I smiled. "Yeah, they did."

He turned away, and we continued to lie there, holding hands, lost in our own thoughts.

And that was how I remembered falling asleep, hand in hand.

CHAPTER FORTY

OLLIE

W HEN I WALKED into English Prep on Monday morning, I was on the prowl. Eric and Christian were behind me as I all but jogged to the front entrance. My hand landed on the willowy handle, and I jumped over the threshold.

I knew Piper was already here. Little Miss Sunshine always got here early, and Hayley was usually right there beside her. What they did before the bell rang each morning, I had no idea, but I was ready to see her.

Piper and I stayed up in my room for the rest of the party on Saturday. When Sunday morning rolled around, she and Hayley had dipped out early, and I knew it was because Hayley wanted the details.

Christian, Eric, and I—along with a few underclassmen who desperately wanted to be in our inner circle—cleaned the house. My dad texted a few times, reminding us that we needed the house "fucking spotless" before our housekeeper showed up today.

I threw all my anxiety and frustration into scrubbing the

kitchen and throwing out beer cans with as much force as I used to throw a football on the field. Christian questioned my behavior, asking why I was so pissed when I'd spent the entire night with Piper, but I brushed him off.

My phone morphed into a heavy boulder in my hand every time I looked back at the text my father had sent. My father had to have suspected that I knew he wasn't my real dad with as many times as I'd gone into their room.

I promised myself I'd deal with my own drama after Saturday, which was going to be a whole ordeal. My jaw snapped closed as I pushed the rising stress down. My throat was constricting, but I grabbed onto my backpack straps and continued walking down the hall.

I found her instantly. Piper was pulling books out of her locker as Hayley was leaning back with her foot propped up behind her. She was laughing at something Hayley had said and shaking those long locks out.

The stress was gone almost instantaneously. *There she was.* We hadn't discussed what really laid between us. Though, Saturday night was a game changer. We were no longer dancing around hidden secrets and hushed truths. We weren't teetering over the invisible line drawn between us.

We were simply *us,* and that was just how it was.

As I stood back and stared at her laughing and full of happiness, I didn't really care if she wanted to pretend Saturday didn't happen. That wasn't an option any longer.

I was in this deep.

Hayley glanced up and moved her attention from me to my brother. She smiled shyly at Christian and mumbled something to Piper before pushing off the locker and coming over.

Piper's head flew up and over to me, and I grabbed onto my backpack straps even tighter.

Hey there, Piper. Remember me?

Her eyes were wide as she froze in place. Her hand was still half inside her locker, resting on one of her books as her lips fell apart. I strode over to her, and even though everyone was pouring into the hallway, gathering their own books, it might as well have been only her in front of me.

"Hey," I said, sliding up beside her. Piper straightened her shoulders at the last second and ran a hand down her plaid skirt. She flipped her hair over her shoulder and then continued gathering her books.

"Hey, what's up?"

I held back a laugh as I rested my shoulder against the lockers. "Is that how you think this is gonna go?" Piper kept digging through her locker. Her bright cheeks were clearly evident, even through the fallen strands of her hair. "I don't think so, Piper."

She slowly brought her books to her chest and peered up at me with those forest-green eyes. I swore they grew even greener under the fluorescent lights.

"What do you mean?"

"Everyone already knows there's something going on between us. You know that, right?"

She sucked her bottom lip in her teeth, and my eyes zeroed right in. I knew Piper was being innocent with her lip playing peek-a-boo in between her teeth, but I really wished she would stop. It was hot.

Piper moved her gaze around the hallway, and I knew without even looking up, that all eyes were on us. Which was perfect. Let them see me claim her.

"Everyone is looking at us," she whispered as her head dipped. Piper wasn't used to the attention. She was used to being on the sidelines, being nearly invisible. She liked it that way, too.

My hands dropped from my backpack, and they found her waist. I pulled her toward me. The only thing between us were her books that were clung tightly to her chest. "Good," I whispered. "Let them see this."

"See wh—"

My mouth was on hers in a flash. The clawing anxiety that had left its scratch marks on my back yesterday instantly healed. The softness of her lips, the warmness of her tongue —it did things to me. Things I couldn't even put into words.

Once I pulled back, she gasped for air. Her eyes were wide, and that fire was burning ever so hot between us.

I reached up and tucked a stray hair behind Piper's ear, and her eyes glistened. "That. That's what I wanted them to see."

A ghost of a smile fell on her lips. "People have seen you kiss a girl before, Ollie. What are you trying to prove to them?"

I cupped my hand around her cheek. "I'm not trying to prove anything to them, Piper. I'm trying to prove it to you."

Piper didn't mumble a single word, and I hated that I couldn't tell what she was feeling. A bout of unease came over me. I'd never laid so much out on the line before. I'd never had a girlfriend. I had fucked girls, kissed them under the bleachers, and taken them in the locker room, but had a girlfriend? Never. It'd never even crossed my mind. Until now.

Piper waited a few more seconds before she reached up on her tiptoes and placed her lips on mine. It was a soft kiss, a chaste one, but when she pulled back and smiled, I was in awe.

She adjusted her books against her chest, and before she grabbed my hand and walked us over to our friends, she whispered, "I guess I just claimed you, too."

Our fingers intertwined.

"But, Ollie?"

"Yeah?" I asked, glancing down at her.

"Don't break my heart."

Pride swelled in my chest. "Never."

But as we walked hand and hand down the hall, the voice in the back of my head reminded me that Saturday was only a few days away.

I was going to break her heart. Just not in the way she thought.

The door to my bedroom slammed open, and I snapped my neck over to my brother. The room was lit by the lamp on my desk as I worked on a paper that was due three days ago. Thankfully, my charm had worked on Ms. Carpenter, because she let out an exasperated sigh behind a smile when I told her I'd have it turned in by tomorrow.

"We need to talk." Christian strode into my room with his arms crossed over his chest. It'd been a while since he'd pulled the I'm-your-big-bro-and-our-dad-is-absent role. But here we were.

"What?" I mumbled, rereading the bullshit line I'd just written regarding the Republican Party.

"What is going on with you? Why are you avoiding Dad so much?"

I stilled, staring at the word Republican for so long it started to look wrong.

"Is it because of the races on Saturday? And yeah, let's discuss that as well. Piper told Hayley that you said you've got it all under control. What exactly is your plan?"

For fuck's sake. This was exactly why I didn't want Christian involved. He needed to be in control at all times, and it was frustrating. For once, he just needed to leave me be.

Just as the thought came through, I regretted it. Christian was a good brother; he always had been, and he deserved better than having me as his brother. I couldn't even be honest with him.

I placed my pen down and leaned back in my chair and acted relaxed. "Can you chill? I have everything under control. Tank is a little bitch, and he's going to wish he never started these races in the first place."

Christian propped himself along the wall and crossed his arms over his chest. "How long have you been racing?"

I fought to keep my eyes on him and my face unmoving. I shrugged. "A little while. I was bored."

Christian pushed off the wall quickly, shaking his head. "That's stupid fucking behavior. Imagine if you were to get caught! You could kiss that football scholarship—that we both know you're getting—away."

I said nothing, and he continued.

"And now, you're stuck in a shitty situation without an out. How is this going to go on Saturday? What? You're going to race one more time, Tank will get back the rest of the money *if* you win the race, and then..."

"Like I said, I have it under control." My voice was beginning to rise. "For once, let me fix my own shit."

His face flinched. "What does that mean?"

My desk chair flew backwards as I stood. "It means you can't always swoop in and save me from reckless behavior. I know I've gotten myself in a stupid position. I fucking know Tank isn't someone to mess around with. I'm not as immature and naive as you think, Christian."

My voice was rising to higher octaves, and I could tell Christian was surprised. Shit, even I was surprised. I didn't lose my temper, but lately, things were piling up, and I was at the bottom of the pile. Part of me wanted to tell him about our dad, but the other part knew I needed to hold onto the secret for just a little while longer. One thing at a time.

"Fine." Christian dropped his gaze for a moment before

leveling me with a glare. "But Dad is on his way home, just for the night, and he said to make sure you're here. He wants to talk to you, and he said you keep avoiding him."

Fuck.

My nostrils flared. "So, what? Are you gonna hold me down until he gets here?" I chuckled, dropping back into my chair.

"No," he answered sharply. "It's been you and me against the world since Mom died. I'm not changing that now, even though he's trying to make amends. I'm not going to stop being there to protect you, even though you're pushing me away. I know the feeling all too well."

Christian: the king of shutting people out. I guess we did have something in common, even if not the same father.

"So, go now if you want to avoid him."

If I left, I was weak. But if I stayed, I was stupid. I wasn't prepared to deal with this right now. Not when I had Saturday to worry about. So, instead of being strong and facing this head-on, I walked over to my bed and snatched my keys, wallet, and phone.

Christian's hand clamped down on my arm as I began to walk past him. "You know I'm always on your side, right?" His tone was almost pained.

I nodded once as I brushed past him.

I wanted to say more, or maybe even mutter an apology, but I couldn't. Nothing would come out. I didn't feel like myself. Stress was rising again, and I didn't like that. I needed something to distract me, or at least to lessen the load. I needed someone to hold my feet on the ground until I started erasing my problems, one by one.

And there was only one person that came to mind.

CHAPTER FORTY-ONE

PIPER

I KEPT TOSSING AND TURNING, my comfy duvet all bundled up in a heaping mess at the bottom of my bed, as I stopped myself from texting Ollie.

Monday passed by quickly, and by the end of the day, everyone in school knew that he and I were a thing. Rumors spread like wildfire; the cheerleaders all stared at me like curious kittens; teachers eyed me with that look in their eye that read, *He's gonna break your little heart.* And maybe he would. Ollie's reputation was stellar in most aspects, but he'd never ever been in a relationship. Then again, neither had I, so what did that say? But apparently, both Powell brothers being "taken" blew everyone's mind. It kind of blew mine, too. A few months ago, I'd never ever imagined I'd be kissed by Ollie Powell in the hallway, or the lunch room, or out in the courtyard before climbing in my car to drive home, but here I was, living the dream.

At this point, part of my life was a dream and the other part a nightmare.

The mere thought of Saturday gave me goosebumps.

Tank gave me a bad feeling. His dark, wandering eyes and pitch of his voice loomed in the back of my head anytime I started to relax. Jason had never left my mind. Even when I was angry with him after I found him in Tank's bathroom, I was still worried about him. I wasn't sure what Saturday would bring. Would there be no hard feelings between my brother and Tank after the money was paid back? That just didn't sound right to me. Tank was a bad guy. I didn't trust him.

I did trust Ollie, though, and for now, that was enough.

Grabbing my phone, I lay back on my pillows and scrolled through my text messages.

I smiled, re-reading the ones from Ollie, but grimaced at the ones with my parents.

They'd texted over the weekend, asking if I'd received my college acceptance letters yet.

I hadn't, but I did end up sending them a picture of me and Hayley in our dresses before we went to the winter formal.

Neither one of them responded.

I glanced at the picture, making sure it had sent. It had.

The innocent girl inside of me that longed for attention from her parents was still buried underneath the fiercely independent girl I was now, and she was hurt.

A depressed breath left me as I pulled my phone in close, pushing the pain away, and then I placed it on the side of my table and put my back to it.

As soon as my eyes closed, my phone vibrated on the table. My eyes flew open, and I turned back around and grabbed it.

Ollie.

It was like he knew I was upset.

"Hello?" I answered.

"Hey." Ollie's voice was hushed, but I could hear the rumble of his Charger in the background.

"Hi," I said, trying to hold back a smile.

"Your parents aren't home, right?"

A hot trickle of anticipation rained over my head. "Right. It's just me."

Ollie answered quickly. "Good, I'm pulling up. Come hang out with me."

Sitting up in bed, I pushed my hair behind my ears and climbed out of my bed. Bright orbs of light shone through the limbs of the tree outside of my balcony, and I smashed my lips together to control my excitement. "Let me get dressed, and I'll be right down!"

Ollie's voice dipped. "Let you get dressed? What exactly are you wearing?"

I rolled my eyes, shoving my pj shorts down. "I'm wearing my pjs, you perv."

He laughed and then hung up the phone. I shook my head, smiling, as I continued to pull my skinny jeans on and an old soup kitchen volunteer t-shirt over my head.

The rumble of his car purred when I opened the front door and disarmed the alarm. His maroon Charger's hood glistened from the light of the moon, and when I pulled open the door and saw Ollie leaning back in the driver's seat with his hat on backwards, I fought a grin. Butterflies swarmed my belly. Being near Ollie suddenly had me feeling like I was on top of the world. I couldn't believe I'd pretended to hate him for so long. Time was robbed from me.

"Hey," I said shyly, sliding into the passenger side. The door slammed shut, and Ollie's hand was suddenly wrapping around my face. He brought my lips to his and kissed me like he hadn't seen me in years.

My back arched, my chest puffing out to hit his. I almost

climbed over the center console just to be closer to him, but he let go at the last minute.

He sent a look my way that made me shiver. "Sorry, I just really needed to kiss you."

I smiled. My cheeks felt like hot embers from a burning fire. "Don't be sorry."

He placed his hand on the stick shift. His sharp jaw was all I could focus on. "I didn't call you for a booty call, though. That's not what this is."

Part of me was disappointed. "Then, what is this?"

He smiled in my direction, and I swore, even though it was pitch black out besides the glow of the moon, I felt like I was touched by the sun itself. Ollie's smile was my favorite thing about him. "I'm taking you out. What do you want to eat? What's your favorite food?" He sighed and shook his head. "I feel like I should know this about you."

I laughed and put my seatbelt on, hearing it click into place. "We know all the nitty-gritty details about each other, not the light and fluffy stuff that *most* people learn while in a relationship."

He smirked as he crept onto the main road. "And that's exactly why we already have an advantage in this. No hidden secrets."

His smile fell briefly, but it was back before I could dissect it. "Now tell me, what's your favorite food?"

I laughed, looking out the window. "Well..."

He gave me a side glance. "Don't tell me."

"What?" I giggled again.

"Fucking chicken nuggets?"

A loud laugh came from me as he grinned. "Did Hayley get you stuck on those? She did, didn't she?"

I nodded, relaxing into the seat. "What can I say? They're good."

"I had never seen two girls eat so much before that night."

Ollie was referring to the night that Hayley got attacked at a football game. He and I rushed to the nearest pharmacy, and we spent over one hundred dollars on medical supplies in an attempt to clean her wounds. That was one night he and I had worked together instead bickering back and forth.

"Do you remember that night?" he asked, driving down the road.

I checked my phone and made sure I didn't have any missed calls from my parents. After the party at Ollie's on Saturday, I began checking my house for cameras, too. It wouldn't have surprised me if my parents started putting cameras up in our house to see if Jason was snooping around. I didn't find any, but I was still a little paranoid.

I came out of my thoughts, putting my phone back down. "Of course I remember that night. It was terrifying. It scared me to see Hayley like that."

Ollie nodded as he turned his blinker on. The sound of some band was drumming through his speakers. "I was in awe of you that night."

My head turned to him, surprised. "Me? Why?"

He glanced at me for a quick second. "I don't know. I guess because you acted fast, and you weren't letting on how frazzled you were. How frazzled we all were. You cleaned up her cuts like you were a trained nurse or something."

I sunk back into the leather seat. "That's because I was used to it."

"What do you mean?"

"I mean"—I tucked a strand of hair behind my ear, staring at Ollie's grip on his stick shift—"I've cleaned Jason up many, many times. Cleaning wounds is my specialty."

"As is caring for others." Ollie's voice was soft and comforting. I peeked up at him and gave him a tiny smile. "You did a good job hiding that part of your life."

I nodded. "That's what my parents taught me to do."

Ollie's hand left his stick shift, and he grabbed mine, giving it a squeeze before letting go and shifting once more. "Well, you don't have to do that anymore. Not with me. Okay?"

A lightness filled my body. My heart grew with his words as if he were climbing inside my chest and making it bigger with his very hands.

The big things in my life, the scary ones, seemed a little smaller with his hand in mine. Things felt right when I was with Ollie.

But for some reason, after we ate our body weight in chicken nuggets and he dropped me back at home, the anxiety was back.

Things felt right yet so wrong at the same time.

CHAPTER FORTY-TWO

OLLIE

THE PIT in my stomach grew deeper as each day passed. A dark cloud was following me around school, to my house...it even hovered over my head when I'd text Piper late at night.

Tomorrow was Saturday, and although I had all the Ts crossed and Is dotted, I still felt sick. I'd questioned if I was doing the right thing, but I wasn't even sure what was right anymore. I knew very well that Tank was a piece of shit who didn't give a fuck about anyone or anything besides himself. He was money-hungry and self-righteous, and he needed to be put in his place.

He fucked with Piper, and I wasn't okay with that. And there was no way in hell I'd be tethered to him for any longer than I needed to be. I wouldn't be racing for him after Saturday; he just didn't know it.

An elephant sat on my chest as I ignored the two notifications on my phone from my dad. I drummed my fingers over the mahogany table in the school library, the rich wood even richer underneath the hanging light. Books lined the shelves, one by one, as I gazed in front of me.

I heard the tick of the clock in the background, the minutes of study hall passing by painfully slow, which did nothing but heighten my rising anxiety.

You're doing the right thing.

But was I?

My intentions were clear, but I wasn't sure they'd appear that way.

I was trying to be a good guy. I was trying to do the right thing and protect the people I cared about: Piper, Christian, the relationship my father and Christian recently formed.

But my hold on being a good guy was slipping. Things were beginning to eat away at me. I felt lost. I was tense. My teeth slid together and ground on top of one another. Sometimes I did this: I lost the battle between good and bad, right and wrong. Maybe it was the side of me that I didn't really recognize yet. Maybe it was the blood that ran through my veins that had me halting and rethinking who I wanted to be.

I liked being the good guy, the happy Powell brother, the one that made people laugh. But other times, I liked to step out of that box and toe the line of being something else. I wanted to dip into the other side—the side that made me want to plummet my fist into Tank's face repeatedly until he slipped into unconsciousness. The side that wanted to hunt down Piper's parents and scold them for not caring enough about their daughter. I wanted to ring Jason's neck until he became submissive and got the help he needed instead of filling his veins with drugs and hurting his sister in the process.

My breathing grew harsher as I pressed my back against the wooden chair, my fingers still drumming agitatedly over the table. A hot sweat started to coat my brow as I fought internally to stay my calm, even-tempered self. I needed to get into that level-headed, everything-will-be-fine mindset.

I shrugged off my blazer and threw it over the next chair. I loosened the tie around my neck.

Not helping.

My eyes found one of the underclassmen boys that I'd played football with last semester. *Kyle? Was that his name?*

My chin tipped in his direction, and his brows shot up. *Yes, you. Come here.*

The freshman slowly stood up from his chair and walked over to me on wobbly legs. I felt better already. My lips twitched as I scribbled down something on a piece of paper. Once I folded it in half, I peered up at the boy. He had thick, black-framed glasses that weren't even sitting straight on his face.

"I need you to do me a solid. Can you do that for me?"

The boy nodded his head vigorously, and I was almost afraid his glasses would fall off the tip of his nose. This was a benefit of being a Powell—of being Christian's brother. I may have been a grade younger than him and Eric, but I was still worshiped just the same. "I need you to deliver this note to Mrs. Sampson's class. Just hand it to her. That's all."

His hand shook as he reached out to grab it. *Jesus. Why is he so scared?*

"You good?" I asked, genuinely concerned.

He looked surprised at first but slowly nodded, eyeing me suspiciously. "Who do I say it's from? Who is it for?"

"It's all in the note, but if she asks, say it's from Head-master Walton."

His thick brows furrowed, but he nodded like a soldier receiving an urgent message from their general. I almost saluted him before he walked away.

A lighter breath left my chest as I stood up and began walking past the several rows of book-lined shelves.

Once I got to the back row of history books, the ones in the *XYZ* shelving, I turned around and leaned against their spines. I began rolling my sleeves up to my forearms, my heart pounding.

God. I didn't like this. I truly felt out of control, a little lost, and I was suddenly regretting keeping everything to myself—the plan for tomorrow, my family shit. My world felt a little tilted...until I saw her.

I saw the shine from her hair as she walked through the arched doors of the library. Her flawless heart-shaped face was stricken with confusion as she searched for Headmaster Walton, per what was written in the note.

Four-Eyes Freshman tried to breeze past her in a scurry, but when her hand landed on his arm, he jolted back, almost falling over his own two feet.

She said something to him, and when he answered, her eyes squinted for a moment before she dropped her hand and hurriedly searched around the library.

When her eyes landed on me, I shot her my best grin, beckoning her to come over. The freshman was long gone, probably worshiping the arm that Piper had touched moments ago.

Once she was in front of me, I felt the wrath of her anger. "Oliver Powell!" Her hands flew to her hips, resting along her plaid skirt. She glanced behind her as she lowered her voice. "What are you doing sending me a note in the middle of class, posing as Headmaster Walton? Mrs. Sampson was so confused!"

My hands found my pockets. I shrugged. "I needed to see you."

Her anger slowly resolved. The lines on her face grew soft. "Why? Is everything okay?" She took a step toward me and whispered. "What's wrong?"

Every bone in my body broke with the need to tell her

everything. To spill everything I had locked away. I wanted to be vulnerable with her, tell her how afraid I was that this shit with my father was going to mess up what little family I had left. How I was afraid he'd taint the memory of my mother even more. How sick I felt that, after tomorrow, she might hate me for taking her brother down, too.

But instead, I grabbed her by the waist and pulled her in close. A gasp left her pink lips as I moved us further into the last aisle of the library.

The corner of the library was dark, the hanging light with intricate designs above it was turned off. We were tucked away where no one could see us—not unless someone was looking for a particular book, at least.

"Ollie." There were worry lines along her forehead, and my hand reached out to smooth them. "Is it Tank? Are you afraid tomorrow isn't going to go how you want? We have the rest of the money from the party, right?"

"Shh," I whispered, placing my finger on her mouth. "Everything is fine. I just wanted to see you."

I could barely see the gold flecks in her green eyes, but I knew they were filled with worry.

"I can tell when you're lying, you know." Her voice was soft as it floated around me. She inched closer to me, and her chest pressed along mine. "But I'm here for you like you are for me, okay? What do you need?"

God damn. I think I might love her.

"You're all I need," I said before dipping my head down to hers. Our lips hovered for a moment before she erased the space between us. Her tongue darted in, and my hands tightened around her waist.

As she sucked on my bottom lip, I grew hungry. Maybe it was that intense need to distract myself from tomorrow, or maybe it was just *her*. Either way, I was lost until her lips were on mine.

My fingers pulled her blouse out of her skirt, and the heat from her skin all but burned my hands. The strands of my hair were tugged as her fingers tore through, and I wished I could say I forgot we were in the library, tucked back behind rows of books, but I knew very well where we were. I just didn't care.

One of my hands left her as she grabbed onto my bicep and gave it a squeeze. I held back a raspy growl and parted her legs with my knee. My fingers itched to find her warmth. My blood was screaming inside my veins with anticipation.

Piper. Yes. Fuck yes.

Her skin was smooth as I trailed my finger up her inner thigh. Both of our heavy breathing filled the abandoned corner, and when I found her wet panties, I pulled away from her mouth and shut my eyes.

A hot swallow went down my throat as I inched her panties away from her swollen clit. One finger dipped in, and she threw her head back and let out a soft gasp. Her pussy tightened around my finger, and I was three seconds from pulling out and putting my dick inside her.

But soon, I lost all control of my inhibitions as Piper started moving her hips over my hand, riding it like it was what she was born to do.

My finger moved in and out as she curled her hips. Her hair was falling down her back as her head was thrown back. It was the hottest thing I'd ever seen—Piper letting go, standing there in her hot, school-girl uniform, knee-high tights, riding my hand until a moan left her mouth. I hurriedly flipped us around and pressed her against the bookshelf, giving her back something to rest along as my other hand left her waist and cupped her chin.

My lips were a breath away from her ear. "Shh. Bite my hand if you have to, but stay quiet."

Her eyes flared open, and something about me whispering

in her ear set her off, because soon, her teeth were sinking into my hand, and her pussy walls were clenched onto my finger.

My stomach dropped out from below as I watched her take in the ecstasy like a champ, keeping her moans quiet.

I was so proud that she'd just let go like that in the library, and I was seconds from telling her so, but she disappeared from my sight and landed on her knees.

"What are you doing?" I hissed as her deft fingers found my belt.

She put her finger up to her lips and gave me a coy smile. I almost choked when her lips wrapped around my dick.

Her warm mouth coated me as she moved up and down. My eyes shut as I grabbed onto the ledge of the bookshelf. My hands might as well have broken the damn thing with the force I put behind my grip. I tried to keep myself in line so I didn't smother her with thrusting my hips, but it felt so good that I had a hard time keeping control.

When I glanced down and saw Piper peeking up at me, all sexy yet innocent, I felt the tug deep within my core. *Holy fuck.* A hot trickle of sweat fell down my chest as she sucked harder, and suddenly, I was biting my lip to keep quiet as she milked me dry.

Her lips stayed wrapped around me until the very last drop, and my mouth fell open from pure bliss when she popped up and wiped her swollen lips with the back of her hand.

"*Jesus Christ,*" I breathed out, gripping her body and pulling her in close.

Her flushed cheeks rose as she opened her lips to say something, but the bell sounded above our head. A rushed breath left her. "Oh my God, Ollie. We're in school!"

My head tilted, dumbfounded. "I know."

"I just gave my first blow job in the library! What has gotten into me?"

Her first blow job? Holy shit.

My lips twitched as I brushed by the thought. "Well...me. I'm what's gotten into you...literally."

She playfully smacked my chest before she began tucking her blouse back into her skirt. "It scares me how wrapped up I get in you. I forget my name, and apparently, I forget where I am." She glanced around the library and shook her head. "You're the only thing I see when I'm with you."

Piper was still trying to put herself together as I stood back with my pants already buttoned. I quickly reached out and ran my hands through her hair, taming the wild mess. "It's like that for me, too."

"It is?"

Precisely why I needed to see you. I nodded. "It's always been that way, Piper. It's you I see. And nothing else." She flashed me a soft smile, and I felt my chest split open.

"Come on," she said as she tugged on my hand. "We'll be late for our next class."

I followed after her, letting her lead me through the book-lined shelves. I couldn't help but feel the anxiety slipping in again as I thought about tomorrow.

It would be here soon, and there was nothing I could do to change it.

CHAPTER FORTY-THREE

PIPER

I STOOD BACK beside Hayley and Christian as the crowd grew crazier. The moon was creeping up past the lined trees with the sun soon setting behind us.

Nerves piled up inside my belly. I picked at the strands of ripped denim on my jeans as I watched Tank throw his head back and laugh. Sky was standing off to the side, looking bored, with her arms hanging down by her sides. My gaze shifted to my brother right beside her. He looked okay. Skinny, as usual, but he didn't have any noticeable marks on him. I did note that he appeared nervous, maybe because he knew tonight was the last race. Maybe he was anxious to see how this would all play out.

He wasn't the only one.

I knew there were a lot of missing pieces when it came to my brother and Tank. I didn't know the whole story between them, and I wasn't sure I wanted to know after tonight. I just wanted this to be over with.

Hayley nudged me. "There's Ollie."

Ollie casually climbed out of his Charger, sporting his nice jeans and gray t-shirt. His golden strands stood out underneath the setting sun and all but gleamed their shine in my direction. He pulled his hat on backwards, and my heart jumped. I liked the preppy, school-boy look he sported at school, especially when he took off his school jacket and rolled up his sleeves, but this look was even better. He went from sophisticated prep student with a dazzling smile to a bad boy in three seconds flat.

"Is he going to tell Tank he has the rest of the money? And that tonight will be the last race?"

Christian turned and glanced at Hayley, shrugging. "I'm not sure. He has been pretty secretive lately." Christian angled his sharp jaw in my direction. "Do you know what's going on with him?"

The nerves were back. My stomach was queasy. "No. He just kept telling me that everything was handled."

Christian's eyes grew darker. Something was up. I could feel it in the air. It was tight and full of unanswered questions.

I bounced my attention between Ollie, Tank, and my brother. Tank seemed completely unbothered by whatever Ollie was saying, even patting him on the back with a slimy smile. *Weird.* My brother stood back, observing the two, but when I saw him catch Ollie's eye, he nodded—just barely, but I noticed it.

"Something isn't right," I mumbled under my breath.

Hayley's voice was low. "I know. I can feel it, too. I've got a knack for these things."

My thoughts were all over the place. I trusted Ollie. I did. I thought I always had, but he was off. I knew it. Yesterday, in the library, I sensed something wasn't right with him, but instead of pushing it, I let it go.

And if I knew anything about Ollie, it was that he was

awfully good at looking okay on the outside when he wasn't on the inside.

As soon as he was finished talking to Tank, he made his way over to us. A few people close by were watching us, probably because we all stood out, being from English Prep, but I ignored them when Ollie appeared.

"Everything good?" Christian pulled Hayley in close, draping his arms around the front of her body.

Ollie didn't say anything. Instead, he stood in front of me and stared with a tight jaw.

"Ollie? What did Tank say? Did you tell him this was the last race? Did you give him the money we got from the party? Is Jason good to go?" I was rambling. Something felt wrong. I looked past Ollie's shoulder, seeing Jason still standing beside Tank, looking even more nervous. His thumb was pulled into his mouth as he gnawed on his nail.

"No. I haven't told him anything yet." Ollie's voice was curt, unlike him.

I took a step closer, canceling out the chaos around us. "What's going on?" My legs were wobbling, the ground suddenly unsteady underneath me.

His Adam's apple bobbed before he forced the words out. "I'm sorry."

I felt stripped. "Ollie."

His eyes were like glass as he looked away. "You know I care about you, right?"

My hand wrapped around his sturdy chin, and I forced him to look at me. My breath was stolen from my chest when we locked eyes. Ollie was upset. Sad. Broken. Worried. It was like I was looking into a mirror.

"What's going on?"

"Answer me," he demanded.

"Of course I know you care about me." I gestured to the races behind his back. "Look at where we are. You're here because of me." Ollie brought his forehead down to mine as I heard a car start up behind us. I knew he was up next. The final race. He assured me that it wasn't a hard one and that Tank actually wanted him to win this one to show people that last week *wasn't* a cheat, but of course, I knew it was.

"Just remember that, okay? Remember I'd do anything for you. I'd do anything to keep you safe and out of harm's way."

Ollie's arms wrapped around me, and it felt like a warm blanket draping over my body. For a second, I let myself fall into his grasp, relishing in the calmness I felt with him being so close, but then he pulled away, and I was torn in half.

"You're not okay. Something is wrong. And I know Jason knows something, too. I can tell."

Ollie ignored me, but I kept a hold on his hand. He glanced at Christian. "Get her out of here when shit hits the fan."

"What?" I shouted. "No! I'm not going anywhere without you."

Ollie wouldn't look at me.

Christian asked, "Do you know what you're doing, Ol?"

Ollie nodded confidently. He pulled out his phone and slapped it into my hand as someone called his name. "Hold on to my phone for me. My dad is going to be calling shortly."

"Ollie!" I demanded again, begging him to look me in the eye. He wouldn't. He was avoiding my gaze, and I could tell it was hurting him.

"Ollie." Hayley left Christian and walked to stand beside me. "Seriously, do you know what you're doing? Tank is not someone you should mess with. Trust me on this."

Ollie's hand slowly fell out of mine. "I know exactly what type of person he is."

"Ollie," I urged again, beginning to feel defeated.

Instead of looking at me, he looked right past my head. "Eric, you know what to do?"

"I got you." I craned my neck back and saw him standing behind me.

When I turned back around, Ollie finally met my eye for a quick second, but then he squeezed his eyes shut and quickly turned around and began heading to his car.

No!

I refused to let him do something that was clearly hurting him. I didn't care about the consequences at this point.

His phone was clutched in my hand when I reached him. I threw my arms around his back and buried my head in his shirt.

"Stop whatever you're about to do, Ollie." My voice was near breaking, and his entire body tightened.

"Ollie, you're up!" someone yelled from a distance.

Ollie turned around in my grasp and hugged me tight. When he wrapped his hand around my face, pressing it to his chest, I could hear his heartbeat. It was hard and fast as it echoed through my ears.

"I love you. Just remember that." He bent down and kissed my forehead and peeled me away from his body. "Go. Now."

Anger sliced through me. "No. I am not leaving."

Ollie groaned, tightening his jaw again. The muscles were jumping back and forth along his temples. He eyed someone from behind before landing back on me. I felt doom approaching. "Don't make a scene, Piper. Please." He was all but begging me. "I need you to trust me."

I do. I do trust you.

Christian appeared at my side along with Hayley. They didn't move a muscle as we all watched Ollie walk to his Charger. My stomach fell to the ground with a thud. I turned and spotted Jason several yards away. Eric was now standing beside him. *What the hell is going on?*

"Why is Tank getting in Ollie's car?" I snapped my attention back to the Charger. Ollie's arm was hanging out of the driver's side as he threw his head back and laughed at something Tank said—as if everything was fine.

Keep your friends close, but your enemies closer.

Ollie's phone vibrated in my hand. I saw several incoming texts from his father.

I swiped open the screen and read the conversation.

Ollie: I know you know I know.

Dad: Which is why I've been trying to talk to you for over a week.

Ollie: So it's true...you're not my real father.

Dad: I'm just as much your dad as I am Christian's, no matter what.

Ollie: I just need to know something.

Dad: Ollie. I'm on my way home. We need to sit down and talk this through.

Ollie: Even though I'm not yours, will you still help me when I'm in trouble?

Dad: Ollie, you are mine.

Ollie: Answer the fucking question. Please. I need to know that when things get messy, you'll be there.

Dad: Always. Now get home so we can talk. I need to explain.

Ollie: Call Michael in twenty minutes and tell him it's time.

Dad: What? Michael who? The family lawyer?

Dad: Ollie?

Dad: Stop ignoring my phone calls. What is going on?

Dad: Son, are you in trouble?

Cars revved in the distance, and when I looked up, Ollie was staring directly at me. He knew I had read the messages, and he knew I was seconds from losing it. He shook his head slightly and mouthed the word, "*No.*"

"Oh my God," I whispered. "What is he planning?"

I heard Hayley ask Christian, "Why does your dad keep calling you?"

"I don't know!" Christian sounded agitated, but I kept my attention trained on that maroon Charger. "I don't know what the hell Ollie is doing. He's been so goddamn closed off. Won't tell me anything. I've been trying to give him space like you said, but something isn't right, Hayley."

"No. Something isn't right at all," I mumbled, my hand covering my mouth. "This is all my fault."

I looked down at Jason and met his eye. Why did I let him drag me into this? Why did I keep fighting for him? Was his safety worth mine? Were his life choices worth the destruction of mine? Or Ollie's?

My head snapped back when I heard a girly, high-pitched voice counting down for the race. Panic seized my heart. My heart very well might have stopped beating. I felt my legs begin to take off, but I was quickly pulled back by strong arms.

"Piper!" Hayley got in front of my face as Christian held my arms. "You're about to get run over!"

"He's going to get in trouble, Hayley!" My voice was rushed. "I am not letting him take the wrap for something he should have never had any part in!"

I looked past her as I heard the cars taking off. Dust flew in every direction, taillights fading as everyone hollered.

"What do you mean he's going to get in trouble?"

Christian continued to pull me back by my arms as people ran out onto the gravel road to watch the cars disappear. I almost shoved the phone in his face, but at the last second, I remembered that Ollie still hadn't told him about being half-brothers. "He told your dad to call the lawyer!"

"What?" His hold began to loosen, and I was seconds

from running to Jason to demand he tell me what was going on. But then I heard a frantic shout. "COPS!"

My hand shot to my mouth. *Oh my God.*

"Run!" Hayley grabbed onto my hand, and we ran after Christian, the tall grass whipping around my ankles.

I glanced back once, and through the billowing dust, I watched as Jason ran beside Eric.

Confusion slapped me in the face as Hayley and I tumbled into Christian's Charger. It started immediately, and we were down the grassy field within seconds. Red and blue flashing lights swarmed the area in the distance, and when I flipped back around, my heart flying through my chest, I pulled Ollie's phone out. I re-read the messages between him and his dad but paused when I heard Christian curse under his breath.

My heart stopped at the scene we were passing. There was Ollie and Tank, along with the other driver, standing outside their cars with their hands above their heads.

Guilt fell over me like an avalanche. It was cold and painful, and I hated myself for getting him into this mess.

I pressed "Call" on the phone and felt nothing but remorse, even with Ollie looking completely unphased as he had cuffs slapped on his wrist. Tank was fuming; he wasn't complying with the police, and that seemed to make Ollie even happier.

"Hello? Ollie?"

My voice cracked. "Mr. Powell?" I took a steady breath as Christian's eyes flashed to mine in his rearview. Hayley whipped around with her mouth agape. "This is Piper. I think it's time you call Michael. Ollie has just been arrested."

CHAPTER FORTY-FOUR

OLLIE

I SAT UNMOVING in a cold room with nothing but a metal table and chair. My hands were still cuffed as I leaned back in the seat, waiting for my fate. I felt eerily calm for having been arrested and thrown into the back of a cop car an hour prior.

Everything moved quickly after I pushed in my clutch and flew down the gravel road, and I had anticipated that, which was why I'd had everything planned the second I pulled up to the races. The only thing I hadn't planned for was the dagger that had been thrust into my chest the second I saw how worried Piper was. My chest ached at the thought, and I was suddenly pissed that the cuffs didn't allow me to rub the dull spot.

Tank was dead to me the second he gave Piper a sideways look that first night at the races, and ever since then, I'd been trying to figure out a plan to take him down while keeping myself and Piper both out of harm's way—especially Piper.

That was where Jason came in. He was the glue to our little problem. He was the one in between Tank, myself, and

Piper. When I'd asked him if he was ready to dig himself out of the hole he'd dug, he was willing.

I just had to sit here and hope that he was following through with his plan. If not, then I was shit out of luck.

The door swung open as I acted casual. Our family lawyer, Michael, entered along with my father and a police officer. *Shit.*

"Good news," Michael said, gesturing to my cuffs. The young police officer walked over and uncuffed me quickly. My hands fell with a thud, and I was thankful to be able to crack my wrists. As soon as the officer left the room, shutting the metal door behind him, Michael pulled out the other chair. "The guy talked. He did exactly what you said he would, and police are on their way to the premises now to corroborate the allegations."

My father stood back along the door, but I couldn't force myself to look at him. I pushed down the sick feeling that was crowding my stomach as I kept my attention on Michael. "And what about the racing? Where is Tank now?"

"He is in custody still. If what Jason says is the truth, it will be unlikely that he'll even get bond. They're pretty hefty allegations—killing a girl and making it look like an overdose? That isn't something to play around with."

I nodded. "And what about Jason? What do you think he'll get?"

This was the trickiest part. The part that I was afraid to hear. Piper was going to be devastated when she learned that Jason was in trouble and that he had turned himself in to take Tank down. And I was the one that had pushed him to do it.

But what choice did he have? Jason would have never been free from Tank, not after he had gotten a glimpse into his world. When I'd first met with Jason, behind Tank's back, I thought I had a solid plan, but Jason's information made it that much stronger.

He beat Tank at his own game. Jason beat him to the cops. Jason was the better man.

This was his ticket out.

"Well..." Michael kicked a leg on top of the other, his shiny loafers catching the glare of the one hanging light above our heads. "It really depends on how good his lawyer is. But considering he was there the night Tank force-fed drugs down a girl's throat and moved her body to make it appear as an overdose, he could get involuntary manslaughter. It's going to help that he came forward, and if the other witnesses do the same and validate Jason's story, proving Tank was the one to do it, he may get a lesser sentence. It truly just depends."

I nodded, the ache in my chest still there.

"And what about him?" It was the first thing I heard my father say.

Michael chuckled. "Ollie is free to go after the paperwork is finished by the arresting officer."

I laid my hands flat on the table. "Wait. What? I'm not in trouble at all?" *That doesn't make sense.*

"You'll have a fine to pay for racing, but that's it. Street racing is illegal, but I was able to pull a favor. You're the least of their worries, and to be honest, they should be thanking you for helping corner Tank. They wouldn't have had a reason to arrest him if it weren't for you asking him to get in the car with you."

Exactly why I did it.

Michael stood up and clasped his hands together. "Well, my job here is done. Unless there is something else we need to discuss?" He looked at my father and waited a few seconds. "Okay, then." He turned toward me. "Oliver, as much as I like the paycheck, stay out of trouble."

I snickered under my breath as he walked out of the room and shut the door, leaving me and my father alone for the first time in weeks.

The impending doom was like an oncoming train, and I couldn't seem to get myself off the tracks. My gaze stayed glued to the metal table as I counted backwards from one hundred. If I looked him in the eye, I was going to explode. Everything that I'd kept locked away was going to come spilling out. The longer I held this in, the bigger it became, and I didn't realize that until recently. With nothing to distract me any longer, I was forced to face what I'd buried deep. I was angry, and confused, but most of all, I was hurt.

Finding out I wasn't his son hurt. It sliced me. He was my only parent left, and we didn't even share the same blood.

"Street racing? Really?" My father's voice was stern, a tone he didn't usually have to use with me, but I'd heard it plenty of times with Christian.

My heart beat hard as I reached up and took my hat off my head. I placed it gently on the table, and that was when I did it. That was when I looked at him.

He was standing back along the wall, his light-blue button-up shirt undone at the top. His dark hair wasn't gelled down like usual; instead, it was standing up in several directions. He looked calm and collected with his hands tucked in his pockets, but I was certain he was fuming on the inside. My dad was a lot like Christian; they were blank canvases—you never had any idea what was going through their head.

"Why, son?"

A small piece of anger flashed throughout. "Son?" I turned away. "But I'm not actually your son."

I heard him push off from the wall and scuffle toward me. "You are my son. Even if not biological."

My nostrils flared as words began to claw up in my throat. The hold on my emotions was slipping. I knew this would happen eventually—that we'd have to have this talk, but for some reason, I wasn't prepared.

"Did you know I found the birth certificate?"

I didn't meet his eye, because from where I was sitting, I would have had to look up to him, and that didn't seem fitting at a time like this.

He sniffed. "I had a hunch. That's why I moved it."

"So, who is my father, then? Because his name wasn't listed."

The chair in front of me screeched as it was pulled out. He sunk down in the seat and began rolling his cuffed sleeves up to his elbows. When I finally did gather the confidence to look at him, it was like looking into a mirror. For the first time in my entire life, we were the same. We were raw. There were no more lies, no more secrets. It was time. I could sense it. He had been in a similar situation a few months ago with Christian. But this time, he wasn't going to hold back.

I asked again, this time keeping our gazes locked and loaded. "Who is my father?"

His eyes dipped away for a moment before they swooped back and pinned me to my seat. "My brother."

My brows came together in an instant. "What?"

He sighed and ran his hand over his five o'clock shadow. "My brother is your father."

My breathing halted. "You have a brother?"

What the hell is with people hiding their brothers?

"Had." My father swallowed, and I heard the gulp from across the table. "I had a brother. He's dead."

A wide range of emotions flooded me, but I couldn't pinpoint exactly how I felt. It was a weird feeling finding out your father wasn't *really* your father, but it was even weirder finding out that your father—who you'd never met—was dead.

That meant that, technically, both my parents were dead.

My hands came up and clasped together over my head. Nothing I wanted to say would come out of my mouth, which was probably a good thing. What was the right thing to say in this situation?

"He died right before you were born."

My mouth opened, but then I quickly shut it, lowering my hands to the cold table.

"I felt wrong signing the birth certificate, because his death was so fresh in my mind. Things weren't good with your mother and me, obviously, but I need you to understand something, Ollie."

The word barely made it out of my mouth. "What?"

His blue eyes drove into me. "The second I laid eyes on you, I knew you were mine. I hated my brother for what he did, and I was angry with your mother, too, but that never, *ever* reflected onto you. You were my son then, and you are my son now. Do you hear me?"

The only thing I could do was nod. I nodded as my stomach tensed. I nodded as I squeezed my fists together. And I nodded as a million and one questions ran through my mind.

I needed to know the whole story, but I wasn't sure if I wanted to know. My mom used to be the light of my life. Even when she'd overdosed, I still thought the world of her. Christian and I blamed the accident and the injuries for her sudden abuse of drugs. We thought—and were told—that she had gotten addicted to pain pills because of the injuries she sustained, but last year, we found out different.

That wasn't the truth.

I hated to admit it, but it ruined the memory of her a little. The perfect image I'd had of my mother was no more. Now, she was like a mirror having a tiny crack near the corner, or like one of Michelangelo's statues with a missing chunk of marble.

I wasn't sure I wanted to know more about my mother's past, or my real father, but in the end, I asked anyway.

"How?"

My father leaned back in his seat, clearly uncomfortable with the conversation. "How what? How did he die?"

"Yes."

He answered short and curt. "Alcohol overdose."

A sarcastic chuckle left my lips. "So, that was why you always got onto me when I partied last year. Addiction runs in the family. On both sides."

My father's voice was stern. "No, I got onto you because you are a teenager who has a bright future ahead of him. And because you are my son."

I ignored him. "You stayed with her after she cheated on you with your brother?"

It was a hard thing to wrap my head around. How could his own brother do that to him? Christian and I would never fucking do that. It was breaking the code. It was wrong on so many levels.

A heavy breath was shared between us both. "Your mother had her ups and downs, Ollie. I loved her when she was up, but I gave up on her when she was down. It led to some bad times between us." He cleared his throat and leaned forward, resting his elbows in front of him. "I'd just found her stash of pills a few months after she'd had Christian. I was livid, threatened to take him away from her. We fought. She left for a few days and came back like a new woman, apologizing. She swore she'd never do them again and that she'd be a good mom from there on out."

"And then what?"

"And then she told me she was pregnant, and I did the math. Long story short, she ended up telling me she had slept with James, my brother. I had no idea how we would proceed. I was pissed as hell. I wanted to strangle them both. We were set to all meet shortly before you were born to talk. I had calmed some, and we all needed to figure out how to proceed.

But he never showed, so I went to his house. That's where I found him, lying face down in a pool of vomit. He drank himself to death and choked on his own puke."

My father's words were like a sucker punch to my stomach. I wanted the conversation to stop. It was too much. So much negativity and pain. I felt for my father. I truly did. It was the first time in my entire life that I looked at him and felt bad.

He wasn't a good dad when my mother died. He was absent and left Christian and me to deal with the trauma on our own, but sitting here looking at him, the broken pieces of his soul were shining so bright I needed to shut my eyes.

Daniel Powell was not a bad man. He was just broken.

"I'm sorry." *There it was.* I had said it. It was in the open. I *was* sorry. He shouldn't have had to go through that. None of it. Maybe it was why he was the way that he was. Maybe that was why he had been absent for so long.

"You have nothing to be sorry about, Ollie. I've been trying to do better by you and your brother. I've been trying to be present. To make up for the way I had acted before." He paused before adding, "I should have told you and your brother all of this a few months ago when some of the truth about your mother came out. But there just never seemed to be a good time."

I nodded, still feeling completely warped inside. "I get it, Dad."

The side of his lip twitched. "So, you're still calling me Dad then?"

A chuckle came out of my mouth involuntarily, and it helped ease the tension just a little. "I guess."

My dad smiled, looking relieved when the door clamored open.

A policeman gestured for us to leave, and my father and I slowly followed after him.

"Let's finish this conversation at home. I think we probably need to include Christian in this, too." I nodded to my father as we walked down the long hallway, trailing the officer.

"They're right outside, you know."

I stopped walking. "Who is?"

"Your brother and Hayley." My dad put his hand on the doorknob after grabbing a slip of paper from the officer with my fine information. He glanced over his shoulder at me. "And the girl. She was the one to call me."

"Piper called you?"

He nodded, ready to push through into what I assumed was the lobby of the station. "Yes. And on my way over here, the first thing I said I was going to do was ask what the hell you four were doing out there street racing, but I've decided I don't even want to know. Just stay the hell out of trouble from here on out. You got it?"

"Yeah, okay," I answered, preparing myself for the worst.

I didn't expect to see Piper so soon after the race, and although my issues with my father were presumably solved, for now, the thought of facing her after I'd encouraged her brother to turn himself in along with Tank had my stomach dropping to the floor.

Piper.

I had no clue what she was feeling or if she hated me, but I was seconds from finding out.

CHAPTER FORTY-FIVE

PIPER

I COULD STILL HEAR the sound of my mother's voice booming in the background of the call I'd made to my father. She was all but shrieking, freaking out, and I was pretty sure she wanted to kill me.

My father was the level-headed of the two, always staying cool, calm, and collected. When he'd thrown Jason out of the house and changed the locks, he didn't act angry. He simply packed up his things, walked them to the front door, placed them on the porch, closed the door, and that was the end of it. Not a single word was muttered from him. I sensed his anger. Saw the redness of his face. But nonetheless, he had stayed quiet. My mother, on the other hand, wouldn't shut up. She was angry and baffled at his behavior, and at one point, I think she even said *good riddance*.

I knew it pained her, though. It pained both of them. That was why they never came home. That was why they buried themselves in loads of work, only checking in on me occasionally. My mother thought that if she checked my bank account and saw that I wasn't spending excessive amounts of money like Jason—the first clue that he was using drugs—that I would stay out of trouble.

I was a good girl. I'd always stayed in between the lines. I knew right from wrong, but now, the truth was beginning to surface. Their perfect, straight-A student wasn't so perfect anymore. They thought my loyalty was to them, but it wasn't. It was to Jason.

Or so I thought.

Crickets chirped in the background of my thoughts as Christian, Eric, and Hayley sat beside me, our backs resting along the side of the police station. Ollie would be coming out any second now, per what Michael, their family lawyer, relayed to Christian a little while ago. Tank was in custody, and Jason... Well, none of us really knew what was going on there, other than Eric dropping him off so he could confess to something that would incriminate him but take Tank down, too. It was all part of the plan that Ollie had whipped up.

And as I nervously sat there, my back against the rough brick, kicking a small pebble back and forth with my shoe, I realized that somehow, over the last few weeks, my loyalty had completely shifted.

I realized that fixing Jason's problems wasn't my job. He was my brother. I didn't raise him, and it wasn't my responsibility as his younger sister to protect him from the choices he made. The person I was most worried about was Ollie.

Oliver Powell.

The boy I used to hate. The boy who stepped in and protected me, who was potentially in some serious trouble for *me*. How could I ever have hated him? He was pure. He was good. And I was pretty certain I loved him. I didn't realize it before, but when I saw him take off down the gravel road, dust flying out from underneath his tires, I saw my life flash before my eyes. Then, when he had cuffs slapped on his wrists, my heart shattered. I would have done anything in that moment to take his place.

It was a scary thought. But it was there.

I was still concerned for my brother. I still cared about him, but Jason had made his bed, and now he had to lie in it. I just hoped Ollie would make it out unscathed.

Suddenly, the door swung open, and light filtered onto the sidewalk. I was the first to jump up, my nerves completely frayed on the ends.

Ollie's dad walked out first, but then I was met with a blue-eyed boy who looked almost fearful to see me standing there. Before I knew what I was doing, my feet took off, and I was in his arms. Air whooshed out of his lungs as I all but tackled him. My arms wrapped around his warm body, and my head buried into his chest.

I whispered, "I'm sorry. I'm sorry. I'm so, so sorry." Tears gathered in an instant, but I clenched my eyes in an attempt to keep them stowed away.

"Hey, hey, hey..." Ollie's voice was like a salve to my wound. He pulled me away, and his troubled eyes cast down into mine. "Why are you sorry? Jesus, why are you crying?" His fingers hurriedly swiped over my cheeks as he brushed away the salty moisture.

My head shook back and forth. "This is all my fault. I was so wrapped up in Jason that I was blinded to what really mattered."

He frowned. "Which is?"

"You!" I shouted frantically, not caring that everyone was watching us, including his dad. "You matter. I should have *never* let you get involved in this. I should have just gone to my parents and been done with it. Jason is not my concern. I'm so tired of fixing his mistakes." I dropped my head and

looked down at my ripped jeans, feeling so incredibly guilty.
"I am so stupid."

"Shh." Ollie pulled me into his body. "Your brother knows
he was wrong to drag you into this. Why do you think he
turned himself in?"

I pushed off his chest and peered up into his face. The
planes of his high cheekbones rose as he gave me a half smile.
"He did it for you, Piper. He's trying to fix his mistakes."

"But what about you?"

In typical Ollie fashion, he chuckled. "Don't worry about
me. All I got was a fine. I'm just glad you don't hate me."

My heart was slowly molding back together. "I could
never hate you."

Hayley snickered behind me. "Says the girl who *swore* she
hated him."

We all laughed, even Ollie's dad who looked a little lighter
than when he had first shown up. I questioned Ollie with a
look, and he gave me a slight nod. He bent his head down.
"Christian, my dad, and I are gonna head home to have a
talk."

Good. This is good. I grabbed onto Ollie's hand and gave it a
squeeze, letting him know I was here for him.

"Eric will take you home?" Ollie looked at Eric for reas-
surance, but I interrupted him.

"Actually...my parents are on the way. I called them as
soon as Eric let us know that my brother was here."

"Oh, good. That's good." He nodded as if he were pleased,
and I glanced at Hayley. "Hayley, will you stay with me until
they're here?"

"Of course."

"I'll catch a ride with my dad and Ol. You can just drive
my Charger to my house when her parents get here, yeah?"
Christian asked. "I think I need to get filled in on whatever is

going on with you." He glanced at Ollie and grimaced. I gave Ollie another squeeze.

"Yeah," Ollie answered, squeezing me back. His palm felt nice along mine, and I hated to let it go, but we both needed to get things sorted out.

His dad and Christian began walking to the parking lot as Ollie stayed back. He tugged me closer as his lips hovered over mine. Our eyes locked for half a second before he pressed his mouth against mine. Things were chaotic, to say the least. Emotions were running high, but with his lips on mine, I suddenly felt grounded. Like everything would be okay.

When he pulled away, he took my breath with him.

"Call me when you get home, okay? The very second."

I wrapped my arms around my middle after handing him back his phone. "I will, and then you can fill me in on that?" I nudged my head to his father and Christian.

"Yeah." He kissed my forehead and started to walk away but not before he whispered, "And when all of this drama bullshit is over...it's you and me, okay? Just you and me."

"Us," I whispered back.

"Us," he repeated, and then he was gone.

Hayley, Eric, and I all went back and sat against the brick wall, waiting for my parents.

We sat silently as I ran my fingers over my lips. The second Ollie was gone, I was back to feeling too much. There was a lot of uncertainty dealing with my parents and brother, and I wasn't really prepared.

Eric's voice had my hand dropping from my mouth. "I'm not gonna lie. Having you two around is a lot like walking into a fucking real-life soap opera. So much drama."

I was the first to snicker, because it was true, and then we all busted up laughing before Hayley popped up, bringing her legs underneath her to sit cross-legged. "No one asked you to stay, you know. You can leave us and our drama fest."

He groaned, pulling his knees up and resting his arms along them. "And miss out on all the entertainment? Yeah fucking right."

I giggled. "Why *are* you still here? You can leave. My parents should be here any minute. For once, they were actually in the state instead of halfway across the world."

He didn't glance at Hayley or me. Instead, he kept his expression in front of him. "I'll wait until they're here, and then I'll take off."

Hayley crooned, "Aw. Eric! I knew you cared about us."

He still kept his gaze straight, but I saw the rise of his cheeks.

I laughed quietly and leaned back onto the brick, waiting patiently for my parents to show up.

The past few days had somehow flown by with minimal fights between my parents and me, but that was only because they were basically ignoring me all together. Things moved quickly as soon as they had arrived at the police station. I sensed the rising disappointment from them when I began telling them what had happened. I started at the very beginning and barely took a breath as everything tumbled out. It was like a waterfall; I couldn't stop the words even if I wanted to.

My father had barely blinked in my direction since that night. And my mother... Well, I'm surprised her teeth weren't cracked with how hard she clenched her jaw anytime I walked past her in the house. They took the entire week off from work to stay home and figure things out, which was a surprise to me.

I assumed they'd rip me out of the police station whilst

putting a tracking device on me and leave my brother there to fend for himself, but that was not exactly what happened.

To be honest, I wasn't even sure what happened. I'd been shut out of all things relating to Jason. He won't talk to me either.

The police released him early Sunday morning, and he'd been here since, but again, I had no idea why. I should have been happy that I was left in the dark, because after all, it was what I'd been wanting since the very beginning, but I wasn't happy at all. My house was like a ticking time bomb—one wrong move and the entire thing was going up in flames.

My phone vibrated against my desk. A tiny bit of happiness filtered through when I saw it was Hayley.

"Hey, Hay."

"Hey, how are things tonight?" Hayley was whispering through the phone, and I had no idea why. I glanced at the clock. It was after ten, so maybe Ann was asleep.

"Things are the same. Jason has barely come out of his room unless my parents drag him out to talk." I sighed, flopping onto my bed. "He still won't talk to me. I don't know, but I will say it still feels like we're on the verge of World War III in our house."

Hayley laughed. "We all miss you at school. Ollie walks around like a lost puppy. I can't believe your parents are having you stay home."

Ah, yes. My parents decided to keep me home for a few days until they sorted things out. Why? I had no idea. I guess they were afraid that people would find out that not only was Jason a troublemaker, but their precious, straight-laced daughter wasn't the princess they thought she was, either.

"I know," I huffed. "But they were so angry with me that I didn't even argue. I did, however, almost go to school today just to spite them." Hayley laughed again. "But seriously, things are weird here, Hayley. So weird." My stomach dipped with nerves, thinking back to this morning when I crept downstairs to find my mom and dad arguing. It was rare. Not the arguing, but just them being in the kitchen on a Wednesday morning. They didn't say a word as I grabbed some orange juice and a granola bar. When I went back upstairs, my nerves coiled tight, I stopped in front of Jason's door only to hear nothing at all. When I peeked inside, I saw him sitting on the edge of his bed with his head hung low. I was certain he knew I was standing there, but he wouldn't turn in my direction. He was icing me out.

At first, I was pissed that he wouldn't talk to me. Part of me wondered if he was angry with me, but once I'd talked to Ollie later that day, he helped me realize that Jason was probably ashamed. He was mad at himself, not me.

Ollie. I missed him. I wanted things to go back to normal —well, semi-normal. I wanted the freedom of seeing him when I wanted.

"Why are things weird?" Hayley asked, still whispering.

"I'm just confused. My parents won't tell me much, and I'm too afraid to ask. Jason won't talk to me." I slowly sat up on my bed and tucked my damp hair behind my ears. "I have a bad feeling, and I can't shake it."

"You know what I think you need?"

"What?"

I could tell Hayley was smiling. "I think you need your best friend...and your boyfriend."

I do. Ollie and I had talked every day since Saturday. In fact, we talked so long on Sunday night that we both fell asleep on the phone. We had a lot to say. He filled me in on what was going on with his dad and Christian, and I filled him in on everything going on at my house. He dropped off my homework yesterday and gave me a quick peck on the lips before leaving me at the door before my parents came.

It only made me miss him more.

I hated to admit it, but part of me felt like I needed him. I needed him to lean on. I needed him to ground me. The thought scared me, because I was so used to being on my own, but it was kind of nice having someone as a clutch. Having someone you could lean on.

"I wish things weren't like this right now," I said. "I want things to go back to normal, before I got involved with my brother's shit and Tank."

All of a sudden, I heard a deeper voice. "But you mean, like, you want them normal, except for you still want us to be *us*, right?"

I almost squealed. "Ollie! What are you doing with Hayley? Are you guys all hanging out without me?" My lip jutted out. It was agonizing that I wasn't with them.

"Open your balcony door, Pipe."

My heart halted. "What?"

"We're coming in to hang. Did you really think I could go this long without touching you? That kiss yesterday was a tease."

I smiled so hard my face hurt. My phone fell from my hand as I jumped up onto my carpet. The balcony door pushed open slowly, and I slapped my hand over my face as I saw three smiling faces staring back at me. *Oh my God. I love my friends.*

And Ollie. I loved Ollie. The feeling that blossomed when I saw his lifted cheek was life-altering. That was what love was, right?

Ollie was the first to jump from the tree limb to my balcony. His arms wrapped around me almost instantly, the breeze of the cool January air coating my bare arms. "Hi," I breathed into his chest.

"Hey, you," he said, kissing the top of my head. "I missed you."

Content. That was what I felt being in his arms. One hundred percent content and full. He filled me up.

"Move, dipshit." I peeked over and heard Christian scoff at our embrace. He was the next to jump and then Hayley. Christian tried to reach over and grab her, but she swatted his hand away and rolled her eyes. *So independent.*

As soon as they were all safe and on my balcony, they shuffled inside my room. Hayley pulled me in for a hug, and I squeezed her.

"You okay?" she asked quietly.

I nodded before letting go. "I love you guys! I can't believe you just snuck into my room!"

Ollie stood back along the wall and just gazed at me. I couldn't help but smile.

Christian flopped onto my bed and acted as if he owned the place, per usual.

Hayley fell down beside him. "Are you kidding? These two are pros at sneaking into places, and believe it or not, it was *their* idea."

"So, you missed me, huh?" I placed my hands on my hips and looked up at Ollie. He shrugged coyly. "You can admit it, you know. We no longer hate each other."

His tongue darted out to lick his lip. "Oh, trust me. I have no problems admitting it. I just wish I could *show* you how much I miss you, instead of saying it."

Christian groaned. "No sexual innuendos allowed. Breakin' the rules."

"What rules?" Hayley asked, looking between them.

Ollie pushed off the wall and went over to sit in the chair by my desk. It only took one tip of his chin for me to follow after him and to sit on his lap. His arms went around my middle, and I sighed happily, leaning back into his hard chest. "When Hayley and he had started dating, and we'd hang out, I had a little heart to heart with my brother here."

"About what?" I asked, tipping my head back.

"I told him he couldn't eye-fuck his girlfriend while we were all hanging out as friends. Or make out with her, because it always turned into something more, and I was forced to leave the room."

I busted out laughing before Ollie slapped his hand over my mouth. "Shh," he whispered along my ear. "Your parents will hear."

Goosebumps broke out along my skin, but I shook them off. He was right. My parents would likely come investigate. I whispered, "Do you remember that time we were at Eric's and they started to make out so intensely that the three of us were forced to go out onto the deck for the rest of the morning?"

"How could I forget?" Ollie asked. "It was chilly. You didn't have a bra on."

I smacked his shoulder, causing Hayley to snicker.

Just then, a loud bang came from somewhere in the house.

"What was that?" Hayley asked, sitting up a little taller.

I jumped off Ollie's lap, fear taking away any bit of calmness I had felt seconds ago.

My ears strained, but I didn't hear a single thing. "I don't know," I hesitantly said. I walked a little closer to my bedroom door. *That was weird.* "I'm going to go make sure everything is okay. Stay here." I glanced at Ollie once before opening the door and peeking my head out. The long hallway was dark, but I saw the light from underneath my brother's door on the carpet. I shoved away the apprehension and mouthed, "I'll be right back," to Ollie, Hayley, and Christian. Ollie's brows were knitted, and his perfect, pale lips were set in a firm line, but he gave me a nod.

Once the door was latched, I crept down the hallway, still listening. I didn't even hear my parents downstairs. *Were they in bed?* It was sad that I didn't know my own parents' sleeping schedules.

I didn't know them at all.

My hand lingered in front of Jason's door with my heart stuck in my throat. It had been at least a year since Jason lived here, but it felt like yesterday that I was standing here, afraid to go into his room to see him passed out from partying.

A heavy breath of air left my lungs as I flipped my hair over my shoulder and pushed through the door. His bed was messy, the covers thrown halfway across the room. My eyes quickly went to the bathroom where the light poured out onto the floor.

"Jason?" I half-whispered, waiting for a response.

Nothing.

The nerves picked up in my stomach; the bile in my throat was rising slowly.

I shook my head. *He's fine. Relax.*

There was no way he could have gotten drugs since he hadn't left the house since he got here. My parents made damn sure of that, I was sure.

Even though my head was telling me to retreat and to go back to my room, something dragged me over the carpet and the bundled-up blanket and into the bathroom.

The door creaked as I pushed it open, and when I saw the orange pill bottle turned on its side on the porcelain vanity top, it felt like I was plunged into ice-cold water.

There, on his side, was my brother, unconscious.

A blood-curdling scream left my mouth, and suddenly, everything went dark.

CHAPTER FORTY-SIX

OLLIE

"WHAT IS TAKING HER SO LONG?" I asked, pacing Piper's bedroom floor. There was a shift in the air the second her bedroom door closed.

I felt cagey and anxious. A lot like I used to feel before I'd race. Something ominous was in the air, and it was eating at me.

"Bro, relax."

"Yeah, Ollie," Hayley said, scooting down to the edge of the bed with her feet dangling. "It's probably nothing."

"I guess," I said, about to sit down, but then my head snapped when I heard the most piercing, terrifying scream I had ever heard in my life.

My shoulders snapped straight, and when I locked onto Christian, we both flew into action.

I ripped Piper's bedroom door open, and I swore I was to her within a second. Somehow, my feet knew where to carry me. I jumped over a mess of blankets on the floor, and when I walked into the scene, all the oxygen in the room ceased to exist. I couldn't breathe. I was stuck, staring at the girl who literally made my heart skip a beat, huddled on the floor, lifting her brother's lifeless head off the ground. There was a mess of yellow vomit around her knees. The putrid smell slapped me into action as Hayley came barreling through.

"Get her out of here!" Hayley screamed as she ran by Piper's side and shoved her out of the way. Piper yelled out, reaching for her brother, tears flowing quickly down her face. *Oh, fuck.* Just the thought of Piper hurt made me want to kill someone, but seeing the look of pure fear on her face felt like every bone in my fucking body was being broken at the same time.

My hands wrapped around her tiny arms as she clawed and reached for Jason, yelling. I swooped her up.

"No! No! Let me go!" She smacked my chest and pushed at my shoulders. I caught the eye of Christian as he already had his phone pulled out, calling 911. Hayley had Jason's head lifted, and she was shoving her fingers down his throat, saying, "Come on, come on. Puke it up. *No, no, no, no.*"

As soon as I pulled Piper out of the bathroom, her parents came through the bedroom door. Her father looked ready to kill me until they saw that Piper was now clinging onto me for dear life. Her mom took one look at us and ran past, screaming when she saw the scene.

Christian was talking quickly into the phone to the dispatcher, but I continued to drag Piper away. I could feel the grief radiating off her body. She was shaking in my arms, and in that moment, I actually turned to God. I'd only ever prayed once in my life, and it was the day Christian and I had found my mother dead in her bedroom. It was pointless then. Our mother was dead and had been for hours. But right now, I didn't care. I prayed that he would take her pain and give it to me. I'd gladly carry it for her, because seeing her like this was one of the worst things I'd ever felt.

"Shh, shh, shh," I hushed her as I pulled her back into her room, shutting the door softly behind us, shoving all the chaos in her brother's room out. Piper's cries racked her body so hard that I had to cradle her head into my chest.

"No, no. He can't—where—no."

Agony wrapped itself around my windpipe. "Just breathe."

She gasped so many times that I wanted to breathe for her. My own lungs constricted. My arms ached as they wrapped around her. The pain. I felt her pain.

God, don't let him die. I knew what it felt like to watch someone die from a silent disease. I knew what it felt like to have someone pick a vice over you. A user took your love and they threw it away. They didn't even mean to, and that was probably the hardest thing to accept. It was something I'd learned years ago, when I finally processed what had happened to my mother.

"Just breathe, Pipe." Piper was still gasping for air, but it wasn't as bad as before. My arms tightened around her as I finally lowered us to the ground in her bedroom.

"Ollie," her voice cracked, and I swore I did, too.

"I know, Piper. I know. Just breathe. I'm here." I kissed her head again as she buried it even harder into my chest. Her small, shaking hand clenched my shirt, and I had to smash my lips to keep myself together for her.

I knew, sitting there in her room as shit unfolded in the worst of ways in the next room, that nothing else mattered but this moment right here. No matter what happened in the next few days, or months, or even years, I would forever be linked to Piper. I would fight like hell to keep her safe and happy. Because the alternative was literal hell in my world.

CHAPTER FORTY-SEVEN

PIPER

ONE. Two. Three. Four. Five. A heavy breath left my lips and floated to the ground as I twisted my fingers together again. *Six. Seven. Eight. Nine. Ten.* Another breath escaped. A large hand came down and rested on my knee, giving it a light squeeze. I glanced up at Ollie's tired face, and he gave me a smile that didn't quite reach the dark circles under his eyes.

I wanted to smile at him. I wanted to tell him how much I loved him. How him being here by my side was enough to keep me from spiraling out of control. But I couldn't even muster up a single syllable. My cheeks refused to rise. My mouth was glued shut. I only hoped that my eyes told the story, because I wasn't sure I'd ever speak again.

I replayed the scene in my head over and over again. Small pieces of broken memories flew at me as I sat in the waiting room with the sound of beeping machines echoing through the hospital. I wondered what I'd done wrong over the years. I wondered, if I had done something differently, if Jason would be here. Regret and guilt started to sneak their way in, and I had no one to blame but myself.

That was the thing about situations like this: they were so uncertain. If my parents would have helped Jason a few years ago, would he have landed in the hospital? Or would their help have just turned into enabling? What if I'd told my parents about Tank, and Jason owing him money? What would they have done? Would he still have ended up like this? Was this the ending he was meant to have?

The ending. Was it the end?

I swallowed back a harsh lump as Ollie's thumb rubbed the inside of my knee. I stared at it, the strokes back and forth somehow comforting me in my state of rising panic.

"How is he? Is he okay? Is he alive?" My mother's voice had me snapping my head up in search of whomever it was she was talking to. The doctor, with his wrinkly tanned face, looked ambushed, but nonetheless, he answered.

I quickly got up and stood by my parents, my father glancing down at me once before looking back at the doctor.

"He is alive. We were able rid his system of the drugs and are giving him fluids now. Your son is tired but coherent enough to talk to you, if you'd like to go back."

My heart leapt in my chest. *He's alive.* But…now what?

My mother began to push forward, but the doctor quickly put his hand up. "Listen." My mother stopped in her tracks. "I say this to all parents and caregivers when we get a case like this." The doctor closed the file in his hand and lowered his voice. "We both are aware that your son needs help. In fact, I have had a lengthy talk with him about what happened, and now is not the time for you and your husband to go in there to reprimand him. Jason is in a fragile state. Not only did he just come close to overdosing, but he did so on purpose. He needs rest and fluids, and tomorrow, I have scheduled for a psychiatrist to come evaluate him and to talk with you two as well." I sucked my lips between my teeth and glanced back at Ollie. Hayley and Christian were huddled beside him, talking quietly.

When I turned back to look at the doctor, he was staring at me. The wrinkles on his face softened just a tad before he turned and glanced at my parents. "You all are welcome to come back now, but please keep in mind that this is not the time to have a yelling match. Jason's health is my number one priority right now, and that will do harm." He began to turn away but not before he said, "If you cannot control yourself and your anger and disappointment, please do not come back." Then, he turned to me and inched his head for me to follow. I felt the small rise of my lips as I trailed after him, not really caring if my parents were doing the same.

Once we got to the window, we both stared into the room. My brother was lying on the hospital bed with an IV hooked up to his arm. His eyes were closed, and the white sheet was pulled up to his chest. He looked so unlike the picture I had of him in my head. When I thought of Jason, I thought of the good times. The times where he was happy and glowing. The times we had fun together. Not this. Not this shell of a person I used to know.

"He's sorry, you know."

I shifted my attention to the doctor. "How do you know?"

He continued peering through the window. "The first words out of your brother's mouth when he woke were, '*I'm sorry, Piper.*'"

My hand came up to cover my mouth.

"It took me a while to figure out who you were, but once he was coherent and I started asking questions, I learned you were his sister."

I said nothing. I didn't really know what to say. All I knew was that my heart hurt.

For a while, the doctor and I just stood and stared

through the window. Jason was sleeping peacefully, his coppery-brown hair matted down to the side of his head. His cheeks had more color, thankfully, but he still looked rough.

"I'm sad," I finally said, barely above a whisper.

And I was sad. I was sad for a lot of reasons. I was especially sad that my parents chose to stay in the waiting room rather than see their son. Did they hate him that much? Or were they sad too?

"It's okay to be sad. It's hard to see someone you love being destroyed by something that's completely out of your control." The doctor cleared his throat before looking down at his phone. "It's hard to love a user."

I stared at his profile as he continued looking at Jason. "Sounds like you know from experience."

"I do," he answered abruptly. "And my only advice to you is to hope for the best, but always expect the worst. I was told that once, and it stuck."

I nodded, taking in his advice like it was actual oxygen. I repeated the mantra in my head as he began to walk away, leaving me to stare at my brother all alone.

But then, that was when I heard the raised voices.

I gave Jason one more glance before rushing to the waiting area, waiting just behind the far wall to listen.

"Ollie, calm down. I've never seen you act like this." *Christian.*

"Yes, I would appreciate it if you calmed down." *That was my dad.*

"I've never acted like this because I've never cared about someone like I do Piper!" Ollie's voice roared over my father's and Christian's. There was a pause, but then Ollie started up again. "You and your wife are standing out here, for what reason? Because you can't hide your disappointment that your son has an addiction? Piper is back there *alone* while you two do what? Sit out here and argue about whose fault it is that he's in the hospital and that Piper is somehow involved in all of this? Of course she's involved!"

"Calm down."

I wanted to peek my head around the corner and see what was unfolding, but I didn't want my cover blown, so I stayed tucked away, pressing my hands to the wall behind me.

"No! I will not calm down." There was a pause. "You two don't even know your own daughter! She cares about people so deeply that she'd do anything to help them. She has been fighting for Jason from day one, and it's because you backed out. If she didn't fight for him, who would?"

My heart squeezed. Ollie. I could hear the protection in his voice.

"I agree with him." My brows dipped at Hayley's voice. "I know all about loving someone with an addiction. And the second you stop loving the person they used to be, they're gone forever. Piper has been fighting for the old Jason, her brother, the one before drugs took over. Don't fault her for trying to help him, for holding out hope. Because that's when resentment comes through, and I can tell you right now, speaking from experience, once that happens, you won't just lose Jason, you'll lose her, too."

"Yes." Ollie again. "Thank you! That's what I'm saying. For fuck's sake, go comfort your daughter. She just found her older brother lying in his own vomit! And if you knew her at all, you'd know that she is hurting."

Tears brimmed my eyes as I listened to Ollie reprimand my parents. In any other situation, having your boyfriend yell at your parents was less than ideal, but in *my* situation, it was as if he was confessing his love for me. Ollie was fighting for me, and there was something about that that had a tear falling down my cheek.

"Where are you going?" My mother's voice wasn't laced

with anger. There was something else in her tone that I didn't recognize.

Ollie's voice was closer now. "I'm going to comfort my girlfriend because *I* fucking love her and know when she is hurting."

Another tear slid down my cheek as I turned the corner and ran straight into his hard chest.

"Umph." His strong hands were on my upper arms, his brows folding until he realized it was me. The deepened lines on his forehead disappeared as he wrapped his arms around me and pushed me back into the hallway. My back was resting along the wall as he took his finger and tipped my chin back. "Are you okay?"

I gulped. "No. But I'm a little bit better now."

His eyes searched my face frantically as his other hand wrapped around my waist. "How is he?"

I sighed. "He'll be okay, for now. But Ollie?"

"Yeah?"

"I love you."

Time froze. We were stuck in a busy hospital with all sorts of sounds coming from various rooms, nurses shuffling back and forth with their carts of supplies, but I was lost in this moment with him.

"I heard what you said. All of it."

Ollie's head dipped just slightly. His blue eyes almost appeared shy.

"And I just want you to know that I love you. I have no clue what the future holds. I know nothing. But I do know that I love you, okay?" I licked my dry lips. "I just need you to know that."

Ollie didn't need to say it back, because I already knew what he was feeling. Our eyes connected, and I felt it in my soul. I felt it last year, and I'd felt it every single day since then. Ollie and I were one.

His lips hovered over mine for a brief moment before his hands wrapped around my face and his mouth was on mine. The kiss was soft but deep. From the outside, it may have looked harmless and innocent, but we both knew it wasn't.

Our kisses were full of hidden words and secrets that only we shared.

And I hoped it would stay like that. *Always*.

EPILOGUE

OLLIE

MY FINGER TRAILED the inside of Piper's arm as she leaned back onto my chest with her legs propped out onto the coffee table. People were starting to show up at Eric's cabin for the party, but part of me wanted to go back to my house so I could have Piper all to myself.

We weren't getting as much alone time as before because her parents were taking the time to make it home more often than not. It seemed my talk (read as: yelling match) got to them. Plus, they were still dealing with Jason's shit.

The case with Tank was just starting to form, and Jason was a prime component of it. But as long as he testified against Tank and didn't recant on his statement, he would be able to continue the rehab program which was set up by his lawyer. When he finished rehab, he'd be on probation, but that was the extent of it.

Piper was happy he was in rehab, but I could tell she was still a little leery. I saw the distant look in her eye every so often, and I knew it was because she was thinking of him.

I did my best to distract her.

After all, distraction was one of my strong suits.

"Did Hayley tell you guys the news?" Christian was beaming, which was completely unusual for his brooding self.

"It's really creepy when you do that," I said.

His brow furrowed as he leaned forward and rested his elbows on his knees. "What is?"

I snickered. "When you smile."

He scoffed. "Fuck off."

Christian and I were still working on things with our father, but now that everything was out in the open, things seemed to be less tense at the house. It was actually pleasant to be home now, and Christian took the news that we were half-brothers a lot better than expected.

Piper sat up a little taller but still kept her body pressed closed to mine. "What's going on, Hay?"

Hayley tried to hold back a smile. She pushed her hair behind her ear shyly. "I got some college acceptance letters back."

"And?" Piper asked eagerly.

"I got a full ride to Harvard."

Piper squealed. "Oh my God! Are you freaking serious?" She flew up out of my lap and rushed to Hayley, wrapping her arms around her shoulders. A bright smile was on her face, and I couldn't look away even if I wanted. "I am so proud of you! This is so deserved, Hayley!"

"Wait, there's more," Christian said smugly.

"More?" Piper asked.

Hayley blushed bashfully. "I also got a full ride to UCLA."

"UCLA?" Piper's lips were parted slightly, and I zeroed in on them. "Wait, so you're going to go to college where Christian is playing football?"

The music got louder in the living room, and I saw Eric

coming down into the den with a beer in his hand. He came to stand behind the four of us on the couch.

Piper grinned. "Is this where you tell me you're going to UCLA, and we're going to be roomies?"

I leaned forward, garnering her attention. "Wait, you got into UCLA? I thought you wanted to go to Stanford?"

Piper bit her lip and looked from me to Hayley, then back to me. "My parents wanted me to go to Stanford. I also applied to UCLA because of Hayley. I got my acceptance letter yesterday."

"Wait, so you're going to UCLA? Why didn't you tell me?"

UCLA was the closest (best) university to Pike Valley in terms of distance, and it was always the plan for Christian and me both to go there and play football after English Prep. But now Piper, too? And Hayley?

Piper played coy. Her light freckles scattered across her tinted cheeks. "I...I don't know. I mean, the plan was to go to Stanford, but then I thought about when I'd have to leave you, or Hayley, or heck"—she giggled—"even Christian or Eric, and it made me feel...lost. I wanted to go to Stanford to please my parents, but now that isn't as appealing. I want to go where *I* want to go." She blushed even harder.

I grinned, standing up from the couch and pulling her to her feet. I tucked my hands into the back pockets of her jeans, cupping her butt. "And here I thought this next year would suck with everyone leaving me behind. You won't be far from me at all."

Her nose scrunched, and her green eyes twinkled. It was fucking adorable. "I don't think I could ever leave you."

She bit her lip and glanced at everyone else.

My voice boomed over the speakers. "Well then, I guess it's decided. The fab five will live on for many years to come. I wonder what other shit we can get ourselves into."

Hayley threw her head back and laughed, making Piper giggle in the process. I pushed her in closer with my hands on her butt and pressed my mouth to hers, sneaking my tongue in there for good measure.

She let out a tiny groan before biting my lip and pushing my chest. "Knock it off, Ollie."

I laughed, pulling us back down to the couch, staying there for most of the night as Eric's cabin became more and more crowded.

It was funny how quickly things could change in just a few months.

Lies were told, secrets were shared, and truths were revealed.

But somehow, through all of that, I found myself the happiest I'd been since before my mother died.

And to think, it had all started with a secret.

Speaking of... My eyes followed Eric as he quietly left the party and stepped out onto the deck. It was hard to see much of anything or anyone outside, except for the roaring bonfire just over the small grassy hill, but I caught the blur of long, blonde hair swishing past the door and a dark figure following after it.

It seemed Eric had some secrets, too.

And I couldn't wait until they unfolded.

The End

ALSO BY S.J. SYLVIS

English Prep Series

All the Little Lies

All the Little Secrets

All the Little Truths

St. Mary's Series

Good Girls Never Rise

Bad Boys Never Fall

Dead Girls Never Talk

Standalones

Three Summers

Yours Truly, Cammie

Chasing Ivy

Falling for Fallon

Truth

All books can be found on Amazon or at sjsylvis.com

ABOUT THE AUTHOR

S.J. Sylvis is a romance author who is best known for her angsty new adult romances and romantic comedies. She currently resides in Arizona with her husband, two small kiddos, and dog. She is obsessed with coffee, becomes easily attached to fictional characters, and spends most of her evenings buried in a book!

www.sjsylvis.com

ACKNOWLEDGMENTS

Joe, Emma & Ripley, I know two out of three of you can't really read this yet but thank you for being my happiness. I love all three of you more than anything in the world and I'm so happy to share this life with you. <3

My grandparents - two of the greatest humans on this earth. There has never been a doubt in my mind how much you both love me. I wouldn't be the person I am today without your guidance and support and I will always be so proud to be your granddaughter.

To my mom, thank you for always being my biggest cheerleader. You are so incredibly supportive and please never stop signing up to be on my ARC team even though you have no idea what that is. HAHA. I love you so much!

To my in-laws, thank you for always supporting me and cheering me on. I love you so much!

Taylor & Kristen- Katie P told me to tell you she loves you. She also mentioned something about send erase the word send but I had no idea what she was talking about.

Laura - I am SO thankful for you and our late night texting sessions. I would be lost without your friendship!!

Thank you to my sweet friend Dana, for helping me with my plot hiccups. Piper and Ollie were difficult and you helped me sort them out!

Megan & Becca, thank you times a million for beta reading for me! I love you!

Jenn, you are the quickest and best editor out there. You make my work shine! I get so excited to do my final read through after you've polished my manuscript! Thank you so incredibly much!

Lastly, to all the amazing authors, bloggers, bookstagrammers, and readers out there. YOU are one of the biggest reasons I continue publishing books. You're my biggest cheerleaders. I love you all so much!

Xoxo,

S.J.

Lightning Source UK Ltd.
Milton Keynes UK
UKHW010712300123
416172UK00004B/286